# Saving Nary

## A Novel

### Carol DeMent

For Princess TTT —
I hope you enjoy reading
this book as much as I
enjoyed writing it!

All the best —
Carol DeMent

*Saving Nary* is a work of historical fiction. Apart from the well-known actual people, events, and locales that figure in the narrative, all names, characters, places and incidents are the products of the author's imagination or are used fictitiously. Any resemblance to current events or locales, or to living persons, is entirely coincidental.

ISBN-13:978-1-522-98290-6
Library of Congress Control Number: 2016900034

CreateSpace Independent Publishing Platform, North Charleston, SC

This book is dedicated to
Myky, Tara and Nouk

# Acknowledgements

In my mid-twenties, I responded to a newspaper ad recruiting volunteers to teach English to refugees from SE Asia. It was a decision that forever changed the direction and tenor of my life, and for that I am profoundly grateful. So to the many refugees who later passed through the programs of the Thurston County Refugee Center, and who thanked me for my assistance, I say no, thank *you*, truly, for sharing your lives and your stories with me.

Were it not for the Puget Sound Writers Guild, this book would still be a partially completed manuscript gathering dust on a shelf in my closet. In particular, I thank Hal Dygert for his comments on structure, Jeremy Ryding and Tim Milnes for their unflagging encouragement, enthusiasm and belief in the story, Mary Vanek for her aversion to exclamation points and comma splices, Daniel Rice for his fine eye for narrative voice, Patricia McClure and Wendy Impett Ervin for their insightful comments on the emotional lives of the characters, and Laura Swan for her leadership.

Much research went into the writing of *Saving Nary*. For conditions in the camps and under the Khmer Rouge, I relied heavily on a series of taped interviews of resettled refugees conducted by Columbia University's Public Health Program on Forced Migration and Health, as well as conversations with my own refugee clients, and written memoirs including Dith Pran's *Children of Cambodia's Killing Fields*, *When Broken Glass Floats* by Chanrithy Him, and *First They Killed My Father* by Luong Ung.

*Terms of Refuge: The Indochinese Exodus and the International Response*, a report commissioned by the United Nations High Commissioner for Refugees and prepared by W. Courtland Robinson provided necessary background information for understanding the Thai border camp situation, as did a research trip I took in 1989 to the Phanat Nikhom Refugee Processing Center in Thailand. There I was graciously received by camp commander Khun Santi Kerd-in, and by United Nations High Commissioner for Refugees Field Officer Leo Glensvig. In addition, two reports by humanitarian agencies, *Refuge Denied*, by the Lawyers Committee for Human Rights, and *Detained, Denied, Deported: Asylum Seekers in the United States*, A Helsinki Watch Report, provided grounding in the legal processes of asylum and refugee resettlement in the United States.

For information on Site 21, the memoirs *One Year in the Khmer Rouge's S-21* by Vann Nath, *Voices from S-21* by David Chandler, and *Survivor*, by Chum Mey were indispensable resources. I wish also to thank REI Tours for arranging for me a special side trip to S-21 and the Choeung Ek killing fields during a bicycling tour through Cambodia in 2012. Additionally, I found the book *The Lost Executioner* by Nic Dunlop to be an excellent resource on the birth and rise to power of the Khmer Rouge, told through the life of Comrade Duch, the infamous warden of S-21.

Understandably, many Cambodians are reluctant to talk about the Khmer Rouge years. "This is between Cambodians," I was told by one person. Respectfully, I must disagree. The story of the Khmer Rouge is for humanity to ponder and to mourn. The story of its survivors is equally, if not more, important for what it can teach us about human resiliency. In this spirit, I searched for and found historical works that provided detailed insight into the internal structures and workings of the Khmer Rouge regime, as well as the psychology behind their bloody policies and practices. Ben Kiernan's *The Pol Pot Regime*, Alexander Laban Hinton's *Why Did They Kill*, Phillip Short's *Pol Pot, Anatomy of a Nightmare* and Joel Brinkley's *Cambodia's Curse* added greatly to my understanding.

Finally, should readers find inaccuracies in the text of *Saving Nary*, I wish to make it clear that any and all errors are mine alone and do not reflect information gleaned from any of the sources mentioned above, or additional sources not listed. And though I based my narrative around actual events in history, *Saving Nary* is a novel. Resemblance of any characters or events to persons living or dead is purely coincidental.

Writing a novel, though primarily a solitary endeavor, relies heavily on the near-heroic patience of friends and relatives. For slogging through the first draft and providing comments and suggestions, I thank readers Sandra DeMent, Diane Langston, Christian Westphall, John Cox, David Beigh, Mary Vanek, Patricia McClure, Nancy Sullivan, and especially, Sue Duffy and Laura Phenix, for all the bike rides spent listening to my plot lines, scoffing at my doubts and encouraging my dreams.

# One

Khath's body hit the ground before his mind registered the reason for it, so ingrained was his response to gunfire. Three years of fighting the Khmer Rouge in his native Cambodia had left an indelible imprint on body and soul.

Tasting dirt, breathing dust, Khath lay still for a moment listening for the whine of bullets overhead, the shredding of vegetation, the thud of lead embedding itself in wood, the spattering rain of dirt thrown up by a near miss burrowing into the earth. All was quiet in his immediate vicinity, but not too far away, he heard more shooting, shouted commands, and cries of protest, pain and fear. Here? In broad daylight?

He heard the sound of approaching voices and watched a group of men in ragged shorts and bare feet run past on the trail, heading toward the shots, sporadic now, slowly dying away like the hopes of so many in this refugee camp.

Khath's days had been free of gunfire in the fourteen months since he and his brother Pra Chhay arrived at Khao I Dang Refugee Holding Center in Thailand. Located a few miles west of the Cambodian border, the camp was staffed by Thai government officers and military personnel, and many foreign

1

volunteers. Khao I Dang in daytime had been relatively safe, a haven for refugees seeking shelter and a chance for a new life.

But at night, after the foreign aid workers left the camp, Khao I Dang was a dangerous place. From the watchtower, the night guards routinely swept the perimeter wire with staccato bursts from their automatic weapons, and in the early mornings Khath often saw bodies scattered along the fence. The guards said those who tried to slip illegally into the camp at night were Khmer Rouge, but Khath wondered. In the dark, one starving Cambodian face looked like any other—how could they tell?

Cautiously, Khath stood and continued down the path toward the camp's administrative buildings, senses alert. Near the open receiving area adjacent to the camp gates, a large throng of refugees milled about, churning up billowing clouds of dust. Most had wound cotton scarves around their noses and mouths to keep their lungs free of the choking powder; dry cough was already rampant in the camp. Loudspeakers mounted on tall poles around the receiving area crackled on overhead, the sound quality distorted and tinny: *Return to your scheduled activities. Do not approach the perimeter fence. Clear the area immediately.*

Khath reached the outer edge of the crowd and stopped an old woman who was walking away, a listless child in her arms. "Tell me, elder sister. What happened?" he said. "Are we under attack? Is it the Khmer Rouge?"

The woman looked at him. "I don't know." She waved a hand vaguely. "They shut the gates." She set the child down on the ground where it stood passively, one dirty hand grasping a fold of the woman's wrapped skirt. The woman placed her hands on the small of her back and rubbed absently. Her feet hung over the edges of flip-flops meant for a smaller foot, perhaps one not so flattened by years of field labor and a starvation diet of rice gruel.

Khath wondered suddenly how old she was. He had used the polite form of address meant for an elder, but everyone in this camp looked old beyond their years, even the children.

Even me, he thought. I am not yet 40 years old, yet my face is withered like a dried-out mango. He dug in his pocket and found the remnants of a box of candied ginger, holding it out to the woman. "For your child," he said.

Edging deeper into the crowd, Khath moved toward the gates until he was blocked by an armed Thai guard. Beyond the soldier, through the iron gates Khath could see two men, supporting a companion who limped between them, making their way slowly back toward the border. The injured man's right foot dragged behind him, shoeless, scraping against the hard-packed dirt road leading to Cambodia. Khath looked away, his brain already too full of accidental images of the everyday pains of warfare. "I try not to notice them; they torment me so," he had said just yesterday to his older brother Pra Chhay, a Buddhist monk and scholar. "Can you help me not to see them?" But Pra Chhay had no satisfactory answers for him.

Khath risked a sidelong look at the soldier blocking his way. Some of the guards were kind, showing compassion for the refugees they were there to protect. Others were cruel and preyed in unspeakable ways on the refugees' vulnerability. Most, like this one, seemed simply to be obeying orders. Not sensing active hostility from the man, Khath ventured a question.

"Khmer Rouge?" he asked, nodding toward the camp gates. Who else would draw the guards' gunfire at this time of day?

The soldier, a mere boy really, gave a faint shake of his head, but that was all. "Clear the area," he said, gesturing toward Khath with his weapon. The conversation was over.

Khath turned away from the soldier and walked toward the thatched bamboo structures housing the offices of the camp commander, the International Red Cross, the United Nations High Commissioner for Refugees and numerous other humanitarian agencies that provided food, medicine and instruction to the residents of the camp. Usually, the veranda was deserted when Khath made his daily pilgrimage to these buildings, but not today.

Drawn by the commotion at the gates, foreign aid workers lined the railing, talking loudly and waving their hands. *What are they saying? What has happened?* The jabber of foreign tongues swelled around Khath as he neared the building, his sense of unease growing. He could tell that these people were upset, anger making their pink faces redder and sweatier than usual.

Keeping to the back edge of the veranda away from the foreigners, Khath made his way toward the cork boards outside the door of the Red Cross office. Today, as it had every day for the last 14 months, his heart beat faster as he neared the boards. Hope, wrapped with fear, squeezed his lungs and forced quick, shallow breaths from his chest. He averted his gaze as he approached the boards and stared at the floor, watching his feet carry him toward great joy or crushing disappointment depending on what he found posted on the cork surface. Centering himself in front of the boards, he squared his shoulders, murmured a prayer and raised his eyes. His pent up breath escaped in a whoosh as he stared, shocked, at nothing. The lists were not there.

Khath passed a hand over his face and looked again. No lists. He stepped back, uncomprehending, then tapped on the Red Cross door frame before entering the room where a lone worker sat typing at a desk. Her yellow hair was tied back from her forehead in a ponytail that swung free from high on the crown of her head in the manner of a schoolgirl, though the lines on her face showed she was long past those days. She did not look up until Khath coughed politely.

"Yes? Can I help you?" she said.

Khath kept his eyes lowered in respect. "The names," he mumbled, pointing toward the door.

"Excuse me?"

Anxiously searching his mind for the English words, Khath tried again. "Every day, I come. Look names. Today, not."

The woman's face cleared. "Oh," she said, and then launched into rapid-fire English for several moments.

Khath watched her lips moving as the sounds tumbled from her mouth. He noticed she had large teeth, very straight and white, evenly spaced with no gaps. Not like refugee teeth. When she stopped speaking, he looked at her helplessly. "Sorry?"

She pointed to a chair against the wall. "Sit. Please," she said. She walked out the door and to Khath's relief soon returned, followed by one of the camp interpreters.

The young Cambodian greeted Khath politely and introduced himself as Youk. "I was just on my way to the canteen for lunch," he said. "Walk with me, and I will tell you what I know." He lit a cigarette as they made their way out of the building. "I recognize you. You come every day to check the Unaccompanied Minors List for new children who have been registered with the Red Cross."

Khath nodded. "My two daughters, Kamala and Sitha are missing. I pray to find their names on the list."

The interpreter glanced at Khath. "I'm sorry," he said. "I hope one day they will come. What are their full names?" He drew a small pad and pencil from the breast pocket of his shirt and made a note, promising Khath that he would watch the lists of arrivals. "When did you last see your daughters?" he asked.

"About eighteen months after Phnom Penh fell," Khath said. "Our work unit was being moved from Khompong Cham to Phnom Bros. The Khmer Rouge took the children to a youth work brigade to dig irrigation ditches." Khath felt his facial muscles tense at the memory and a twitch began to plague his left eye. "My daughters were eight and ten years old, but their bodies were so small, with stick legs and big bellies. There was so little food by then…" He stopped walking and turned to face the interpreter. "How could they expect such little girls to work so hard?"

Youk let the question pass. "Phnom Penh fell in 1975. You last saw your daughters in 1977? Four years ago?"

Khath nodded, hating the sound of defeat that had crept into Youk's voice. Four years wasn't such a very long time, was it? "I searched for them in Cambodia in 1979 when the Vietnamese soldiers drove the Khmer Rouge into the jungles. For almost a year, my brother and I went from village to village, searching the streets and orphanages. We checked the border camps as well when it was safe to do so."

"Any trace of them? Any sign at all? Were you able to find where the Khmer Rouge took them?"

Khath shook his head and sighed heavily. "No, nothing. But I always felt we should go to the next village, and the next. Because they could always be there, at the next village. Or the one after." Khath saw the now familiar pitying expression begin to spread itself over Youk's face and dropped his eyes. "I would know if they were dead," he said defensively.

They stood outside the canteen, an open air thatched roof pavilion filled with orderly rows of eight-foot tables and plastic chairs. Around the edges of the pavilion, Thai venders sold snacks, beverages and meals, mostly to foreign aid workers. There was no electricity in the canteen. Hot meals were made with single burner stoves fueled by portable propane tanks; refrigeration consisted of bins of ice, refreshed twice daily.

"We will continue to watch for their names," Youk said. "But I am afraid that there will be no more lists for a while."

"What do you mean, no more lists?" Khath asked.

"Well," Youk said. "You heard the shooting this morning?"

"I thought it was Khmer Rouge attacking the camp like they do at the border," Khath said.

Youk shook his head. "No, the Khmer Rouge would not dare to enter Thailand to attack Khao I Dang."

Tell that to the guards, Khath thought. Obviously, this boy went home at night with the foreign aid workers, even if he was Cambodian. He'd not seen the bodies outside the fence in the early morning hours. Of course he hadn't. The guards always carted them away before the foreigners returned to camp. Khath envied the boy his innocence. "Then what was the commotion this morning?" he asked. "Who were they shooting at?"

Youk looked uncomfortable. He cleared his throat. "You know that Khao I Dang is filled to overflowing—over 100,000 people, yet still more refugees come," he said. "Now that the camp is officially closed, the refugees bribe the supply truck drivers or even climb into the trucks when the drivers aren't watching. Other countries are too slow to accept our people for resettlement." Youk tossed his spent cigarette on the dirt, then paused to grind it into the earth. "So now Thailand is strictly enforcing its policy not to accept any more refugees. This morning, a large group was caught sneaking through with a supply truck. Once inside, the guards pushed them back to the gates but they refused to leave."

Khath stared at Youk, aghast. "The guards were shooting at the refugees?" he asked. An image of the man with the dragging foot flashed in his mind.

Youk lit another cigarette. "Not exactly," he explained. "They aimed high. I heard the commander tell the soldiers to aim above their heads. Just to frighten them back to Cambodia."

"But the Khmer Rouge will kill them for trying to escape!" Khath stared at Youk angrily.

Youk nodded his head. "I know. It is a terrible situation. But this is all political, don't you see? Once the international news gets wind of this, it will force other countries to take more refugees for resettlement. At least, that is what the Thai government is hoping to accomplish."

"No. This can't be. It is too cruel." Khath was filled with the horror of what awaited any returning refugee unfortunate enough to be caught by the Khmer Rouge forces still hiding in the border jungles. It was forbidden to try to escape to Thailand and the Khmer Rouge liked to make examples of those who disobeyed the rules. Tears filled his eyes. What if his girls tried to come to Khao I Dang now? They would die, if not at the hands of the Khmer Rouge, then surely from pure despair. "Thailand is supposed to help us," he cried. "Not send us back to be murdered."

Youk reached out a soothing hand, but Khath backed away from him. "How long?" he asked, his voice hoarse. "How long will the borders remain closed? How many of us must die before we're allowed back in?"

Youk took a quick drag on the cigarette, looking down and away as he blew the smoke from his lungs. "I don't know. No one knows. We must hope for the best outcome," he said, still looking at the ground. "Please," Youk gestured toward the canteen. "Come drink some tea with me and calm yourself. I've done wrong to upset you like this."

Khath studied the young man for a moment. No one who had lived under the harsh rule of the Khmer Rouge could be so matter-of-fact about this. "You've been away from Cambodia for a long time, haven't you?"

Youk blushed. "My father was a diplomat. He sent me to France to study when the war broke out, and would not let me return. He was killed when the Khmer Rouge captured Phnom Penh."

Khath nodded. Many wealthy Cambodians sent their children abroad to keep them safe when the war drew too near. Those who didn't probably regretted it until their dying breath, which, for them, usually occurred not long after the Khmer Rouge entered a town.

"Your father was a wise man," he said to Youk. "But I have no time to drink tea. This new policy of Thailand…it changes everything."

# Two

"Go back to Cambodia?" Pra Chhay stared at Khath with puzzled eyes.

Khath nodded. "What choice do we have, brother?" he said. "Our people are being forced back across the border into the arms of the Khmer Rouge. My daughters will have no chance now to get into Khao I Dang. We must go back to continue our search for them."

Pra Chhay, dressed in saffron monk's robes and cracked rubber sandals, stood framed by the setting sun outside the open doorway of the bamboo and thatch shelter he shared with Khath and five other families. The odor of too many human bodies crowded into a small living space hung heavy in the air spilling across the threshold.

The rectangular shelter was partitioned by side walls into six open-faced cubicles, three to a side, facing a center corridor running the length of the shelter. There was no privacy other than what could be attained by turning one's back to the open side of one's cubicle or crawling inside a mosquito net hung over the thin kapok sleeping mattresses on the floor. The shelter's only doors were located at each end of the central corridor, opening directly to the outside.

With no way to secure themselves or their meagre belongings, the refugees lived in helpless fear of night visits by bored Thai soldiers, whose transgressions ranged from theft to rape. Pra Chhay and Khath occupied an end cubicle by the door, making them even more vulnerable to unwanted attention from the soldiers, but because of Pra Chhay's position as a monk, they were usually left alone.

As Pra Chhay slipped his calloused feet out of his sandals, stepping barefoot into the corridor, a gentle breeze puffed out the hem of his robes and blew camp dust into the shelter.

Khath motioned to Pra Chhay to shut the door. Careful not to waste a drop of the day's ration of precious water, he barely moistened the corner of a rag and ran it over random surfaces in their cubicle that might attract and harbor dust: the wooden altar in the corner, the cracks and edges of the bamboo slats that formed the walls of the hut, the straw mats that covered the floor. A squat wooden bench, left behind by the prior resident, completed the amenities of the living space.

Pra Chhay took off his outer layer of robes and hung them on a sliver of bamboo pulled out from the wall to serve as a peg for clothing. Turning, he watched Khath rub his cloth over the wooden bench, back and forth, back and forth, harder and harder, the knuckles gripping the cloth turning white with effort.

"Khath, stop it. You will polish our only seat away to nothing," Pra Chhay said. "Tell me exactly what you heard today that makes you say we must return to Cambodia." The monk settled himself comfortably on the floor.

With an effort, Khath slowed his rubbing and carefully folded the rag and laid it on his lap. His eyes followed the tiny particles now dancing in the single ray of golden sun that slipped through the crack between the outer door and its frame. He laced his fingers tightly together to stop their reaching for the rag as, mesmerized, he watched the motes settle onto the areas he had just cleaned. The sight of dust on surfaces where it ought not to be was still intolerable to Khath, though nearly six years had passed since his obsession was born on the day the Khmer Rouge killed his wife and son.

"Silence that boy," the soldier had said to his wife on that awful day. Khieu gathered their son Bunchan into her arms, but how is one to soothe a toddler who cries from hunger when there is no food? Khath, Khieu and their three children had been walking for three days in the heat and humidity, shoulder to shoulder with thousands of other refugees inching their way out of Phnom Penh by order of the Khmer Rouge. Already hunger, thirst and exhaustion had thinned their ranks: the elderly and the ill simply dropped along the sides of the road, patiently awaiting the mercy of death.

Given only minutes to prepare for their exodus, the food Khath and his family carried was gone in a day. After that, they bought, scavenged and bartered for whatever nourishment they could find along the way. Now, they stood next in line before a table of grim-faced cadres in the simple uniform of the Khmer Rouge: black cotton shirts and pants with *kramas,* red-checkered scarves, wound around their heads or necks. The cadres were checking identity papers and quizzing the refugees about their prior occupations.

Bunchan's incessant crying enraged the soldier. "Silence him or I will," he warned Khieu.

Khath saw the man's tight lips and clenched jaw and stepped between his wife and the soldier, doing his best both to shield his family and appease the angry cadre. "Please," Khath said. "If you could spare just a few grains of rice. Or perhaps there is some place nearby I could buy or trade for food. I will go immediately. The child is hungry, that's all."

Khieu's frantic attempts to calm Bunchan had the opposite effect. Red faced, the toddler screamed his hunger to the skies above.

The soldier flicked his eyes to one side, turning slightly. Following his gaze, Khath saw a man standing a little apart from the check-point, watching the scene impassively. As Khath waited, his heart thudding inside his chest like the heavy, dread beat of a death knell, he saw the man glance at the position of the sun and cast a look at the road behind Khath, densely packed with men, women and children yet to be processed through the checkpoint.

The man rubbed his left jawline as though he had a toothache, but perhaps it was his ear, missing its earlobe, which was causing the pain. At any rate, he frowned and seemed to come to some sort of decision, for he looked at the soldier and gave a barely perceptible nod.

At that, the soldier moved quickly, brushing past Khath and yanking Bunchan from Khieu's arms. "You had your chance," he said to Khieu, and began striding toward a large tree not far off the side of the road, the bawling toddler slung under his arm.

"My baby! Give me my baby!" Khieu screamed and rushed after the soldier, grabbing at Bunchan, whose angry howls had turned to terrified shrieks.

Khath's daughters, crying, tried to run after their mother but Khath held them back. A terrible dread filled his heart as he watched the scene rapidly unfolding before him for he knew that the Khmer Rouge were ruthless when crossed. He pressed the girls' faces to his body to shield them from what he feared would follow.

The soldier swung his rifle and knocked Khieu to the ground where she sprawled, tears streaming down her face, her arms reaching for Bunchan. She grabbed for the soldier's leg and held on, moaning "My son. Please, oh please give me back my son."

Struggling to manage both his weapon and the squirming child, the soldier's face darkened in anger; his eyes narrowed. He drew himself up, trying to shake Khieu off of his leg.

Khath stood transfixed, knowing a line had been crossed. "Khieu," he whispered. He gripped his girls in a rigid embrace as the world narrowed to a tight circle encompassing himself, his daughters and the scene before him.

The man with the missing earlobe burst into Khath's world, standing beside the soldier, the drawn revolver in his hand pointed squarely at Khieu's forehead. "Rubbish," he spat, and pulled the trigger. Khieu was flung backwards by the shot, a tidy red hole in her forehead belying the spray of brain, blood and bone that spewed out behind her as she flopped back onto the ground. "Rubbish," the man said again, and kicked dirt toward Khieu's face. An eerie silence descended over the scene.

Dangling from the soldier's grasp, Bunchan stretched his chubby arms toward Khieu's body. "Maa," he wailed.

The soldier whirled, took the remaining several steps to the tree, and grasping the crying child by the legs, swung him in the air. A dull squashy thud silenced Bunchan's cries, followed by a soft thump as the earth received his lifeless body, tossed aside by the soldier.

The man with the missing earlobe turned his cold eyes toward Khath. "Clean up this mess," he said.

A roaring filled Khath's ears and he fought the urge to vomit. His pores opened and acrid sweat soaked his clothing. Still shielding his daughter's faces, he urged them with trembling hands to the side of the road and sat them down with their backs turned toward the carnage. "Hold each other tight," he whispered, squatting down beside them. "Do not turn around. Do not make a sound. Do you understand?"

The girls nodded, their frightened eyes brimming with unshed tears.

"Wait for me. I won't be long," Khath said. He hurried back into the road and dropped to his knees beside Khieu's body. He tried to brush away the dirt from her clothing, but it merely settled into the neckline of her blouse and the dark tendrils of hair that curled about her neck. He reached out a hand to lower her eyelids, but stopped in horror at the sight of a light sprinkling of dust and dirt particles kicked up by her killer and stuck fast to the orbs of her eyes. "Blink, Khieu. Oh, my dearest, please cleanse your eyes," Khath moaned. He glanced helplessly toward the line of refugees still shuffling along the road and saw only averted faces. Scooping Khieu up in his arms, Khath carried her a little way into the roadside field and laid her gently beside some bushes. With dread in his heart, he approached the tree where the soldier had taken the life of his son. The sight of Bunchan's crushed skull brought the bile back to Khath's throat and he swallowed hard. Then in a rush of panic, he spun around to check on his daughters, finding them still huddled on the side of the road as he had left them.

There was no time to spare in grieving. Khath cradled his son's body in his arms, saying a prayer as he hurried back to where he had laid Khieu to rest. He placed the boy in the crook of Khieu's right arm, then drew a length of Khieu's long wrapped skirt from underneath her body, bringing it up across her chest to cover Bunchan. Pausing, he stroked the face of his dead wife, then, gently drew the cloth up and over those dusty eyes, tucking it carefully around her head.

A pain in his hands made him glance down, and he saw only a damp rag twisted around his fingers here in this hut in Khao I Dang.

"Are you all right, Khath?" Pra Chhay squatted down and began to untwist the rag from Khath's grip. "Have some water."

Khath took the proffered glass and raised it to his mouth with a hand that trembled. Then, clearing his throat, he began to tell Pra Chhay what he had learned that morning from the interpreter. "So you see," he said as he finished. "We must return to Cambodia, otherwise, we will never find my Kamala and Sitha."

"Perhaps," Pra Chhay replied. "But I think we should talk directly to the Red Cross and not base such an important decision on the words of an interpreter."

A dull brown lizard, about six inches long from snout to tail tip, clung to the interior wall of the Red Cross office. The lizards were a common sight around the camp, useful for catching beetles, killing their prey with a rat-a-tat-tat banging of the struggling insect against the wall. At times, the lizards would lose their grip and fall—plop!—on top of whatever surface was below them, whether it be the floor, a desk or someone's head. They would lie stunned for an instant before scuttling off to seek shelter.

Khath imagined that was what it would feel like to be resettled in another country—one just fell from the sky into a new land, gathered one's wits, and then tried hard just to carry on with life.

Seated on uncomfortable wooden folding chairs, Khath and Pra Chhay waited silently while the officer at the desk, identified as Mr. Ames by a badge on his chest, rifled through the contents of two slim file folders: dossiers on him and his brother. An interpreter sat nearby, an older man who emanated sadness and looked beaten down and tired. And who wouldn't be, listening to the sad stories of so many thousands of refugees day after day, Khath thought.

Finally, Mr. Ames closed the file folders and mopped his face with a handkerchief. "Damn this heat," he muttered. He leaned forward and, with the help of the interpreter, began to speak with Khath and Pra Chhay. "Given your histories," he said, "you would both be granted preference for resettlement. As a monk," he nodded his head toward Pra Chhay, "you would receive favorable treatment under the Religious Persecution category. And you," he said, turning to look directly at Khath, "would certainly merit Political Persecution status because of your history as a government soldier fighting the Khmer Rouge. Especially, and correct me if I misunderstood this part..." Mr. Ames paused, peering over his spectacles at Khath, his arched eyebrows and wrinkled brow suggesting dubiousness mixed with awe. "What I mean to say here is that your file indicates that you were held at Tuol Sleng prison in Phnom Penh for some time. About six months, wasn't it? Is that accurate?"

Khath nodded, noticing the interpreter's sharp intake of breath and narrowed eyes as he received, then interpreted, this bit of information.

Mr. Ames sat back in his chair. "But how on earth did you survive…when so many others…" His voice trailed off.

Eyes welling, Khath looked at his hands now curled in his lap. These battered hands had saved his life.

"My brother had skills," Pra Chhay jumped into the silence. "He was a railroad mechanic. It says so in his file. He can fix anything and the Khmer Rouge found that useful. They kept him alive and forced him to maintain the equipment in the prison. It was not his choice. He was their slave." Locking eyes with the official, Pra Chhay's stern expression dared the man to suggest that Khath might have been a Khmer Rouge sympathizer.

Stroking his chin, Mr. Ames considered this information. Then he nodded and picked up Khath's file and made a notation in it. "So far," he said, closing the file, "we know of just four other survivors out of the 20,000 who were imprisoned and tortured at Tuol Sleng. One was an artist, of all things, who was put to work painting pictures of Pol Pot. Did you know him?"

"I saw him," Khath said. "We were not permitted to speak. I am glad that he survived."

"Well, at any rate, I would suggest we forward your documents to the US consulate for resettlement consideration, since you were a soldier in the US-backed Lon Nol forces," Mr. Ames said. "That would be the most logical place to start. Is that what you would like me to do?"

"No!" Khath's head jerked up. "My daughters…"

Laying a restraining hand on Khath's leg, Pra Chhay said, "Before we decide, Mr. Ames, we have questions about how best to find my brother's daughters. We searched for them in Cambodia for nine months before coming to Khao I Dang about a year ago. Every day Khath checks the Unaccompanied Minors List, but so far we have not found them here, either. Is it true that no more refugees are allowed to enter Thailand?"

"Temporarily, yes. But, listen, if you've been looking for this long and haven't found them, your best bet might be to go to the US and register with the Red Cross over there. Our program is pretty local here."

Mr. Ames waved his hand around the makeshift office. "As you can imagine, we've had lots of technical difficulties here in Khao I Dang. It's possible your daughters might have already been sent abroad."

Khath's eyes widened in shocked disbelief. "Alone? Without their family?"

Mr. Ames spread his hands apart, palms up, a slight shrug of his shoulders acknowledging the brashness of the act. "It was a nightmare when all these starving, sick kids arrived at the border," he said. "We were desperate to save them, and sending them abroad by the planeload was the only way we could think of to do that, initially. They needed medical care and we had nothing to offer. Of course it's different now with the clinic and children's center here. But back then there was nothing. Don't worry, though. Those kids are not lost. We are tracking them."

He waved Khath, who had half-risen from his chair, back into his seat. "This is what I'm saying. You go to America, you register with the International Red Cross there. Get yourself in their computers, and then they can search our offices all over the world for your daughters. Meanwhile, you establish yourself, build a new life. That way, you can sponsor your daughters directly so when they are found, they've got a safe place to go and a much shorter wait to get there."

"I don't know," Khath said. He tried to imagine his daughters loaded aboard a plane of child passengers, sent off to a foreign land to be raised by strangers. How terrified they would have been. His stomach clenched as his world crumbled just a little more.

"Believe me, it's your best option. With your histories, you could be on a plane bound for the US in three to four months." Mr. Ames waited for a response.

With a question in his eyes, Khath turned to his brother.

"I think he's right," Pra Chhay said, after a moment. "I think we should leave. We can always come back later if we need to. But it's your choice. We will do as you wish."

A heavy silence descended, and then Khath sighed. "All right. Give them our files. If they accept us, we will go."

# Three

As the sun rose, Khath sat cross-legged in a lotus position in the small Buddhist temple nestled below Khao I Dang Mountain. The barbed wire perimeter fence separated the mountain from the refugee camp, but the mountain lent its power to the area nonetheless. Pra Chhay and two other monks chanted the Heart Sutra, a prayer of enlightenment, the rhythmic drone rising and falling in a soothing and familiar hum as the scent of incense hung heavily in the hot, humid air. About thirty refugees sat on the straw mats covering the wooden floor of the bamboo temple. The lips of many were moving as they softly chanted along with the monks.

Khath's lips remained still, his heart empty. If asked, he would not disavow the teachings. He believed the teachings, yet the words of the Buddha had lost the power to move or to comfort him. He felt somehow distant from the teachings, as though they controlled behavior on a different world from the one he inhabited. It was a very lonely feeling.

The monks chanted on, a background hum that began to irritate Khath. He might as well be listening to the drone of mosquitoes as he toiled on the dikes under the watchful eyes of the Khmer Rouge, their guns aimed and ready, afraid to brush the insects away from his face lest he be beaten for not putting full attention into his work.

Observing the others in the temple, Khath envied them their faith. Pra Chhay often said there were two levels of Buddhism, one being the simple devotions taught to uneducated villagers; the other consisting of the higher practices and theories studied by the scholar monks.

Neither, Khath reflected sadly, could shed much light for him on the blood lust that had gripped Cambodia under Pol Pot. Abruptly, Khath stood and backed out of the temple, keeping his head low, hands clasped and body bent over as tradition demanded, never turning his back to the Buddha. It did no harm to be respectful when doing otherwise would be a useless insult that served only to draw attention and anger toward him.

The temple, run by camp residents, stood next to a Christian church operated by foreign missionaries and refugee converts. As Khath passed the church, a man about his own age came down the steps towards him. Tall and lanky, in contrast to Khath's compact body, the man fell into step beside Khath.

"Leaving so soon?" he asked.

Khath glanced at the man and kept walking without responding.

"I used to go to the temple," the man said. "But the Buddha …he just sits quietly on the lotus throne, yes? Maybe he naps, happy, calm. Not like me. My world is gone, my family gone, and Buddha still sits, calm and happy. What can he know of the pain in my heart?"

His interest piqued, Khath stopped and faced the man. "And what about the Christian God? What does he know?"

"Oh. Everything. They say he is everywhere, all the time. And that he is very powerful, and can do anything. He can make a big flood, and destroy the earth. Khmer Rouge is nothing for him." The tall man grinned. "But he loves the good people, so nothing to fear."

The man's smile was infectious. Khath felt the corners of his own mouth twitch upwards. "How does he know who is good and who is not?"

"Oh. Easy. They sprinkle some water on you, make a mark, and then God knows."

The man's smile faded and he shrugged. "I don't know if it's true, but the people are nice. Sometimes I feel happy there. And the pastor says it might help us to find a sponsor from a church in America."

A flutter of excitement started in Khath's stomach and moved upwards. Only yesterday he had agreed to go to America if the US would take him. Now, a man stood before him offering him a way to improve his chances of finding an American sponsor.

He had passed this church a thousand times on his way to and from the temple and never before had anyone approached him. Was it a sign? An omen confirming that the decision to search for his daughters from America was the correct one?

Khath glanced back down the road, longing to run into the temple and consult the oracle sticks about this new development. The slender bamboo sticks, each imprinted with a number, were gathered into a long bamboo sleeve off to the side of the altar. Many times when grave decisions were necessary, Khath had shaken the sleeve gently, the soft, hissing rattle of the dry sticks muting the sound of his whispered prayers until one stick broke free of the others and fell to the floor. The numbered stick was then matched with a corresponding sutra verse or parable. Khath always found the advice of the oracle sticks to be profound and relevant. He turned his gaze back to the tall man beside him.

"Why don't you come see for yourself?" the man said. "We have Bible study at 3:00 this afternoon." He touched Khath briefly on the arm. "There's no harm in it, and we can help each other. I get points if I bring new people to church. You might have some happy times. The stories are interesting—something different to think about, and they usually serve a little food afterward."

At the mention of food, Khath's stomach rumbled. He agreed to attend the Bible study and hurried back to his hut to eat a little rice before heading to the water tanks to collect his daily ration of water.

It was mid-morning when Khath joined the queue of refugees waiting for water. A solid row of eight foot square metal water tanks were positioned next to each other in the dirt, each one with a round trap door on the top, the heavy metal clasps secured with padlocks. Khath knew from chatting with the drivers that the water was trucked in from various villages anywhere from thirty to sixty miles away. A fleet of sixty tankers made two trips per day to meet the needs of the camp. It seemed like a lot of water, but each resident was only allotted ten liters per day.

Khath saw Pra Chhay ahead of him in line, getting his bucket filled. He waved and Pra Chhay waved back and went to sit under a tree so the brothers could walk home together. Along the way, Khath told Pra Chhay about meeting the tall refugee outside the Christian church.

Pra Chhay nodded his head. "Yes, I have heard that some Christian leaders place great emphasis on recruiting members to join their churches."

Khath stopped for a moment to switch the heavy bucket from one hand to the other. "But did you know that converting can help you get a sponsorship to America?"

"I suppose that makes sense," Pra Chhay said. "But your tall friend did not seem to have much faith in the teachings. I would think the church leaders would be offended by pretenders."

They walked in silence for a few minutes. Sweat rolled down their faces as they trudged with their heavy buckets.

"I'm going to go there this afternoon," Khath said, his words plopping into the silence like pebbles tossed into a pond.

Pra Chhay said nothing.

"I'm going to meet the pastor later," Khath said. A hint of aggressiveness tinged his voice, as if daring Pra Chhay to object.

Pra Chhay stopped walking and brought the end of his robe up to wipe his face. "I know you are struggling, Khath. If the Christian teachings bring you comfort, I would support your conversion with a happy heart," he said.

"You should come, too," Khath said. "The sooner we get to America, the sooner we can register with the Red Cross there. If the pastor will help us find a sponsor, I am willing to sit in his church and pray to his God. And for the sake of Kamala and Sitha, I think you should be, too."

"Khath, I am a monk. Are you asking me to give up my vows?"

A muscle in Khath's jaw twitched as he stared stubbornly at Pra Chhay. "Think of the girls," he said. Would Pra Chhay be so unwilling if their roles were reversed?

Pra Chhay turned away and continued walking, their hut coming into view now. After a few moments, he said, "The Red Cross says we already have protected status and that there will be no problem getting visas to go to the US." Pra Chhay stood now with his hand on the door knob of the hut, facing his brother. "We do not have to lie our way into the country."

"But we need sponsors." Khath dropped his bucket to the ground in frustration, sloshing a good portion of his water ration over the edge of the bucket and onto his feet. "We can't just go there. You know we need someone to sponsor us before they will let us in, even with visas. Who's going to sponsor us, Pra Chhay? Who? We know no one in America."

"Brother, calm yourself," Pra Chhay moved toward Khath and placed an arm around his shoulders. "You know I cannot do what you ask, but we will find a way. I promise you that. Go to your meeting, get information. I will see what information I can gather as well." He squeezed Khath's shoulders, giving his brother a gentle shake. "Don't despair, Khath. We will get to America soon, I promise."

Swallowing hard, Khath nodded and picked up his bucket again. He buried his frustration deep in his heart where it burned with an almost physical pain. His veins throbbed with the effort to contain this anger, building year after year since the Khmer Rouge had destroyed his country, his life, his love, everything he held dear. He passed a hand over his face, and rubbed—hard—to distract himself from his thoughts.

Following Pra Chhay into the hut, Khath's senses were immediately assaulted by the odors of garlic and sweat mingled with those of stale, unwashed clothing. Babies wailed, adults snarled and snapped at one another, and miraculously, an occasional laugh split the air. Scratchy music from cheap transistors thumped and throbbed in the background. The first few moments inside the hut were always jarring, but today, in his agitated state, the shrill of humanity seemed even more disturbing than usual.

Across the corridor, an elderly woman with gray-streaked hair tied back in a wispy bun lived with her two grandsons, one a teenager of sixteen; the other, a boy just eight or nine years old. Khath had grown accustomed to the old woman's tuneless humming as she went about her daily chores. She seemed to have a fondness for him and Pra Chhay, welcoming them with a gap-toothed smile and betel-stained lips whenever they entered the shelter. More than once she had shyly offered some delicacy from the market to Pra Chhay as a sign of her respect for his vocation.

But today, Grandmother moaned and cried and pulled at her hair, while the eldest boy tried to soothe her. The younger boy crouched in the corner of the hut, huddled silently against the wall, his eyes fearful as he watched Grandmother cry.

Pra Chhay had already crossed the hall and was kneeling beside Grandmother. "What is it? What has happened?" he asked.

Grandmother lifted her tear-stained face. "They're here," she sobbed. "I saw them."

"I don't understand," Pra Chhay said as Khath joined the group. They looked for clarification at the teenager as he awkwardly patted Grandmother's shoulders, but he shrugged and shook his head. He didn't know what was going on either.

Khath brought a mug of water to the distraught woman. "Here, Grandmother, drink this. Dry your eyes and let us help you," he said.

Slowly, the old woman sat up and rubbed her eyes. "The Khmer Rouge," she whispered. "They're here in the camp." She glanced around fearfully. "There was a boy, from my village, named Mith. He turned Khmer Rouge. He joined them and did terrible things, terrible." Her eyes welled up again, but as she recalled the past her anger surfaced and she brushed away her tears impatiently. "They brought heads into the village and hung them on poles to warn us not to resist. I saw my friend, the schoolmaster, on a pole." She drew her finger across her neck. "For days. He rotted on a pole. No one dared to take it down. I hate them." Then, her face crumpled again. "Today I saw him. I saw Mith at the camp market."

Khath's stomach lurched. Rumors were rife about different people in the camp. Camp bullies were commonly accused of being Khmer Rouge behind their backs. Pointed fingers, suspicious glances—no one really trusted anyone else. A thin veneer of civility was all that separated the gentle smile of the mouth from the raging fire of the soul. No one wanted to peer underneath the surface for fear of what they might find there.

"But are you sure? How can you be certain?" Pra Chhay was saying. "Perhaps you just thought you saw him across a distance. It's a hot day, the market was crowded…"

Grandmother shook her head, weeping again. "I saw his watch. I made that watch. I sewed beads in the shape of a lotus on the leather band. I bloodied my fingers on that watch!" Grandmother held her gnarled and bent fingers up for inspection. "When the Khmer Rouge killed my son, they took his watch, his rings. Now, Mith wears the watch like a prize."

"Did he see you?" Pra Chhay asked.

Miserably, Grandmother nodded. "I cried out when I saw the watch. The shock was so great. I saw a wrist wrapped with that beautiful lotus band—he was reaching for a mango—and I thought for a moment it was my son, come back to life. Instead it was that awful man. He looked up, saw me, laughed in my face, then walked away. Now, maybe he will kill me, too."

"No." The grandson leaped to his feet, a wild look in his eye. "No one is going to kill you, Grandmother. I remember Mith. He went to University in France and came back a communist. But without his guns, he is a coward and a bully. I will bring back father's watch. I am his son. I should be the one wearing it."

Grandmother struggled to her feet and seized the boy's arm. "I forbid you," she hissed. "You must swear to the Venerable One that you will do no such thing. Think of your future, your brother. I forbid you to throw your life away on more killing." She turned to Pra Chhay. "Please. Stop him," she said, her voice breaking. "I cannot bear another death in our family."

———

Khath made his way slowly toward the Christian church, his thoughts churning. It had troubled him greatly to see Grandmother's distress. How were the Khmer Rouge making it into camp? Were they sneaking in at night, bribing the guards to let them in? His heart twisted. Would he look up some day and find himself staring into the faces of the men who'd killed his wife and his son? He pressed his hands to his temples and shook his head. He did not want to enter a church and meet its leader with thoughts of bloody revenge raging in his mind.

As he approached the church, he saw his acquaintance of the morning leaning out over the veranda, craning his neck and staring up and down the street. When he saw Khath, he broke into a big grin and came to meet him.

"Ah, good. You are here with time to spare. Would you like a cigarette?" He flipped open a pack and extended it to Khath.

Khath helped himself to a cigarette, nodding his thanks to this kind-hearted stranger.

They smoked in silence for a moment, then the man nodded at Khath. "This morning, I thought you looked troubled. Now, even more so. It is a good day to meet a pastor, yes?"

"I am honored to meet him," Khath said automatically, his mind elsewhere. He blew a long stream of smoke from his lungs. Feeling calmer, he said, "How do you suppose the Khmer Rouge are entering this camp?" Khath spoke casually, as though it were no big deal to him, just a passing reflection on a known phenomenon, like the weather.

The tall man grinned. "Oh. Easy," he said. "The bosses here, they tell us to watch for Khmer Rouge. Big points to convert a Khmer Rouge! You know Sakeo Camp? On the border? It was overrun by the Khmer Rouge; they took control of it. The United Nations, they don't want to give help to the Khmer Rouge. So they close the camp. Bus the refugees here. They think the Khmer Rouge will go back into the jungle to fight some more; only the real refugees come here." He took a drag on his cigarette and winked at Khath. "Maybe some of those Khmer Rouge are tired of fighting, yes? They'd rather come here and get a ticket to America. So they tell a little lie. Who's going to stop them? Who's going to know? Only the refugees know and they are too afraid to say anything." Flicking the stub of his cigarette into the road, the man smiled a sad smile at Khath. "Better just to let God figure it out, yes?"

Khath followed his companion toward the church, wishing he had not asked about the Khmer Rouge. Now, again, his stomach was churning and the blood pounded in his head. Big points to convert a Khmer Rouge? The thought horrified him. There was no converting those people. Not that it mattered. No one could lie better than a Khmer Rouge. We're just taking you out for some fresh air, they said to their victims as they led them to the killing fields. You can go back to the city in three days, they promised as they began their four year reign of terror. Oh yes, I believe in your God, absolutely I do, they would insist as they plotted their escape to America. Maybe his lanky guide was right. These problems were beyond the scope of man.

Entering the building, Khath found himself in a short hallway with offices on either side. The hallway opened up to a large room partly filled with wooden chairs. A lectern holding a book bound in black leather with gilt-edged pages faced the chairs, and a large wooden cross dominated the wall behind the lectern. A plain altar with flowers on it was positioned under the cross.

To one side, six or seven people sat on chairs arranged in a circle. Khath saw a soft-looking foreign man in slightly wrinkled clothing sitting beside a thin white woman perched on the edge of her chair. They stood up and welcomed Khath into the circle, speaking in simple Cambodian. Khath had never heard a foreigner speak Cambodian before. It pleased him and he smiled at them. Maybe he would have some happy times here. Khath settled into a chair and waited to see what would happen next.

The man introduced himself as Pastor Tom. The woman was his wife. They said how happy they were to see such a nice group coming to study the Bible and learn about God's love for them. The woman looked at them with a yearning gaze when Pastor Tom spoke of God's love. She seemed to want to enfold them all in a motherly embrace. Khath looked down, embarrassed, until the woman took her seat to let her husband begin his preaching.

"The Lord God loves you as his children," Pastor Tom said, speaking in stilted Cambodian. "He loves you so much he sent his own son to be your Savior, to die on a cross for you." Pastor Tom swept his arm back to point at the cross on the wall.

The gesture seemed practiced to Khath, and he realized that Pastor Tom was reciting a learned speech. Still, he was making the effort and Khath appreciated it.

"In return," Pastor Tom continued, "God asks only that you take him into your heart, and show him through your actions that you renounce your sins, that you love the Lord as your Savior. If you do these things, there is nothing to fear on the Day of Judgment. You will rise. You will rise high into the heavens and sit at the right hand of the Lord, surrounded by angels and glorious music. Let us pray."

Pastor Tom fell silent and stood with his head bowed for a moment. Then he looked around and smiled upon the group. He said something in English to Khath's tall friend, who laughed and translated: "Pastor Tom has run out of his Cambodian vocabulary and now he must use a translator. Please be patient. The translator has gone to get special study Bibles for you all and will be here any minute."

Pastor Tom said something to his wife, who jumped up and left the room. Khath assumed she had gone to track down the wayward translator. The group waited respectfully with downcast eyes. No one spoke and the only sound was the rustling of pages as Pastor Tom busied himself reading and making notes in a pad he pulled from a briefcase beside him.

A few minutes later, the sound of hurrying footsteps announced the return of the pastor's wife, followed by a young man, his arms laden with notebooks. He was dressed as any working Cambodian male would be in a similar situation: black pants, a long-sleeve starched white cotton shirt, and a thin black tie. His short hair was slicked back from his forehead. He reminded Khath of the Red Cross interpreter he'd met on the day the guards had fired upon the refugees at the gate.

"Ah, here we go," Pastor Tom said, closing his pad.

The young man murmured an apology in English and Cambodian for his lateness and began passing out the notebooks around the group. In front of each new student, he bowed and, speaking his native Cambodian, bid them welcome and said, "Praised be the word of the Lord," as he handed them their notebooks.

When he got to Khath, the young man repeated his litany, but Khath heard nothing, staring riveted at the wrist protruding beyond the young man's cuff as he stretched out the arm holding a notebook toward Khath. A slender, well-formed wrist, wrapped around with a leather watchband, beautifully beaded with the image of a lotus. Khath gasped and pushed backwards in his chair, which scraped loudly on the floor. He stared at the lotus watchband in slack-jawed disbelief.

"Are you unwell?" the young man asked.

Khath tore his gaze from the lotus and found himself staring into a pair of hard, flat, hooded eyes that narrowed slightly as their gazes locked. A gentle smile of concern was fixed upon the young man's lips, completely at odds with the expression in his eyes. Sweat broke out on Khath's brow as his heart began to skitter inside his chest like a mouse trapped in the same room as a hungry cat. He dropped his eyes quickly, aware that everyone in the room was watching him. "Forgive me," he said in a hoarse voice he hardly recognized as his own. "A fever has taken me…" He lurched out of his chair, and stumbled toward the door, blinded by the memory of Grandmother's face awash in tears.

Once outside, Khath hurried away from the church, drawing deep breaths of hot, humid air into his lungs. The air cleared his head, but the heat fueled his rage, and soon he was running past startled faces, running with a desperate need to burn off the anger before he exploded with the force of it. Finally, spent, he stopped, sweat soaking his clothing, his chest heaving. He wiped his face with his sleeve and pulled his shoulders back, a new resolve hardening in his heart. Grandmother would not need to worry about her eldest grandson and his blood debt. He, Khath, would solve that problem.

# Four

Khath lay on his mattress, the mosquito netting providing a thin veil of privacy. The bamboo group house was quiet, poised between the stirrings of those who'd arisen early and left before dawn, and those who slumbered on with no reason to get up and begin their day. He had much to think about and the dim coolness of early morning cleared his mind.

After his encounter with Mith at the Christian church yesterday, Khath had roamed the camp for hours, walking his way through memory after painful memory. As the afternoon passed into early evening, Khath's mind quieted, honing in on one simple problem: How was he going to get the lotus watch back into the hands of its rightful owners? To do nothing was unthinkable. After four years of powerless terror, he had been given an opportunity to strike back at his blood enemy on an equal footing, to right a wrong. Khath viewed this situation as a gift from the ancestors, another omen that the tide was beginning to turn in his favor.

If he succeeded in this small act of retribution, Khath thought, it would bring him one step closer to Kamala and Sitha. Again and again, his mind replayed the image of his girls being herded away from him by a woman dressed in black with a red and white checkered *krama* wrapped around her neck.

Kamala had carried a crying Sitha on her hip, looking back at him with a sad and knowing look. *Goodbye* her eyes had said, wise beyond their years, aged by the abrupt and difficult turn her life had taken on the day the Khmer Rouge had entered her world.

Through striking back at this foe, Khath believed his spirit would grow and reach out to his girls. They would know that he was still searching, that he had not given up, that he was coming nearer to them. He saw little Sitha's face, tear-streaked, her arms reaching out to him, and pushed the image away, setting his grief aside. Grief would weaken him. Khath needed strength for the task ahead. Strength, cunning, and above all, secrecy. This was something he must do alone.

His decision made, Khath had slept deeply and awakened full of purpose. He said nothing to Pra Chhay about discovering Mith at the Christian church. To allay questions about his own long absence the prior evening, he had brought home some treats from the canteen along with a story of making a new friend from the church and eating together. Today, he would consult the oracle sticks at the temple. He would wait until the morning chanting was finished and the food offerings made to the monks. The worshipers would eat together then, the monks sitting apart and chewing mindfully, the refugees clumped companionably and sharing the latest camp gossip. Only then, after the simple rhythms of temple life were completed and the temple stood empty, would Khath venture inside.

By midmorning, the last worshipers filed slowly out of the temple, with the sleepy satisfaction of those who have breakfasted well. Khath waited a little way down the street until he saw the temple caretaker come out. The man stretched and rubbed his eyes—Khath knew he'd been up since well before dawn and would now amble to his own lodging for a well-deserved nap. Satisfied that he could safely attend undisturbed to the task at hand, Khath moved quickly down the street, his feet raising small puffs of dust as he walked toward the temple.

Once inside he performed three quick prostrations, inhaling the crisp, woody scent of the dry reed mats as he pressed his forehead to the floor with each prostration: one for the Buddha, one for the *dhamma*—the teachings of the Buddha—and one for the *sangha*, the community of Buddhist believers.

As his hand closed around the bamboo container holding the oracle sticks, Khath saw a shadow darken the entrance to the temple.

"Going back to the Buddha now, yes?" Khath's tall Christian friend entered the temple and performed the traditional prostrations, then sat cross-legged on the floor. His gaze rested on the serene face of the Buddha. "You are feeling better now, I hope?" he said to Khath.

Sitting down beside the man, Khath began shaking the oracle sticks, which rattled softly against the bamboo container. "I feel quite well now," he replied.

The tall man nodded at Khath and clasped his hands together, murmuring a mantra. "It is odd, a coincidence no doubt," he said, pausing in his recitation. "But now it seems that Mith is unwell, too. His mind is very restless and quick to anger. He asks many questions about you."

Khath glanced at the tall Christian and continued shaking the oracle sticks until one slender stick fell to the floor. Picking it up, Khath moved to the numbered cabinet where the matching sutras were kept. "And what do you tell him?" he asked.

"What is there to tell? I met you. I brought you to our church." The man cocked his head, watching Khath closely. "But now I think, perhaps, it would be best for you if you do not return." He stood up and gestured toward the stick in Khath's hand. "And what does the oracle say?"

Khath pulled a slip of paper from the drawer that matched the number imprinted on the oracle stick. He smoothed the worn paper and read aloud: *"Whatever you have started to do, accomplish that very thing first."*

"I see," said the tall man. "Then I beg of you, friend, be very careful what you start." Giving Khath a rueful smile, the tall one slipped out the door and was gone as silently as he'd appeared.

That evening, Pra Chhay entered the group house accompanied by the teenage boy from across the hall. Khath watched as Pra Chhay said something to the boy, who smiled and bowed to Pra Chhay, his hands clasped at chin level as he backed respectfully into his own cubicle.

"You are befriending him, just as Grandmother asked," Khath said. "How is he doing?"

Pra Chhay removed his outer robe and sank gracefully into a relaxed lotus position before answering. "He's a fine boy, with a bright future in America. His aunt married an American soldier and lives in California. She has sponsored them all to come live with her. They are just waiting for visas and could be leaving any day. And not a day too soon, now that they know Mith is in the camp."

Khath grunted his agreement, careful not to show too much interest. "Do you think you can keep the boy from tracking him down and demanding the watch back? It's important that there be no trouble when they are so close to getting out."

"I will try. I think he understands. He's a smart boy." Pra Chhay gazed across the hallway as Grandmother handed the teenager a sticky rice roll wrapped in a banana leaf. "I think he knows it would break Grandmother's heart for something to go wrong now."

"You think? You must be sure, Pra Chhay. You must not let that boy near Mith."

With an effort, Khath kept his hands relaxed in his lap. He shrugged his shoulders and softened his tone. "I mean, you never know what a man like that might do if challenged. The boy might get hurt." He felt Pra Chhay's steady gaze on him, and forced his own eyes up for a moment, a casual glance he hoped.

"Don't be concerned, Khath. I won't let that happen, all right?" Pra Chhay yawned, crawled inside the mosquito netting and lay down on his mattress. Within minutes, he slept.

---

The morning sun wilted the produce at Khao I Dang's Wednesday market. Soon the vendors would be packing their unsold wares and leaving the camp. Reaching for a melon, Khath *felt* Mith's presence before he saw him, a prickle among the hairs of his neck, a sudden readiness in his muscles and a quickening of his senses—the innate response of an animal to danger. Khath could not begin to count the times that these primal instincts had saved him, both during the war against the Khmer Rouge, and later, as their prisoner. Turning slowly, the melon in his hand held ready to be flung in self-defense if needed, Khath began a sweep of the area with his eyes. There. Slouched against the side of a delivery truck, his arms crossed over his chest, Mith stared at Khath, a sneer twisting the planes of his face. Khath felt the slow burn of hatred in his chest, but he merely nodded at Mith, a neutral acknowledgment of the man. *He doesn't really know what I know. He suspects, and it worries him, otherwise he wouldn't be here looking for me. Good.*

Khath continued to browse slowly through the fruits and vegetables, watching Mith from the corner of his eye. He saw Mith straighten and walk toward him.

"Well, look here. It's the man with the fever."

Mith's eyes were dark holes, a perfect reflection of the blackness of his soul. Khath shuddered inwardly. "Said the man with the beautiful watch," he responded. "Wherever did you find such a unique watchband?" He kept his gaze innocent and open, admiring the watch on Mith's wrist.

Mith frowned a bit, watching Khath intently. "It was given to me by an old acquaintance." He paused. "In a manner of speaking." His eyes never left Khath's face.

Forcing a chuckle from his throat, Khath smiled. "Sounds like someone lost a bet. A little friendly gambling?" To his relief, he saw Mith relax and soften. *Excellent. He is letting down his guard; he thinks I am harmless.* Khath turned back to examining the fruit, lifting one melon after another.

"Will we see you again at church? Learning about the Christian God has been a great comfort to me," Mith said.

Like an actor in a play, Khath thought. Mith is settling into his role as Christian convert and emissary of the Lord. Even his eyes have brightened. He's very good.   Those innocent Christians have no chance against one so skilled at deception.

"We would all be very happy to see you again, especially after your unfortunate illness the last time. Pastor Tom and his wife were quite concerned." Mith smiled at Khath with great earnestness.

*He's enjoying this. He thinks I am stupid, a toy for his amusement.* Khath smiled back. "Thank you. I will see you again soon."

Khath waited until Mith had gone, then followed him at a distance, hoping Mith would return directly to his assigned group house. For his plan to succeed, he needed to know where Mith lived in the camp, and what his daily routines were. He hoped that Grandmother and her family would not be issued their visas too quickly for him to learn Mith's habits and decide the best location to confront him. Khath flexed his arm thoughtfully. He was still strong, still hardened, battle-ready. He was confident about his ability to quickly overpower the smaller man and take the watch by force if need be, nor was he concerned about being caught in the act by the camp guards. The guards rarely patrolled at night and if they did, it was not for the purpose of protecting the residents of the camp. Scuffles between refugees were of no matter to them.

Khath's only concern was that he would run out of time to do this properly. At times he wondered at himself. How was it that the lotus watch had come to assume such a momentous importance? He could no longer think of the watch without seeing the faces of his lost girls, Kamala and Sitha. They loved pretty things, shiny beads and baubles. In the time before the Khmer Rouge seized power, he would take them to the market and buy them pretty barrettes and ribbons, little Sitha riding on his shoulders, clutching his ears for balance, while Kamala skipped along beside him, her small, sweet hand engulfed in his.

After a short distance, the part of Khath's mind that was not carried along on his daydream alerted him to the fact that Mith was entering a group house.

Quickly, Khath stepped behind the corner of a nearby building. Was this where Mith stayed or was he just visiting someone?

Khath settled down comfortably to wait and keep watch. He pulled a small knife from his pocket and began whittling a piece of bamboo, just another bored refugee with nothing much to do except carve whistles to sell at the market.

The days passed, each one very much like the one before it. Khath would rise early in the morning and station himself down the street from Mith's group house. He discovered that Mith mostly kept to himself. Apart from participating in the Christian church, Mith had made only a few friends in the camp that Khath could see. He rarely visited them, nor did he eat with anyone at the canteen. Mith was a loner. All the better for Khath.

One evening Khath returned home to great rejoicing in the cubicle across the hall.

"We are leaving!" Grandmother twirled across the hallway to him, clutching an envelope in her gnarled fingers. "We have our visas! We leave in three days. We're going to America!" Tears of happiness and relief rolled down her brown, wrinkled face.

Khath smiled broadly. "We must celebrate," he said.

"Yes, yes!" Grandmother sang out happily. "Your brother has gone to trade for treats and incense. He will begin special prayers for us tonight."

"Sit down and tell me all the details," Khath said. "I want to know exactly when you will leave the camp, so I can be sure to send you off at the gate."

Grandmother rattled on with great excitement. Soon, Khath knew what she planned to wear on the day she and her family departed Khao I Dang forever. He knew what food she would pack along, how she would dispose of her meager belongings in the camp, and how she planned to spend each and every day before she left. Satisfied, he nodded. He had two days to implement his plan. It was enough.

———————

Dusk had fallen and Khath stood hidden near the entrance to Mith's group house, waiting. It was Tuesday night, the night that Mith led a small group of converted refugees in a prayer meeting at the church.

Khath again thanked the ancestors for the way events had played out. Tomorrow morning, Grandmother and her grandsons were boarding a bus out of the camp that would take them to Bangkok for final processing and departure to America. Khath and Pra Chhay would escort them to the bus. Just before helping Grandmother to board, Khath would press a small package into her hands with instructions not to open it until she was on the plane bound for her new life in California. He imagined her gasps of surprise when she saw the lotus watch. Would she try to guess what the gift was before she opened it? Would she shake it or feel for the outline of the contents with her fingers? He must be sure to package it in a way that no clues would lead them to guess correctly.

Grandmother would cry tears of joy, he knew, to have this last loving memento of her son. She would turn the watch over and over in her hands, examining it in wonder and gratitude until her grandson took it from her and strapped it onto his own wrist to wear with pride.

Khath smiled. What little risk he was taking this evening was well worth it. Not just for Grandmother, but for himself as well. His quest to retrieve the watch had given him an attainable goal. He felt like a man again, he realized, no longer a helpless refugee dependent on others for survival. Kamala and Sitha would be proud of what he'd done, and he knew that this was the lesson he was supposed to take from this task. *When I see them again, I want to be able to tell them how I lived my life in a way to make them proud of me, as their father.*

Footsteps padded softly on the street, and Khath edged to the corner to peer out and see who was coming. As expected, it was Mith. He appeared reasonably alert, as anyone would be walking alone through the camp at night, but not excessively so. Khath reached for the kitchen knife he had wrapped in a rag and secured to his body with a length of rope twisted around his waist. Quietly, he unwrapped the knife and stuffed the rag into his pocket until he was ready to use it. It would make a handy gag. The rope he wrapped around his waist again, tucking the ends into his pants. He flicked his thumb along the edge of the blade to test its sharpness, an unnecessary gesture since he had spent thirty minutes with a whetstone this afternoon honing the blade to a fine edge.

Moving silently to the very corner of the group house, Khath stood poised, knife in his left hand, rag now in his right. He knew from practice that it would take just two steps to cover the ground between himself and where Mith would stand, his back turned, to remove his shoes before entering the house. Silence was crucial, and earlier Khath had made sure to remove all the twigs, scraps of paper, plastic, bottles and stones that might possibly crunch, crinkle, snap or twang if he stepped on them.

Mith came nearer, he was almost to the door now, and Khath saw him yawn. He turned away from Khath, bent slightly, NOW. One step, two, the ground was crossed. Before Mith could turn Khath slid his right arm over Mith's and pressed the rag into Mith's mouth, while his left hand held the blade of the knife against Mith's throat. "Do not make me kill you for a wrist watch," he hissed into Mith's ear. Mith's body was rigid in Khath's grip. "We are going to step around the corner now, and just so you know, this blade is very sharp. It would be very easy to accidentally slit your throat."

Power coursed through Khath's veins, and he realized with some disgust that he was enjoying this moment of victory.

Together, the two men moved ever so gently around the corner of Mith's group house. Out of sight of passers-by, Khath gave a tiny sigh of relief. The first phase of his plan had gone very well. Cautiously, he moved the angle of the blade so that the tip was positioned under Mith's jawline over the vein now throbbing frantically with the beat of Mith's heart. He could feel the pulsing of it pushing against the knife blade. Applying the tiniest bit of pressure, Khath carefully broke the skin so that a thin tickle of blood ran down Mith's throat. "Do you feel that?" Khath asked. "Blink twice if you feel the blood."

Mith blinked twice, squeezing his eyes shut and opening them wide. His breath came in little gasps.

"Do you understand now how very sharp this knife is? Blink twice."

Mith blinked.

"Good. Because I want you to unstrap the watch from your wrist, hold it in your hand and then clasp both your hands behind your back. If you do anything but that, you will die. If you make a sound, you will die." Khath watched carefully as Mith fumbled with the wrist band, his fingers shaking. As Mith reached behind him, Khath stepped to the left, removing his hand from Mith's mouth as he did so. "Not a sound," he whispered, sliding the knife a hair deeper into Mith's skin. He grasped a fold of skin from Mith's neck with his thumb to stabilize the knife blade, and gently took the watch from Mith and stuffed it into his pocket. Instructing Mith to hold one end of the rope, he wrapped the rest of it tightly around Mith's wrists. Then in one swift move, he withdrew the knife and yanked up on the rope, using his left hand now to shove Mith down into the dirt, where he quickly straddled him. *The boy was right. Without his guns and his Khmer Rouge pals, there is no courage, no fight at all in this man.* Mith lay absolutely still, his face turned to the right, scarcely daring to breathe.

"I know who you are," Khath said. "And I know how you got that watch." This was the part in his plan where he trussed Mith's feet and arms together behind his back and rendered him unconscious with a well-placed blow of the knife handle. Not a killing blow, just enough to allow Khath time to get away undetected. But in all his planning, he had not taken into account the tremendous desire he now had to end this man's life, this Khmer Rouge tormentor of his people. He stared at the knife in his hand. It would be so easy to finish this now. *But you are finished. You have the watch. You have honored your daughters. It is done.*

Below him, Mith squeezed his eyes shut, a grimace drawing his lips back from his teeth, waiting. The rank stench of fear rolled off of him. Khath brought the knife down slowly and laid the tip of it gently, caressingly, at the corner of Mith's right eye. "Have you any idea what your Khmer Rouge brothers did to people in Tuol Sleng prison?" he asked. "I saw people with half their faces carved away. I wondered how they could go on living like that, even for a minute, a second. But some of them lived for days. And each day they would return to their cell a little bit less of a person, in their mind as well as their body."

Mith moaned.

Khath pressed the tip of the knife just hard enough to draw blood. "So I say to you, Mith, do not let me see you ever again in this camp. If I see you again, I will do to you what your people did to mine. I promise you that."

The knife moved swiftly in the dark. Handle met skull with a dull thump and Mith sank into oblivion. Quickly now, Khath finished wrapping the rope around Mith's feet and hands, and tied the rag around his mouth. "I hope the fire ants find you before your housemates do," he muttered and melted into the night shadows.

# Five

The diesel engine rumbled, muffling the cries of goodbye and good luck as the throng of those left behind stepped back to make way for the bus loaded with departing refugees. A high pitched *toot-toot!* sounded, shrill and insistent, as the bus began to inch toward the camp gates, a silly sound for such a large and lumbering vehicle, Khath thought.

He and Pra Chhay stood waving at the bus, which now resembled a large centipede with the arms of so many reaching through every window, fingertips straining for one last touch of the friends and loved ones who stood outside with outstretched hands. With a final blast of the horn, the bus pulled out of the camp gates, bound for Bangkok, great billowing clouds of dust marking its passage down the road and around the corner. As the bus disappeared, a depressed silence settled over the crowd, punctuated by the sound of sniffles and throat clearing as the refugees slowly began to leave the area.

"I saw you give Grandmother a packet as she boarded the bus," Pra Chhay said to Khath. "What was in it?"

"Just a memento."

"Of life in Khao I Dang?" Pra Chhay laughed. "This is a place that one tries to forget. I would be surprised if she kept it beyond the first corner in the road."

Khath spread his hands in a gesture of resignation. "It is her choice to keep it or not."

"Come, brother, what did you give her? The Buddha teaches us that needless secrecy is a sign of arrogance." Pra Chhay stood smiling, his hands on his hips, facing Khath.

"If you must know, it was a watch."

Pra Chhay's smile froze on his face and he paled. "A watch?" he said carefully. "Something from the market? Surely not Mith's watch."

"No, it was never Mith's watch." Khath began moving past his brother. "He had no right to that watch."

Pra Chhay grabbed Khath's arm. "Khath, what have you done? Tell me."

Khath wrenched his arm free. "What have I done?" He faced his brother. "I have done nothing except to bring joy to a family that had none. I have given a grieving mother a remembrance of her lost son. I have done what all your prayers and chants could not do. I have brought them some peace, that's what I've done." Khath's voice broke. "How I wish someone could do the same for me."

"I wish this for you as well, brother," Pra Chhay said. "But I can promise you that antagonizing the Khmer Rouge is not going to bring peace to you in this camp. You don't know how many there are. You don't know how much power they wield in this camp. You have put your life, and mine, in danger by this foolish action."

Khath glared at Pra Chhay, uncomfortably aware that his brother was saying much the same thing that his Christian acquaintance had: *Be very careful what you start.*

He turned away from Pra Chhay, but his brother followed.

"Khath," Pra Chhay said. "Do you really have no concerns over what you have done?"

"I can handle Mith," Khath muttered. "Have a little faith in me. I was fighting the Khmer Rouge while you still said prayers in your temple. I can protect you."

"Brother, you insult me," Pra Chhay said. "I will be fine, in this life or the next. It is your karma that concerns me, not my own."

"It is not your concern," Khath said, his anger making his tone more curt than he had intended. They were passing the water tanks now, and already the line for water was growing. He hated life in this camp, this waiting and waiting for something to happen. He was glad he had confronted Mith, no matter the consequences. He gestured at the line. "We'd best get our water before the supply runs out," he said.

Pra Chhay nodded. "Fine," he said. "But we must talk about the watch, Khath. You cannot keep this to yourself."

As they made their way back from the water tanks lugging the day's ration of water, Khath told Pra Chhay the details of how he'd gotten the lotus watch from Mith, leaving out nothing, from the weeks of careful watching to the lengthy session of knife sharpening. Pra Chhay listened quietly to the entire tale without interruption, a small frown creasing his forehead.

Khath felt a fog lift from his mind as he unburdened himself, and a growing uneasiness about his own actions. "I feel now almost as though I was gripped by an evil spirit, Pra Chhay," he confessed. "Was I behaving oddly these last few weeks?"

"No." Pra Chhay shook his head. "In fact, you seemed content, calmer and happier than I've seen you since the Khmer Rouge were driven into the jungles. I thought you were feeling hopeful about leaving this camp, looking forward to the future." He glanced at his brother. "Instead, you were going back into the war, stirring up the hatred."

Khath dropped his eyes, feeling shame.

"I am afraid of what you may have stirred up, Khath," Pra Chhay continued. "If there is one Khmer Rouge in this camp, there are many—the rumors are true. I do not think that Mith will take his defeat meekly. He will gather the others and come after you, Khath."

Khath nodded. "You are probably right," he said. He set his water bucket down and stood thinking, his eyes wandering over the dreary sights before him: a dusty road, lined with group home after group home, a bunch of children in ragged clothing listlessly kicking a rattan ball between them. The smell of the latrines hung faintly in the air, mingled with the starchy aroma of steaming rice. It was an unpleasant combination.

"Maybe we should go talk to the Red Cross again," Khath said. "Perhaps they can help us leave this camp before Mith has time to plan his revenge."

Pra Chhay looked pleased. "Yes, that's a good idea. If we tell them our new situation, there may be a way we can be moved up on the wait list for sponsors. And Khath, we should stick together now. Two men are harder to attack than one."

Continuing toward their group home, the two brothers devised ways to meld their separate routines into one seamless unit for the safety of both in the coming weeks. After depositing their water buckets at the group home, they set off for the Red Cross office.

The same brown lizard they had seen on their first visit, or one very much like it, still clung to the wall above Mr. Ames' desk.

"So you see, Mr. Ames," Pra Chhay was saying, "We have reason now to fear for Khath's safety if he remains for long in this camp."

Mr. Ames flicked his gaze toward Khath. "I remember you," he said through his interpreter. "I remember you both, the monk and the brother who survived Tuol Sleng prison."

Pra Chhay nodded, and Khath sat up a little straighter at the mention of Tuol Sleng, a scowl darkening his face. He wished he would never hear those two words spoken again, so vile were the memories they triggered. He focused his eyes on the lizard and concentrated hard, trying to stop the cascade of gruesome images before they could fill his mind. He saw himself carefully turning the broken bodies of little children, compelled to check, to make sure, somehow, that the mangled and bloodied faces were not those of his daughters. He saw the rows of prisoners, lying on the floor, shackled by their feet to an iron bar running down the center of a prison cell, lined up like so many fish arranged in a basket at the market, ten on each side of the bar. He saw . . . *no. The lizard. It's big and brown, clinging to the wall in this office. And the man behind the desk is asking me a question now.* Khath cleared his throat. "I'm sorry?" he said.

"Do you have proof that this man Mith is Khmer Rouge?" Mr. Ames doodled on a notepad as the interpreter translated his question.

"Proof? I'm sorry, no. I have no proof. Especially now that Grandmother and the watch are gone."

"I see. What a pity that you didn't come to us instead of taking matters into your own hands. Now there is nothing to be done." Mr. Ames drummed his fingers against his desk top for a moment, looking unhappy. "We are not here to care for the Khmer Rouge," he said sternly, pointing his pen at Khath. He sighed and ran his hands through his thinning hair. "Well, it's a moot point now," he continued, rummaging through a pile of files on his desk and extracting one. "It turns out that your cases were high enough priority as it were, helped along by Thailand's closing her borders. We've had a surge in sponsorship offers and I'm in the process of confirming your placement now." He glanced inside the file. "You've been sponsored by a church in Glenberg, Oregon, USA. I'm just waiting for a telegram for final confirmation." He grinned. "Congratulations. Unless they suddenly change their minds, you should be out of here in less than a week."

Khath's mind whirled. Did he hear that correctly? He looked at Pra Chhay for confirmation and watched a big, slow smile spread across his brother's face as Pra Chhay got to his feet and bowed low to express his thanks to the Red Cross official, bringing the tips of his clasped hands to nose level. Only the Buddha rated a more respectful bow than that.

Turning now to his brother, Pra Chhay reached down and gripped Khath's arm, hauling him to his feet to face the beaming Mr. Ames. "Did you hear, Khath? We are leaving."

Mumbling his "thank you" in English, Khath too offered a bow to Mr. Ames, but his mind was elsewhere. With less than a week left in Khao I Dang, Khath had one final task to accomplish before he could board that bus. Until then, he was not going anywhere.

---

On the other side of the world, in the small town of Glenberg, Oregon, Sareth Mom examined his reflection in the bathroom mirror and ran his comb one last time through his slicked back hair, still thick enough thanks to the daily scalp massages he enjoyed from his wife Chea. Though his temples had grayed, Sareth knew he looked younger than his 62 years and it pleased him to hear others remark upon it.

A soft footfall barely disturbed his thoughts, and he absently extended a wrist toward Chea, who had come to help with the final details of Sareth's appearance. Moving around him, she fastened first one cuff link, then the other, and as he turned toward her, began to knot his tie.

Sareth angled his head slightly to watch Chea's reflection in the mirror, mesmerized by her long agile fingers playing delicately over the silk tie and the gentle clink of silver bangles sliding down her slender forearm. He had chosen her ten years ago from an entire village of lovely virgins after his first wife had died in childbirth, taking his unborn son with her. A wealthy, educated Cambodian male had many options when it came to acquiring a wife. His young bride, now 28, had ripened beautifully.

Perhaps too beautifully. Sareth thought of the many glances he'd seen American men giving his young wife. So far, to his knowledge, she had not glanced back. He knew her girlfriends had pitied her all those years ago being married off to a man so much her senior. But Sareth could see that wealth and status had suited Chea, especially knowing that now her old friends were widowed or saddled with maimed and bitter soldiers who had returned home broken in spirit. A kindly, older husband was not the worst fate that could befall a young girl.

Even though Sareth had lost much of his wealth in the fall of Cambodia, he could still provide his young wife a position of status here in her new community. Educated abroad, fluent in English and comfortable in the ways of Westerners, Sareth had quickly become Father Ralph's right hand in the resettlement project.

Sareth was proud of the fact that within days of his arrival in Glenberg, Father Ralph had begun paying him a stipend for his services as interpreter, cultural adviser and language instructor.

"Will you be gone long, *Bong?*" Chea asked, using a respectful form of address rather than Sareth's name.

"Several hours I would think, my dear. Father Ralph has received the files on the last of our countrymen he plans to sponsor. Today we are going to discuss these newcomers and decide if we should accept them into our community or not."

"How many are there?" Chea asked.

"Just two. Two brothers. That's all I know at present." Sareth stroked Chea's hair back from her forehead and watched the way her long lashes lay feathered against her cheekbones as she lowered her eyes gracefully in response to his touch. He longed to know what lay hidden behind those lowered eyelids. Was it love? Tolerance? Scorn? He dared not ask, dared not show such weakness to his wife.

Bidding her a pleasant day, he gathered his jacket and vinyl portfolio and set out on the ten minute walk to the church.

It was a mild late August day in northwest Oregon. The leaves on some of the trees were turning golden, reminding Sareth that nearly a year had passed since he'd been resettled in Glenberg. He remembered how Chea had been astounded to see yellow and red leaves on trees. She'd never experienced autumn before.

As he neared the back doors to the church, Sareth consulted his watch. His timing was excellent. He would arrive two minutes early, just as Westerners preferred. How strange it was that such a powerful nation should be so ruled by the sweep of a second-hand.

As he approached the door to Father Ralph's office, he heard the murmur of prayer. Unwilling to interrupt Father Ralph's devotions, Sareth paused outside and listened with idle curiosity. What was the good Father praying about today? Father Ralph's rich baritone rolled out into the hallway:

*Father in Heaven, let thy wisdom be my guide as I work with these refugees. Fill my actions with the divine essence of your glory, such that they, too, will feel the power of your love and lift up their souls to rejoice in you. And finally, O Lord, I ask that you give me strength to carry this burden, to remain strong in the face of human suffering, and to be steadfast in my devotion to you. I pray this in the name of the Father, the Son and the Holy Spirit. Amen.*

Sareth heard Father Ralph's knees crack as he rose from his prayers. A moment later, the priest appeared from around a screen that shielded a private alcove and waved Sareth into his office. Sareth envied the man his height and physique, for Father Ralph towered above him and looked lean and strong, with an aquiline nose separating large gray eyes.

"I'm sorry to keep you waiting, Mr. Sareth. Have you been standing there long?" Father Ralph moved toward his desk, pouring himself a small cup of aromatic, freshly brewed coffee from the pot on his credenza. "Coffee?"

"Please," Sareth said. He accepted a cup and added sugar and cream, and then settled into a chair across the desk from Father Ralph. "I'm happy to report to you that I had a most satisfactory visit with the Widow Hendrix yesterday. She assures me that the house on Blackberry Street will be ready for the newcomers, stocked with linens, kitchenware and the like, by

Tuesday. Once you tell her the confirmed arrival date, the good ladies of the auxiliary will add a five pound sack of rice and stock the refrigerator."

"That's great. Thank you," Father Ralph said. "You've done an amazing job getting the ladies better organized, Mr. Sareth. I sure appreciate it. And your social calls make them feel valued. I'm afraid Americans have lost the habit of making formal calls on each other. It's a pity but we're always too busy to pay much attention to one another. "

Sareth sipped his coffee. "It is true that Americans do not seem to relax overmuch. This need to be busy is like an illness. You yourself look very fatigued much of the time, Father Ralph."

Father Ralph's attention had already turned to the work at hand. He murmured, "Do I?" in a distracted tone of voice, then reached for a thin file on his desk and handed it to Sareth. "Our final refugees look pretty interesting," he said. "They've both got some education and experience outside of village life. It says this man Pra is a monk and teacher. Do you suppose he will speak English well? I'd love to talk religion with him."

Sareth looked over the bio data sheet and accompanying photo quickly, careful to keep his expression neutral. At 43 years old, Pra Chhay looked like a typical monk, with serene eyes and a soft, round face. His shaved head had sprouted a quarter inch growth of black hair that stood straight out from his scalp, making him look pleasantly fuzzy. He had a tenth grade education, but Sareth knew that serious monks studied scripture for years after their formal education ended. An educated monk would almost certainly pose a challenge to Sareth's own authority in the Cambodian community, and weaken his influence with Father Ralph. He would have to tread cautiously here, try to discourage the priest without appearing to have an interest.

Sareth sighed. "There is so little information to go by…" he murmured, tuning the single paper over to examine the back, though he knew full well it would be blank, as it always was. It was insulting, really, the way a man's entire life was summed up in two or three sentences on these forms. "He appears to be a monk," he said, letting the tiniest bit of doubt creep into his voice. "He uses the title 'Pra,' which is an honorific just as your parishioners call you 'Father.' But we do not ever use only the honorific, so you must say 'Pra Chhay' always."

"Okay, thanks for telling me that. What else can you see from the form?"

"Well, I'm guessing he's the older brother, correct?"

Father Ralph nodded. "How did you know that?"

"It is common for a family to send their eldest son to the monastery, to give him up to the monkhood. Some boys go willingly. It is a great honor in our culture, and both the parents and the boy, if he is sincere, will gain much merit and a higher rebirth from their mutual sacrifice."

"If he is sincere?" Father Ralph asked. "Are you saying that many are not?"

Sareth leaned his arms on the table, pressing the fingertips of his two hands together. "Always, in our human endeavors, we have the ideal and the reality, do we not?" he said delicately. "I am sad to say that some monks in Cambodia fall very far short of the ideal. And with so many people trying to get out of the country, well, it is easy enough to put on a robe and shave one's head."

Father Ralph stared in dismay at Sareth. "So he might not even be a monk?"

"I am, shall we say, cautiously optimistic that he is who and what he says he is. I hope my candidness has not offended you."

"No, of course not," Father Ralph said. "I'm just disappointed. It never occurred to me that he might just be working the system. I was quite excited at the thought of sponsoring him."

"And so we shall give him the benefit of the doubt." Sareth paused. "I only felt it my duty to mention the alternative. I would not want your generosity to be abused. Shall we go to the next file?"

Father Ralph handed over the second file. "What do you make of this one? It looks like he may have some transferable skills from his work history."

Opening the file, Sareth studied the black and white photo of a man named Khath Sophal. Khath had thick, heavy eyebrows shielding eyes that stared fiercely into the camera, eyes that were perhaps a little fearful behind that fierceness. He looked thin, the skin stretched tight over cheekbones and jawline. Reading on he learned that Khath was 38 years old, had a tenth grade education, and was a "railroad worker." Like many of the male Cambodian refugees, he was also listed as a soldier in the Lon Nol government forces. In the section labeled "Family," a single word, *deceased,* spoke volumes without actually saying much. Sareth looked again at the photo, drawn to Khath's eyes.

Father Ralph leaned across the desk. "Did you see that handwritten note at the bottom? Tuol Sleng survivor. What does that mean?"

Sareth's head snapped up. "What? Impossible. No one survived Tuol Sleng." He stared at the page where Father Ralph's finger was pointing at a smeared scrawl in faded ink. "This is very strange," he said, staring at the form. A shiver ran down his back at the very thought of the notorious Tuol Sleng Prison. Who could this man be to have come from such a place? Whose side was he on? After a moment, Sareth looked at Father Ralph. "You have never heard of Tuol Sleng, otherwise known as Site 21?"

"You mean the prison?" Father Ralph asked. "I heard about it, of course. Saw the news reports. I didn't recognize the Cambodian name."

"It is an evil place, a hideous place, a place of torture and death. Men, women, even children, so many children. All forced to write false confessions and then taken to the killing fields and executed. No one ever came out. No one." Sareth stared again at Khath's photo. No wonder those eyes held fear.

"Where exactly is it?" Father Ralph asked.

"In Phnom Penh." Sareth smiled sadly. "Right there, in our most beautiful city. It used to be a school. Some of the classrooms were turned into group cells, others were divided by crude brick walls into tiny individual cells, barely large enough to lie down in."

"How could this man survive such a place?" Father Ralph asked.

Sareth frowned, shaking his head rapidly. "This I cannot answer. When the Vietnamese invaded, the staff all ran away—who would admit to working in a death factory like that? I cannot fathom who this man is, or what he did or didn't do to survive Site 21." Sareth gave the file back to Father Ralph with a hand that shook slightly. This was shocking information.

Father Ralph got up and poured two new cups of coffee, handing one to Sareth. They sipped in silence for a while, unwilling to rush this important decision. Then the priest said, "Well, Mr. Sareth, are these the kind of men we want to round out our community here? We've got six families already. Perhaps that's enough."

Sareth took a calming breath. "I would fear for the sanity of anyone coming out of Site 21. And I tell you honestly, his arrival would disrupt our community. People would question, as I do, who this man really is, where his sympathies lie."

"Then perhaps we should only accept his brother, the monk."

Shaking his head emphatically, Sareth said, "No, no, that would never do. They are brothers. They would not separate."

"So we take them both, or not at all. Is that what you're saying?"

"That, I fear, is the situation." Sareth said. Perhaps his concerns about the monk usurping his authority in the community could be laid to rest. He felt a degree of tension resolve in his shoulders. "It is regrettable, of course, but it seems quite impossible to bring them here."

Father Ralph swiveled his chair around to gaze out the window. After a moment he spoke. "But we are a house of God," he said softly. "Jesus did not turn away from the afflicted." He turned back to Sareth. "If we do not help these men, who will? I hear your concerns, Mr. Sareth, but my faith tells me I must take positive action on their behalf."

"As you wish," Sareth bowed his head slightly, as much to hide his frustration as to acknowledge his subordinate status. "It is not my decision to make, and I am thankful for that. I would not want the future of these men to rest in my hands." Sareth picked up the files and opened them to gaze at the faces of Pra Chhay and Khath—two brothers, one calm and serene, the other tormented and fierce. He felt the tension return to his shoulders and a dull headache began in his temples.

"I will take full responsibility, Mr. Sareth, but you will help me, won't you? Because no matter what decision is made in this room, we are affecting their future." The priest swiveled around to the window again. "I can't help but ask myself why God has delivered these two souls into my care. What new cross is the Lord preparing for me now?" He turned back and smiled at Sareth. "I believe we must accept them, Mr. Sareth. Go ahead and send a telegraph to the Red Cross office at Khao I Dang. Please tell them that we look forward to welcoming Khath and Pra Chhay to Glenberg."

# Six

Clutching a small packet in his hand, Khath stepped from the shaman's hut into a moonless tropical night. He paused to let his eyes adjust to the lack of light before moving. The holy man's rituals had taken far longer than Khath anticipated. Pra Chhay would be sick with worry, wondering where he was on this all important night: the eve of their departure from Khao I Dang. Khath grinned into the darkness. Pra Chhay would be even more worried, and very angry, if he knew where his brother stood at this moment. And rightfully so, Khath thought, his grin disappearing.

Moving as quickly as the light would allow, he set off down the path through the jungle, knowing his chances of slipping back into Khao I Dang under the perimeter wire lessened dramatically as the camp settled down for the night and quiet descended. Noise traveled far in the stillness and Khath would have to bide his time carefully to coincide his scramble under the wire with some other disturbance in the night. A baby crying, an argument, a woman's screams as she is raped by a neighbor or guard. Khath hoped it would not be this last scenario. He would rather wait all night in the darkness than have to listen one more time to this act that shamed all men.

56

He had discovered the old shaman's hut months earlier on his forays to find food in the jungle before the Thai government had made Khao I Dang a closed camp. Back then, it was easy to wander in and out. Khath had sought the old man's counsel on several occasions in his search for his daughters. Did the shaman feel their spirits, and if so, in which realm did they reside? Were they yet burdened with human form or had they been freed from this life of pain? On this night, the shaman had been vague. He sensed a transition, he told Khath, but was unable to decipher the meaning. He chanted and prayed long and hard to lift the veil but without success. As he solemnly prepared and blessed the two amulets, he promised Khath that as long as he carried the charms, his bond with his girls would never be broken no matter where on this earth, or beyond, Khath's travels may happen to take him. Only with this assurance was Khath willing to leave the land of his birth and begin his search for his daughters from America.

A branch cracked to his right and Khath froze, listening, sniffing the night breeze for the rank odor of a predator. The air was heavy, damp, and rich with the mingled scents of night blossoms and rotting vegetation. He heard the rustling sounds of a small animal and the hooting of an owl as he paused, alert to danger. Patting his pocket to reassure himself that the precious packet was still there, he hurried on. At the edge of the jungle, an open field stretched fifty feet to the camp fence. Khath waited in the shadows, watching the play of the search light as it stabbed the darkness with random thrusts. He oriented himself carefully, counting seven fence posts to the left of the watchtower. A small undulation in the soil several yards back from the fence between the sixth and seventh posts would provide some cover from the restless light—it was there that Khath planned to wait for the opportunity to slither back inside Khao I Dang.

Keeping his eyes on the beam of the searchlight, Khath crouched and ran, his heart pounding with fear, toward the fence. Diving face first into the hollow behind the rise, he curled himself into a small round ball, pulling his jacket up over his head to disguise his shape. He wanted to look as much like a rock or shadow as he could, and the outlines of a human form would spoil the illusion. He knew the guards would shoot first and investigate later. The night stretched on for…hours? Minutes? Khath's fear played tricks with the passage of time. Whenever the searchlight neared his hiding spot, time raced, each precious second possibly the last he would ever know. As the light arrived and probed the nooks and crannies of his rigid body, time slowed, toying with him the way the searchlight did, making each heartbeat last an eon until finally, darkness came again and he was safe until the next sweep of the light.

Finally, the diversion that Khath prayed for presented itself. Raucous laughter and taunting erupted into the night air as a group of men, probably drunk, sauntered slowly along the perimeter road, from left to right, drawing the searchlight upon themselves as they strolled. This was perfect. The men were pulling the attention of the guards away from Khath's line of travel toward the fence.

Rolling out over the edge of the rise, Khath scrambled for the fence and slid under, then dashed for the nearest building. To his right he could still hear the men creating a ruckus. One had fallen and his companions shouted at him to get up. Khath reached the safety of the building and paused to catch his breath. Now he was just another refugee, foolishly walking through the camp after dark.

Khath began his trek along the dirt roadway toward his section of the camp. Off to his right he heard the sound of swearing and a scuffle and assumed that the man who had fallen was being helped along none too gently by his companions. A few minutes later he saw that he was right. He could just make out the shapes of three men coming toward him on the street, the one in the middle, his head hanging low, supported and half-dragged by two larger men, one on each side. Khath moved to one side of the narrow street to make way as the men weaved and stumbled their way along.

As the men neared, the one closest to Khath flashed an apologetic smile in Khath's direction, turning slightly towards him as he did so. This appeared to be a mistake as the smaller drunk man lurched, off-balance, and pitched headlong toward Khath, the force of his fall dragging his companions in his wake.

Khath stepped forward to steady the group and as he did, a fist lashed out and caught him full in the stomach. Khath bent double with pain, gasping to breathe, and another blow caught him in the face, throwing him backwards onto the ground. Confusion muddled his brain. A shoe thudded into his ribs, more pain, and then hands grasped him under his arms and hauled him roughly to his feet.

"Did you think we would let you leave without saying goodbye?" Mith stood before him, a sneer curling his lips, and now Khath recognized him as the small man being dragged along by his companions. A hot wave of hatred flared through Khath's body, clearing his mind. He spat out a mouthful of blood.

"You're not wearing your watch tonight," he said, though it hurt to talk. It hurt to do anything, so what had he to lose? He knew he would probably not survive this encounter anyway. A profound sadness softened his knees, and he sagged. So this was how it would end. To have survived so much and for nothing, after all.

"Take him behind the building," Mith said to the two men holding Khath's arms.

Khath felt himself half pushed, half dragged out of the street. The men shoved him up against the back of the building and let him slide down until he sat, legs splayed out before him, back propped up by the wall. Mith squatted down and faced him.

"I and my comrades have been following you for weeks, you know," Mith said. "You and your brother, always together, always protecting one another. We were afraid we would have to take you both. But we were patient. We waited, we listened, and we found out your plan." He lit a cigarette and blew smoke in Khath's face. "You made it very easy for us tonight." He laughed. "So we returned the favor by helping you get back under the fence."

Khath stared at him dully. So it was all a planned diversion, that perfect opportunity to get back inside Khao I Dang? He should have known. His luck had not been so good in recent years—why would it change now? "Did you bribe the guards?" he asked.

Mith's hand flashed in the night and the force of a hard slap sent fresh waves of pain rolling across Khath's bloody face.

"I did not give you permission to speak," Mith snapped. He rose and stepped back away from Khath. "Hold him upright," he said to his companions.

Khath's head swam as he was yanked to his feet. He would have fallen if not for the solidly built men gripping him under the arms. As if from a far distance, he watched Mith make a fist and draw it back. Like cocking a pistol, Khath thought. In hazy slow motion he watched that fist coming toward him. At the last moment he decided to resist the blow by clenching his stomach muscles. If Mith was going to beat him to death, at least the man would walk away with sore knuckles. The blow landed, and then another, and another. Bile burned in Khath's throat and he gagged. Mith stepped back.

A gentle cough sounded above the rasping of Khath's breath.

"Brother Mith, you forget yourself, yes?"

Khath raised his head and tried to focus his eyes. He recognized the calming drawl and drawn out cadences of his lanky friend from the Christian church, the one who'd tried to recruit him, and then warned him to stay away after the trouble with Mith started. Yes, it was him. There he stood, towering over Mith, like a slender stalk of bamboo shooting upwards toward the heavens. As Khath watched, Mith struggled to control himself. He passed a bandana over his face, wiping away moisture of some sort, Khath's blood or possibly his own frothy spittle, and then cleared his throat.

"Brother Oum, you have come at an unpleasant moment. My friend here," Mith nodded toward Khath, "has challenged me to settle a personal disagreement." A scowl settled on Mith's face. "Why are you here?"

"Pastor Tom's orders, Brother Mith." Oum shrugged. "He has been worried about you these last few weeks, worried about your absences. Concerned for your safety. He asked me to follow you, to make sure you were not in trouble. The camp is a dangerous place at night, yes?" Oum's gaze lingered on Khath and the two men holding him upright. "It seems you have won the fight. I doubt that this man will give you any more trouble. Perhaps it is time to let him go."

"Perhaps I am not yet finished," Mith said, a hardness entering his tone.

*He will not be finished until I am dead.* Khath's mind formed the words but all his body could manage was a moan. *Surely Oum knows that. Funny that I have not known his name until this moment.*

"Pastor Tom will want a full report of what I have seen tonight," Oum said. "It would be a shame, Brother Mith, if he removed you from the sponsorship lists. You've been waiting a long time, yes? Longer than most. But the good pastor tells me he has some lingering doubt about the..." a slight, mocking pause, "depth of your love for the Lord." Oum raised his eyes heavenward. "Praised be his name."

Mith snorted. "Why do you care about this man? What is he to you?"

*Yes, why do you care?* Khath wondered this, too.

"It is not your business," Oum replied. "But if you leave him now, in my care, I will report to Pastor Tom only that you have been visiting a friend who is leaving the camps."

"See that you do," Mith said, and motioned his cronies to let go of Khath. "Drop him," he ordered curtly, but instead Khath felt himself lowered, if not gently at least slowly, to the welcoming earth.

A few moments later, Oum was kneeling beside him. "Can you walk?" he asked.

Khath shook his head, scattered thoughts flickering through his mind as he teetered on the edge of consciousness. *Is it over? Am I to live after all?*

"Rest here then. I will get your brother to help us."

Oum disappeared into the night, or perhaps Khath passed out, he was not sure. But the next thing he knew, it was daylight, he was back in his own bed, and Pra Chhay was standing before him, holding a plate of rice with a fried egg on top of it.

"How do you feel?" his brother asked.

Khath sat up. His lips felt pulpy and one eye was swollen, as was his nose. He looked down at his body and saw bruises and scrapes on his arms and trunk. Where were his clothes? The amulets! His gaze jerked around the room, searching, until he saw them safe beside his mattress, placed on top of a leather pouch.

"Yes, they are safe," Pra Chhay said, his voice bitter. "You risk your life, and our future, for such charms. I don't understand you, Khath." He sat down on the floor next to the mattress, and handed the food to Khath. "Your friend, the one who saved your life, insisted that we put the charms right beside your bed, so you would see them first thing."

Khath found that he could open his jaws about half an inch. He pulled the egg into strips and poked them into his mouth, sucking the grease eagerly off each morsel and using his tongue to massage the egg against the few places inside his mouth that didn't hurt in lieu of actual chewing. He was afraid he would lose his teeth if he chewed. He was surprised to find himself so hungry.

"Where is he?" he mumbled through stiff lips.

"He has gone to beg some ice from the canteen. If we cannot bring the swelling down in your face, they will not recognize you from your photos, and then where will we be?"

Khath nodded his response. I don't understand me, either, he wanted to say. But he was too hungry, and it hurt to talk.

Pra Chhay moved to his own mattress and sat, chanting softly, his prayer beads clicking, until the door of the group home swung open and Oum stepped in, a small plastic bag of ice leaving drips on the floor.

"Look who's up and eating," he said, his slow lazy smile splitting his cheeks. "Bet it hurts to chew, yes? Hurry and finish so we can put this ice on. There is no time to lose."

Khath put his plate aside and reached for the ice bag. He focused his good eye on Oum. "Why," he croaked, "did you save my life?"

Oum sat back on his heels and studied Khath's swollen face. "Mith is a rotten man. This, I know. There is no help for Mith. He is lost, better dead, yes? Mith, and men like Mith, Khmer Rouge, will be scattered on the wind to far places—America, France, Australia. Their rotten seed will grow and spread like it did in our country." Oum's face darkened and he leaned forward and touched Khath's knee. "Men like you will stand up to them, stop them. So I help you. Maybe God is watching. Maybe I make some good karma too, yes?" Rising to his feet, Oum bowed to Pra Chhay, and then turned to Khath. "Goodbye, my friend," he said. "I hope you find your daughters."

---

Gail Marsh sat on her front porch in Glenberg, Oregon, wishing she could go for a walk in the mild afternoon sunshine. Hell, I'd settle for crossing my legs, she thought, stroking her dachshund, Zeus, who lay curled in a furry ball on her lap. A soft woolen blanket was tucked around her and she wore a light windbreaker zipped to the neck. She chilled easily since the accident and felt a touch of autumn cooling the late August breeze.

Careful not to disturb Zeus, she leaned forward to watch her sister, Teresa, who was kneeling by the picket fence in the side yard closest to the alley. Teresa had put in a garden bed and planted some late season kale there. A small pile of weeds was evidence of her morning labors. But now, Teresa spoke softly and held a plucked dandelion flower outstretched toward the fence.

Although Gail couldn't see clearly through the pickets, she knew that a little refugee girl crouched low in the weeds on the other side of the fence, her fingertips curled around the slats, glossy black bangs partially obscuring dark eyes. Teresa had been trying to befriend the girl for weeks.

Unlocking the wheels of her wheelchair, Gail pushed forward, eager to catch a glimpse of their little visitor. As she rolled out from behind the solid porch railing and onto the ramp, she heard a sudden rustling in the weeds and saw a flash of color. Teresa held a hand up to stop her, but it was too late. The child had bolted and was running back down the alley, her flip-flops making slapping noises against the soles of her feet, each footstep raising a puff of dust in its wake.

"Damn. I scared her off, didn't I? Sorry."

"That's okay. I need to get changed and get going soon, anyway," Teresa said, rising and brushing the dirt off of her jeans.

"Has she said anything yet?" Gail asked.

"No, but I think she was going to take this dandelion from me. That's progress." Teresa walked up the ramp toward Gail. "She sure is a cutie."

Gail backed her chair up to make room for Teresa to pass. "How old do you think she is?"

"Judging from her body size, I'd say about nine or ten, but she might be small for her age."

Gail rolled her eyes. "Ya think? Last I heard, refugee kids don't have the best diets in the world."

"Smarty pants," Teresa said, then flinched slightly at her choice of expression and turned away to hurry into the house.

There's that elephant again, Gail thought. Her sister tried never to do or say anything that might draw attention to Gail's inert legs. *It makes me feel worse to see you flinch than it does to hear you say something related to legs*, Gail had told her more than once, to no avail. Now she paused to give Teresa time to collect herself. A moment later, Teresa called out to her from inside her bedroom.

"Come help me figure out what to wear to this interview. You know, I've never actually talked with a priest before."

Skillfully, Gail maneuvered through the house and into Teresa's bedroom. It helped to have a sports chair, smaller and more agile than a regular wheelchair. Her regular chair just made her feel old and defeated. She parked herself just inside the doorway and watched while her sister surveyed the clothing in her closet.

"So what do you think I should wear?" Teresa asked.

"Hell, I don't know," Gail responded. "Nothing at all sexy. You're not supposed to wear sexy things when you go see a priest. Especially not when he's a young, handsome priest, eh?" She grinned at Teresa and waggled her eyebrows up and down.

"He's not that young. He's got gray temples." She held up a dark blue belted cotton dress. "How about this?"

Gail shook her head. "No, not that. Wear pants. Something casual and comfortable. You're not going to ask him for anything. You're offering to help with the refugees. You don't have to dress up." Honestly, sometimes Teresa was so prim. "What does he want you to do, anyway?"

"Father Ralph said the last two refugees will be arriving in a couple days. He said he might need help picking them up from the airport, and that the project always needs more tutors to teach English. I'd enjoy being an English tutor."

Teresa pulled on a pair of forest green corduroy pants and selected a sweater set to go with it. "Will this do?"

Gail nodded her approval. "Too bad all this resettlement stuff is being organized by churches. I bet some of them are just trying to convert people. Think of the power you'd have over someone if you rescued them from a refugee camp." She sure wouldn't want anyone to have that kind of power over her. Even unable to walk, a situation she hoped would not be permanent, Gail fiercely defended her independence. "So," she said with a teasing grin, "I guess it's good that a heathen like you is getting involved. No ulterior motive."

Shortly thereafter, Gail shooed Teresa out the door, assuring her she would be fine at home by herself, she didn't need a glass of water (or if she did she could get it for herself), she wasn't hungry, not too hot, not too cold, and God forbid, no, she did not want to come along. Shit. Would Teresa ever lighten up? It had been six months and she didn't blame Teresa for not being the one who got hurt, so when would Teresa stop blaming herself?

Gail studied her own reflection in the living room window. Apart from the wheelchair, as if anyone could miss that, the only sign of the accident was the scar, a light jagged line that started to the left of her mouth, ran diagonally across her cheek, up to her temple and finally disappeared into her hairline. Thank God her eye had been spared. An interior designer needed both eyes and she fully intended to get back to work one of these days.

Sadness welled up, threatening Gail's resolve as she remembered the squeal of automobile tires, the glare of headlights bearing down upon the vehicle, her mother's screams eerily truncated as the life was slammed out of her body, the utter silence of her father, before, during and eternally after the accident. Teresa had escaped unscathed, protected by the mounds of clothing and linens piled on her lap, ready for donation to the Goodwill. "Guess I didn't make out so well, eh

Zeus? Should have put the pots and pans and knives in the trunk like Dad said."

Sighing, Gail scooped Zeus gently out of her lap and pulled her 'gripper,' an extendable mechanical hand, out of the umbrella stand by the door. "C'mon Zeus. Might as well go watch the garden grow."

Rolling down and off the ramp, Gail wheeled slowly about the yard, stopping with her gripper to snap a dead flower head here, pluck a weed there. Teresa had insisted they put down wide, finely graveled walkways around the yard soon after the accident. Gail had protested the expense at the time, but now she was thankful for these pathways to nature. She paused, leaning back in her chair and letting the sunshine warm her face. After a moment, she continued on toward the side yard. Nearing the kale patch, she spied a large garden slug sliming his way through the tender shoots, leaving a trail of destruction in his wake.

"Shit. I knew there was a reason for me to come out here. Sic 'em, Zeus!" she cried, pointing in the direction of the slug with her gripper. Zeus wagged his tail, cocked his head and sat down.

"No, Zeus! No! The slug! He's destroying our baby kale!"

Zeus yawned and slid down onto his tummy.

"Well. Some guard dog you are." Gail feigned indignation, thoroughly amusing herself with this little drama. Gotta take your amusement where you can get it when you're all gimped up. "If you're not up to the task, I'll do it myself," she announced grandly to the dog. "I think I can just about reach him."

Twisting her body in the wheelchair and leaning sideways, gripper in hand, Gail stretched, straining toward the voracious slug. Suddenly, the chair teetered. Flailing, she felt her body pitch forward helplessly. Before she had time to get her arms in front of her to break her fall, she smacked face first into the garden bed.

Gail lay stunned for a moment, eyes closed, smelling and tasting dirt. Tears of frustration seeped from underneath her lids. Her left arm was pinned underneath her body, her right was flung over her head by the force of her fall. Her wheelchair lay on its side, wheels spinning, halfway on top of her legs.

A wet tongue lapped at her face; a cold nose pushed at her ear. Zeus whimpered, and clambered over her prostrate body, seeking a response to his pokes and scratches.

"It's okay, Zeus. I'm all right, I think, but how am I going to get back up in that chair?"

She wriggled her left arm free and rolled slightly over onto her side, her back towards the fence. "Ahhh, that's better. At least I can breathe without getting a nose full of dirt."

Lifting her head, Gail took a closer look at the wreckage below her waist. Her legs were splayed and twisted, entangled in the underpinnings of the wheelchair.

"Holy shit. Never mind how I'm going to get up in the chair. Let's start with how I'm going to get the damn thing off of me."

A twinge of anxiety arose in Gail's mind. She had no feeling in her legs, so how could she know if the weight of the chair was causing more damage? Maybe she was bleeding somewhere that she couldn't see and couldn't feel. What if her bones were broken and jutting through her skin and clothing into the dirt? Jesus H. Christ. She could practically feel the infection setting in now. What if — *Calm down,* she told herself firmly.

"Hey, Zeus. What is it, boy?" The dog's body had tensed, his ears pricked, and a small "woof" escaped his throat. Gail grabbed his collar.

"Hello? Excuse me, is anyone there? I need some help, please," Gail called out. Silence.

Zeus whined and tugged against her grip.

"Shhhh, Zeus, cut it out. You're making me nervous." Gail struggled unsuccessfully to raise herself up. "Hello?" she called again.

She heard the squeak of rusty hinges as the old picket fence gate swung open behind her. Someone was coming. Zeus yapped frantically.

"Who's there?" Gail shouted. *Why don't they answer me?* Her heart pounded, partly in fear and partly with the exertion of trying to twist her body around to see who was approaching.

"Allo?" The soft voice spoke timidly. Footsteps crunched around behind her and soon a child's dusty brown feet were visible, shod only in flip-flops. Bare legs disappeared into a colorful sarong wrapped snugly around the girl's small body. A dirty pink tee-shirt completed her ensemble. "You fall?" The child squatted down next to Gail.

"Hello! It's you. You *can* talk." Gail forgot her discomfort in the surprise of seeing the little mystery child Teresa had been working so hard to befriend. "Boy, am I glad to see you. Listen, can you pull this thing off me? I was trying to reach this slug that was eating all our kale. Eeeeww, I hope I didn't land on him." Gail stopped. I'm babbling, she realized. The poor kid probably doesn't understand a word I'm saying.

The child remained squatting, gazing impassively at Gail. Then she reached out and touched Gail's shoulder.

"You wait," she said, and nodded her head vigorously. Then she stood and trotted out of the yard, the sound of her flip-flops fading as she hurried away down the alley.

# Seven

Phally lugged the vacuum down the hallway into the living room. Another machine, she thought, longing for the simplicity of a wood hut, where a quick going over with a straw broom followed by a damp rag was all it took to keep the floor clean. She gazed at the scruffy brown shag carpet with distaste. Why would anyone cover a good hard floor with this fuzzy cloth that tickled one's feet and smelled of dust? Some of her Cambodian neighbors in Glenberg had covered their carpets with woven mats, but with her daughter Nary to care for, Phally had no money to buy frivolous things.

Unwrapping the electric cord from the neck of the machine, she tried to remember how the vacuum worked. It had sat unused in the closet for months, until recently when one of the church ladies had happened by while she, Phally, was vainly sweeping the rug with a broom, sweat dripping from her brow as debris bounced up from the rug and settled back down among the fibers, defying her attempts to clean the shag. The woman had laughed, though not unkindly, and Phally knew now how silly she must have looked.

Positioning the machine in the center of the room, Phally looked around for a place to plug it in. She found an outlet near the sofa. With a backward glance at the silent vacuum, Phally approached the wall socket and timidly inserted the plug. Nothing happened. Puzzled, she went back to the vacuum and examined it more closely. She discovered a lever near the base that, when pressed, allowed her to move the handle of the vacuum up and down. Then Phally noticed a small black switch near the top of the handle. Firmly, she pressed it. With a roar, the machine came to life. Jumping back in fright, Phally tripped over the electric cord and landed on her rear with a thump. The vacuum continued its awful racket. Unable to think with all the noise, Phally reached up and pressed the switch again. Quiet descended, marred only by the ringing that lingered in Phally's ears after the roar of the vacuum was silenced.

Phally stood up and glared at the vacuum. What a strange and difficult country. All these machines made her feel disconnected from the real things of life. She had cooked over a fire in the back yard for the first week after being resettled in this house that the church had arranged for her, uncomfortable with the knobs and dials of the electric stove in the kitchen. When Mr. Sareth found out, he scoffed at her country ways and said she must use the stove or she would insult her sponsors who, after all, had provided it for her. But it was not until she found her young daughter Nary experimenting in the kitchen that Phally was convinced that she must learn these new ways. How else could she guide her child in this foreign land?

Her eyes roved over the interior of the living room, skipping over the sagging tan sofa pushed against one wall, the table that stretched lean and low in front of it. An overturned cardboard box shored up with blocks of wood held her English picture books and easy readers; a cassette recorder sat on top with her lesson tapes beside it. Two straight-backed chairs, pushed out of the way against the wall on either side of the fireplace, completed the room's sparse furnishings.

As they always did, Phally's eyes came to rest upon the small shrine atop the fireplace mantle. Her husband's face, along with those of her father, mother, sisters and other deceased relatives gazed back at her. She sighed. Boran would have loved this new adventure. The machines alone would have delighted him. He had been so full of life, so brave and so devoted to saving his country from the Khmer Rouge. Not many in her village had heeded the call of the *Pu Yi Ban* to spy on the Khmer Rouge when they slipped into the village under cover of darkness and held their meetings. But when the village headman had asked, Boran said yes. She remembered the nights when he would dress himself in black, wrap his neck with a red checkered *krama*, kiss her forehead and disappear into the night to infiltrate the enemies of his beloved country. Phally would lie awake all night, scarcely breathing, until just before dawn when Boran would slip silently into bed beside her and fall quickly into an exhausted sleep.

A tear rolled down her cheek, and Phally dashed it away angrily. *I miss him so much. My heart bleeds with sorrow at every dawn and continues until I am drained empty by nightfall. And the next day it begins again. When will it stop?* With a sigh, she switched on the vacuum and ran it over the carpet until the noise of the machine and the dust it raised made her head ache.

Turning to the slightly open window for a breath of fresh air, Phally caught a glimpse of her daughter Nary trotting breathlessly into the yard. This daughter of hers weighed heavily upon her heart. Almost eleven years old, yet she exhibited none of the modesty of a properly raised Cambodian girl. Four years under the Khmer Rouge and six months in the refugee camp had turned a charming child into a wild and boyish survivor. Look at her now. Sarong trailing in the dust, grime embedded in her shirt, her hair snarled and dirty, running down the street in public.

Setting her mouth firmly, Phally stepped to the door. Mr. Sareth had told her yesterday that a holy man, a monk, was coming soon to join their community. Perhaps this monk would give classes to teach the children respect for the Buddha and for their culture. I will be the first to enroll my daughter if he does, she thought.

"Nary," Phally began sternly as the girl dashed up the steps.

Nary's breathing was labored, her eyes anxious. "Mama...Mama," she panted. The soft rolling cadence of the Cambodian language was harshened with Nary's urgency. "Please Mama, come with me. The American lady, she can't walk, Mama. She fell."

Nary tugged at her mother's hand, pulling her down the stairs and out onto the road. "Hurry, Mama."

"What American lady? Nary, where are we going?" Phally pulled free of Nary's grasp and slowed to a walk.

Wringing her hands, Nary danced impatiently in front of her mother. "I told you, Mama. You remember about the lady who always sat on the porch while the other one worked in the yard. Here, it's just around the corner. Hurry, Mama, we have to help her."

Wondering what mischief Nary had gotten into now, Phally lengthened her stride to keep up as her daughter sprinted around the corner and darted into a dirt alleyway behind some homes. As she rounded the corner herself, she saw Nary up ahead disappearing through a gate into the yard of one of the houses. Oh no. Phally's heart thumped in fear. Mr. Sareth had warned them that Americans were very private and did not want people walking up to their houses unless they were invited. Was Nary's boldness putting her in danger?

Panicky now, Phally broke into a run. She had failed to protect Nary from the Khmer Rouge. She would rather die than fail in her duty again.

Grabbing the gatepost, Phally flew into the yard and skidded to a stop in surprise at the scene before her.

Nary was kneeling in the dirt, her hand on the shoulder of a young American woman who lay sprawled awkwardly on her side. A fancy wheelchair made of metal and rubber, not at all like the bamboo chairs shared among the amputees in the refugee camp clinic, was half on top of the woman and appeared to be pressing heavily into her back and legs, which lay askew in the underside of the chair. Yet the young woman smiled at Nary, even though tear stains made tracks through the dirt smudged on her pale white skin. A strange looking little dog, very long in the body, began to bark at Phally until the woman calmed it.

Clucking in sympathy, Phally hurried to woman's side and, after bobbing her head at the woman in a way that she hoped would be seen as reassuring, began to run her hands over the woman's legs, feeling for bumps, breaks or the dampness of blood. "Ask her if it hurts," she said in Cambodian to Nary.

"You pain?" Nary said to the woman.

The woman pointed to her legs and shook her head. "No pain," she said. Then she pointed to her left wrist. "Here, pain."

Phally nodded. "Okay." Gently she began to untangle Gail's legs from the wheelchair, moving slowly and carefully until she was able to lift the chair and set it upright.

"Thank you," the woman said. "Ahhh." With her right hand she rubbed her back where the arm of the chair had been jabbing her, and carefully sat up. "Thank you so much. My name is Gail." She pointed to herself and repeated, with a smile, "Gail."

Phally looked purposefully at Nary.

"My name Nary," the child said. "This," pointing to Phally, "my mother."

Phally smiled, pressed her palms together at chest level and bowed her head gracefully in Gail's direction, at the same time managing to shoot a glare at Nary from under the cover of her half lowered lashes. Nary hastily dropped a Cambodian style bow in Gail's direction.

Tucking her sarong tight against the backs of her legs, Phally now lowered herself easily into a comfortable squat beside Gail's legs, laying one hand lightly on Gail's knee. She turned to Nary. "Sit behind her, child, and let her lean against your back for a little support." Once Nary was situated, Phally moved her hand to the hem of Gail's pant leg and pulled up slightly, to expose bare skin. "Okay?" she asked.

Gail nodded.

Phally pushed Gail's pants up to mid-thigh, running her hands over Gail's legs, one at a time. *So thin,* she thought. *She has no muscle. This is not a new injury. Most people died quickly under the Khmer Rouge if they were unable to work. But later, when the Vietnamese came and there was medical care, more survived. She'd seen plenty of withered limbs after that.* She felt around Gail's knees and ankles and gently moved the joints. There were many bruises and a few scrapes, but nothing seemed broken.

Phally pointed at Gail's left wrist. "I look?" she said.

Again, Gail nodded her permission.

This time, Phally noticed Gail wincing when she examined the swollen wrist. But Gail could move it and shook her head when Phally said, "You go doctor?"

Now Phally moved the wheelchair close and made sure it was stable in the soft dirt. She squatted behind Gail and put her hands under Gail's arms, but the young woman shook her head vigorously and said 'no' and a lot of other things Phally didn't understand.

Puzzled, Phally came around to look Gail in the face. Surely this woman didn't think Phally wasn't strong enough to lift her? *I have lifted sacks of rice that weighed more than you.* But the woman was smiling and pointing to a small lever on the arm of wheelchair.

"I think she is telling us how to take the arm off, Mama," Nary said. "So it will be easier to get her back into the chair."

"Go ahead, Nary. Do as she says," Phally watched closely as Nary removed the wheelchair's arm. "Good," she said. "Now, I will lift her while you guide her legs."

Compared to the labor Phally had been forced to perform for the Khmer Rouge, it was a simple task to reposition Gail in her chair and roll her back up the ramp to her house, while Nary and the little dog followed.

Phally had never been inside the house of an American before. The church ladies often came to visit, bringing food and other useful things, but none of them had thought to invite her to their houses.

Curiously, she gazed about as she pushed Gail inside, kicking off her shoes before entering, as was the Cambodian custom. The first thing she noticed was the comfort of a hard wood floor, instead of carpet, under her bare feet. The second was the overwhelming sense of abundance and life in the home. Pictures adorned the walls, comfortable looking chairs with cozy blankets folded over the backs clustered in the main room. Phally noticed a TV set and radio, and many books on shelves along one wall. Live plants, even a small tree, thrived near the windows.

Through an arched doorway, Phally could see a large kitchen, with a varied assortment of pots and pans hanging from a rack in the ceiling. Jars of spices and canisters of dried beans, noodles and flour lined one counter, and a large basket of fruit sat in the middle of a big table. She wondered how many people lived in this house and how it was that Gail could stay so thin and pale surrounded by all this food and comfort. She had much to learn about these Americans and their ways.

---

Khath shuffled after Pra Chhay down the long narrow airplane aisle, clutching a small suitcase to his chest, half empty despite being packed with the worldly belongings of two grown men. A woman in a blue uniform directed them to their seats, her gaze lingering on Khath's bruised face and torn, puffy lips. Pra Chhay was right. Khath was painfully aware that he would not be making a good first impression on his sponsors in America.

Pra Chhay bowed his thanks to the woman while Khath slipped into the window seat. To Khath's surprise, his brother was very nervous about the flight and wanted nothing to do with gazing out a window so high above the ground. "I plan to sit with my eyes closed and my prayer beads in my hand the entire flight," Pra Chhay had said to Khath. "If I should be so lucky as to fall asleep, please don't wake me. My feet were made for this earth and I hope to dream of walking on solid ground for as long as I am airborne."

A ripple of excitement passed through Khath as he settled into his seat—he had learned to love engines when he worked in the train yard in Phnom Penh before the war years. He looked out the small window into the brightly lit night and watched as baggage was loaded aboard the jet. His precious amulets he carried in a pouch on a string around his neck.

The plane's public address system hummed with the soft, musical tones of the Thai language, followed by rapid-fire, unintelligible English translation. The uniformed woman who had shown them to their seats was now standing in the aisle, smiling wordlessly as she pulled gadgets out of a kit and demonstrated their use, presumably in concert with the voices over the loudspeakers. She pointed to various features of the plane, then held the two ends of a seat belt high over her head, fastening it, unfastening it and pulling one end to tighten its loop. Khath checked his own seat belt and leaned over to inspect Pra Chhay's, as his brother sat rigidly in his seat with his eyes squeezed shut, clicking his prayer beads.

Satisfied with the state of the seat belts, Khath returned his attention to the woman. To his horror, she next pulled out some sort of plastic bag which she placed over her nose and mouth, using a small elastic cord to fasten it to her face. Khath quickly averted his eyes but it was too late. His breathing quickened and his throat felt tight as painful memories crowded out conscious thought. He saw the faces of those he had watched the Khmer Rouge murder with a plastic bag placed over the head and fastened tightly round the neck, their mouths open wide, straining for air and finding none, their desperate struggles intensifying in one last mighty effort to live, then fading away to stillness.

A slight jolt startled Khath as the plane began to move. Released from the grip of his memories, he peered out the window at the passing buildings. The plane slowed, turned, then gathered speed with a scream of the engines. Khath gasped as an invisible hand pressed him back against his seat. Beside him, Pra Chhay moaned and his hands abandoned his prayer beads to clutch at the arm rests as the plane tilted sharply upward. Khath patted Pra Chhay's hand and whispered, "There's nothing to fear, brother. Feel how smooth it is." A thrill coursed through Khath's body and he could not help but grin. They were flying. He, Khath Sophal, was flying in an airplane.

Peering out the window, he saw the ground dropping away below him, and the enormity of what he was doing crashed over him, a wave of tangled emotion surging through his body. For a time, Khath sat quietly, eyes closed, one hand grasping the amulet pouch over his heart. "Be with me, my daughters," he murmured. He summoned their faces from memory and pledged never to give up his search. A firm determination gripped him and he opened his eyes. Better start getting accustomed to this new life as quickly as possible, the better to start his search at once when he landed in his new home.

For several minutes, Khath continued to pat Pra Chhay's hand until his brother's grip loosened and he fell asleep, his head lolling.

Satisfied that Pra Chhay was settled, Khath began to explore his surroundings. He peered into the pocket on the seat back in front of him and pulled out a paper sack, several magazines, a stiff and glossy piece of paper with brightly colored pictures on it, and a plastic bag containing a pair of headphones. Khath flipped through the magazines, glancing at a few pictures of people and landscapes, then stuffed them back into the pocket.

Paper was scarce in Cambodia. He marveled that there were well over 100 people on this plane, and it seemed that every one of them had two magazines to look at. One would be more than enough, he thought. In Cambodia, a single newspaper would be passed from hand to hand until it was in tatters.

Khath next examined the paper bag. He sighed. Even the paper bags were different, modern. The most prosperous merchants in his childhood village used to fold newspaper remnants to make bags, and no one ever bothered to glue the edges. In truth, they had rarely used paper bags. It was easier to wrap things in banana leaves and tie them with a bit of string, or even with narrow strips of more banana leaf.

Tucking the bag back into the seat pocket, Khath looked now at the headphones inside the sealed plastic bag. A quick glance around at the seats nearest him assured him that the headphones were there for the use of the passengers and he quickly figured out how to plug them in, adjust the volume and select a station. What a disappointment. Apart from one station featuring classical Thai music, nothing he heard even remotely resembled the traditional music of Cambodia. The rest of the stations sounded to Khath like noisy children banging with sticks on metal and he soon lost interest. He removed the headset and rubbed his ears. Beside him, Pra Chhay slept on.

Finally, Khath turned his attention to the last item he had taken from the pocket, the stiff and shiny paper covered with colorful drawings. He studied the pictures and realized with a shock that this was some sort of instruction sheet for what to do if the plane crashed. He gazed in alarm at the picture of men and women perched on a raft in the ocean, while the plane floated nearby. He had heard many horrible stories at the refugee camp about Thai pirates who swooped down on hapless refugees in their rafts, violating the women and girls, killing the other passengers. With a hasty glance at the sleeping Pra Chhay, Khath quickly buried the page behind the magazines in the seat pocket. Then moving carefully in order not to awaken his brother, he removed the instruction sheet from the pocket in front of Pra Chhay and hid that one as well.

The disturbing pictures reminded Khath that they were indeed flying above the ocean, just as the refugee camp staff had said they would. He turned to the window, curious to see what all that water would look like from above, but saw only darkness. He had forgotten it was nighttime.

Khath craned his head—so much blackness outside the window. Where were the stars? A vague anxiety tugged at his heart. Did the stars shine only above Cambodia? He shook his head in irritation at this stupid thought. Of course there were stars all over the world. Peering upward, Khath caught a glimpse of the moon and knew then that it was only the glow of the moonlight drowning out the twinkle of the stars. Reassured, he settled himself more comfortably in his seat and let his mind wander back to other moonlit nights, nights when it was still safe to walk about in the evening and admire the silvery gleam of moonbeams reflected on rice paddies, banana trees and coconut palms.

Weariness caused his eyelids to sag, and soon Khath, too, slept soundly as the plane hurtled him toward a new life.

# Eight

Sareth stood near the Delta Airlines counter, studying the arrivals monitor. He frowned. The plane was delayed in Los Angeles and would not be arriving in Portland for another ninety minutes.

He was anxious to meet these two newcomers, anxious to assess what challenges they might bring to his authority in Glenberg's refugee community. The monk could definitely be a problem, especially since Father Ralph was so eager to meet and befriend the man. The brother was a complete unknown as far as Sareth was concerned. According to his file, his experience of life under the Khmer Rouge was quite horrific. Sareth guessed he would be either a broken man, or a hardened one. Either way it could be trouble.

He sighed and turned to watch his wife Chea standing beside Father Ralph near the entrance of the concourse. His heart clenched. She was so lovely with her dazzling sarong and long shining hair, staring with unabashed curiosity at the streams of people swirling about in the airport. He followed carefully the sweep of her eyes. Did they linger on one man or another? He counted the times he saw men stutter in their steps, their pacing askew as their eyes were pulled toward Chea's startling beauty.

In Cambodia, Sareth had felt pride in the envy of other men, secure in his possession of Chea. Wealth and prestige had wrapped his wife in their embrace, and he had no fear of losing her. Now, stripped of his wealth and failing to find much of importance on which to build his influence within the sleepy community of Glenberg, Sareth feared his hold on his young wife was weakening. At least, as Father Ralph's assistant, he could still provide Chea opportunities for amusement unavailable to the other refugees, like this trip to the airport.

Sareth glanced again at his watch. They were waiting for Teresa, the new volunteer, to show up. They could have squeezed six into Father Ralph's sedan, but it would have been uncomfortable, and the church van was in the garage. Besides, the monk would need to avoid proximity to the women. Of course, the obvious solution would have been to leave Chea at home, but she had so wanted to come and these days Sareth did not dare to disappoint her in these small matters. When Teresa offered to take Chea back to Glenberg in her car, the problem was solved.

Sareth broke off his musing as he saw a smile crease Father Ralph's face. Teresa had arrived. Sareth watched her recognize Father Ralph and give a cheery wave. She was not unattractive, though when she stood next to Chea, it was abundantly clear that she was not beautiful, either. She had pretty hair, golden brown and shoulder-length. But, in Sareth's opinion, she was under-dressed, as he had come to expect of Americans. Her brown pants and tan sweater revealed her figure. Not fat, like many Americans, but soft, with a well-fed look. Sareth had yet to meet a lean American woman over the age of thirty.

Approaching the group as Father Ralph was introducing Teresa to Chea, Sareth watched critically to see if his wife had mastered the American handshake yet. He groaned inwardly as Chea bowed with clasped hands and lowered eyes, completely missing the fact that Teresa was extending her hand toward Chea.

In two steps Sareth had moved to Chea's side and placed his hand upon her elbow, propelling her upright. Turning to Teresa, he said, "You must forgive my wife. She is not yet accustomed to the American style greeting." He extended his hand to Teresa and smiled. "I am Mr. Sareth. You must be Miss Marsh?"

"Call me Teresa, please. It's a pleasure to meet you, Mr. Sareth."

"Father Ralph tells me that you are volunteering to teach English. On behalf of my community, let me say how grateful we are for your gracious assistance." Sareth offered a slight bow in Teresa's direction. As expected, he saw a flush creeping up Teresa's neck. He had noticed early on that American women were easily flustered, and very soon afterward, charmed by the formal courtesies so freely expressed in his country. And Sareth had learned decades ago as a young man that a charmed woman was a pleasant and compliant one. It was a lesson he never forgot.

Father Ralph spoke up. "Mr. Sareth has truly become my right hand in this resettlement project, Teresa. You'll be seeing lots of him, I'm sure. Feel free to ask him any questions you like about the project or about Cambodian culture. He can help with any translation you need, as well."

"It is as he says, Miss Marsh. I am at your service. Indeed," Sareth gestured at the arrival board, "it is my unhappy duty to inform you both that the plane has been delayed by more than an hour."

"Why don't we have some tea and get acquainted then?" Father Ralph said. "There's an Asian restaurant near the gate."

Sareth spoke in Cambodian to Chea, explaining the new plan. A smile broke across her face and she fell into step between her husband and Teresa.

"*Bong,* does the American lady come often to the airport?" Chea asked Sareth.

Sareth smiled at his wife. "Go ahead, ask her. Practice your English," he said.

"You come here, many time?" Chea asked Teresa.

"No, it's my first time." Teresa held up one finger. "How about you?"

"I come two time." Chea pointed at Sareth. "My husband, he come every time." She touched her hand to her chest. "Me. I stay home, cook. I cook for you, sometime."

As they arrived at the restaurant, Sareth fell to the rear, ushering the women ahead of him. Father Ralph chose a table by a window overlooking the runway. It was a good choice, Sareth thought, one that would allow Chea to watch the planes and not be too bored while the rest of us talk in English. Father Ralph was getting much better at handling these mixed language level situations.

The priest ordered cups of tea for them all, and then smiled across the table at Teresa. "Thanks again for coming today. It's a big help."

"My pleasure," Teresa responded. She turned to Sareth. "You speak English beautifully. Do you mind my asking where you learned?"

"You flatter me, Miss Marsh. My accent is very poor." Sareth shook his head sadly but allowed a smile to hover at the corners of his lips and eyes. "However, since you ask, I was educated in France, primarily, and took my baccalaureate degree in political science there. It was many years ago, perhaps before your birth, even." Sareth shook his head again but this time his sadness at the passage of time was real. "Things were different then," he said. "Did you know, Miss Marsh, that Phnom Penh was known as the "Pearl of Southeast Asia?"

"No, I'm sorry. I really don't know much at all about Cambodia. I'm rather new at all this." She sounded regretful. "It must be very beautiful, then?"

"Indeed it was, before the war destroyed so much of it. Very ancient, yet modern in some respects as well. Perhaps someday I can share my photographs and my memories with you, Miss Marsh."

"I'd love that. You must have fascinating stories to tell." Teresa leaned forward eagerly, but the conversation was interrupted by the arrival of the waitress with four cups, a small cut glass bowl of lemon wedges, two large white ceramic pots of tea, and a matching sugar bowl and creamer.

Sareth nodded at Chea, who immediately took the role of tea server. She filled first Father Ralph's cup, then Teresa's, then Sareth's. Her own cup she left empty. Sareth enjoyed watching the graceful way she poured, not splashing or spilling even a single drop.

Murmuring his thanks, Sareth placed the tea condiments directly in the center of the table within easy reach of all, and sat back to watch. You could learn a lot about people just by observing their manners at table, he thought, and especially by their ways of preparing tea, a very versatile beverage.

Only Teresa used lemon in her tea, and added a teaspoon of sugar as well. Father Ralph drank his straight. Sareth added two precise teaspoons of sugar to his, along with a dollop of cream. To his dismay, Chea filled her cup nearly halfway with cream, then added three heaping spoonsful of sugar and just enough tea to lend a light tan color to her drink. Of course this was how she took her tea at home, but he had not expected her to display such childish tastes in public. Feeling slightly embarrassed for her, he made a mental note to speak to her about it in the privacy of their home.

Taking a deep sip of his tea, Sareth pronounced it excellent and then turned to Teresa. "And yourself, Miss Marsh? Have you family in Glenberg?"

"I live with my sister Gail in my parent's old home." Teresa paused. "They, uh, they were both killed in a car crash about six months ago."

"I'm so sorry for your great loss." Sareth's response was immediate and sincere. He murmured a quick translation into Chea's ear.

Chea laid her hand on Teresa's arm.

"Thank you." Teresa's face grew pink. "They had a good life. They were happy together. I can't imagine one without the other. Maybe it's better this way."

"Quite true." Sareth nodded sympathetically, yet his brain churned at this ridiculous notion. This woman obviously knew nothing of the will to live. It took far more than the loss of a loved one to quench that fire. Why, if that were true there would not be a single soul left alive in Cambodia. No one's family had come through the war untouched. No one's.

With an effort, Sareth quieted his raging mind and turned his attention back to what Teresa was saying. Something to the effect of worrying about her sister.

"Your sister is grieving heavily?" Sareth asked in a tone of concern.

"Well, it's hard for both of us, of course, but Gail was injured in the accident. Her spinal cord was damaged. She'll most likely never walk again."

"Ah, that is very difficult. A very difficult situation indeed." Sareth clasped his hands together and studied them intently. An idea was stirring in his brain.

Father Ralph leaned forward. "I should have realized how tough it's been for you and your sister from some of the things you mentioned in our interview, Teresa. I am sorry. I just didn't connect the dots. I feel we should be helping you, not the other way around."

"Precisely," Sareth said crisply. "Chea will help you to care for your sister." He turned to Chea and spoke to her in their native tongue, his voice low and urgent. Chea nodded her head and stroked Teresa's arm.

"What? No, wait… I didn't mean …"

"Chea is an excellent nurse," Sareth said. "She's very gentle and knows many herbal remedies."

"But Gail doesn't need a nurse," Teresa protested. "Really, Mr. Sareth, Chea, you're very kind but it's not necessary. But thank you. It's very generous of you to offer."

"A companion, perhaps? Someone to stay with your sister when you're not at home?" Sareth leaned back in his chair and studied Teresa from across the table. She looked back at him, a troubled expression on her face.

"Gail's pretty independent, although sometimes it does get her into trouble. I know I'd feel better if someone were there," Teresa admitted. "Just the other day she had an accident in the garden."

"Well, that might work then," Father Ralph said. "Maybe a couple of mornings a week or something."

"Maybe," Teresa said, stirring her tea slowly.

Father Ralph stroked his chin. "You know, it would be good for Chea, too. She'd improve her English being around your sister. She'd have a chance to practice more."

"We would consider it a favor, Miss Marsh," Sareth said. "Please think it over." He cocked his head. "And now, if my ancient ears do not deceive me, I believe they are announcing our flight."

A few minutes later, the group stood at Gate 23, watching as the jumbo jet taxied up to the terminal. Soon a dense stream of disembarking passengers flowed into the arrival area. Cascading over the noise of the public address system, a jumble of languages swirled on the air, pierced now and then by a scream of delight as relatives met, surging against or ducking under the rope barrier that separated the arrivals from those who awaited them. Beside him, Sareth saw Teresa straining to see through the crowd of arrivals, searching for the monk and his brother. He touched her arm to get her attention.

"Do not worry, Miss Marsh. They will be the very last to arrive. An attendant will bring them out and entrust them to our care, before the plane continues on its way. It is an arrangement the Red Cross has worked out with the airlines."

Gradually the crowd around them began to dissipate. The flow of disembarking passengers became a trickle, then stopped altogether. Next out came a parade of wheelchairs, bearing the elderly and disabled into the arrival area. Any minute now. Sareth felt his breathing quicken. Teresa stood with clasped hands, leaning forward to peer down the walkway. Father Ralph straightened his posture. Only Chea was unaffected, staring at a posted sign about baggage allowances and size requirements. Her lips moved as she struggled to sound out the words.

"Here they come." Father Ralph was the first to spot them.

Sareth relaxed his body, the better to receive the first impressions these two newcomers would make upon his conscious and unconscious mind.

The monk came first, gliding along under saffron robes that hung wrinkled after 20 or so hours in transit. His arms, poking out from his robes, were well-muscled, his gaze intelligent despite the fatigue that lined his face. When the flight attendant spoke to him, he nodded and gave a gentle smile, revealing gleaming white teeth. He carried no luggage, just a bulging cloth pouch that was slung across his chest to hang at waist level. He held a strand of prayer beads in his right hand, and rotated them smoothly between his thumb and first finger. His feet were broad and hung over the edges of a pair of brown sandals that appeared to be about two sizes too small. *He'll need new shoes.* Sareth's mind supplied this thought automatically, but nothing else about the man's appearance or behavior jumped out at him. He seemed to be what his file claimed he was: a simple Buddhist monk.

Sareth turned his attention next to the brother, following close behind the monk. The man pulled a small suitcase along on rusty wheels that screeched across the linoleum floor, an annoying sound that he seemed not to notice. He's overwhelmed, Sareth thought. A man in his right mind would pick up that tiny bag and stop the hideous noise. Dressed in murky clothing that hung from his spare frame, the man carried himself tightly, rigidly, in marked contrast to the monk, whose movements had seemed effortless. His face was turned away, watching a tall blond woman in high heels click her way down the terminal. When he turned toward the waiting group, Sareth heard Teresa gasp.

"Oh my God," she said softly.

The man's lips were swollen and scabbed. Fresh blood seeped from the edges of one particularly thick and clotted area on his lower lip. But these injuries paled in comparison to the multi-hued, shiny flesh stretched tight over his swollen nose, and the runny slit that passed for his right eye.

I wonder what the rest of his body looks like, Sareth thought grimly.

Father Ralph had hurried forward, identification in hand, to meet the flight attendant. Sareth, after a stiff bow in the direction of the monk, joined Father Ralph to help take care of the formalities, while Teresa and Chea hovered in the background.

"He was in a lot of pain on the flight," the attendant was saying to Father Ralph. "We did our best with what little ice we had, but, well, a long flight is tough even in the best of circumstances."

"I am sure your care was exemplary," Sareth said. "We thank you for your trouble."

The attendant smiled. "No trouble," she said. "But I'm glad you're here waiting." She glanced at the trickle of passengers now boarding the flight. "We're trying to make up lost time on the next leg. The Captain was fuming over the delays in getting here. He's raring to go now, so I better get back on."

She turned to follow the last passenger onto the flight, then paused. "Hey, good luck," she said. "It's really nice what you all do for these folks." She disappeared down the ramp, and a moment later, the desk crew clanged the big doors shut behind her.

Now comes the awkward part, Sareth thought, as silence descended over the little group. But the monk stepped forward and bowed deeply, first to Father Ralph and Teresa, then to Sareth and Chea.

"I am Pra Chhay," he said in Cambodian. "And this is my younger brother Khath. I apologize for his appearance. He had…an accident…just before we left Khao I Dang."

There's the first lie, Sareth thought. But he translated, dutifully, for Father Ralph and Teresa. There would be plenty of time later to ferret out the truth.

"We want to say thank you, and to promise that we will work very hard to repay our debt to you," the monk continued.

Father Ralph nodded at the translation and touched Sareth's arm. "Please tell him thank you, Mr. Sareth, and how very happy we are to welcome them to America. Assure them that we will all be working very closely with them to help them settle in to our community." He paused. "Tell them we're very happy they've arrived safely. Right, Teresa?"

Teresa smiled and nodded. "Very happy."

"Do they have any checked luggage?" Father Ralph asked.

Sareth spoke quickly to Pra Chhay and Khath, who shook their heads. No one ever had extra bags to check. It was a silly question, but it had to be asked. They prepared to walk, and Sareth, seeing Khath tighten his grip on the pull strap of his noisy suitcase, leaned forward to pick it up and said, "Allow me, please."

Khath mumbled a thanks and released the strap, his freed hand now creeping up toward the base of his own neck. As Sareth watched, Khath's fingers took on a life of their own as they fanned wide and lazily patted his chest, then began to scrabble more urgently among the buttons, collar and plackets of his shirt. With a look of unease, Khath brought both hands up to his shirt collar and pulled it away from his body, looking down at his chest beneath the shirt. A look of horror crossed his face. He stood stock still for a moment, and a garbled moan escaped his mouth. The others stopped to look back at Khath, staring in consternation as he stood frantically patting his pockets and body, muttering the same phrase over and over in Cambodian. "Where is it? Where is it?"

"Have you lost something?" Sareth asked. "What is the trouble?"

Pra Chhay moved quickly to his brother's side and placed a restraining hand on his arm. Khath flung it aside, and his chest heaving, backed away from the group, a low wail rising from deep inside his chest. Suddenly, he whirled and dashed back toward the doors of the gate, with Pra Chhay at his heels.

The gate attendant stared at the two men charging toward her, a look of alarm on her face. She ran to the desk and picked up a phone. Above the gate door, a red light began flashing.

Sareth and Father Ralph hurried after the two brothers.

"What's going on?" Father Ralph said. "Did he forget something?"

"I don't know," Sareth said, as he reached the door where Khath now stood, pushing fruitlessly against the steel, oblivious to Pra Chhay's attempts to calm him.

"Stop!" Sareth hissed, grabbing Khath's arm and putting all the authority he could muster in his voice. Out of the corner of his eye, Sareth saw uniformed men approaching rapidly. "You must stop this now. The police are coming."

At the mention of police, Khath sagged against the door, and Pra Chhay and Father Ralph moved in quickly to support him before he fell.

Sareth turned toward the officers, his hands raised, palms out. "I am so sorry for the disturbance," he said. "Our friend is overwrought, such a long flight, I'm afraid he became disoriented." He smiled humbly, gesturing to Father Ralph. "I believe the good Father has things in control now."

Father Ralph approached. "Officers, I'm sorry about all this to-do." He nodded toward Pra Chhay and Khath. "They've just arrived from Cambodia this very minute. Kind of overwhelming, I guess. I think he might have left something important on the plane."

At this bit of information, the faces of the officials cleared. The gate attendant stepped forward with forms to fill out and numbers to call. The officers spoke on their radios and the red light over the gate door ceased to flash.

Sareth turned to Pra Chhay. "What did he lose?" he asked.

"Amulets. Protection charms to keep his missing girls safe, and to keep their bond unbroken." Pra Chhay sighed. "He got them from a shaman just before we left Khao I Dang."

"I see," Sareth said. "Well, perhaps they will be returned by the airline." He looked at Khath, who leaned quietly against the gate door, head thrown back and a look of utter despair upon his face.

Broken, Sareth thought. This one is definitely broken.

# Nine

A dank smell assailed Khath's nostrils as he sank deeper into the mud, trussed and flung into a buffalo wallow by Khmer Rouge soldiers, who lined the banks jeering and placing bets on how long it would take for the filthy sludge to invade his mouth and nose. Desperate, Khath heaved his body up against the bonds that held him captive. He felt the tightness across his chest give way with a ripping noise and his eyes flew open, staring into darkness. He gasped and flopped back as the realization sank in. Another nightmare, brought on this time by the unaccustomed softness of a Western-style mattress beneath his body. Clawing his way out of the tangle of sheets and blankets binding him, Khath got up to wash away the sweat of fear and clear his mind of the unwanted images lingering from the dream.

Chilled now as the cool night air struck his damp skin, he wrapped a blanket from the bed around him and groped his way into the bathroom on bare feet. He shut the door quietly, trying not to wake his brother, who snored peacefully in the other bedroom. Sliding his hand along the wall, Khath found the light switch and squinted as the electric glare filled the room.

Sareth and Father Ralph had given him and Pra Chhay a quick orientation tour of their new home when they arrived late

93

that afternoon, explaining how to operate the appliances and adjust the heat. But numbed by fatigue, pain, and grief over the loss of his amulets, Khath had paid scant attention.

Now, he studied the single silver faucet over the sink in puzzlement. Where were the knobs? The handle moved easily from side to side, but no water came from the tap. He spied a little round knob behind the faucet and pushed down, but the knob did not move. Next, he twirled it. Again, nothing. When he tried pulling it upwards, the stopper in the basin lowered, sealing the sink. Perhaps the water would flow if he pumped the main handle? With this thought, Khath yanked upward on the faucet. A burst of water splashed into the sink, and after a moment, turned scalding hot. Khath hissed and jerked his hands out of the water as steam rose upward, fogging the mirror above the sink. Through a process of trial and error, Khath adjusted the water temperature and splashed his face, neck, chest and arms with tepid water, patting himself dry with a corner of his blanket. A proper bath would have to wait until tomorrow.

Returning to his bedroom, Khath eyed the bed as if it were a trap. He leaned forward and pushed down on the mattress, which yielded easily beneath his hand. No wonder he'd dreamed he was sinking into mud. With a guilty sigh, he wrapped himself in the rest of the blankets from the bed, grabbed the pillow, and stretched out on the floor, comforted by the familiar feel of hardness beneath his bones.

He was awakened by Pra Chhay, who shook him gently by the shoulder. Khath opened his eyes slowly, pleased that his facial swelling had gone done enough to let him see through both eyes almost equally. He noticed sunlight seeping around the edges of the bedroom curtains, splashing the floor with thin streams of brightness.

"Get up, Khath. Mr. Sareth is here and he says we must hurry so we won't be late for our appointment with Father Ralph this morning." Pra Chhay looked around the room. "Why are you sleeping on the floor?"

Khath groaned and pushed the mess of blankets aside, rising to his feet stiffly. "I'll tell you later," he said and stumbled toward the bathroom.

Breakfast was hurried, with Mr. Sareth clucking his tongue and taking many worried peeks at his watch. "You must learn to be punctual," he told them in a stern tone of voice. "It is rule number one regarding any official business you have in America. You must be on time, even a little early." He hustled them out the door for a brisk fifteen minute walk to the church offices.

Trailing behind Pra Chhay and Mr. Sareth, Khath looked around with wary interest as they walked along the shoulder of a roughly paved and patched road. Houses made of painted wood lined the tree-shaded street, some with well-tended fenced yards, others full of dried grass and weeds. Here and there, dogs barked. Once, a cat slunk across the road in front of them, but there were no people on the streets, no farmers riding past on bikes laden with vegetables for the market, no street vendors selling their wares, no smoke from cooking fires, no signs of human life at all. The doors were all closed and not even the sound of a crying baby reached Khath's ears. What kind of a town was this?

"Where is everyone?" Khath whispered. He felt as though he were back in Lon Nol's army, a government soldier on patrol, entering a town from which all the residents had fled, or were in hiding.

"Dear me," Mr. Sareth said. "Must I begin again?"

Pra Chhay's lips curled upward slightly, in a placid look that others might take for a smile but that Khath had learned to interpret as irritation. With whom was his brother annoyed? With him? With Mr. Sareth? He hoped it was Mr. Sareth, for the patronizing tone of voice he had just used. We may be fresh from the camps, he thought, but that does not mean we are stupid.

"Forgive me, brother," Pra Chhay said. "I have been hogging the ear of our guide. Come walk beside me, so you can also hear." He motioned Khath to walk between him and the interpreter. "Mr. Sareth has just been explaining that everyone is at work, at school or at centers where parents leave their children when they cannot care for them. He said the neighborhoods are quiet during the day, but even at night, because it is colder here, it will seem very quiet to us as most people stay indoors. Not like Cambodia at all."

They turned onto a bigger, busier street with concrete sidewalks lining the edges of the road. Cars flowed past in an orderly way, no honking, everyone staying in their own lanes, no one in a rush. Khath assumed it was because America was a wealthy country. A man with money had no need to rush in Cambodia. Such a man let others rush to him. That is, until the Khmer Rouge came and hunted the rich ones down, killing with an unquenchable bloodthirst. A little rushing then might have saved some of those rich men.

Lost in his thoughts, Khath lurched off the curb as the sidewalk ended and they crossed a street. Cursing inwardly, he forced his mind to attend to his current surroundings, dismayed at how easily, day or night, his thoughts drifted back into the churning nightmare of the Khmer Rouge years. He envied Pra Chhay's decades of monastic training that enabled him to place his mind where he wanted it, and keep it there. Perhaps the Buddha did have something to offer Khath, after all.

Climbing a short hill, the three men passed by a gas station and came upon a brown brick church, set back from the road with a parking area in front and a lofty bell tower. They had arrived. Approaching the heavy wooden door, Khath paused to study an ornate stained glass window arching over the entrance, depicting a man with a globe of light around his head—Jesus, he supposed—standing with arms outstretched in welcome, dressed in flowing robes. The man was tall and slender, his lanky build and open posture reminding Khath of Oum, his Christian protector in the refugee camp. It was a comforting thought. Taking a deep breath and squaring his shoulders, Khath followed his brother and Mr. Sareth inside the imposing building.

"Welcome, welcome." Father Ralph strode across the lobby toward them, a smile on his face, hand outstretched. Pra Chhay hesitantly held out his own hand, which Father Ralph engulfed with the two of his.

The priest continued to speak, far too rapidly for Khath to understand, but Mr. Sareth had moved to stand half a step behind Father Ralph, and began a simultaneous interpretation of the priest's words. It was almost as though Khath *could* understand the conversation, so skillfully did Mr. Sareth handle the interaction. Though Khath had little experience speaking to Westerners, he could see that Mr. Sareth was very smooth, very polished in his delivery. Much better than the interpreters at the refugee camp. For the first time, he wondered what work Sareth had done in Cambodia.

"First, Father Ralph apologizes that Teresa is not able to be here today," Mr. Sareth said. "She phoned to say she was ill." Mr. Sareth paused for a moment, listening. "He says that he looks forward to getting to know you, Pra Chhay, and sharing opinions about religious beliefs." Turning to Khath, he continued, "And he wants you to know that you are looking much better than you did last night. He hopes you are feeling better as well."

Khath offered his hand to Father Ralph, who shook it gently. Father Ralph's hand was warm and smooth. Khath felt embarrassed at his own cold, work-roughened hands. At least they were clean. He had made sure to scrub them well this morning, in anticipation of his first American handshake. He had a lot to make up for, a lot of face to recover. *He probably thinks I'm baa-baa-bo-bo after last night. Another crazy refugee.* Khath felt his fingers curling into fists, and with an effort, relaxed them.

Father Ralph ushered them into a quiet room with a gleaming wooden table surrounded by comfortable leather chairs. A tray with ice water and glasses sat at one end of the table, along with several pads of lined paper, pens and some file folders. A sink and cabinets were recessed into one wall. The smell of coffee rose from a bubbling pot, and a plate of cookies and fruit sat on the counter, with napkins. A row of long windows lined one wall, each one topped with arching stained glass. Outside the windows, a well-tended garden sparkled with dew in the morning sunlight.

A sense of peaceful abundance pervaded the room. Khath felt tears rise to his eyes. This was a place that had never known war, nor torture, nor even simple want. It felt so *safe*. If only Kamala and Sitha could experience this. A desire to bring his girls to America rose so savagely in Khath's chest that he felt strangled and had to cough to clear his throat. It was just as well. The coughing fit would explain the tears he wiped from his eyes with his sleeve, until Mr. Sareth handed him a napkin to use. Another mistake. Baa-baa-bo-bo.

The interview of Pra Chhay went quickly, with Father Ralph asking questions and Mr. Sareth translating and sometimes clarifying. After all, what was there to tell? Pra Chhay had entered monastic life as a young boy, gotten a monastic education, and spent his life in one monastery or another. It was a common enough story. When the Khmer Rouge had come, he'd been living in a temple in Srey Santhor district, part of the Khmer Rouge's Eastern Zone, and was allowed to continue living as a monk for about two years.

"Really?" Father Ralph interjected. "I thought the Khmer Rouge were against religion. I thought they killed monks."

Pra Chhay and Sareth spent a moment discussing Father Ralph's question. After finishing, they both turned to face Father Ralph.

"As a general statement, you are correct," Mr. Sareth said. "But, there were different factions of Khmer Rouge. Some were very cruel. Some were not so bad, more idealistic, especially in the beginning. The leaders of the Khmer Rouge in the Eastern

Zone were among the better ones. They worked alongside the villagers and did not commit the type of atrocities committed in other zones. The Southwest Zone was the worst, very savage. The leader there, Mok, was…" Mr. Sareth paused and studied his fingertips, "Well, I suppose one must call him a barbarian. In the end, there was a great deal of fighting among the different factions of the Khmer Rouge. Purges among the leadership were common."

"So what happened to Pra Chhay after two years?" Father Ralph asked.

"Khmer Rouge tell me, 'Go, work in fields,'" Pra Chhay said. He spread his hands. "Not any more monk. Same as everyone. Work hard, starve like all the people." He said something in Cambodian to Sareth, who translated.

"He says he could scarcely believe that he was still a human being. He felt he'd been suddenly reborn as a mongrel, full of lice and fleas, no food to eat, scrabbling in the mud to catch a minnow or frog, then gobbling it quickly—raw—before anyone saw. The Khmer Rouge punished people for "wasting time" looking for food to eat, even pausing for a minute to grab a bug from a blade of rice."

For some moments, the only sound was that of Father Ralph's pen scratching notes on the pad in front of him. He reviewed what he had written and nodded to himself before looking up again to ask another question. "And when the Khmer Rouge were driven out by the Vietnamese in 1979," he said, "did you resume life in your temple?"

"No, not go to temple." Pra Chhay shook his head and gestured at Khath, continuing in his native tongue.

"He says he began to search for his brother, who working in the railroad yards in Phnom Penh before the war. He had not seen or heard any news of him for over four years, but he had to try," Sareth interpreted.

"Of course," Father Ralph said. "Well, perhaps we should hear from Khath at this point in the story."

At the mention of his name, Khath felt his stomach muscles tighten. He dug into his pants pocket and pulled out a thin billfold, extracting a small square of shiny, cracked paper. "My daughters," he said, holding the photo out to Father Ralph in a hand that trembled despite his best efforts to steady it. "I look my girls." He pointed to some words and numbers printed on the back of the photo. "Names. How old. You can help me?"

Father Ralph glanced at the photo then set it down on the table. "They are lovely," he said, through Mr. Sareth. "Such sweet faces. And we will certainly contact the Red Cross about finding them, but first let's hear a bit about you."

When Mr. Sareth translated this, Khath's anxiety surged. How could he make the priest understand that every minute of delay was another minute that Kamala and Sitha might slip back into the forests and give up hope of finding their father forever? Tripping over his words, even in his native tongue, he tried to explain about the amulets, about the broken spirit bond, about the urgency. He pushed back his chair and began to rise with the intent of falling onto his knees to beg the Father to hurry, but found Pra Chhay's hand clamped onto his thigh with an iron grip.

"Let's allow Mr. Sareth to explain, brother," Pra Chhay whispered to Khath. "It will be better this way. The priest trusts Mr. Sareth. He does not yet know that we, too, are honest men. Let Mr. Sareth convince him of the need for haste."

A long conversation ensued between Mr. Sareth and Father Ralph. Khath watched as hands gestured, eyes glanced his way, chins were rubbed and heads nodded. The English language sounded to his ears like so many snakes hissing. He was unable to catch a single word of the conversation. He felt powerless and scarcely dared to breathe as the most important thing in the world to him was discussed, and decided, by two strangers.

Finally, Father Ralph turned to Khath, a kind look upon his face. Using Sareth to translate, he said, "I promise you, Khath, that when we are done here, I will immediately call the Red Cross and inform them about your daughters. And, I will get an appointment for us to visit in person. But I need to know a little more about you and your situation before I call them. Do you understand? I will help you, I promise, but this is the best way to do that."

Knowing there was no use in arguing, Khath nodded and began his story while Mr. Sareth translated. Before the war he had lived in Phnom Penh with his wife, son and two daughters, working in the central railroad yards. Life was good. He enjoyed his work and his home was peaceful, loving. Then in 1972, he'd been drafted by the government army, and sent to the jungles to fight the Khmer Rouge for two years before being assigned back to Phnom Penh to guard the royal palace.

When the Khmer Rouge invaded the city in 1975, he was able to slip away from his post, gather his family and a few provisions, and leave with them when the Khmer Rouge gave the order to evacuate the city. The streets were packed with people. It took an hour just to travel one city block, but no one was allowed to go back to their homes a few paces away to wait for the crowds to clear. There were soldiers herding them along, and Khath and his family were funneled onto the road leading toward the Southwest Zone.

"The Southwest Zone?" Father Ralph murmured, a look of dismay on his face.

Khath's eyes turned dull and he stared at the table as he recounted how their food had run out in a day, how hungry his little boy, just a toddler, had been, how he had cried. Looking up now at Father Ralph, tears rolling unheeded down his cheeks, he said, "They didn't need to kill him. He was just so hungry. They smashed his skull against a killing tree and shot my wife when she tried to stop them." Again, Khath wiped his eyes with his sleeve. This time, no one bothered to correct his manners.

Pra Chhay poured Khath a glass of water and laid a hand on his brother's sagging shoulders. Sareth suggested a short break but Khath shook his head. "No," he said, "Let me finish." He took a deep breath and rushed on, telling his tale in a wooden voice. "They sent me and my girls to a work camp where we lived together for a year. Then the Khmer Rouge took them from me, made them go to a youth work brigade so they could brainwash them, turn them against me. This was their plan, to break apart families." He gave a long heavy sigh. "I have not seen them since."

Sareth's voice droned on in a soft murmur, explaining Khath's words to the priest, who scribbled furiously on his note pad.

"I was denounced by someone in the camp, who told the Khmer Rouge that I had education, skills from working on the railroad before the war. I thought they would kill me, but railroad workers were needed." Khath gave a short, bitter laugh. "They drove everyone from the cities, then realized they had no one left to run the trains. So the Khmer Rouge sent me back to Phnom Penh."

"To the train station?" Father Ralph asked. "There's a note in your file that you also worked in a prison in Phnom Penh?"

As Sareth interpreted the priest's question, Khath's face darkened. "Site 21," he spat. "I cannot speak of that evil place. They took me from the train yard because I am good at fixing things. They forced me to work in their death jail." Khath covered his face with his hands, shaking his head violently. "No, do not make me recall that place. I cannot. I will not speak of it." Head bowed, he rocked from side to side in his chair, struggling to stop the images that flooded his mind at the mention of Site 21.

Father Ralph dropped his pen and pushed his chair back from the table, the scrape of wooden legs on the hard floor causing Khath to raise his head.

The priest stood before him. "All right," he said. "All right. We do not need to talk of this now." Then his face brightened and he scooped up the photo of Khath's girls. He spoke rapidly to Sareth and laid a hand on Khath's shoulder, then turned and left the room.

Mr. Sareth turned to Khath. "Father Ralph says we will take a break and he will go call the Red Cross now, immediately, about your daughters."

Khath nodded, the hope of finding his girls crashing up against the horror of Site 21 and leaving him breathless. He felt dizzy and dry-mouthed. He and Pra Chhay whispered together for a moment, then Pra Chhay turned to Mr. Sareth. "He asks me to tell you the rest of his story," he said. "He was there at Tuol Sleng prison for about six months, a slave to the Khmer Rouge. He's only alive because they needed his skill to keep the prison operating, the lights on. He's very talented mechanically." Pra Chhay paused to refill Khath's water glass. "Drink, brother," he said. "You will feel better."

Turning back to Sareth, Pra Chhay continued. "So, when the Vietnamese liberated the city, Khath went back to the train yards and that's where I found him, a broken man, wandering around, living on garbage, sleeping in the streets. I took him to one of the refugee centers the Vietnamese set up, and as soon as he was able, we began walking through the country, looking for his daughters. For nine, ten months we looked, then, we went to Khao I Dang. The Red Cross in Khao I Dang said we'd have a better chance of finding the girls if we came to America. So, here we are."

Mr. Sareth leaned back in his chair, his arms crossed over his chest, gazing at Khath and his brother. The interpreter's face was unreadable. "Indeed," he murmured. "Here you are."

Khath sat silently then, allowing the peacefulness of the room to settle over his raw nerves like a soothing balm. Beside him, Pra Chhay clicked his prayer beads.

When Father Ralph returned to the room, he informed them through Mr. Sareth that a Red Cross case manager would look into the situation and call him back in a couple of days to make arrangements for a meeting.

Half an hour later, Khath and Pra Chhay stood outside the church, getting final instructions from Mr. Sareth about the route back to their house. They set off down the hill and passed by the gas station at the edge of town.

"Look, Khath, there are some teenagers," Pra Chhay said, gesturing toward three adolescent boys coming out the gas station store. "Our first look at American children."

"They look very messy," Khath said, pausing to study the youths, who wore blue jeans and shirts with the tails hanging out. One of the boys had a scraggly beard and was smoking a cigarette. He seemed to be the leader. He noticed Khath watching him and stared back, a scowl on his face. He shouted something and began walking with long strides toward Khath and Pra Chhay. As he came closer, he began pointing at Pra Chhay's robes and spoke to the two boys behind him. All three began to laugh and point.

Khath and Pra Chhay looked at one another in confusion. "I think he said *girl*." Pra Chhay said. "Does he think I'm a girl? Because of my robes?"

"I don't like this," Khath said, uneasily. "The priest wears robes, too."

"They're just boys, Khath," Pra Chhay said. "Don't overreact."

By now, the youths had formed a rough half-circle around Khath and Pra Chhay. The bearded one spoke.

Pra Chhay smiled at him. "I'm sorry," he said. "I don't understand."

The boy muttered and spat on the ground.

Sensing danger, Khath clenched his fists and moved forward slightly in a protective stance. He'd learned in the refugee camp that Pra Chhay could diffuse nearly any situation with a smile and a soothing comment, but his brother's words were useless here.

One of the other boys spoke, a sneering grin on his face. The leader grinned back, nodded, then lunged forward and grabbed the edge of Pra Chhay's robe, lifting it high and exposing the monk's legs.

Pra Chhay gasped and clutched at his robe, a look of shock on his face. Khath sprang forward and shoved the boy back, jerking Pra Chhay's robe from the youth's fingers.

Then Khath saw a blur of movement darting toward him from the side of the road. Before he could react, a small child with disheveled black hair and a pink t-shirt rushed forward, brandishing a long whip-like branch. She twirled the limb ferociously above her head, shouting "Leave him alone!" in Cambodian.

Soon the boys were howling as the slender branch tore at their skin through their thin shirts. They stumbled backwards, their arms raised to protect their faces. The leader scowled, made a rude gesture, then turned and ran up the hill, followed by the other two boys.

"Enough, child. Enough," Pra Chhay moved in to stop the girl from chasing the boys up the street. "Thank you," he added.

The girl stood motionless for a moment, staring wide-eyed at Khath and Pra Chhay, panting, her chest heaving. Then she ducked her head and disappeared back into the bushes.

# Ten

"Come sit with me, Nary, and let me brush the tangles from your hair."

Phally sat on the porch step, enjoying the warmth of the sun toasting her back, yet careful not to let its rays touch her bare skin and darken it to the color of a common field laborer. She'd tried to teach her daughter to take the same care, but Nary stood now in the full glare of the sun, inside the small vegetable garden that the church ladies had helped Phally to plant back in the spring. The child's attention was focused on the cherry tomato plant, her small hands plucking the red balls and popping them into her mouth. She chewed and swallowed each tomato rapidly, without apparent enjoyment or pause, one after another. This was survival eating, the urgent foraging of a child who has known starvation. It broke Phally's heart to see Nary eat with such grim determination. She patted the step beside her.

"Come, child. It is very pleasant here on the step. We can rest a while before we eat our lunch." Phally inhaled deeply, savoring the smells of garlic and curry wafting out from the kitchen, mingling with the sweet scent of jasmine rice as it neared the point of being perfectly steamed.

"Besides, I cannot bear to sit opposite you while we are eating when your pretty hair is so wild." Phally spoke in a teasing tone of voice, but even still she sensed the anxiety rising from her little girl, whose hands plucked even faster upon being called to leave this food source. Phally sighed. Nary was in one of her moods, usually triggered by an unpleasant event. She would have to tread carefully. "Bring some tomatoes with you. You can eat them while I brush your hair. Maybe you can share some with me, too, little mouse."

Nary's eyes flicked upward to her mother, and she nodded, pulling her pink tee-shirt away from her body to form a pouch into which she dropped a dozen or so tomatoes.

How thin she is, Phally thought. So tiny and stunted from years of hunger. She has the body of an eight or nine year old child, not a girl of eleven. Will she ever catch up? Phally pondered the sad irony of how the war had trapped her daughter in the youthful body of a small child while at the same time prematurely aging her mother.

Approaching the house, Nary carefully counted out half of the tomatoes and placed them on the top step beside Phally, then sat down on the step below her.

"Good girl, Nary." Placing a hand firmly against the child's scalp to lessen the pull of the brush, Phally began to work through the snarls in Nary's hair. She noticed bits of leaves and twigs tangled among the strands of dark hair. It seemed her daughter had been creeping through the brush again. Carefully keeping the annoyance out of her voice, Phally continued, "You took a long time to buy salt at the little market, child. What kept you? Did you see something interesting?"

Slowly, Nary nodded her head. "I saw the new people."

Phally frowned at Nary's use of the words "new people." That was what the Khmer Rouge had called the city dwellers forced to march into the countryside and live in the villages. The Khmer Rouge said that new people, tainted by the Western world, were inferior to villagers. "Don't call them that, mouse.

They are going to become our friends and neighbors. They are Cambodians, just like us. Not new, not old, just Cambodian."

Nary popped more tomatoes into her mouth.

"I hope you greeted them properly, child. Especially the monk."

Nary sat silent.

"Well? Tell me, little mouse. Where did you see them? What did they say to you?"

In a torrent of words, Nary blurted, "Those boys were attacking them, Mama. They pulled the monk's robes up. So I got a stick and chased them away."

"What? You didn't!" Phally stared, scandalized, at her daughter. "What boys? What stick? Was anyone hurt? Where did this happen?" Phally took a deep breath to calm herself. "Nary, turn around and tell me what happened."

"I was outside the market," Nary said. "I saw the new...I saw them coming, so I hid in the woods to watch them."

"Again? Oh Nary, what have I told you about that? You must stop all this hiding and creeping around. It's time you start behaving like a young lady now."

Nary's eyes flared. "But Papa told me..." Then she looked down, her lips clamped together.

Phally's heart skipped a beat. Nary never talked about her father. "Yes, child? Go on. What did Papa say?" Phally's voice was as gentle as she could make it.

"He said always to hide until I was sure. He taught me to walk silently in the woods, like a hungry tiger. We played games so I could practice." A tone of pride entered the girl's voice. "Papa said I was very good. He said I must be the most hungriest tiger to be so quiet."

Phally's eyes filled with tears. She drew Nary close and hugged her. "I am sure you learned Papa's lessons very well, Nary. He was always proud of you." She stroked Nary's hair. "But child, your Papa taught you those things so you could hide from the Khmer Rouge, not from ordinary people. We are in

America, now. There is no need to practice being quiet in the woods. We have to learn new ways now. Do you understand?"

Nary dropped her eyes. "Yes, Mama."

"Good," Phally said. "Now go and wash up for lunch, and remember that we are going to see the American girls later." She thought about what Nary had said, and a frown creased her forehead. "Nary," she called.

The child stopped and looked back at her.

"When did Papa teach you all these things?" Phally asked. "Where was I?"

Nary's eyes grew dull, as though shuttered from within. "I don't know," she said in a small voice, then hurried into the house.

———————

Gail sat in her wheelchair on the front porch, reading a mystery. A teapot wrapped in a cozy, four mugs, and a plate of cookies and nuts sat on a small wooden coffee table next to her chair. Her satchel, filled with a selection of books, pens, writing paper and stamps, rested on the floor near her feet. The sound of bees buzzing among the flowers below the porch made a pleasant background hum, punctuated by the chirps and chattering of various birds in the yard. A flutter caught her eye and she watched a small brownish bird hop along the porch railing for a moment before flying up into the maple tree that marked the corner of the yard. A rhythmic thumping drew her attention to Zeus, who lay on his side beating his tail in response to something too faint for Gail's ears to pick up. A moment later, she heard it, too, and smiled. Her guests had arrived.

"Hi, Phally. Hi, Nary. Have a seat. How are you two?" Gail beamed as she waved the two into chairs.

"I am fine," Nary grinned. "And youuuuuu?" Her childish voice rose an octave or more as she trilled the "you" as though trying to encompass an entire scale in a single word.

Gail laughed. "I'm fine, too. What's in the bag?" she asked, nodding at Phally, who held a grocery bag stuffed with papers in her lap.

"I don't know," Phally replied. "Every day, letters come. More, more. I no read. I keep. Maybe good, maybe bad. I don't know. You can read for me?"

"Sure. First, tea, then we'll look. OK?"

The porch door opened and Teresa joined them. Gail took the cozy from the teapot and Phally poured the tea into the cups. Teresa took hers standing, gazing out at the yard. "Look at those weeds," she muttered.

Gail laughed. "It's killing you, isn't it? Go ahead, maybe Nary can help you."

Teresa nodded. She finished off a handful of nuts and wiped her hands on her jeans. "Good idea. Do you need anything here, Gail?"

Gail shook her head. "No, I'm fine," she lied with a smile. *Actually, I'm stuck in a wheelchair on a beautiful day while you get to go play in the yard. Sucks to be me.*

Teresa turned to Nary. "Hey, kiddo. Come work with me in the garden. Let's pull weeds." She held her hand out to Nary and they wandered off into the yard.

Gail opened the paper sack and began sorting through Phally's mail. As she suspected, most of it was just junk. From the garden, she could hear Nary laughing.

Beside her, Phally smiled at the sound. "Is good," she said. "Nary. Your sister. I want her make friend. Forget Khmer Rouge. Sometime, Nary very sad." Phally tapped her head. "Think, not good. Not right. Sometime, very angry. No talk." Phally sighed heavily, seeming to droop under the burden of motherhood in a strange land.

Gail set the mail down. "She can come here anytime, Phally. Both of you. We want to help." She hesitated. Should she ask? Would that make things worse or better?

"Phally, what happened to you and Nary in Cambodia?"

Phally looked at Gail for a moment then pointed to the pad of paper in Gail's satchel. "I can write?"

Gail handed her the pad and a pen.

Phally drew a circle on the paper. "We live here, in village. Me, my husband, Nary." She drew three stick figures in the circle. "Very happy. Very nice family. Then, many Khmer Rouge come." Phally drew several big stick figures with angry faces and big guns inside the circle. "Eight month, not so bad. Work hard. Then they take my husband, kill him." She drew an "x" through her husband's stick figure. "Many city people come." A stream of arrows appeared on the page, all pointing toward the circle. "Stay village. Too many people. No food. Me, Nary, we very hungry, work so hard." She scowled at the memory.

"Then Khmer Rouge take Nary, too. Go to work group for children. Three year, I no see Nary." Phally drew an arrow from Nary's figure to a small circle up near the corner of the page, and then paused, her head bowed. "Three year, my heart break. Where Nary? Khmer Rouge take her far away, teach her many bad thing. No love Mama. No love Papa. Love only Khmer Rouge big boss. They call Angkor. Live for Angkor. Die for Angkor. Kill for Angkor." Phally's fist struck the table with each statement. "Khmer Rouge kill my Nary's heart. Take her mind, her..." Phally stopped, searching for a word. She looked at Gail. "How you say it? Body dead, but ..." she gestured outward and upwards with her hand.

"Soul," Gail said. "I think you mean soul."

"Soul," Phally repeated. "Khmer Rouge take her soul. Now Nary empty. I hope, I try, every day, bring her back. I come here, for save my child, have better life, better school for my girl." A tear trickled down Phally's cheek. "But how I can save my Nary? She so far away." She wiped away her tears and began gathering up the sorted mail and putting it back into the sack. "I go now. Thank you. I very happy have friend now." She bowed her head to Gail, and raised her clasped hands to the level of her nose.

Gail reached forward and took Phally's clasped hands in her own, pulling them down gently. "I'm very happy, too," she said, blinking back tears of her own. Maybe sitting on a sunny porch in a wheelchair wasn't so bad after all.

A few minutes later, Phally and Nary set off for home and Teresa joined Gail on the porch.

"What a nice family," Teresa said. "Oh, and that reminds me. Mr. Sareth called earlier. He's going to stop by about 7:30 this evening to fill me in on the newcomers, since I missed the intake. I think he also wants to arrange a schedule for his wife Chea to come by a couple times a week to practice her English while she runs errands for you."

Gail nodded. "I'm excited to meet them, especially now that we've gotten to know Phally and Nary some. It'll be good to meet some of the other Cambodians."

"Well, Mr. Sareth and Chea are not at all like Phally and Nary," Teresa said.

Gail looked at Teresa, hearing a bit of reservation creep into her sister's voice. "What do you mean?"

Teresa shrugged. "Mr. Sareth is very formal and cultured, very European in his manners, and his English is perfect. He's quite charming, actually. And Chea, well, I've only met her the one time at the airport."

"And?" Gail said.

"She's younger than Phally, a lot younger than Mr. Sareth." Teresa paused. "She's drop dead gorgeous, for one thing. I felt quite dowdy beside her. She's elegant, and at times seems very sweet, and other times, I don't know. Maybe she's playing a role. Who knows what she really thinks."

Gail nodded. "That makes some sense if she's married to a much older man. Maybe?"

"Could be. There's kind of a funny dynamic between the two of them. He's definitely the lord and master, kind of has her under his thumb, but I think that's partly just the culture. He sure watches her closely though. Lots of men in the airport were making fools of themselves over her, and it seemed to bother Mr. Sareth a bit. She's got the kind of beauty that stops men in their tracks."

"So maybe Mr. Sareth is nervous about hanging on to her," Gail said. "Maybe he's right to be nervous."

"I don't know," Teresa replied. "Maybe I was tired and misinterpreting everything, and they're a normal loving couple, whatever that looks like in Cambodia. Anyway, you'll meet them tonight and you can see what you think."

"Right," Gail said. "I think we should pay her for helping me, don't you?"

Teresa began to stack the plates and cups on a tray. "I agree, but I doubt they will accept. We can try."

———————

Sareth guided Father Ralph's sedan onto the grassy shoulder in front of Gail and Teresa's house. He turned off the engine, which died with a rattle. He was proud to be the sole licensed driver in Glenberg's Cambodian community. Although most of the other men could drive, none could speak English well enough to take and pass the exam at the Department of Motor Vehicles. He picked up his vinyl portfolio and glanced at his watch. 7:27 P.M. Perfect.

Exiting the car, he let himself in through the picket gate and strode up the sidewalk, noting the neatly tended flower beds and lawn. A wheelchair ramp angled discreetly from the side of the porch to the driveway, and a finely graveled path fanned out from the ramp and wound along the yard's perimeter between the lawn and the flower beds. Quite nicely done, Sareth thought, examining the ramp. He was sure Chea would be able to push a wheelchair up the ramp, as long as Teresa's sister was not overly large.

Ignoring the steps, he strolled up the ramp, crossed the porch and knocked on the door.

Teresa answered Sareth's knock and greeted him, then looked behind him, a puzzled frown on her face. "Isn't Chea coming?" she asked.

"I'm afraid my wife is feeling unwell this evening and sends her apologies," Mr. Sareth said, the lie slipping easily from his mouth. The truth was that he had decided to come first and assess the situation at Teresa's house before bringing Chea. He wanted to be able to set the stage a little as well, let the girls know what sort of help they could expect from his wife. He certainly hoped they were not expecting her to clean or do other menial chores. That would not do at all.

Teresa led him into the living room. "Mr. Sareth, this is my sister Gail," she said. "Gail, Mr. Sareth. Unfortunately, Chea is sick tonight."

"A pleasure to meet you…" Sareth was at a loss for words, which he covered nicely with a slow and elegant handshake. What to call this young woman? It would be too confusing to address them both as Miss Marsh. Miss Gail and Miss Teresa it would have to be. "Your sister has told me so much about you, Miss Gail, I feel as though I already know you," he finished smoothly.

Gail smiled. "Likewise," she said.

Teresa disappeared into the kitchen after directing Mr. Sareth to a comfortable arm chair. He looked around the house and was pleased with what he saw. Books, a piano and the absence of a large, blaring television set in the middle of the room assured him that these women would be suitable company for Chea. He did not want her becoming vulgar as she associated with Americans, so many of whom seemed to take a perverse pride in what they called casual manners. It seemed to him that American casualness was nothing more than a fancy name for laziness and a lack of graciousness.

"What a lovely and functional home," he said, nodding at the transfer pole he had just noticed strategically placed to the right of Gail's seat. He could see at once that it would allow Gail to swing herself from the chair to her wheelchair with minimal, if any, assistance.

"Oh, this?" Gail said, patting the pole. "We've actually got these tucked away in all kinds of places in this house."

Teresa returned to the room, bearing a tray loaded with a bottle of Perrier water, sliced limes, a bottle of burgundy, and glasses. "Gail is amazing," she said. "She gets around this house as well as I do." She pointed to Gail's wheelchair, tucked between Gail's seat and the wall. "She's got the sporty version of chair. It's thinner, turns on a dime, weighs less and really scoots around. It's the kind athletes use for playing basketball."

"How very practical for someone as petite as you, Miss Gail." Mr. Sareth glowed with satisfaction. This was far better than he could have imagined. It would be perfect for Chea. "Indeed, I'm quite impressed."

Gail waved aside the compliment. "Enough about me," she said. "Let's hear about those newcomers. Teresa felt so bad to miss the first meeting with them."

Mr. Sareth chose his words carefully as he described the morning's meeting with Khath and Pra Chhay. In his role as community spokesman, Sareth felt compelled to provide an accurate rendering of the two men's experiences, yet he also did not want to depict them as overly tragic figures. It would not do to bias Teresa and Gail too strongly in the newcomers' favor, to the point that they would pester him and Father Ralph with special requests. Or worse, question Sareth's authority and judgment regarding the refugees in Glenberg. As he wound down his narrative, Sareth pressed his fingertips together and cleared his throat. He gazed at Teresa, who was blinking rapidly and had a strained expression on her face.

"You must not be so distressed, Miss Teresa," Sareth said. "Although this story seems terrible to you, please remember that it is only too common among your refugee neighbors. They have all lost family members. They have all faced starvation and the threat of death."

Gail leaned forward. "Yes," she said, pulling a sheet of paper from a pouch hanging over the arm of her chair. "Phally was here this afternoon with her daughter Nary. She was trying to tell me about her experiences."

Mr. Sareth sat back in his chair. "Really? Phally and her child came here? How have you become acquainted with them?" He arranged his features to convey pleasant surprise. Inwardly, he fumed at the thought of that coarse village woman and her wild child forcing their attentions on this home, the home he had chosen for Chea's acculturation.

Indeed, not a day went by that Chea did not complain to him about Phally—her failure to pay respect to Chea as wife of the community's acknowledged leader, her assumed role as community matriarch because of her position as eldest female. "Can't you do something about that woman? Send her away, or at least put her in her place," Chea would whine to him about Phally's daily failures of etiquette and decorum. "I should not have to put up with these slights, *Bong*." And now, it appeared that Phally had usurped Chea in befriending these Americans.

Gail chuckled. "I fell out of my chair into the lettuce patch. They rescued me."

"How very fortunate," Mr. Sareth murmured. "But I hope they are not imposing on your generosity now. If they are, I am always more than happy to intervene." He spread his hands apologetically. "Village culture makes assumptions, sometimes." This was worse than he'd expected. A debt of gratitude had been incurred and would have to be honored.

"It's not a problem at all," Gail said, shaking her head. "I like them."

"Nary is very helpful in the yard," Teresa offered. "She helped me weed the garden today. But, we'll be sure to tell you if it becomes an issue," she added.

Sareth smiled at Teresa, appreciating her diplomacy. "Please don't hesitate, Miss Teresa," he said. "These matters can sometimes become a bit delicate, but you need never fear of offending me. I am always happy to be a bridge between our culture and yours." He chuckled and directed his next comment at Gail. "Even, if it comes to it, between my wife and you, Miss Gail. Have you had a chance to decide upon a schedule for Chea's visits with you?" He placed his calendar on the table and sat poised, pen in hand, to mark the dates and times.

At the question of payment, Sareth shook his head firmly. "I am afraid it would be quite impossible to accept a stipend for Chea's services as a companion and helpmate," he said. "I fear that she will be much more the beneficiary of her time in this house than you." He looked sternly, in a fatherly matter, first at Teresa, then Gail. He wagged his finger solemnly at them. "You must promise me, if this arrangement becomes burdensome, to let me know. I cannot adequately express how meaningful a kindness this is to my wife and me." He drained his wine of the last sip, and glanced at his watch as a prelude to ending the evening.

Teresa spoke up quickly. "Before you go, Mr. Sareth, I was thinking of popping in on Khath and Pra Chhay tomorrow, to see if they've settled in comfortably. Do you think that would be okay?"

"Ah, you bring me to my last point, Miss Teresa," Sareth said. "Normally, a brief visit would be fine, but given Khath's state of mind, and Father Ralph and I discussed this thoroughly, we feel it might be best, for the time being of course, to limit your interactions with Khath to the ESL classes. Father Ralph and I will take care of the home visits."

"Really?" Teresa said, her face expressing concern. "Why?"

Sareth studied Teresa's earnest face with its furrowed brow. A seed, really. He would just plant a seed of doubt in her mind, to encourage her to come to him with her thoughts and concerns, so he could monitor things until he had a better understanding of these newcomers. Considering the lingering problem of Khath's Site 21 experiences, one couldn't be too cautious. Common sense suggested that Khath would have needed more than just good handyman skills to survive a place like that.

"As you know, Miss Teresa, when there are communication barriers, misunderstandings can arise so easily. And our new friend, Khath, has had some difficulty already." Sareth paused to let his words sink in. "Naturally, we have every faith that he is a fine man, merely struggling to cope with trying personal circumstances."

Sareth tipped his head to the side and put a thoughtful tone into his voice to suggest this idea had just come to him. "Actually, Miss Teresa, you could be very helpful to us as we try to help Khath settle into our community. Just stay in touch with me. Let me know how things are going, and if I can be of assistance in any way. You may notice things as you spend more time teaching him." He smiled at her warmly. "Together, I am sure we can help Khath transition smoothly."

# Eleven

Khath's footsteps made a crunching noise as he walked briskly along the unpaved shoulder of the road. He was feeling pretty good physically. The cut was nearly healed on his lip, though it would leave a scar. His eyes were no longer puffy and the travel fatigue had worn off. It was his third day in America and he had awakened wanting to explore the countryside.

Tonight he and Pra Chhay would begin attending ESL class at the church, but until then, he was free to wander about and begin to get his bearings. He chose to avoid the town after that run-in with those nasty boys yesterday. Out here in the forests and farmlands, he could easily slip off the road and hide himself in the heavy underbrush if he needed to get out of sight quickly.

He thought again of the sneering, scowling teens who had harassed him and Pra Chhay last night. And for what? Because a man wore robes? Those boys were foolish to attack grown men like that, without fear. Why, he could have snapped their necks, one, two, three, dead. Not that he'd wanted to, but didn't that possibility even occur to them? And yet they had run away from a little girl in pink twirling a flimsy stick in her hand. It all seemed so upside-down. Boys attacking men. Girls attacking boys. He began to laugh as the image replayed itself in his mind.

How silly he and Pra Chhay must have looked, standing there aghast as the drama swirled around them.

Khath's smile faded. The little girl. Seeing her had made his heart ache. Were Kamala and Sitha somewhere in America, too, learning how to survive in this upside down country? Who would protect them from unkind strangers? And what about the little girl in pink? Would she be a target now because she had defended him and Pra Chhay? She was plenty tough, obviously, but if those boys ganged up on her, ambushed her, things could go badly for her. He would make it a point to find out more about her and keep an eye out for her safety for a bit. It was the least he could do. He owed her a debt now.

Out of nowhere, a small deer bounded into the road in front of him. In a single leap it stood poised on the shoulder, then sailed easily over a barbed wire fence that was strung along a stretch of forest running beside the road.

Khath's heart thudded inside his chest and a sense of delight spread through his body. He felt his lips spread wide in a grin, stretching the new skin on his lip. A deer. It was the first familiar thing he had seen since leaving Khao I Dang. It wasn't a large animal, but even a deer that size would feed him for weeks. Pra Chhay wouldn't eat meat, but Khath could sell or trade the excess with the other Cambodians to get eggs and vegetables for his brother. He stood still, listening for the crackle of underbrush or thud of hooves but his deer was long gone. There were sure to be others, though. He could track it now, get a sense of the trails the deer were using and return later to set a snare or trap of some sort. Were there rules about catching deer in this country? Probably. He'd have to remember to check with Mr. Sareth later.

Glancing up and down the road, Khath made sure there were no cars in sight, then slipped carefully through the strands of barbed wire and entered the forest. This forest was very different from the jungled mountains of Cambodia. Tall, sparsely limbed trees towered over him with short stubby needles instead of leaves. The air felt cool and moist, almost soothing against his face. A bird fluttered and squawked in the branches nearby, and a rich, earthy scent filled Khath's nostrils. He inhaled deeply and felt himself really relax for the first time in days, maybe months.

Stepping with caution, Khath moved behind a tree and out of sight of the road. The ground was littered with fallen and decaying branches, making the footing treacherous. Filtered sunlight dappled the forest with areas of light and dark. Looking around, he studied the vegetation. Ferns grew thickly in clumps, and he saw many types of shrubs. Carefully, he fingered the unfamiliar plants, seeing which types bent easily and rebounded, which ones snapped or had thorns to snag an animal's fur, which leaves tore and which didn't, all so that he would know what signs to look for as he tracked the deer.

Checking again for cars, he searched along the fence line and picked up the trail easily, marked by a tuft of fur caught in the barbed wire and a divot of earth displaced where the deer's hooves had dug into the ground as it landed after leaping the fence.

Following the signs of the deer's passing, he moved deeper into the forest. Within ten meters of the road, the deer's trail intersected a more traveled pathway. Though still barely visible to the casual eye, the path was now simple for Khath to follow using the tracking skills he'd learned in the war. He strolled along, noticing that the trail was leading him gradually downward and away from the road. He could see the trees thinning ahead, and was grateful for the deer trail, for with the increased sunlight the underbrush had thickened and grew nearly to Khath's waist. Without the path to follow, it would have been tough going.

The ground became soft under Khath's feet, and now he realized the reason for the thinning of the trees. Ahead, a small pond sparkled, and as he drew near, a flock of colorful ducks quacked loudly as they swam hastily away from him, their movement rippling the still surface of the water. Khath grinned, his mouth watering at the thought of fresh duck eggs. Maybe even fish. Perhaps his karma was changing.

Standing quietly in the shadow of a tree at the edge of the pond, Khath let his eyes roam the perimeter. A water source could attract all kinds of creatures. It was never a bad idea to wait in stillness upon arriving at such a place. He'd already been careless in startling the ducks. Lucky for him they had not taken flight, causing anyone in sight to wonder what had frightened them. His eyes returned to a spot one quarter of the way around the pond from him, to an area of deeper darkness, an area that defied the sunlight's penetration. He relaxed the muscles around his eyes, lowered his lids slightly to sharpen his gaze, snuffed the air for hints. Was it a boulder? A fallen tree? A cave?

Khath began to work his way toward the darkness, placing each foot with care, bending and weaving his way through the underbrush until he was close enough to define the shape in front of him. It was a hut, a cabin. Old and moss-covered, with plants growing out of a swaybacked roof, the cabin's wooden door hung crookedly ajar. Tall grass and thorny berry bushes grew undisturbed across the partially open door, reassuring Khath that nothing much larger than a rat had passed through that opening in recent times.

Pleased, Khath moved forward to explore his discovery. He found that he could lift the mat of berry bushes and creep under them to the door. Using a twig, Khath swept the obvious cobwebs and debris from around the opening, and then slipped inside by turning his body and scooting through the narrow space between the door and the frame. Until he knew more about this place, he was not going to make it obvious to outsiders that he had been here.

Inside the cabin, it felt surprisingly dry, though he had been right about the rats. A sour odor invaded his nostrils and he heard the rodents rustling in the dark corners. One small window of thick, blurry glass admitted a dim light, but he would need candles or a flashlight to do a thorough job of exploring. His stomach rumbled loudly, announcing the passage of time. Surprised, Khath glanced at the glowing dial of the watch on his wrist, one of the items that Mr. Sareth had placed in the "Welcome to America" basket he'd left with Khath and Pra Chhay on their first night in their new home. It was 1:30 PM already. He'd been rambling about for three hours. He crawled out of the cabin, plucked a handful of black berries from the vines across the door and found a log to sit on. Reaching into his pocket, he drew out the packet of rice and the apple he'd brought for his lunch. Supplemented by the berries, it took the edge off his hunger nicely.

A sense of satisfaction enveloped Khath as he thought over his morning's activities. He'd found several potential food sources, and now this, a place to come and find peace when the strangeness of this new country threatened to overwhelm him. Would he share this with Pra Chhay? Should he? He decided to wait, to see how things played out. For now, he would slowly begin to clean up the cabin, not spending enough time here to raise questions, covering his tracks when he came. It would give him a project, something to focus on while he waited to hear about Kamala and Sitha. He imagined bringing them to this place, heard them squealing with delight as they splashed in the water on a hot day, looking for minnows perhaps, or duck eggs. They could make a little fire and cook a meal to share together.

Feeling happy, Khath prepared to return along the deer path, but this time, he decided, he would follow the trail along the road a ways to see if there was a better way to enter the forest. He didn't want to leave an obvious trail running from the road into the woods.

Walking steadily, it took Khath twenty minutes to pass the spot at which he'd left the road to enter the forest that morning. He moved on, timing himself. The deer trail continued to run roughly parallel to the road. A short distance later, the forest ahead seemed to stop abruptly.

Approaching the edge of the woods, Khath saw a dirt road forming a border between the forest and a field of tall corn, fenced by barbed wire. The hum of farm machinery reached his ears. A tractor, perhaps? A dozen or so meters to his left, the field ended, bordered by the paved road he had walked on that morning. This was perfect. All he would have to do is slip through the barbed wire fence and along the dirt road to the deer path. The wire strand fences puzzled Khath. In Cambodia, the wealthy built concrete walls with glass shards embedded in the top around their homes to keep intruders out. What good was a three- or four-strand wire fence against a determined intruder?

As he stood there musing, he saw movement along the paved road. To his surprise, the small stick twirling girl was darting toward the fence. She climbed through in one fluid movement, holding her sarong bunched at knee level to keep it from catching on the fence. Slung over her shoulder was a large cloth satchel. She wore a white tee-shirt today rather than pink, but Khath knew it was the same child. Why wasn't she in school? He worried that she was roaming too widely, too far from home. As he watched, she scrambled down the embankment from the road, paused for a moment on the edge of the cornfield, then darted inside. A few meters in from the edge of the field, Khath saw the tassels on the top of a corn stalk shake slightly. A moment later, another tassel quivered in the vicinity of the first.

Khath grinned. Smart child. She was picking randomly, one ear here, one ear there, to lessen the chance that the farmer would notice her theft. And she had moved far enough into the field that she wouldn't be seen from the road. Then, he noticed more movement in the field, more tassels shaking a few rows away from the child. One after another, the stalks trembled. There was something, or someone, in the field with the little girl.

Moving quickly, Khath left the shadow of the trees, crossed the dirt road and slipped through the fence into the cornfield.

The corn was well-tended, with wide pathways between each row. He worked his way across the rows, peering down each, searching for the child. He became aware that the noise of the machinery had stopped. At the same moment, a dog began to bark to his right.

Past the next row of corn, Khath saw a strange sight. The girl, her satchel bulging with stolen corn, stood transfixed at the sight of an odd-looking animal waddling toward her, barking loudly, yet wagging its stumpy tail all the while. The dog was brown and white, low to the ground and immensely fat. Its skin was loose and baggy, its long, floppy ears dragged on the ground. The dog's short, thick legs were barely long enough to keep its stomach from scraping the earth as it moved steadily and loudly toward the girl. As the dog came nearer, Khath could see that even its face drooped with the weight of its jowls pulling the skin away from the creature's eyes.

Slowly, the girl began to back away from the dog. She had yet to notice Khath, now standing several meters behind her in the same row.

A sharp whistle pierced the air. The dog ignored the sound. Khath heard another whistle, followed by shouting. A stout and bearded farmer appeared at the end of the corn row, clutching a rifle in his right hand. He stopped, staring toward Khath, his mouth dropping open.

"Hey!" the farmer yelled. He raised the rifle over his head and shook it threateningly. He yelled something else and began to run down the row.

At the sight of the angry farmer, the little girl whirled and was already in mid-stride when she saw Khath. She skidded to a stop, now trapped between the two men, her eyes darting wildly around.

Khath reached his hand toward her. "Hurry," he said in his native tongue. "Come quickly, child."

She hesitated a moment longer, gave one short nod of her head and reached for Khath's hand.

Khath grabbed the satchel from her, tucking it under his left arm, and pulled her behind him as he ran, slipping through the rows of corn, toward the edge of the field closest to the forest. Behind him, the man's shouting grew fainter, and then stopped. A moment later a shot rang out. *He's just firing into the air,* Khath thought, his mind registering the lack of any sound that a bullet would cause as it ripped its way through the dense cornfield. *Or, he's a very poor shot.*

Reaching the fence, Khath tossed the satchel over first, then lifted the girl and swung her over. Grasping the wooden post, he lightly vaulted over the wires. The girl had retrieved the satchel, and he wondered if she was going to make a run for it on her own now, but she handed it back to him, clasped his outstretched hand and let him lead her into the forest along the deer trail. After several minutes, Khath stopped, standing still to listen for the sounds of pursuit. All around them, the forest rustled and breathed, branches creaked in the breeze, a bird called out, another answered. *As it should be,* Khath thought. *We are safe.*

For the first time, he allowed himself to study the child. She would be pretty if she were not such a mess, dirt smeared on her face and clothing, hair tangled and full of twigs. She appeared to be about nine years old, but Khath guessed she was small for her age, like most children who survived the Khmer Rouge. At any rate, she seemed to be just a bit older than his daughters had been when they were taken from him. His heart softened. "Are you all right?" he asked.

Her eyes flicked up to meet his for the barest instant and she nodded her head.

"You should not be out here by yourself," Khath said. "Come with me. We will go together back to town."

The girl's lips twitched at this, but she said nothing, and fell into step behind him.

Khath stifled a grin. *She'll follow me meekly to the ends of the earth as long as I'm holding the corn,* he thought. He walked slowly, staying close enough to see the road, leaving the deer trail when it veered into the forest and finding a way through the brush. He could hear the vehicle approaching long before he saw it, so loud was the motor.

"Stay hidden, child. It may be the farmer."

Khath moved closer to the road and peered back toward the cornfield. A blue and white farm truck was approaching, a meaty arm poking out the open window. If Khath had any doubts about the identity of the driver, they were dispelled at the sight of the brown and white dog hanging its head over the frame of the truck bed, jowls and ears flapping in the wind.

As the truck disappeared around the corner, Khath gestured to the girl. "What is your name, child?"

"Nary," the girl muttered, looking at the ground.

"Well, Nary. You seem to know your way around. Do you know of a path that will take us back to town without using the road?"

Nary pointed up the road. "Up there."

"Show me," Khath said, pleased that his instincts had been right. This girl was a survivor. Whoever had taught her knew what they were doing.

Reaching Nary's path, they walked briskly now, soon arriving at a dirt lot on the edge of town. Nary stopped and turned to Khath. "You go that way," she said, pointing down the road, but her eyes were fixed on the satchel of corn that he still carried.

He looked in the direction she had pointed and could see the church tower in the distance. Good. He knew his way now.

"Go straight home now, child. No more wandering," Khath said firmly, draping the satchel of corn over her shoulder.

She stood before him, clutching the corn, looking uncertain. Then she grabbed several ears and thrust them into his hands, turned and darted away.

Feeling a lightness in his heart, Khath headed toward the church and home. Meeting this child was a good omen. He glanced at his watch. Plenty of time to get home, eat and come back to the church for ESL class. He pictured Pra Chhay's pleased surprise at the sight of fresh corn and walked faster, eager to share this bounty.

A familiar bark stopped him dead in his tracks. He looked around in dismay. There, parked in the church's lot was a blue and white pick-up truck with old floppy ears in the back.

# Twelve

"Think, thank, thought," the woman, Teresa, said, pointing to words on a sheet of paper as she spoke.

"Tink, tank, tot," Khath repeated. He was seated across from Teresa at a small table at the back of the classroom. Sareth stood at the chalkboard, speaking a mixture of Cambodian and English, explaining the grammar of a sentence on the board to a group of about 25 men, women and children, including Nary. The child sat next to a pleasant-looking woman, no longer young but with traces of faded beauty evident in her careworn face. Her mother? It was unwise to make assumptions when so many families were pruned of entire branches by the Khmer Rouge. The woman could be an aunt or distant relative. So far, through unspoken agreement, neither Khath nor the girl had acknowledged one another. Pra Chhay sat with the group, having had his turn with Teresa earlier.

Teresa smiled and shook her head. She drew a picture of a man in profile, showing his teeth open with tongue slightly protruding. "Like this," she said. "Thhh. Understand?"

Khath nodded, trying to look pleasant and interested. He was worried about the farmer. What had the man told Father Ralph about the cornfield incident?

"Try again," Teresa said, pointing to the three words. "Think, thank, thought."

"Tink, tank, tot," Khath intoned stubbornly. Good manners would not permit him to stick his tongue out at this woman.

"Hmmm," Teresa said. She touched Khath's hand, her finger pale against his dark skin. "Look at me. I'll show you. Thhh."

The tip of her moist, pink tongue squeezed out between her upper and lower teeth, like flesh protruding from the ragged edges of a freshly bashed in skull. Like his son's skull.

Embarrassed and horrified at the image, Khath dropped his eyes quickly to the table. He felt moisture gathering at his hairline as a flush prickled up his neck and into his scalp. And then, he felt a firm hand on his shoulder, fingers digging slightly into his skin. While the rest of the class worked on an assignment, Sareth had wandered back to check on him and Teresa.

"How are we doing back here?"

Sareth's voice was smooth, oily, slippery. It's a wonder his tongue doesn't slide out of his mouth and down his chin, Khath thought, hating the way Sareth's lips smiled while the man's fingers clawed into his shoulder.

Teresa's eyes were bright as she replied, speaking slowly to help Khath understand. "Khath's doing great." She grinned at Khath. "Almost perfect."

Khath blinked, surprised. He knew he was not doing great. His performance was barely acceptable. He raised his eyes and met Teresa's, gazing steadily into his. Such a direct gaze would be unsettling were it not so kind and gentle. She's protecting me, he realized. She's on my side.

Mr. Sareth pulled up a chair, releasing Khath's shoulder. Khath resisted the urge to rub it. He sat quietly while Sareth and Teresa spoke in English for a few minutes, then Mr. Sareth turned to him and spoke in Cambodian. His mouth smiled for Teresa's benefit, but his words were stern.

"Listen carefully, Khath. When your teacher speaks, raise your eyes and look at her to show your respect. It is the opposite from Cambodia. I know you are new here, but you need to learn these American ways, or you will bring shame upon our community. Do you understand?"

Khath nodded.

"If your teacher tells you to put your tongue between your teeth, do it. If she tells you to stand on your head, do it. If you don't understand, ask me later and I will explain. As I told you before, I will do what I can to help you learn the ways of this country, but you must trust me and do as I say."

Sareth stood up and looked down at Khath with slightly hooded eyes. "I am sure you understand how disappointed Father Ralph and I would feel if we had to send you back to Cambodia."

Khath lifted the corners of his lips and let the well-worn mask of amiability settle down over his features. Behind the mask, his thoughts were protected and safe. *Again with that threat. Did Mr. Sareth even have the power to send him back to the camp?* As from a great distance, Khath saw his voice and body go through the motions of thanking Sareth for his assistance and assuring the older man that he, Khath, would be a model student and citizen of this new country. No return plane ticket needed, thank you very much. Again, he felt the weight of Sareth's hand as the interpreter clapped him heartily on the back before returning to the chalkboard.

Feeling pressure in his chest, Khath realized he was holding his breath. He exhaled slowly. He needed to remember that his sole purpose in coming to America was to find his daughters and bring them to safety. If he had to stand on his head to do it, he would.

Teresa touched his hand. "Are you okay?" she asked.

"Yes, okay," Khath said, nodding. He pulled the page with the words on it toward him. With grim determination, he thrust his tongue between his teeth. "Thhhhink." Spit flew from his mouth and spattered the paper. Mortified, Khath swiped at the page with his sleeve.

"Very good," Teresa said. "Try again. Softly. Think, thank, thought."

Khath put his tongue between his teeth. "Thhink. Thank." He paused. "Thank you," he said.

Teresa's face glowed. "You're welcome," she smiled. "I think you've got it now. Let's take a break."

Once outside, standing on the raised covered veranda that ran the length of the south side of the church building, Khath smoked a cigarette, drawing the calming smoke deep into his lungs, releasing it in a stream through pursed lips and watching as the breeze snatched it away, scattering it to nothingness. Like his family. Carried away on currents they had not seen coming, did not understand, and could not control.

His gaze drifted over the church garden below, noting a gracefully curved brick walkway that led to a small rock-rimmed pond, with a statue of a robed man at the edge. Concrete animals played at his feet, and as Khath watched, a live rabbit hopped out of the foliage and nibbled at the grass along the edge of the pathway. A sweet scent hung over the garden, and he wondered which of the many blossoms to thank for it.

Hearing footsteps, Khath turned to see Teresa walking toward him. She was attractive in a soft, plushy sort of way. He liked her hair, golden with hints of copper. It had the sheen of well-polished metal.

Khath felt a flicker of curiosity. Who was this kind woman? He smiled and nodded at her, pinching his cigarette out as she came up and stood beside him, looking at the garden. What do Americans talk about, he wondered?

He waved his hand vaguely toward the garden. "Very nice. Flowers. Smell good," he ventured. He took a deep breath to illustrate his meaning, just in case.

"Very beautiful. Very nice," Teresa agreed.

"You have family, children?" Khath asked.

Teresa shook her head. "No children. No husband. I live with my sister."

"Your sister, have children?" Khath was puzzled. Where were the babies, the toddlers, in this town? Eventually, through pantomime and guesswork, he learned that Teresa's sister was hurt recently in a car crash that killed their parents and that the sister could no longer walk. Teresa helped to care for her sister. He looked at her with new interest. Tragic death and injury. These were things he understood.

They returned to the classroom and for the next hour, he and Pra Chhay worked with Teresa at the back of the room. Towards the end of the hour, just as Khath was beginning to relax, Father Ralph walked through the door. The priest apologized for interrupting the class, then took Sareth aside for a brief conversation. Watching out of the corner of his eye, Khath saw the two heads swivel toward him. He noticed Sareth's lips tightening and the curt way the older man nodded at the priest, and his heart began to beat faster.

Moments later, his fears were confirmed. As the priest left the room, Mr. Sareth turned, smiled coldly at him and said, "A word, please, Mr. Khath. You, too, Phally, and Nary as well. The rest of you may go."

---

Sareth turned away from the small group and began to erase the chalkboard. It was a bittersweet task that mirrored his life, each beautifully lettered word, each grammatically perfect sentence obliterated, swipe by cruel swipe, leaving only a blank slate. His evening's work, like his life's work, simply gone.

In his former life, Sareth had climbed the bureaucratic rungs in Cambodia's Ministry of Health to a position of influence and power. And now, at an age when he should have been relaxing among his leather-bound books, surrounded by gleaming teak and mahogany in the comfort of his elegant home, his every need tended to by house servants and an obedient wife, he found himself instead forced to start anew. He felt the burn of resentment deep in his chest and needed an extra minute to settle himself before facing the group behind him.

When he was ready, Sareth placed the eraser in the chalk tray and turned to the silent, waiting Cambodians. He noticed that Pra Chhay had chosen to stay, along with his brother. The monk stood erect, calm, his left hand rolling his prayer beads while his lips moved to the rhythm of a silent chant. Beside Pra Chhay, Khath stood with head inclined downward, arms crossed over his chest in a gesture of respect. Sareth made a mental note to remember to tell Khath that Americans would likely view that posture as defiant or defensive. He must learn to stand with his hands at his sides, or he risked being branded as sullen and uncooperative.

Sareth's gaze now shifted to include Phally, who stood with an anxious expression on her face, her left hand clutching Nary by the shoulder. The child, looking scruffy and unkept as always, stared out the window as though longing to escape.

"Shall we sit?" Sareth perched on the edge of a desk while the others sat in a row facing him. Looking down on the group, he continued. "Father Ralph had a visitor today, a farmer. He said you two," Sareth nodded toward Khath and Nary, "were stealing his corn this morning. Is it true?"

Phally's jaw dropped and she turned on her daughter. "Nary! You said the nice man gave you that corn. Did you lie to me? Did you take his corn? And you never said anything about Mr. Khath." She gestured to Khath. "Explain yourself, child."

Nary stared mutely at the desk top, a muscle jumping in her clenched jaw.

Phally's face flushed. She leaned across the aisle and pulled her daughter's desk around to face her. Sareth saw Khath flinch at the harsh scraping noise of metal legs on linoleum. Phally's hand closed around Nary's upper arm and she shook it. "Answer me, child!"

Sareth watched this scene with growing disdain. Such clumsy, brutish behavior. Just as he would expect from a village woman. But then again, the child was willful. He silenced Phally with a dismissive wave of his hand. "Enough," he said. "Perhaps another perspective would get us further along here." He turned to Khath. "Well?"

Before Khath could respond, Pra Chhay spoke up. "If I may?" he said, inclining his head toward Sareth.

At least this one has manners, Sareth thought. "Go ahead."

"My brother was tracking a deer this morning and came to the edge of the forest by the cornfield. He saw the child enter and heard a dog barking. Fearing that the child might be attacked, he went after her. It was then that the farmer saw them and began to chase them and shot his gun. Khath helped the child to safety, that is all."

"And helped himself to some corn," Sareth countered.

At this, Nary's head shot up. "I gave him the corn. He did not take any himself."

Pra Chhay smiled at Nary. "Good girl," he said. "Never fear to speak the truth."

Sareth studied the group before him. He did not like the way the others seemed united against him and protective of Khath. There was a unity between them all that excluded him. But it had always been this way, the weak banding together against the powerful. Besides, it was always a disruption when newcomers entered the community. But over time, alliances would be built, broken and reformed, and a new pecking order established.

As long as he remained at the top, Sareth thought, his life in this town would be tolerable. But these two, this monk and his damaged brother, might prove more challenging to his authority than most. It was a contest Sareth was determined to win.

He turned to Khath. "Have you anything to say?"

Khath raised expressionless eyes in his direction. "Nothing to add, no. It happened as they have said."

Sareth sighed. "I suppose it is too late to return the corn?"

Brief smiles flashed around the group. "The corn is gone," Pra Chhay confirmed.

Khath spoke up. "We can work to pay off our corn debt."

"Perhaps," Sareth said, "though I doubt the farmer will want you on his land again. We shall soon find out." He glanced at his watch. "It is ten minutes to the hour. At seven o'clock, the farmer will return to the church to meet with you all, so you can offer him your sincere apologies and assure him that it will not happen again. I suggest you tidy yourselves," Sareth looked pointedly at Nary, "and meet me in the lobby just before seven. Do not be late."

As the clock struck the hour, the five Cambodians trooped into the sitting area of Father Ralph's office.

The farmer, talking to Teresa, fell silent as they entered, staring closely at each of them in turn. "Yep. That's them. Them two are the ones that was stealing my corn this morning." The farmer pointed to Khath and Nary as he spoke. "I'm just glad it was me that saw them and not my son, Lawrence. He's a vet, served his country damn straight, and now his country ain't doing nothing to help him readjust. If he'd a seen those two, he wouldn't have pointed the rifle at the sky, that's for damn sure. Poor son of a bitch." The farmer glanced at Teresa. "Excuse me, miss. But my son ain't been the same since the war and it's a damn shame."

Teresa nodded.

"Mr. Taylor." Father Ralph leaned forward. "I'd like to introduce you all properly. Teresa you have already met, of course. This is Mr. Sareth, our interpreter and my assistant in the refugee project."

Sareth rose and stepped forward, his hand outstretched, a thin smile on his face. "A pleasure to meet you, Mr. Taylor."

The farmer looked startled and heaved himself to his feet as well. "Nice to meetcha," he responded. "I didn't know any of you all could speak English."

"You will find varying degrees of proficiency among our community," Sareth said. "We have classes in the evening twice a week to help the newcomers learn." He felt the farmer's sweaty, callused hand engulf his own, and his arm was yanked up and flung downward again as the man stepped back away from him.

"Glad to hear it." Farmer Taylor wiped his palm on his overalls. "Anybody comes to this country, they oughta learn to speak the lingo." He sat back down in his chair and folded his arms across his beefy chest, the bulge of his stomach providing a handy ledge on which to rest his limbs. "Now, about that corn."

Sareth sat back in his chair and stared coolly at the farmer. What an oaf. He glanced at Father Ralph, who looked equally appalled at the man's rudeness in ignoring the rest of the Cambodians. Perhaps the priest would end this charade quickly, and they could all go home.

As if reading Sareth's mind, Father Ralph dispensed with further formalities. "Mr. Taylor," he said. "I had Mr. Sareth discuss the matter with Khath and Nary thoroughly and explain our laws about trespassing and property rights. They have assured us that they now understand and nothing of this kind will happen again. Mr. Sareth also tells me that they have asked us to convey their deepest apologies for the incident. And, of course, I will reimburse you for the cost of the corn."

Father Ralph turned to Sareth. "Do we know how many ears were taken?"

Sareth turned to Khath and translated the question. At the answer, he felt a wave of anger. All of this commotion over eight ears of corn. In Cambodia, the Khmer Rouge would kill swiftly over such an infraction for an ear of corn could feed several workers. But here? Americans seemed determined to extract their justice on the basis of legal principle rather than common sense, robbing a man of dignity over a trifle. How absurd. He watched grimly as the farmer and the priest haggled over just compensation for the eight ears of corn and the angst Mr. Taylor claimed to have suffered over the incident.

At last, Father Ralph reached into his wallet and extracted some bills, handing them to Mr. Taylor.

Money in hand, the farmer became affable. "I gotta tell you, Father, there's a lot of folks not so happy about you bringing all these commies and Khy-mer Rooj here to Glenberg. I just figure you oughta know."

"Khmer Rouge? Oh, no, Mr. Taylor. These people are not Khmer Rouge."

Father Ralph went on, explaining the refugee project, but Sareth was watching Khath closely. The man had jumped so at the words Khmer Rouge. Now, Khath turned intense eyes to the interpreter.

"What is the farmer saying about the Khmer Rouge?" Khath whispered to Sareth.

"Nothing," Sareth said. "He is an ignorant man. Pay no mind."

"But what is he saying?" Khath insisted.

Irritation crept into Sareth's tone. "He says Father Ralph is bringing Khmer Rouge to Glenberg. He is a fool."

Khath's eyes narrowed. "Are you sure?" he said. "I heard things in the camps."

Sareth shifted in his seat, turning his body away from Khath. He was not going to indulge this man's paranoia. At least, not right now. Turing his attention back to the priest, he saw to his great relief that Father Ralph was concluding his conversation with the farmer.

A few minutes later, the meeting broke up. Sareth stayed behind just long enough to bid the Father a pleasant evening, then made his way out the doors into the chilly night air. He looked forward to the short stroll to his home a few blocks away. He wondered what meal his young wife Chea had prepared for him tonight, for he had not yet eaten. It was unfortunate that Chea was an indifferent cook, but food was food and he was quite hungry. Lost in his thoughts, he did not at first notice Khath and Pra Chhay standing and talking on the sidewalk half a block ahead, but in the still evening air, Sareth could hear their voices clearly.

"But Khath," Pra Chhay was saying, "Mr. Sareth told you clearly the farmer was wrong, that he was a fool."

"Even a fool can stumble upon the truth," Khath replied. "I hope you are right, brother. But if there are Khmer Rouge in this town, I will hunt them down. I will not rest until they are gone."

# Thirteen

Khath dipped the soft sponge into the bucket of soapy water, feeling useful for the first time since his arrival in Glenberg. Raising the dripping sponge, he applied it to the roof of the church van, creating big swirls of muddy foam as he scrubbed at an accumulation of pollen and bird droppings.

Pra Chhay was inside the church with Father Ralph, studying the vocabulary of religion with the priest, eager to share ideas about large topics: creation, sin, penance, death, karma, reincarnation.

Khath, knowing how dirty the van was and anxious to make restitution for the corn, had come along with his own, less lofty, idea of providing some simple manual labor.

The priest had appeared delighted with Khath's offer to clean the vehicle, and quickly moved the van into a shady spot, producing more rags, buckets, hoses, soaps, polishes and scrub-brushes than Khath had ever seen assembled for a simple car wash. Before the war, at his railroad job in Cambodia, he could have washed an entire train with less equipment.

He missed working with machinery. Perhaps when the priest saw how beautifully he could clean a vehicle, he would entrust Khath with more jobs to do around the church. With

that hope in mind, Khath was determined to make the van spar-
kle inside and out. He was uncomfortably aware that he was not
making a good impression in these first weeks in Glenberg, and
he badly wanted to turn that around. He needed help to find his
daughters, and he was not naive enough to believe people would
whole-heartedly help him as long as he continued to make
mistakes and get into trouble.

What were Kamala and Sitha doing now? Khath pictured
them sitting in a camp somewhere, safe from harm. Perhaps
Kamala was brushing her little sister's hair and fastening a
flower behind Sitha's tiny ear, teaching her the graceful ways of
a budding young Cambodian girl. The man from the Red Cross
in Khao I Dang said there were special camps and programs for
children separated from their parents. He imagined a kindly aid
worker taking an interest in their welfare, protecting them from
harm. He hummed as he worked on the car, comforted by the
images in his mind.

Khath washed and rinsed the body of the car, scrubbed the
hub cabs and the sidewalls, cleaned the bugs from the headlights
and taillights. He sprayed the engine carefully and cleaned the
underside of the hood. He scraped the corrosion from the
battery and made sure the radiator was full. With a damp rag he
wiped down the dashboard and vinyl seats, washed the running
boards and removed the rubber floor mats, shaking them free of
debris and scrubbing off the dried mud stains.

Searching among the various cleaning products, Khath
unscrewed caps and sniffed the contents until he found the one
he wanted —polish—and set about making the van shine, inside
and out. When he was done, he rinsed the brushes and rags,
coiled the hoses up and carried all the supplies to the back door
of the church, setting them quietly in a sheltered area near the
door.

Glancing at his watch, Khath saw that he had 20 or 30
minutes to while away before Pra Chhay rejoined him. He
glanced about, taking stock of his surroundings.

An open meadow of mown dried grass dotted with trees swept down the hillside behind the church. Crisscrossed by many paths and worn bare of grass in areas, it was evidently a favorite play area for local children. A group of four or five kids was down there now, and Khath saw from their clothing and physical appearance that they were Cambodian. He wondered if Nary was with them and decided to go take a look. It would be pleasant to hear children playing games in his native tongue.

Strolling a little ways down a path, Khath paused by a shady tree that gave him a good vantage point of both the rear of the church and the playing children. He squatted comfortably and leaned his back against the trunk.

Lighting a cigarette, Khath watched the activity below him. Two older boys were throwing rocks at a stump, while three girls squatted around a splash of color on the ground. He wondered what it was, and his curiosity was soon satisfied when one of the girls, her glossy black hair fanning out against the blue of her tee-shirt, picked up the bundle, dusted it off and cradled it in her arms. It was a doll, and a treasured one at that, judging from the way the girls fussed over it.

Khath grinned to himself. He was not near enough to see the faces of these children clearly, but he was confident that the wild child Nary would not be found among a group of girls toting a doll around. And yet...he swept his eyes slowly around the hillside. Ah. There she was, sitting not far from him, half hidden among some nearby shrubs, watching the scene below. What an odd child Nary was, never a part of the action but always aware of it. The girl seemed to have been aged by the war into something not quite adult, but certainly far more than a mere child. He caught her eye and nodded at her. She gazed solemnly back.

Khath squinted his eyes against the cigarette smoke swirling lazily toward him, pushed by the light breeze. He softened his focus, letting the world blur beyond the fringe of his lashes, his thoughts flitting between his lost daughters and Nary. He and his wife Khieu had worked hard to raise proper Cambodian girls: modest, polite and respectful of their elders. He smiled, remembering how sweet his eldest, Kamala, then seven, had looked all dressed up in a traditional sarong and golden headdress, performing the simple dances taught to little girls. Several times each day, Khieu had gently stretched the child's tender fingers backwards, training her youthful ligaments into the graceful arch of a traditional dancer's hand.

Would four years spent under Khmer Rouge control have transformed Kamala and her little sister Sitha into wary tomboys like Nary? Would it have erased all traces of his and Khieu's early influence on the girls? What horrible things had they survived during the war?

For the first time, Khath wondered if reuniting with his daughters would bring worse heartache than losing them had, a thought that only strengthened his resolve to find them and protect them from further harm.

The gentle hum of childish voices had turned harsh while Khath rested against the tree. He heard shouts and opened his eyes. The two boys were carrying sticks now, brandishing them over their heads as they shouted at the girls. The littlest girl had begun to wail. One of the other girls took her hand and began pulling her along, walking with stooped shoulders and cringing steps along the path indicated by the boys. The girl with the doll tossed her head defiantly, turned her back and began to walk away, clutching her precious bundle to her chest. The biggest boy grabbed her by the arm and spun her around, pushing her into line after the other two girls.

Khath's body tensed. This was getting rough. He hoped he would not have to go down there and chastise those boys for behaving so brutishly. He wondered who their parents were and if they allowed such behavior. As he watched, the scene below quieted. The girls had settled down on a patch of dried grass beside the path, a nearby tree offering some shade. The boys sat close by.

After a few minutes, the older boy nudged the smaller one, who got up and approached the girls. Holding out his hand, he beckoned for the littlest girl to take hold and come with him. After a moment's hesitation, the child complied. The boy smiled at her and they walked over to the first boy, who gestured for her to sit with them. The boy in charge reached out and took the little girl's hands, examining her palms, then shooed her back to sit with the other girls.

Khath frowned. It was almost as if…no. He pushed the thought away before it could fully surface. Pra Chhay would say he was letting his imagination color his view of the world around him.

And maybe Pra Chhay was right. It was peaceful down there. The children were playing quietly. Why borrow trouble? He watched idly as the boys repeated their actions with another of the girls. Ignoring the turbulence in his heart, Khath told himself that it was some new game the children were playing, perhaps an American game.

So what if the children's play resembled a Khmer Rouge checkpoint, where the presence of callused palms—proof that one was not a member of the wealthy, Westernized classes—could save your life. How many times had Pra Chhay scolded him for jumping to such conclusions?

Below him, the boys' attention turned to the girl with the doll. They beckoned her over. She shook her head. The leader stood up, leaning casually on his stick. This time Khath could hear his loud command. "You will come here now."

By the time the smallest child began again to wail, Khath was on the move. But the young leader was already closing in on the girl in blue, grasping a handful of hair and pulling her to her feet. Through it all, she clung to her doll, though she, too, was wailing now.

The boy wrested the toy from the girl's grasp and, holding it by the ankles, began twirling the doll around his head, moving toward the tree that cast its shadow over the girls.

"Noooo!" The scream wrenched itself from Khath's throat as his legs launched him down the hillside, his feet seeming scarcely to touch the ground. "Stop it. Stop it. Stop it."

Again and again he hurled the words like darts toward the children, who paused, frozen, as Khath hurtled down the hillside, screaming. Before they could scatter, he was among them, collaring the leader in a choke hold. "Stop this evil play. How dare you mimic the Khmer Rouge. Where is your decency?"

Khath's horror and outrage spewed forth like floodwaters breaching an irrigation dike during monsoon. "Give her back the doll."

With an arm that shook, the boy thrust the doll toward the girl in blue, who looked questioningly at Khath. At his nod, she reached out timidly, then snatched the doll from the boy's hand and retreated a few steps.

The stench of fear assailed Khath's nostrils, wafting up from the body of the boy he held firmly against his chest.

With an exclamation of disgust, Khath flung the boy from him, into the dirt. The youth scrambled to his hands and knees, his head hanging, drawing in gasps of air as a long rope of snot hung from his nose. He coughed, the movement causing the mucus to swing wildly before it dropped into the dirt.

The second boy began to snivel, and Khath turned on him. "Be quiet," he snapped. "And you," nodding at the boy still on the ground, "Stand up. Stand up and apologize for the wrongs you have done here today."

As the boy began slowly to rise, Khath's brain swirled, awash with images of violence, of smashed skulls and limp bodies, of burns and beatings and shots to the head, of flesh sliced cleanly or flayed to tatters. Shame crashed down upon him as he saw the boy's fearful eyes and halting movements.

With his mind tangled between the past and the present, Khath knew he'd been too rough on the child. He forced himself to concentrate and dug his fingernails into his palms, the discomfort helping to anchor his mind to the scene in front of him. "Go on," he said gruffly. "Ask for forgiveness."

The boy seemed contrite, the swagger gone. Was it an act? His words tumbled into the stillness. He meant no harm. He was truly sorry. Between each statement, he glanced anxiously at Khath, as if to ask, "Is it enough? Shall I continue?" He seemed prepared to go on until sundown, if that was what it took to appease Khath's anger.

"All right," Khath said. The children stood uneasily, casting little glances at one another. Khath cleared his throat and ran his hands over his hair, saddened to see eyes widen and muscles tense at his movement, like deer poised at the edge of flight. He sighed. When the children told their parents of this incident, he would be cast as the village madman who terrorized the weak and the vulnerable. His every action seemed to backfire in this new land.

"I have frightened you, and for that I am sorry." Khath looked at each child in turn and spoke sternly, choosing his words carefully. "The Khmer Rouge killed my son in the same way that you were pretending—his skull smashed against the trunk of a killing tree. He was only two years old. Such evil is not meant for a game of pretend. You must never play such terrible games again. Believe me when I say you do great harm with these games and bring dishonor upon your families."

Khath paused and again looked deeply upon the ring of faces, turn by turn. He wanted so desperately to make them understand. The girl with the doll did, that much was clear. Wanting to soften their fear, he tried to smile at them through lips that felt stiff and unwieldy, like slabs of putty around his mouth. "You have a fresh start in America. Make your families proud. Now go. Go home and play nicely together."

Khath watched the children back away to a safe distance and then turn and walk somberly up the path. Rubbing his hands over his face, he tried to compose himself, taking several deep breaths.

"My friend's brother, he died like that, too." The words were spoken softly, offered hesitantly as a comfort.

Nary. Khath had forgotten all about her. She stood in front of him now, looking at him directly with the gaze of an adult.

"Why did they kill him?" he asked.

She shook her head. "It was too sad. The Khmer Rouge took us to a work camp for kids. Then they said there was not enough food to feed everyone, so one day they just killed the ones too small or too sick to work."

"My daughters went to a youth camp," Khath said. He dug in his wallet, pulling out the well-worn photo and handing it to Nary. "I am still looking for them."

Nary studied the photo. "What's wrong with her foot?" she asked, pointing to a dark shape splotched over little Sitha's ankle.

"Just a birthmark," Khath replied. "Look how it's shaped like a star. No one ever had such a pretty birthmark." A wild hope surged in his breast. "Have you...did you ever see my girls? In your camp?"

Nary looked even more closely at the photo then frowned. "I don't know. These girls have too much flesh. I never saw anyone who looked like that in the camp. Everyone was sick, skinny. We ate bugs, dirt, anything to fill our stomach. I saw many girls die, maybe your girls, too. I don't know. In the camps, in the fields, they would just fall down and die." She handed the photo back to Khath. "Maybe you look too hard, too much. So many people died. Maybe you should stop."

Shocked, Khath stared at Nary. Stop? How could he stop? No. Stopping was not possible. He raised his eyes, suddenly unable to meet the gaze of this child. As he did so, he saw a flash of color on the hillside above him. Pra Chhay, his robes flowing, was hurrying down the path toward him.

"Is everything all right?" Pra Chhay called out as he came within hearing distance. "Father Ralph and I heard shouting. What happened? Khath?" Pra Chhay pulled a handkerchief out of his pouch and mopped his face with it, panting slightly from his rush down the hillside.

"I saw children playing," Khath replied. "I thought it would be nice, peaceful to watch them. I wanted only to relax while I waited for you to finish your lesson."

He looked down and his shoulders sagged. "I don't know what is wrong with me, brother. Nothing I do here turns out the way I intend it. I feel as though I am trying to get to the other side of a mined field, afraid to move in any direction for fear of causing an explosion of some sort."

Feeling utterly defeated, Khath began to draw another cigarette from his pack and noticed that his hands were shaking, even as they still clutched the photo that Nary had returned to him. The girl was nowhere in sight. She must have slipped away when Pra Chhay approached.

"Let's go home, Khath. You can tell me what happened on the way," Pra Chhay said, draping his arm over Khath's shoulder. "You are not alone here, you know. You have Father Ralph and your tutor. They want to be your friends and help you. If you could try to trust them a little more, you would feel better and they can explain how to do things here. It is too confusing to try to figure it all out by yourself."

The two brothers set off toward home, Khath telling Pra Chhay about the children's game and his reaction to it as they walked.

When Khath finished, Pra Chhay sighed. "What a terrible reminder for you. My heart hurts to think of it. No wonder you were upset."

"I was too harsh."

"Yes, but you apologized. And you had a witness, right? Didn't you say Nary was watching?

Khath nodded. "It is just as Oum predicted, brother. The hateful spirit of the Khmer Rouge lives on, even here in America. It sickens me. When I find out who is behind this…" His voice trailed off.

Pra Chhay stopped and faced Khath, blocking his way. "You will do nothing. Do you hear? I mean it, Khath. As your elder brother, I forbid you. You will do nothing."

"Then *you* should." Khath's frustration burned. He felt his whole body vibrate with the force of it. "You are the religious leader in this community now," he said. "You are the one with the authority to teach the children. Forget your study sessions with the priest and focus on your own people. We need you more than he does."

After a moment, Pra Chhay nodded. "You are right, brother. I should take more responsibility, and I will. Thank you for opening my eyes."

The two men walked on in silence for a while, and then Pra Chhay took a deep breath, stopped under a tree and turned to face Khath. "I understand your concerns, brother. I do. We must teach the children about life in our country before the Khmer Rouge. But you are wrong, Khath, if you think we can do this without the priest's help. He is our sponsor and I believe he means well by us, don't you?"

"I have no reason to doubt his intentions. He seems a kind man," Khath admitted.

"Good. We agree then," Pra Chhay said. "I will tell Father Ralph what happened in that field today and share our concerns about the type of games you saw. I am sure he will help us get some classes and activities started for the children. All right?"

Khath nodded, feeling relieved. At least it was something. And this way, maybe he wouldn't be branded the village mad man.

"But remember, Khath," Pra Chhay said. "If you see or hear anything more, you are to do nothing. Let me handle it."

As they neared their home, Pra Chhay turned to Khath. "Are you ready for some good news now?"

"More than ready," Khath said. Whatever the news was, Pra Chhay seemed to be having a hard time containing it. His eyes sparkled, and a radiant smile spread across his face.

"Father Ralph has gotten an appointment for you with the Red Cross in Portland. We go there in two days. Then the search for your daughters can really begin."

# Fourteen

"No, no. That won't do at all." Sareth studied his wife's appearance, a slight frown wrinkling his brow.

"I don't understand, *Bong*," Chea replied. "We are visiting the American women. I thought you wanted me to look nice."

"And you look lovely, my dear. But," Sareth searched for the right words. "In a small town like ours, people do not make formal calls. One should not dress as though it were a fancy occasion."

Chea raised her eyebrows high, their perfect arch accentuated with just the right touch of make-up. In matters of style and beauty, no one could come close to Chea. It was one of the qualities that made Sareth choose her as his bride, knowing she would never embarrass him at important social functions related to his work in Cambodia.

But here in America, Sareth found himself wishing that Chea were not quite so beautiful, not quite so attractive to the virile young men of Glenberg. He was tired of seeing the lustful stares and putting up with the excessive amount of customer "service" Chea received from male store clerks. Worst of all were the raised eyebrows and disbelieving looks he himself received when he asserted his relationship with Chea.

"Go on," Chea said, smoothing the silk of her best sarong, her manicured fingers tracing the shimmering blues and golds of the fabric.

Sareth patted the sofa. "Come sit, Chea. Let me explain about visiting in America."

Chea rustled over to the couch and then lowered herself gracefully. Sareth admired her fluid movements, the sway of her hips, her delicate stride. Unbidden, an image of Phally popped into his mind. Why Chea felt so threatened by a common village woman was a source of frustration to him. Their rivalry used to amuse him, but now it was just another thing to worry about as he strove to keep his beautiful wife contented with her life here, with him.

"First," Sareth said, "we must take them a present, some flowers or a gift of fruit or sweets. So we will stop by the market on our way."

"But you are the headman of our community here, *Bong*. Won't they feel honored that we are paying them a visit? Won't they be offering us gifts?"

"Perhaps," Sareth said. "But here it is different. People are more casual about social status. And have you forgotten? It's not purely a social call. We are going to…" Again, Sareth struggled with his wording. He dared not say that Chea would essentially be working for Gail in trade for English lessons. As the wife of an upper echelon government official in Cambodia, Chea had never worked a day in her life. He doubted she would care to take up employment now. On the one hand, her superior attitude was good. It showed that she still saw him as he had been, an important man, accustomed to commanding others. She had not yet realized his diminished status in this new land, and he dreaded the day when she figured it out.

Chea waited for him to finish his sentence, a questioning look on her face.

"To confirm your schedule, my dear. So that Miss Gail can offer you private tutoring to improve your English. Of course, it would be a kindness, a much appreciated kindness, for you to assist her in any small way that she needs due to her unfortunate injuries."

Chea nodded. "Yes, I recall. The woman is crippled. I don't mind helping her out and providing her with some company." Chea stood up. "So, what should I wear?"

Sareth thought back to his initial visit to Gail and Teresa. Both women had worn pants, casual shirts. Neither wore make-up to define their features or enhance their appearance. Chea would outshine them draped in a burlap rice sack. "Wear your simplest clothing for today, my dear. Once you have met Miss Gail and seen their home, I trust your instincts entirely in these matters."

While Chea changed her clothing, Sareth thought ahead, running through the possible scenarios of the visit, the pitfalls associated with each. First of all, he would have to make sure that Chea understood how sensitive Americans were about physical imperfections. It was silly the way one had to pretend not to notice if a person was missing a limb or had an ugly birthmark or burn splotching the entire face. In Cambodia, injuries and mutilations were common so that people gazed upon them frankly, satisfied their curiosity, and moved on to other topics. But Sareth had noticed that Americans were offended if one looked too pointedly or asked questions too soon. He would have to make sure Chea did not stare at Gail's legs.

The only other issue that he could think of was money. If they offered to pay outright for Chea's services, he would have to refuse. But did he have the cultural skill, he wondered, to refuse emphatically, yet at the same time make it clear that, tendered properly, gifts of money would be gratefully accepted? In his culture, it was a simple thing to give money, as a patron or friend, without shaming the recipient. But he was not sure if this custom existed in America. For the sake of his meager bank account, he hoped it did.

After a few minutes, Chea was ready to go, emerging from the bedroom dressed in a simple cotton sarong of subdued colors, and a white blouse. Her hair was held by a carved wooden clip at the nape of her neck, and flowed in an ebony stream down her back.

Sareth resisted the urge to reach out and fondle that shimmering hair, to draw its sleek strands through his fingers. Time enough for that later. Instead, he merely nodded at Chea. "Much better," he said.

At the market, Sareth pointed out suitable hostess gifts and allowed Chea make the final selection of a bright bouquet of inexpensive, yet fragrant, flowers.

As they were exiting the store, past a stand of papers for sale, a headline caught Sareth's eye. He paused to read, and Chea proceeded out the door ahead of him, unescorted. Absorbed in his reading, Sareth did not at first notice that Chea had walked out without him. As the fact registered, he felt a faint annoyance at her disrespect. But perhaps she hadn't realized that he had stopped. He stepped quickly to the door, emerging from the building just in time to hear a long, low admiring whistle, directed at Chea.

Angered, Sareth looked toward the sound and saw a few young men in jeans and tee shirts, laborers of some sort, judging from their dusty clothing and heavy boots. Sareth could not help but notice the men's muscular arms straining the cloth of their shirts. Did Chea notice this, too?

He saw his wife, startled, look up from the flower bouquet she held, her wide gaze sweeping over the men and Sareth, in turn, before lowering her eyes modestly.

Sareth's heart lurched and he hurried to Chea, placing a hand on the small of her back, pressing her to walk away from the men. "Pay no mind, my dear. They are ill-bred laborers, no manners at all. Disgraceful." He paused. "Chea, my dear, you must be careful not to wander alone."

"Yes, *Bong*," Chea murmured.

Her eyes gazed up into his briefly, the expression contrite. But the bouquet, held so carefully to her nose, could not quite hide the sly smile tugging at the corners of her mouth.

Behind him, one of the men called out, "Way to go, Granddad!" amid general laughter.

Sareth felt his anger and anxiety rise, not yet ready to counter such insults to his manhood. He needed more time to build the prestige that would bind his wife to him in this new land. He cringed inwardly at the thought of Chea comparing him physically to younger, more virile men. Would she have smiled at those laborers, favored them with a glance, if he were not at her side? *Watch your step, Chea. I am still your husband.* Sareth allowed his hand, now grasping Chea's arm just above the elbow, to tighten slowly, squeezing her flesh until the ugly smirk on her face was replaced with the calm mask of submission. It did not take long. His message had been received without a single word spoken. He wished it were that easy to communicate with Americans.

A few minutes later, Sareth and Chea drove up outside Gail and Teresa's house. Sareth had filled the drive with admonishments and advice in last minute preparation for Chea's introduction to Gail and American home life.

"Are you ready?" Sareth asked. "Have you any final questions for me before we go inside?"

Chea shook her head and looked around the yard and neighborhood. "It's very pretty," she said. "I think I will like spending time here. Thank you, *Bong*, for arranging this." She smiled, and Sareth felt a slight easing of the tension in his shoulders. Chea could be difficult at times but so far, things were going well enough.

They entered the yard. The windows of the house were open to the slight breeze. It was a perfect autumn day.

"You see, Chea," Sareth said. "Here is the ramp for Miss Gail's wheelchair. It is well made, not too steep. I think you should have no trou…"

Sareth's words were drowned out by a loud crash and clatter from inside the house. For a moment, there was frozen silence then a woman's voice, a rich, melodious Cambodian voice, scolded gently. "Nary, child, look what you have done. Is it broken?"

It was Phally. Sareth's heart sank. His wife Chea stood rigidly beside him, an expression of dismayed anger on her face. He felt the force of her glare as she hissed, "What is *she* doing here?"

"Letting her child run wild, apparently," Sareth said. "Come, Chea. Let us get to the bottom of this." He strode up the steps, crossed the porch and pressed the doorbell button. From inside the house, he heard footsteps, and then the door was pulled open and Teresa stood before him, a smudge of flour on her cheek and a startled expression on her face. She glanced down at her wristwatch and said, "Oh my gosh," and then looked up at Sareth, her smile of welcome competing with the guilty flush creeping up her neck.

"Mr. Sareth, Chea, welcome. Come in, please, come in. I'm so sorry—we completely lost track of time."

Flustered, Teresa ushered them into the living room and toward the couch. "Please have a seat. What lovely flowers. Thank you so much." Teresa took the bouquet. "I'll get Gail and, oh, here's Gail."

Sareth stared at the spectacle of Gail flying into the room in her agile sports chair, Nary standing backwards on the edges of the foot bar, clutching Gail's shoulders and squealing as Gail twirled to a stop. He heard Chea gasp.

A moment later, Phally appeared in the kitchen doorway. Her eyes widened when she saw Mr. Sareth and Chea. "Nary," she snapped, reaching a hand toward her daughter. "Come here beside me and show your respect to Mr. Sareth."

Sareth arranged his features into an expression, he hoped, of benevolent tolerance as he waited for Phally and her child to sort themselves out and pay due respect to him and Chea. "Such an energetic child," he murmured in English to Teresa, standing beside him.

"She's really opened up in the last few days," Teresa said, smiling. Then her eyes widened as she noticed what Phally and Nary were doing. "Oh my, what a formal greeting."

Phally and Nary both stood, hands clasped before their faces, bowing in the Cambodian manner first to Sareth and then to Chea, their eyes lowered, demeanor subdued. Sareth and Chea returned the bows, though far less deeply and more briefly.

"It is our custom, Miss Teresa. A form of paying respect," Sareth explained, turning back to Teresa. "Now, let me present my wife Chea to your sister." He drew Chea forward and introductions were made. To his relief, Phally and Nary had withdrawn to the kitchen. He could hear Phally whispering instructions to Nary to gather their belongings quickly and quietly.

A moment later Phally appeared in the doorway and bowed again. "Sorry, we go now," she said, speaking to Teresa and Gail. "We come back later, clean." Making dish washing motions with her hands, Phally smiled, then turned and headed toward the back door, pushing Nary along in front of her. Teresa followed, thanking Phally and insisting there was no need for her to return to clean up the kitchen.

Turning from the scene in the kitchen, Sareth found Gail watching him with cool eyes. She gestured to the couch, and Sareth, conscious that by standing he was rudely forcing Gail to crane her head upwards to look at him, seated himself and Chea.

"It appears we have interrupted an activity, Miss Gail," Sareth said. "I do apologize if this is an inconvenient time for you."

"No, not at all," Gail said. "Phally was teaching us how to make those delicious Cambodian egg rolls. It took longer than expected, with the language barrier and all. We sure had some funny miscommunications along the way." A smile suddenly lit up her face, a brief chuckle escaped her throat, as she appeared to recall one of those moments.

Sareth was struck at how Gail's smile changed her entire appearance, making her really quite attractive. Green eyes, curly auburn hair, a spate of freckles across the bridge of her nose. Why had he noticed none of these qualities on his first visit? He felt Chea stir on the couch beside him, and noticed an answering smile soften the tension in her face.

Teresa returned to the room, bearing a tray with tea cups and small plates, forks and napkins, condiments and a plate of fresh hot egg rolls, cut into bite-sized pieces. "Our first egg rolls," she announced. "Chea, Mr. Sareth, please have some and give us your professional opinion. How are they?"

As Gail and Teresa busied themselves serving and passing plates, Sareth briefly translated for Chea. He saw a look of annoyance flit over her face, and tried to make a joke. "Phally didn't know *we* were going to be eating them, dear. At least we need not fear the ingredients."

The corners of Chea's month twitched upward at that, and Sareth nodded at her in approval. Good girl. Chea was too well trained ever to make a scene in front of these American women, but judging from her response to him, she would not even be blaming him for this turn of events later.

The growing rivalry between the two women was subtle but fierce, for each had legitimate claim to the coveted role of village matriarch: Phally, by virtue of her maturity, her widowhood and the general competence she was showing at getting along in America, despite that delinquent child of hers; and Chea, with her elegance and the status conferred by her marriage, nearly overcoming the disadvantage of her youth.

With great ceremony and a twinkle of his eyes at Gail and Teresa, Sareth lifted a morsel of egg roll to his lips. He inhaled the aroma of cilantro, pork, and crisply fried wrapper, and felt a flood of saliva moistening his mouth, readying itself for the treat to come. Placing the savory bite into his mouth, Sareth closed his eyes, all showman now. His teeth crunched through the wrapper and released an explosion of flavor. In truth, it was delicious, far better than anything Chea could produce, but what fool of a husband would admit a thing like that? Like a wise sage, he nodded his head as he chewed, drawing out the moment. Beside him, Chea giggled. At last, he swallowed and opened his eyes, ready to render a verdict. Three sets of female eyes gazed expectantly at him. He touched a napkin to his lips before speaking.

"A very commendable effort," he said. "My congratulations. But let us hear what Chea thinks." He gestured to his wife, who popped a tiny bit of egg roll into her mouth, swallowed almost without chewing and nodded her head.

"Very good," she said with a gracious smile.

Sareth was sure no one but he could discern the effort it took her to praise food made under the tutelage of her enemy. It was time to move on, and quickly.

"Miss Teresa, I have a message that Father Ralph wished me to convey to you. We will be taking Khath to an appointment with the Red Cross in Portland tomorrow."

"Oh, that's wonderful news," Teresa said. "Khath must be so excited."

"Yes, well, Father Ralph wants you to know that he'd be pleased if you are able to accompany us, though we understand this is short notice. We leave at 9:00 AM and can pick you up if you are able to come."

Teresa nodded. "I'll see if I can make that work. Shall I call you or Father Ralph to confirm?"

"Either would be fine. We are in constant communication," Sareth said. It never hurt to emphasize this point.

Gail leaned forward. "Mr. Sareth, there is something that puzzles me. The other refugees, people like Phally and Khath, have such terrible stories to tell. I don't get that sense from you. How did you come to be in America?"

Teresa nodded. "I've wondered that, too," she said.

"Ah, you are both very perceptive," Sareth said.

He turned to Chea and said, in Cambodian, "Patience, my dear. They want to know about our background. We will get to your schedule as soon as I have shared our history with them. I promise to be brief."

Chea nodded.

Sareth took a sip from the cup of tea Teresa had placed before him then turned his attention to Gail. "As you may know, I was a public servant in the Cambodian Ministry of Health. Chea and I lived in Phnom Penh, where I worked on matters of health systems policy. You can well imagine how deluged with work we were. Our hospitals were overflowing with wounded soldiers and victims of land mines. Many of our people had lost limbs, and so I was sent to attend a conference in Chicago on advances in prosthetics. We were looking for artificial limbs that could stand up to the conditions of life in Cambodia. Lack of sanitation, high humidity, monsoon season and so forth. This was in late March, 1975. After the conference I stayed to tour some American veterans' facilities and visit the prosthetics departments."

"So you were abroad when Cambodia fell?" Teresa asked.

Sareth nodded. "I had taken Chea with me on the trip, feeling it unsafe to leave her behind when the Khmer Rouge were approaching the capital."

"Good call," Gail said. "So what happens when someone's country is overthrown when they are abroad? It seems like it would be a bureaucratic nightmare."

Sareth chuckled. "And so it was," he said. "One minute we were Cambodian citizens, the next, stateless refugees. We lost everything, of course. Our home and furnishings, our wealth. Anything we hadn't packed in our suitcases was gone.

"I can't even imagine," Teresa said. "How terrible for you both. In a different way, of course, but still. You must have been so worried, frantic really, for news of what was happening." She cast a look of sympathy at Chea.

"Precisely," Sareth said. "The Red Cross put us up in Chicago for a while, but we needed to be closer to home. Chea had a sister living in Thailand near the Cambodian border. She and her husband took us in, and we lived there illegally for nearly four years until the United Nations began opening up refugee camps on the border. So we entered the camps and applied to come back to America. We've been here just eight months now."

Sareth glanced at his watch, deftly changing the subject. "I fear we are taking up too much of your time. Shall we confirm a schedule for Chea's visits with Miss Gail? I know she is very much looking forward to practicing her English and helping out as you see fit."

"I was thinking about that," Gail said, leaning forward in her chair. "I could use help with shopping. I can never reach the things on the higher shelves. If Chea went with me, we could relieve Teresa of that chore. She's been doing everything around here lately and I'd like to free her up some."

"Well, I'm all for that," Teresa said with a grin.

Sareth nodded slowly, though the image of the three lust-filled laborers loitering about the grocery store was still uncomfortably vivid in his mind. Would the presence of Gail in her wheelchair make that situation worse or better? He couldn't even begin to puzzle it out. He was tired, he realized suddenly, bone tired from the stresses of the day. Eager to be done and go home, Sareth moved the conversation along briskly, setting up a tentative visiting schedule for Chea of two mornings per week.

With smiles and thanks, Sareth and Chea rose to leave. The beginnings of a headache were stirring around Sareth's temples. He would ask Chea to rub his head with scented oil when they got home. Stepping onto the porch, Sareth drew a deep breath but before he could even release the air from his lungs, Teresa's voice was tugging him back.

"Oh, Mr. Sareth, I almost forgot." She hurried after them. "Phally wants to have a big welcoming party for Khath but especially for his brother, the monk. To honor him, you know, pay respect. She wants to have it at her house and wondered if that would be all right with Father Ralph. Maybe you could discuss it with him?"

"What a splendid idea to formally welcome the monk into our community. I should have thought of it myself," Sareth said lightly. He bowed slightly. "Consider it done."

He turned away, his headache flaring. Phally again. This idea of hers was nothing more than a ploy to elevate the monk in the community in order to diminish his own influence. He was sure of that. What a pushy woman, especially now that she had the Americans on her side. Too many things were slipping out of his control. Something would have to be done about that.

# Fifteen

Khath sat up, clutching his head, his stomach churning. The dream was so real he was having trouble clawing his way free of it. His eyes were open, he saw his room in Glenberg, yet the greater part of his brain was still immersed in the horror of Site 21. Bodies sprawled in a long trench, limbs twitching in weak protest as still more people cascaded over the edges, clubbed or shot, smothering the life from those who yet breathed. And now, what was that tapping sound? Some poor soul perhaps, convulsing against a rock, or even worse, vainly signaling life in a deluded belief that those who threw him in might pull him out.

Khath dug his fingernails into his scalp, wishing he could reach clear into his brain and rid himself of these vivid, crushing images. More tapping.

"Khath, are you up? It's Red Cross day. Father Ralph will be here in an hour to pick us up."

Khath watched mutely as his bedroom door swung inward, and the morning smile dropped from Pra Chhay's face.

"Oh, Khath. Not another nightmare? Tell me." Pra Chhay crossed the room and sat beside Khath on the bed. "Are you dreaming of your wife and son?"

Khath shook his head. "No. Site 21." He heard Pra Chhay's soft intake of breath, not quite a gasp. And why not? Even he himself was surprised to hear those words pass from his lips. He'd never before uttered them willingly to a living soul, though others spoke them, in tones ranging from fear, revulsion and, inevitably, suspicion at the dawning realization that Khath had passed through those gates and come out alive.

Haltingly, in snatches, Khath described his dream to Pra Chhay. "But the killing and torture in real life was much worse than in my dream," he muttered, staring at the floor. "And still people begged to live. I heard them. I saw them, reaching their hands out toward their torturers. It made me vomit sometimes. It was so pitiful, so painful to witness. And so useless."

Rolling his prayer beads between his thumb and first finger, Pra Chhay sat beside Khath, his lips barely moving as he murmured his mantras. Khath had noticed his brother working his beads hard whenever a conversation veered into painful territory. Maybe he was seeking inspiration, or just erecting a shield against the grief of others. He had explained once to Khath that the Pali word *mantra* meant "mind protection."

Pra Chhay cleared his throat. "Perhaps it is not so useless, brother, when seen in the proper light. I think perhaps your strong emotions have obscured your vision, causing you to misinterpret what you witnessed."

"What do you mean?" Khath said. The violence he'd come across at Site 21 had always seemed horrifically clear to him.

"The higher teachings tell us that, ultimately, a plea for mercy can be seen as a karmic gift from the victim to the one doing the harm," Pra Chhay explained. "Whether such pleading is done consciously in this spirit or not, at its essence it reflects the innate human goodness, the Buddha nature, of one person reaching out to the Buddha nature of another. Do you see? By asking for mercy, the victim is offering, with their very life, one last chance for the tormentor to honor their own Buddha nature and turn away from such hideous behavior."

Khath stared at Pra Chhay, his brow furrowed. "So you are saying that the one who begs for mercy makes more merit than the one who meets death in stoic silence?"

"Yes, Khath. What greater merit could one achieve, facing the threat of death with compassion for the killer?"

"No." Khath shook his head. "Those people were pleading for their own lives, not thinking of the Khmer Rouge's karma."

"On the surface, yes. But on a deeper level, the level of ultimate truth, there is much more going on than that," Pra Chhay said. "In moments that determine life or death, you may see in the victim's eyes the light of the Buddha."

"I would like to think you are right, brother," Khath said. "But I pray that I will never again have to witness such things."

"Yes," Pra Chhay said. "Not in your waking life, or in your sleep." He stood up. "Do you know, this is the first time you've really talked to me about Site 21. I think that's a good thing, Khath. Don't you?"

Khath nodded. He did feel some relief. And what Pra Chhay had said was worth thinking about. It was the first time the monk had offered a religious teaching that Khath felt was even remotely comforting. Maybe Pra Chhay was slowly figuring things out, too.

----

Sandwiched between Khath and Pra Chhay in the back seat of Father Ralph's sedan, Sareth listened with growing dismay to Teresa chattering on about the party she was helping Phally organize for the monk and his brother. Chea would be furious to be left out of the planning for a community event like this. The insult to her position was intolerable. Did these Americans have no sense of protocol at all?

Thankfully, Pra Chhay and his brother were each gazing out the car's side windows. They seemed entranced by the passing farmlands and paid no attention to the rapid-fire English conversation between Father Ralph and Teresa. And with the road noise of the car muffling the clarity of the conversation, Sareth doubted that the two newcomers understood more than a word here and there. At least he was spared the indignity of public embarrassment.

"Phally is so worried about Nary," Teresa was saying. "Being taken so young by the Khmer Rouge, then living in a refugee camp, now being in America. She's afraid Nary will totally forget all the good things about Cambodian culture."

"I'm sure it's a valid concern," Father Ralph said.

"And now that Pra Chhay is here, he can start some culture classes and teach the kids some traditional morals. She's so grateful to have a monk who can serve the community." Teresa paused and Sareth watched a flush creep up her neck. Finally, the woman had stopped talking long enough to actually hear what she was saying.

"Oh. I mean, of course she's grateful for all the help you've given her as well. I'm so sorry. I said that poorly. I didn't mean to suggest…" Teresa's apology was cut short by Father Ralph's laughter.

"No offense taken. I completely understand, and I agree. I have been at a loss trying to tend to the spiritual needs of the refugees. We are very lucky to have Pra Chhay joining our community."

Resentment tinged with anxiety tightened the muscles of Sareth's upper back and neck. As he had feared, the priest was eager to pull Pra Chhay into a leadership role in the community. The question was, how much would his own role be diminished by this newcomer? And how could he, Sareth, set the parameters for how the power would be divided?

Beside him, Sareth felt Khath shift in the seat and watched how the man's hands writhed in his lap like the coils of two entwined snakes. Perhaps Khath was the answer to his dilemma. Clearly, the monk was devoted to his brother. And Khath was in an unstable state of mind. The more unstable Khath was, the more time Pra Chhay would spend watching out for him and the less he would be able to involve himself in the community. Sareth decided to focus his energy on getting to understand Khath, to ferret out his strengths and weaknesses. And then, he would see.

Father Ralph slowed the car. Up ahead on the two lane highway, a tractor pulling a load of hay lumbered across the road. Father Ralph raised his voice and turned his face slightly to the rear. "Mr. Sareth, have you been following what Teresa is talking about? This welcome party for the newcomers? We need your input."

Finally. At least Father Ralph gave him his due. Sareth leaned forward to join the conversation. "I picked up a phrase or two," he replied. "Though, of course it was not my intention to eavesdrop."

Teresa turned sideways in her seat to include Sareth in the conversation. "Phally has recruited several of the women to help her cook," Teresa said. She began listing the menu.

Sareth nodded, his mind working furiously. He had to find a place for Chea in all this organizing. Something where she could be in charge, wield some influence. But it would never do to insert her into the culinary doings. He could imagine eager hands snatching food from the trays prepared by other women, while Chea's sat barely touched. She would be shamed, humiliated.

No, cooking was not Chea's forte. Her tray would be beautifully arranged, attractive and disappointing in taste. She lacked a talent for blending the intricate flavors of spices and herbs, and had no interest in learning. Sareth credited that disinterest with helping him avoid the paunch of middle age, for it was rare that he was ever tempted to over-indulge in a home cooked meal, no matter how appealing it looked. And there, he realized, was the answer.

"Chea is very artistic," he blurted. "She has quite a talent for arranging things nicely."

Teresa stopped in mid-sentence and looked at him.

Sareth cleared his throat. "What I mean to say is that she could be in charge of decoration."

"Decoration?" Teresa said. "The party will be at Phally's house. I'm not sure what sort of decoration is required."

"Well, let's think this through, Teresa," Father Ralph said. "You need a place to hold a ceremony of sorts, right? Didn't you say Phally wanted Pra Chhay to do some chanting and give some blessings? Her house won't be large enough to hold all the food, plus have room for 50 folks to sit and meditate."

Teresa drummed her fingers on the dashboard. "You're right," she said. "I didn't think of that. There really isn't room in Phally's house. She'll be so disappointed. Could we do all the ceremonial activities in the church hall and then come over to Phally's?"

"I have a better idea," Father Ralph said. "One of my parishioners owns the Ford car dealership in town. I believe he has one of those tents for outdoor events. It's plenty big enough. We could pitch it in back of Phally's house, and warm it up with some heaters if the weather turns nasty. We do the ceremonies there, and set up the food tables and some seating inside Phally's house. Folks will group up to eat inside and out. It should work nicely. Plus it will give the kids a safe play space and get them out of harm's way when the ceremony is over."

"A splendid plan," Sareth said, feeling a surge of gratefulness toward Father Ralph. Whether he realized it or not, the priest had just performed a small miracle in saving face for Chea and him. "My wife will do a wonderful job creating the perfect backdrop for the ceremonies. I can assure you it will be quite beautiful when she is done with it."

"What a good idea. It's actually a great fit," Teresa said. "Gail was doing interior design work before the accident. She can put together some design ideas and Chea can help her set it all up for the party. They can get it all planned out during Chea's visits."

Sareth smiled. "How very fortunate." He looked at the men sharing the back seat of the car with him. "And now, shall I let our guests of honor in on the secret?"

———————

When Khath heard Mr. Sareth's announcement, he felt a momentary flush of pleasure for Pra Chhay. It was a nice gesture, appropriate, for the community to welcome his brother with a party. Khath knew full well that he was being included by default. He hoped they wouldn't make a big deal over him. He much preferred to stay out of the limelight. Putting a pleased expression on his face, he let the conversation flow around him while he settled back into his own thoughts.

Would he find his daughters today? It was possible. The Red Cross officer might type his girls' names into the computer and say, "Ah, here we go. Yes, they are in..." and name some town on the other side of America. Or, maybe even on the other side of the world. The Red Cross was working hard to reunite children and parents through a special program, the official had told them in Thailand. Maybe they would take his information and then call him in a day or two with the happy news.

But what if they didn't? What if the news was not happy at all? What if there simply was no news? He had to be prepared for disappointment as well as joy. But he knew his girls were alive. He believed fiercely that he would feel it, know it, if they were dead. They had to be alive. Hope and fear collided in his chest, making his breath shallow and his hands alternately sweaty and icy cold. He tucked them between his thighs and flicked his eyes toward Pra Chhay, nodding cheerily at him. His jaw ached from maintaining a pleasant half smile on his face.

Round and round his thoughts twirled, like a dog chasing its tail. Khath's mouth was dry. He felt slightly dizzy. Would they never arrive at their destination? They were nearing the city. Traffic was heavy now, and buildings began to crowd out the trees and farms. Just when Khath felt he could not sit in the car a moment longer, he realized in a panic that he would never be able to raise his body from the car seat. Fear kept him rooted, immobile. He was not ready to hear what the Red Cross might tell him. He would never be ready.

"We're here," Father Ralph announced, turning into an underground parking lot.

Teresa turned in her seat and looked at Khath. "Are you okay?" she asked. "Ready?" Her voice was gentle, eyes steady, direct, calm.

Khath remembered Pra Chhay's words from the morning—*Look at the eyes. See the goodness*—and was seized by a thought: How strange it is that we Cambodians are taught to avoid eye contact, taught to look down as a sign of respect. Perhaps if we'd really looked at one another, seen one another, the war would not have happened as it did. And he would not be sitting in this car. He took a deep breath and nodded his head. "Okay," he said, reaching for the door handle.

Their footsteps echoed in the corridor as they followed the receptionist to a room on the far end of the building. Father Ralph and Sareth went first, with Pra Chhay, then Khath, following. Teresa brought up the rear.

As they entered the office, it became immediately clear that they were not all going to fit inside at once. The room was dense with stacks of paper cluttering the tops of three filing cabinets, and a large desk took up much of the floor space. Two straight-backed chairs faced the desk, and a woman, also large, sat behind it.

"I'll wait outside," Teresa said, and Khath felt a sense of loss as the click of her heels faded away. He was beginning to believe that Teresa was a friend, and that he could trust her to help him if she could. He had been heartened to see her in the car this morning, and it seemed like an ill omen that she was forced to leave at the moment when he most needed a friend by his side. It was a bad way to start out.

Following Pra Chhay, Khath crowded with his brother against the rear wall of the office. It felt good to have something solid against his back. Sareth and Father Ralph sat in the chairs, ready to provide documents and information to the Red Cross worker.

The woman smiled a toothy smile and squeezed around the corner of her desk to shake hands, causing a general shuffle as Father Ralph and Sareth jumped up again, their chairs scooting backwards and pinning Khath and Pra Chhay against the wall. The woman took Khath's hand and pumped it firmly. Her hand was soft, plump and moist, which was good because Khath's own palms were now hot and sweaty. She didn't try to shake Pra Chhay's hand, instead giving him a brief nod, her hands clasped under her nose. Khath found this small display of cultural knowledge very reassuring. Maybe things would work out after all.

After everyone was settled again, the woman began speaking with Father Ralph and Sareth, dividing her attention between them and the computer on her desk. Khath tried to read the expressions that rippled across her face. Was it going well? Now she seemed to be asking questions and typing the answers into her computer. It all seemed to be very routine, as far as Khath could tell. He wasn't sure if that was good or bad. He wished his English was better so he could understand what was happening.

Finally, Sareth turned to him. "She wants you to give a brief history of your family life before the war. Where you lived, your daily activities, pets, anything unique about your family. She said they use these facts to verify the identity of people who might respond to the bulletin she will send out about your daughters."

"Verify?" Khath asked. "You mean someone might claim to be my child when they are not?"

Sareth translated and listened to the woman's reply. "She says it happens all the time. People are so desperate to get out of the camps, they'll try to bluff their way out any way they can."

Khath nodded. Of course. People like Mith pretending to be a Christian convert. He mentioned Sitha's star-shaped birthmark, and how her big sister Kamala would make up beautiful stories about stars when Sitha cried because someone teased her about the mark on her ankle.

Sareth translated but the woman shook her head and spoke for several minutes, clarifying. "She wants something more current, now that the girls are grown," Sareth said, turning in his chair to explain to Khath. "She is concerned that they might not remember things so far back in their childhood."

A terrible coldness jolted Khath's heart. "But the girls are not grown," he whispered. "They are just children. They were nine and seven when I last saw them." He watched with dread as a strained expression came over the large woman's face.

"What about the special program for finding lost children?" Khath said. "Ask her, Mr. Sareth. What is the trouble here? What about that program?" His voice boomed and cracked, no longer in his control.

Khath felt Pra Chhay place a restraining hand on his arm. "Slowly, brother. Slowly," the monk said.

With a sense of despair, Khath watched as the woman's expression became regretful, she held her hands out, palms up in a gesture that implied there was nothing she could do, that it was out of her hands.

Mr. Sareth and Father Ralph both nodded and then spoke insistently, rapidly. What were they saying? Khath's fists balled with impotent rage. With the last shred of control he had, he stepped up to the desk, interrupting the flow of conversation and staring boldly into three sets of startled eyes. "Mr. Sareth," he said. "These are my daughters you are discussing. You need to tell me what is going on right now."

"Yes, of course," Sareth said. "I do apologize." He turned to Father Ralph and spoke rapidly.

"Khath, I'm sorry. Please," Father Ralph gestured vaguely in Khath's direction and said something to Mr. Sareth.

"He says you were standing so silently and politely he quite forgot you were there," Sareth explained.

They are stalling, Khath thought. Whatever it is, it is so bad they don't want to tell me.

Sareth took a deep breath. He nodded toward the Red Cross Officer. "We have just been informed that the Unaccompanied Minors program is no longer in existence."

Khath gasped and clutched the desk for support.

Mr. Sareth forged ahead. "I'm sorry to have to tell you that it was disbanded shortly after you left the camp. Within days, actually. What Father Ralph and I are doing now is trying to ensure that all available measures will still be taken to find your daughters."

"And what will those measures be?" Khath asked, holding himself rigid, bracing for more bad news.

"Well, unfortunately it puts some responsibility on your daughters for finding you as well," Sareth said. "They will need to register with the Red Cross that they are searching for you, and then possibly a match will be found. I'm sorry, Khath. It may take many years."

Khath felt his eyes brim with tears that spilled down his cheeks when he tried to blink them away. Without the special program, who would bother to tell his girls to register with the Red Cross?

The woman behind the desk spoke up, a hopeful sound to her voice.

"She says that shortly after the camps were opened, a plane load of unaccompanied children was shipped off to foster homes in France. She can notify that group at least, and see if there were others. You brought your picture, didn't you? She can make a copy of that to send along with the inquiry."

Silently, Khath handed over the photo. It was no use. He turned and walked out of the office, down the long corridor, past Teresa in the lobby. He needed to get away from this place of false hope. Dimly, he was aware that Pra Chhay and Teresa walked with him, but no words were spoken. He could not have responded anyway.

A heavy silence lay over the car for most of the drive home. Khath closed his eyes and leaned against the window. His mind was drained, his thoughts a muddy pile not worth sorting through. Though he was content to exist in this bleary state, he was startled into alertness when a sharp sound punched through, jolting his brain. Someone had said "No!"

He opened his eyes and watched Teresa bouncing around in the front seat, waving her arms, talking with great passion. She pointed to herself and then shook her finger at Father Ralph until he slowly nodded his head and began to speak, softly and slowly at first and then with greater emphasis. She swung round to Mr. Sareth and pointed at him until he too began to nod his head. Finally, she gestured toward Khath. "Tell him," she commanded.

Mr. Sareth chuckled. He turned to Khath. "It seems your tutor is a very determined woman," he said. "She is going to help you find your girls. She says we don't need the Red Cross, that we can write our own letters. And she is right. Father Ralph can get lists of the churches who have accepted refugees. We all have friends and relatives who have resettled in other cities. And I suspect Miss Teresa will think of other ways as well."

Khath looked up at Teresa. She was smiling and nodding at him. A bit of the chill left his heart.

"Okay, Khath?" Teresa said. "We will try, okay? We will start tomorrow."

Khath felt drawn into Teresa's eager, shining eyes. Such good eyes. It seemed dishonest to lift the corners of his mouth in a smile when his heart still cowered in his chest, afraid to hope, almost afraid to beat. But he could nod. "Okay," he said.

# Sixteen

Khath studied his living room, frowning. The coffee table looked cluttered, its dents and scratches strategically covered with cups, paper napkins, a plate of fruit and graham crackers, and a pad of lined paper. The room's one lamp, perched on an overturned box as close to the couch as its cord would allow, cast a dim circle of light that barely illuminated one end of the table. He had tucked a blanket over the worst of the stains and frayed edges of the couch, but still the room and its furnishings looked makeshift and shabby. Khath opened the curtains wide, but it was a cloudy day and little light came through.

It was no use. He would have to move the couch and coffee table. Bending, he lifted the corner of the couch and dragged it closer to the lamp, then did the same with the coffee table, careful not to dislodge any of the items set out on the surface. It gave the room a skewed look to have everything bunched over in one corner, but it couldn't be helped.

Pra Chhay came into the room. "Why are you moving the furniture?"

"We need more light to work on the letters."

"Right," Pra Chhay said. He looked around. "I have a cloth we can use to cover that box under the lamp. It will look nicer."

He disappeared for a moment and returned with a brightly patterned piece of blue cotton that he arranged under the lamp.

"Don't worry, Khath. She knows we've just arrived. Be glad there is a couch for her to sit upon. Americans don't seem to sit on the floor very well."

Nodding, Khath rubbed his hands on his shirt nervously. He didn't have much to offer his guest. He hoped she wouldn't be insulted. He was worried, too, that he might do something rude or break a cultural taboo by accident. It was a mistake to have Teresa come here. They should have met at the church.

"Sugar," he exclaimed. "She might want sugar instead of sweetened milk in her tea."

Khath rushed off to the kitchen, searching for something to pour a bit of sugar into. It would look bad to set the entire ten-pound sack on the floor next to the coffee table. He may have been forced to live like an animal for the past six years, but he wasn't a savage.

He rattled around in the kitchen for a bit, and when he returned, sugar in hand, Pra Chhay was just greeting Teresa at the door with a low bow. She was carrying a box, but when Khath hurried forward to take it from her, she shook her head, laughed and said, "It's not heavy."

Teresa followed Pra Chhay into the room and glanced around, her gaze coming to rest on the coffee table with its pens and pad of paper. "Here?" she asked.

Khath nodded, eyes downcast, feeling shame. At least the house was clean, as clean as a day of scrubbing and sweeping could make it.

Teresa sat down on one end of the couch, placing the box on the floor beside her. She folded her hands in her lap, then looked up and smiled.

Khath stood silently, shyness making him mute. The room felt uncomfortably intimate with its dim lighting. He needed this to go well, needed Teresa's help to search for Kamala and Sitha, but all he could think of was how shabby and wrong the setting felt. Beside him, Pra Chhay cleared his throat. "Would you like some tea, Miss Teresa?"

"I would love some," Teresa said, as if tea were the answer to all her prayers.

Khath hurried into the kitchen to fetch the thermos of hot water and some tea bags. He was so glad that Pra Chhay was here, calmly gliding in to fill the gaping void in his own manners.

Why hadn't he offered Miss Teresa tea himself? His brain felt paralyzed, unable to think, his jaw clenched. From the corner of his eye he watched Pra Chhay set the fruit and cookies in front of Teresa.

Khath took a deep breath. Why couldn't he just rise to the occasion like Pra Chhay? Look at him, sitting down on the other end of the couch from Teresa, smiling and nodding. One would think the monk entertained foreign women in his home all the time.

Calmer now, Khath returned to the living room. He could do better than this. Sitting on the floor across from Teresa, he lifted the corners of his mouth in a strained smile. "You like cookies?" he asked. He had not been sure what type to buy.

"Very good," Teresa said, swallowing. She leaned forward and touched his hand briefly. "Khath, how are you?"

Khath raised his eyes and found he could not lower them. She was looking at him, directly into his eyes like Americans did, and though he should have felt embarrassed, he felt oddly soothed. He trusted those eyes, and felt his tension melt away. It was all right.

Teresa was his teacher. The shabby room, the chipped cups, none of it mattered. Khath realized that now and felt ashamed of himself for thinking otherwise. She was still waiting for his answer.

How was he? "I am happy," he said, surprised to find that, in this moment, this was true. It had been so long that he almost hadn't recognized the emotion.

A huge smile washed over Teresa's face. "Shall we get to work finding your girls, then?" she said, and opened up the box beside her.

First, she pulled out a small lamp and an extension cord. "Do you think we need this?" she asked, handing it to Khath. "I didn't know if you already had a work light." She spoke slowly and clearly to help him understand.

Khath nodded and set up the lamp. To his surprise, it emitted a very bright light from its tiny bulb. He turned it off and picked it up to examine it more closely for a moment. "It makes very much light," he said. "Thank you for bring."

Next Teresa pulled out a stack of envelopes and several pages of what looked like addresses. A roll of stamps followed, and a clean pad of paper. With Pra Chhay's help and the use of a Cambodian/English dictionary, Teresa's plan was made clear.

Father Ralph had given her the contact names and addresses of all the Catholic churches across the country that had resettled Cambodian refugees. She and Khath would compose a letter explaining the situation, along with copied photos of Khath and his girls, and ask if anyone had resettled any girls who might be Khath's daughters. Father Ralph and Khath would both sign the letters.

"This is just the start," she said. "We can get lists from other churches. The Baptists resettled a lot of people, too. And we can send letters to government agencies. Khath, maybe you can address the envelopes. It will be good English practice for you." She drew the shape of an envelope on the pad. "Let's practice. Try one." She handed the typed address list to Khath and pushed the pad toward him.

Khath studied the list. Carefully, he printed out the lines of type onto Teresa's drawing of an envelope, and then slid it across the table for Teresa's inspection.

"You have beautiful handwriting," Teresa said. "Better than mine. Look how your letters are all so evenly sized. Where did you learn to write so nicely?"

"In my country, I study machines, how to fix, all the pieces, the names, in English and Cambodian," Khath said. "Draw a picture. Write the names."

"Like a draftsman?" Teresa asked. She wrote the word on the pad and Pra Chhay looked it up in the dictionary.

"Yes," Pra Chhay confirmed. "Like that. But…" he flipped the pages of the dictionary again, and then pointed out a different word. "Then he worked, like this."

"Mechanic," Teresa read aloud. "That's great." She wrote it down. "Did you fix cars?"

"Not cars. Trains. Later, army trucks and other things."

Teresa pulled a sheet of paper out of a file folder from the bottom of the box. "Father Ralph gave me this," she said. "It's the information he got from the camps about you." She slid it across the table. "Is it correct? The town names and dates are important. Someone might remember you or your family."

Khath studied the paper and nodded. "It is correct."

Pointing to some words scrawled in pencil at the bottom of the page, Teresa asked, "What does this mean? Is it important?"

Pra Chhay leaned forward. "I think, for this letter, it is not important, Miss Teresa."

Khath watched Teresa absorb Pra Chhay's words. She did not seem satisfied, and all at once Khath wanted very badly to tell her about those words. "Very big Khmer Rouge prison," he blurted out. "A very bad place. Many people die. Khmer Rouge hurt them so bad. Then kill them. Smash them. Throw them all in hole, one, then another." Khath held out his hand, palm down, then slapped his other hand on top of it, and continued alternating hands, one, then another, to show how the bodies piled up.

"Oh," Teresa said, her expression tense. "Father Ralph told me about this." She raised her hand as if to stop Khath. "Pra Chhay is right. It is not important for this letter."

But Khath could not stop. She had to hear, had to understand. "Khmer Rouge make me work there, fix things. I did not want to. But they kill me if I say no. All night, I hear people cry. I want them stop it. Sometime I want to die too. I cannot bear it. They cry and cry, pain so bad."

Khath lifted his hands and covered his ears, squeezing his eyes shut. When he continued, his voice felt flat, drained. "Then one day when I wake, it is very quiet. Too much quiet. Everyone gone. Khmer Rouge forget about me. I don't know what happen. So I leave, too. Go back to train station." Khath looked down at his hands, clenched tightly in his lap. With an effort, he relaxed them.

"I found him there," Pra Chhay said. "When he was strong again, we began to look for Sitha and Kamala."

"Nary and Sitha, the same," Khath said, looking up. "Same age, both go to Khmer Rouge work camp. Sometime I think, 'Nary is my child?' But this I know not true. Just hope." He dug in his pocket, pulled out his wallet and carefully removed the photograph of him and his girls. "My Sitha, she have mark on her leg, a star for Sitha." He pointed to the little girl's birthmark. "Nary, she don't have. But I think, Nary not die in Khmer Rouge camp. My girls, they can live too."

It was late afternoon when they finished composing the letter, and Teresa suggested they drive to the church to make copies of Khath's photo. Emerging into the dusk from the back of the church afterward, Khath gestured toward the open fields.

"I go home now," he said. "I can walk. By car, it is long. This way, not far."

Teresa's gaze followed the direction of his hand, and then she said, "What's that?"

Khath looked, and saw a figure dart from the trees at the far end of the field and run along one of the paths crisscrossing the area. The small form occasionally glanced over a shoulder, as if fearing pursuit, hands reaching forward, stumbling at times. At each trail junction, the runner hesitated and then plunged randomly forward along a new trail, as if lost or confused.

"It's a child," Teresa said. "He seems frightened."

A moment later, the child fell, then sat in the dirt and began to wail, pounding the earth with clenched fists.

Khath's breath caught in his throat. He knew that voice. "Nary," he whispered. *Sitha,* his heart cried.

———

Phally cleaned carefully around the pictures on her fireplace mantel, then paused for a moment to contemplate Boran's face. He would be proud of her, she thought, making her way in this new country.

"Is that your husband?" Gail had rolled up beside her in her sports chair, finally finished with diagramming the interior of Phally's house to help with planning the party decorations. She was out practice, and it had taken her longer than she expected.

Phally smiled, remembering how difficult it had been getting Gail and her chair up the steps into her house. She and Chea had argued about how best to accomplish the task. In the end, she had insisted Chea hold two planks steady to form a ramp up the stairs while she pushed and Gail worked the wheels of the chair. Now Chea was gone and Gail was waiting for Teresa to come pick her up. Going down the ramp would surely be easier.

Phally took the framed picture down and handed it to Gail. "Yes, Boran, my husband. He a good man. Some Cambodia man, not so good. They beat their wife, children, too much." Phally shook her head. "Boran don't do like that. Very good man. He like take care me, Nary."

"I wish I could have met him," Gail said. "I'm sorry that he died."

"Khmer Rouge take him to forest one day. Later, we find many bodies there. Khmer Rouge lie. They say, 'We take you go work in forest.' But Khmer Rouge kill them all."

Feeling suddenly tired, Phally looked once more at the photo in her hand. It needed cleaning. The frame's glass had a smear on it and something was smudging the black lacquer frame. Perhaps Nary had picked it up with dirty hands? Phally set the photo back on the mantle.

Come to think of it, where was Nary? Phally frowned. The child had told her this morning that she would be late getting home because of some special activity her teacher had planned, but Phally had expected her by now. Maybe she would ask Gail or Teresa to call the school if Nary didn't arrive before dark.

Turning to Gail, she smiled and said, "Your sister come here soon. I make tea now." She took two steps toward the kitchen, then turned back and retrieved the picture of Boran. Better bring it into the kitchen and set it by the sink as a reminder to clean it this evening, or she might forget.

A few minutes later, Phally heard a car pull up outside. She went to the door and opened it, smiling as Teresa stepped from her car. But Phally could see the shape of someone else in the back seat. Had Chea returned? Looking more closely, Phally's jaw fell open at the sight of the monk's brother emerging from the car carrying Nary. She rushed to the car as the man gently set Nary on her feet. The child stood swaying for a moment, her face tear-stained.

"Nary, child, are you hurt?" A wave of fear for her child swept over her. She put a protective arm around the girl and faced Khath. "What has happened?" She led them inside, her hands running over her daughter's body, searching for cuts, blood, bumps, clues to what had transpired.

Nary stood passively under her touch, then muttered, "I want to go to bed."

"Are you ill, little mouse?" Phally murmured.

Nary shook her head.

"Then maybe a warm bath first?" Phally coaxed. "And then I will bring you something to eat and rub your back until you sleep. All right, mouse?"

Nary nodded, and Phally walked her to the bathroom, her hand resting on the girl's shoulder, so bony under her fingers. Phally's heart trembled, but she knew better than to press her daughter for answers now. Only when Nary was ready would she talk. She ran the bath water and gently peeled Nary's clothing off, relieved not to find any serious marks or injuries.

With her daughter in the tub, Phally returned to the living room to find that Gail and Teresa had made and served tea.

"Is she all right, Phally?" Gail asked.

"Yes, she not hurt, but not talk."

Phally turned to Khath. Without her having to ask, he quickly told her in their native tongue what he and Teresa had seen.

"But why was she so afraid?" Phally asked.

Khath sighed. "This I don't quite understand. She said the teachers made them go outside to where they were blindfolding the children and swinging clubs. Why would they do that at school? Is it a punishment?"

Phally looked horrified. "Blindfolding children? At school?" She shuddered. Being blindfolded in Cambodia meant you were going to die. "Your English is better than mine. Ask them. Maybe it is their custom?"

Khath smiled sadly. "I cannot explain it. I hoped never to have to learn such words here," he said. "Do you have a paper and pencil? I can draw it to make it more clear."

Phally watched Khath draw a picture of what Nary had described, her thoughts drifting while the words flowed around her and over her.

Anxiously, she recalled Nary's tear-stained face, her thin body sliding into the tub, sucking in her breath with pain when the hot water met the scraped areas on her knees. It was so unlike her tough daughter to show pain, to cry. Whatever had happened at school today had shaken the child to her core.

A silence had fallen. Phally turned her attention to these new friends sitting around her. They all stared silently at the picture Khath had drawn, their brows furrowed.

Then Gail said, "A piñata. It's a piñata."

"Oh my God, that must be it," Teresa said.

Gail turned to Phally. "It's a game," she explained. "There's a, a, like a ball filled with candy. The children try to break the ball with the stick, so the candy falls out and they can eat it." She turned to Teresa. "We better call the school so they know that Nary is safe here. Her teacher is probably frantic."

Phally sat, her head spinning. A game. A simple child's game had sent her little mouse scurrying for cover. Oh, Nary. How can you survive in this world with such innocent terrors lurking around every corner? Phally dropped her head into her hands.

She heard Khath speak to Gail and Teresa. "Nary say Khmer Rouge do like that to her father when they kill him. She say she watch them do this."

What? Phally raised her head. "No," she said. It seemed important that her husband's death be honored truthfully. "Not like that. Khmer Rouge no..." she mimed tying a blindfold around her head. "Nary make mistake. So many people die like that. Not Boran."

# Seventeen

Phally stood near the living room window, a deep satisfaction welling up from within her as she viewed the activity in and around her home. Home. Not since the fighting in Cambodia had begun had she had felt such a secure sense of community and belonging. And this party for the monk, Pra Chhay, was solidifying the small Cambodian community like nothing else had in the six months she'd been here.

And not just the Cambodians. Teresa and Father Ralph were out doing more grocery shopping for the party, and Mr. Sareth would be here in an hour to direct Father Ralph's friends in the placement and setting up of the big tent in the back yard. The priest said that many of the church ladies and town leaders were planning to attend the party to extend a formal welcome to the refugees.

Phally would make sure that no one left hungry. The thunk of chopping knives against cutting boards, punctuated by bursts of laughter and chitchat, drifted out from the kitchen as her Cambodian neighbors cut up bushels of vegetables for curries, egg rolls and stir fries.

"S'cuse me!"

Phally grinned and stepped back as Gail flew by on her sports chair. Zipping from room to room, a pad of paper in her lap and a pencil tucked behind her ear, Gail held one end of a measuring tape while Chea trotted after her, her brow furrowed and hair askew, trying to keep up. From the looks of it, two dainty feet unaccustomed to hurrying were no match for four rubber wheels.

Stifling a laugh at the sight of Chea's flushed cheeks and rumpled clothing, Phally offered to help.

"Chea, you look out of breath and in need of a rest. I can help Miss Gail if you'd like a break." Phally tried to speak respectfully, but it was difficult. Chea was dressed in a silk sarong and shiny shirt, as though she'd expected to be supervising this job, rather than getting her own hands dirty. Well, if anyone could knock those superior attitudes out of her, it was Gail. Phally had noticed that Gail didn't *grant* respect to anyone. If you wanted Miss Gail's respect, you had to earn it.

A tight smile lifted the corners of Chea's mouth, but her eyes smoldered. "How kind of you to offer, but there is no need," she replied. "I am quite happy to be Miss Gail's assistant." Chea was a scant quarter inch taller than Phally yet somehow she managed to look down her nose at the older woman. "I'm sure you are aware that most of the fabrics we will use to decorate your house come from my personal collection. Naturally, I should be the one to advise Miss Gail on their use."

"Of course," Phally said. "You've been very generous to lend your things." Phally stared coolly back into Chea's eyes, something she would never have dared to do in Cambodia. The rules have changed, Chea, she thought. And I like these new rules much more than the old ones.

Across the room, Gail gave a sudden, playful tug on the tape measure, causing the end of it to fly out of Chea's hand. Chea gasped and scrambled after the slithering tape. Gail looked at Phally and winked, then rolled sedately toward a pile of fabrics on the couch with Chea in tow.

Going to the kitchen, Phally inspected plates of precision-cut vegetables, covering some with wrap and putting them in the refrigerator and dumping others into large pots on the stove. The vegetable cutters had been hard at it for more than an hour without a break, so Phally brought two large bottles of cola from the pantry and poured glasses all around. She found a box of cookies and shook a dozen or so onto a plate, setting them into the center of the table. She chatted for a few minutes and thanked the women for their help, then got a tray and poured two more glasses of cola and fixed a small plate of cookies. It was time to feed the carpenters.

Phally stepped out to the porch, leaving the door open behind her. The sun shone brightly, but its warmth did not penetrate the shadows. She stood quietly, watching the scene in front of her. Since Khath and Teresa had brought a shaken Nary home two days ago, Khath had set about building a wheelchair ramp from the sidewalk to Phally's porch, and Nary was helping him.

No doubt he'd been horrified at the steep and unsteady planks Phally had laid over the porch steps to get Gail into the house earlier that day. In fact, when it came time to help Gail back to Teresa's car, he'd stopped, shaken his head, turned to Gail and said, "I carry, okay?" Then without waiting for an answer, he'd stooped down and hoisted Gail up as easily as if she'd been a feather and carried her to the car.

And why not? During the Khmer Rouge time, he surely had lifted heavier loads than Gail even when he was half dead from starvation. Carrying Gail must have seemed like a simple solution to a small problem. Phally wondered what it would feel like to be carried in those arms, and quickly pushed the thought away.

Now, Khath stood, shirtless in the warm sun, his back to Phally, bent over a small plank on a makeshift sawhorse, cutting the wood with a hand saw. Phally watched the muscles rippling under the scars that crisscrossed his back. She'd seen scars like that before, fresh ones. And she had tended to the festering and bleeding wounds on more than one man beaten by the Khmer

Rouge with bundles of wire that tore at the flesh with every stroke. Not all of them survived such a beating. She pressed her lips together. She would not think of those things now. She would not spoil this lovely day with thoughts of death and torture.

Where was Nary? Phally glanced around and saw her half hidden behind Khath's body, crouching near the end of the ramp, busily sanding the wood smooth. Khath had taken a block of wood and wrapped sandpaper partially around it, nailing the edges to the sides of the wood block so Nary's hands were protected from the paper and she had a larger sanding surface to work with.

As Phally watched, Khath paused in his sawing, and Nary looked up at him. He nodded at her, and murmured something, and a small smile curved the girl's lips upwards.

Conflicting emotions battered Phally's heart at the sight of Nary's smile. She was wary of the closeness that was developing between Khath and Nary. Should she allow it? Clearly, the girl trusted Khath. In fact, they seemed to share a bond that excluded her. And while she rejoiced to see her little mouse comforted and calmed by this man's presence, she wondered where it would lead. She knew Khath missed his own daughters terribly. What if he found them and left abruptly? How would Nary deal with yet another loss?

And yet, Khath was so kind to the child. Surely it would be wrong to deny Nary the benefits of his kindness, even if it was temporary. After all, everything in life was impermanent. That's what the Buddha taught.

And who knows? If Khath never found his girls—Phally felt shame at even acknowledging such harmful thoughts, yet her mind galloped on—if he never found them, he might stay. Phally's heart thumped a little faster and her cheeks grew warm. She should get to know this man, to see for herself if he was worthy of Nary's trust. Gripping the tray firmly, she stepped out of the shadows of the porch.

"You both must be thirsty, working in the sun like this," she said, walking down the new ramp toward Nary and Khath.

Khath smiled and put down his saw, then lifted his shirt from the end of the saw horse and slipped it on, covering his torso and buttoning one or two buttons.

Nice. It was just enough to show some respect in the presence of a woman, Phally thought. She liked a polite man. She offered him the tray, and he took a glass of cola and a handful of cookies, murmuring his thanks.

Nary jumped up, her eyes widening and a smile stretching her cheeks at the sight of these treats.

"Just two cookies, Nary," Phally said.

"But I'm working so hard, Mama. We are almost finished."

Phally smiled. "All right. Four." She looked more closely at the ramp, then turned to Khath. "The ramp is beautiful. Very strong. I think Miss Gail can come up it without even needing someone to push."

Khath nodded. "That was my hope as well. I studied the one she has at home so I could get the right slope. Luckily, your porch is not very high."

Pointing to the pile of cut wood pieces by the sawhorse, Phally asked, "And those? Where do they go?"

"They are just decoration. I'll show you." Khath gathered a handful of the pieces and brought them over. He crouched beside the ramp, arranging the pieces on top of its raised borders, forming a geometric design as he laid them out. "We will paint them in a pattern to match the trim and body color of your house. It was Miss Gail's idea. She wanted something nice for you. Do you like it?"

Khath was looking up at her from his crouched position, and Phally felt her heart clutch as her gaze brushed against his and was caught, snared. For a brief moment that seemed to stretch into eternity, she was unable to look away. How long had it been since her eyes had been captured by a man's gaze like this? How long since her heart had stirred with the tender flames of desire rather than the scorching heat of hatred or the icy grip of terror? Flustered, she dropped her eyes and turned slightly to study the design he had laid out, imagining how it would look painted. It would be beautiful to her, no matter what it looked like, a reminder that she had found friendship in a foreign land.

"I like it," she said. "I like it very, very much."

———————

Sareth put his signal on well before the turn and glanced in the rear view mirror to make sure the pick-up truck with the tent was following him. He was late. He was supposed to be at Phally's house 30 minutes ago, but someone at the dealership had misplaced the key to the storage shed where the tent was kept. He hated to be late, especially when it was someone else's ineptitude that caused the delay. Pulling up a few minutes later in front of the house, he waved the truck toward the driveway and watched as the man behind the wheel began a laborious process of turning and backing into the narrow drive. Four Cambodian men crouched in the bed of the truck, their waving hands directing the driver's efforts. I'd better give them plenty of room, he thought, and parked the car on the other side of the street.

As he waited for the engine to click and rattle its way to a complete stop, Sareth glanced out his window and was pleased to see Chea and Gail together on the front porch. He wanted that relationship to flourish for Chea's sake. Keeping one eye on the progress of the truck, he watched as Gail held one end of a tape measure while Chea, holding the other end, backed toward the edge of the porch. Too late, Sareth noticed Nary crouching in Chea's line of travel, pouring something into a pan. Neither was aware of the other, and Khath, bending over the ramp with a paintbrush in his hand, was paying no attention to anything except his work.

"Oh no," Sareth murmured. He jumped from the car to shout a warning. "Chea, look out!"

His timing could not have been worse. Chea whipped around toward the sound of his voice just as Nary stood up with the pan of paint. Chea's outstretched hand caught the edge of the paint pan, knocking one end loose from Nary's grasp, and despite the girl's best efforts to hang on, the pan tipped and splashed a thick streak of creamy white paint down the front of Chea's beautiful sarong.

For a moment, everyone froze and stared in horror at the mess ruining Chea's clothing. Then Chea shrieked. The door burst open and Sareth saw Phally appear in the doorway, looking panicky, just as Chea's face contorted with rage.

"Oh no, oh no," Sareth muttered. He saw the stiffness of Chea's spine and prayed that she would contain her anger long enough to let him reach the porch and take control of the situation. His breath wheezed as he hurried across the road, the tent forgotten.

"You worthless, worthless girl!" Chea screamed. "Look at what you've done." Her hand drew back, and she delivered a stinging slap to Nary's face.

Sareth threw dignity to the wind and flat out ran to stop his wife from making more of a spectacle of herself than she already had. But nothing could have prepared him for what happened next.

The child had staggered backwards from the force of Chea's slap, but now she gathered herself, and with a howl of pain and defiance, launched herself at Chea, her scrawny arms and clenched fists flailing as she punched at the woman.

Phally and Gail both rushed forward, but Khath was quicker still, springing onto the porch in a single agile leap, one strong arm encircling Nary's waist and lifting the child off the ground while the other pinioned her arms to her sides. He strode off the porch and around the corner of the house, the wailing child in his grip.

Sareth reached the porch and grasped Chea's arm, but to his shock and anger she wrenched free of him and turned furiously on Phally. "That girl is a menace," she snapped. "Running wild, attacking people. My clothes are ruined."

"You had no right to slap my child." Phally's voice was low, threatening, almost a growl. Sareth saw that her hands were clenched at her sides.

"Hey, hey now, we're all friends here." Gail rolled her chair between the two women, physically forcing them each to take a step back and creating a neutral zone between them.

"Indeed we are," Sareth said, in English, drawing himself up and trying not to pant. Turning to Chea, he again grasped her arm and pulled her to face away from the others, saying, "Let's take a look at the damage here. Perhaps it is not as bad as we first thought."

Then softly, but very sternly, he said in his native tongue, "Chea. You are behaving like the common villager you were before I lifted you out of that life. Have your years with me taught you nothing? Calm yourself at once before you ruin everything I have worked so hard to create for us here." His knuckles ached from the pressure he was exerting on her arm, but he did not loosen his grip until Chea closed her eyes, nodded once, and took a deep breath.

All right, now for the other one, Sareth thought. But when he turned back to deal with Phally, she was gone, and only Gail remained, sitting silently with her hands folded in her lap.

At Sareth's questioning look, she said, "Phally went to check on Nary."

"Of course," Sareth replied. "I hope the little girl is all right."

"She had a bad shock at school the other day," Gail said. "I think she just snapped when Chea…" Her voice trailed off.

"It appears there was a lot of snapping on this porch today," Mr. Sareth said with a rueful smile. "I am afraid my wife loves her pretty clothing more than she should."

"I can probably fix that for her," Gail said, gesturing at Chea's sarong. "I have all kinds of special cleaners at home. Interior designers end up cleaning up a lot of messes. It's just part of the job."

"Could you?" Mr. Sareth said. "I know how much it would mean to Chea. That particular sarong holds much sentimental value for her." This was turning out better than he'd expected it would.

Gail gave Chea a little nudge. "C'mon, Chea. Let's get you cleaned up." She nodded at Sareth and turned her chair.

"Miss Gail," Sareth said, striving for a tone that conveyed warmth and just a touch of humor. "I do apologize for all the drama. I suspect the women are tense, wanting things to go well at the party tomorrow."

# Eighteen

"Let me show you the tent," Gail said. "It's completely transformed."

Bouncing over the uneven lawn in her sports chair, Gail led Teresa into the back yard. Pausing in the entrance of the make-shift temple, she ushered her sister in with a sweep of her arm. "Ta da. You'd never know it was a used car sales tent, would you?"

"Wow," Teresa said. "No, you wouldn't."

Wide panels of glowing silk in complementary hues hung from rods between the vinyl windows of the tent. Cinched in with sashes at the midpoint, the fabric created a brilliant diamond pattern against the tent's white walls. Gail had arranged the darker silks toward the back of the tent, the lighter ones at the front. The effect was to pull one's eyes forward toward the altar, the centerpiece of the room.

"It's nice of Chea to lend all these fabrics," Teresa said.

"I think Mr. Sareth made her do it," Gail said. "I didn't realize it at first, but there's a lot riding on this party. Father Ralph wants to showcase his work and use it as a starting point to begin generating a few simple jobs for these folks. Plus, he's hoping it will settle things down in the community—there's been some weird tension among the refugees since Khath and

194

Pra Chhay arrived. Have you noticed?" Gail plucked a strand of lint off of one of the silk panels.

"I have," Teresa said. "Father Ralph is worried that Mr. Sareth's nose will get pushed out of joint with all the fuss over Pra Chhay. I helped him create the program for the ceremonies and he kept insisting that Mr. Sareth be given a big role and an important one."

"That, and this whole competition thing between Phally and Chea," Gail said. "I feel quite pulled between the two of them sometimes. Maybe if this event goes well, everyone will realize that Glenberg is big enough for all of them."

She pointed to two curved rows of padded folding chairs on either side of a center aisle. "That's where the townfolk will sit. The refugees will sit on the mats up front. Phally and Chea both insisted we let them sit on the floor, so they'd feel comfortable. I think it's the only thing they've agreed on today. Over here against the sides of the tent is overflow seating, and up by the podium the dignitaries can settle in."

Gail had hated to put the podium in but Father Ralph had insisted. "The mayor is coming to welcome the refugees," he had said. "He's going to need something to stand behind and hang on to when he sees all those brown faces and dark eyes staring at him."

Gail had laughed, but Father Ralph was serious. "He fought me on this project all the way," the priest had told her. "It's a huge step for him to make this gesture. We need to make sure he feels it was worth it." Then the priest had smiled. "I'm counting on Phally's egg rolls to help convince him."

Teresa's gaze drifted toward the altar. Swirls of scented smoke danced around slender joss sticks protruding from small silver bowls of rice along the altar's lowest tier. She moved closer and inhaled. "Sandalwood?" she asked.

Gail nodded. Reaching out, she brushed a few rice grains off the dark red fabric draped over the altar. Offerings of fruit and flowers were arranged on the lowest tier, along with the incense, tea candles and a line of seven silver bowls. On the top tier, gazing over the room through half-lowered eyelids, a gilt statue of the Buddha sat in a meditation posture on a traditional lotus pad, hands cradled in his lap with a serene half-smile curving his lips. More flowers—fresh, plastic and silk—cascaded over the edges of the altar, with a string of tiny twinkling lights woven throughout the blossoms and foliage.

Hearing voices approach, Gail turned her head and saw some townspeople peering into the tent uncertainly. "Show time," she said.

Thirty minutes later, the tent was full. Near the podium, Father Ralph was introducing Mayor Hancock to Mr. Sareth and Pra Chhay. Mr. Sareth must have coached the monk, for the introductions went off seamlessly with none of the mismatch between bowing and handshaking that often occurs when East meets West.

Nice compromise, Gail thought, as she watched the monk grasp the mayor's outstretched hand with both of his, managing a humble half-bow while still keeping his eyes trained on the mayor's face. Then Father Ralph, Mayor Hancock and Pra Chhay sat down, while Mr. Sareth stepped to the microphone.

"Welcome, friends and neighbors, and thank you all for coming to our gathering today. I am Mr. Sareth, the spokesman for Glenberg's Cambodian community, and I will provide interpretation for our program today." He spoke briefly in Cambodian to the refugees seated on the rush mats, and then turned the mike over to Father Ralph.

Gail's attention drifted during what she thought of as the back-patting portion of the ceremony. She had parked her chair along the edge of the tent, near the front and opposite to the podium, where she had a good view of the townsfolk, the refugees and the officials. She let her eyes rove over the seated Glenberg folk, curious to see who had come.

The ladies from the church auxiliary were out in full force, of course. And there was Mrs. Tibbets, her bulk spread out over two chairs. She was a latecomer to the refugee project, according to Teresa, but like all new converts to a cause, she was generous with her time and money. Most of the refugees could thank Mrs. Tibbets for the stocked pantries and furnished rooms they found upon first arriving in their new Glenberg homes.

Daniel Olsen, the lanky white-haired proprietor of Dan's Fountain and Grill, sat in the back row, "Too dang tall to sit anywhere else," as he liked to say. Teresa said Father Ralph had Dan targeted as a possible source of employment for the refugees. Same deal with the guy who was loaning them his tent today: Glen Kooney of Kooney Ford, where trade-ins were fair or hats would be eaten. Maybe Khath could get a job there detailing cars or something.

She shifted her gaze to the refugees sitting comfortably on the floor, the men with crossed legs, the women with their legs tucked to one side. Gail envied them their flexibility and strength. It took muscles to hop up effortlessly as she'd seen Phally do so gracefully.

Many of the women had tucked flowers into their hair. Most wore thin short-sleeved blouses with lace trim along with their best sarongs. Some had shawls tossed over their shoulders as well. Chea, as ever, was gorgeous. Her silky hair was swept back from her face and left loose to cascade down her back. Her tawny arms were encircled by heavy gold bracelets, and precious stones glittered on her fingers.

Gail wondered if the bracelets were positioned to cover bruises left by Sareth's fingers gripping his wife's arm on the porch the other day. She'd seen the man's knuckles grow white from the force of his grip and had been about to intervene when Chea had nodded submissively and been freed.

Phally stood at the rear of the tent, near the door, ready to rush out and serve the food the minute the service was over. Nary, standing by Phally's side caught Gail's eye and grinned, causing Gail's throat to tighten.

Those two, she thought. They crept right into my heart while I wasn't watching, and now they're there to stay, that's for sure.

She noticed the refugees all sit up a little straighter. Pra Chhay had stepped to the microphone, with Mr. Sareth standing off to one side, ready to assist with interpretation as needed.

Gail sat forward. Teresa had helped Pra Chhay write a short speech and had coached his pronunciation relentlessly. Would he pull it off?

The monk's voice was soft but confident.

"Hello. My name is Pra Chhay. I have been trained as a monk from childhood. My heart is full of grat-ti-tude." Pra Chhay's voice slowed as he struggled to wrap his tongue around the unfamiliar word. Gail saw the fingers of his left hand tapping out each syllable, making sure he enunciated them all.

That was a close one, Gail thought. She noticed how the townsfolk had leaned forward, as though willing Pra Chhay to spit the word out, almost like a sporting event.

"...at the kindness we refugees have received from the people of Glenberg." He stopped briefly to let Mr. Sareth translate for the Cambodians who, as a group, began nodding and swiveling their upper bodies to face the townsfolk, bowing their heads, hands clasped at the level of their noses. Glenberg's citizenry smiled and waved, seeming a little uncertain about how to respond to the refugees' tribute. A few of them awkwardly clasped their hands together too and bowed back. They're trying, Gail thought. That's nice.

With Mr. Sareth's help, Pra Chhay explained the prayers he would chant. "First, we will do a recitation, three times, of the Refuge Prayer. This prayer affirms our faith in the Buddha, the teachings and the community of practitioners. Then I will recite the Heart Sutra, which encourages one to look past the suffering of daily life and find meaning and peace beyond such things."

Mr. Sareth spoke briefly to Pra Chhay who nodded and stepped back from the podium. With a smile and a slight bow,

Mr. Sareth said, "Pra Chhay agrees with me that I should warn you that there will be some soft clapping of the hands during the Heart Sutra. This symbolizes steps along the path of going beyond our normal existence to find peace. Truly we are a humble people. We are not applauding ourselves." Mr. Sareth crinkled his eyes in a teasing manner and the citizens of Glenberg chuckled.

He's good, Gail thought. I wish I trusted him more. He's almost too good.

Pra Chhay approached a square cushion on the floor in front of the altar and stood behind it, his back to the audience. The refugees all stood up as well. As one, they began touching their clasped hands to forehead, nose and chest, then dropping to the floor and touching their foreheads to the mats. Three times they repeated this gesture of respect, and then resettled themselves on the floor while Pra Chhay took his place on the cushion, facing the audience now. The monk produced a small bell from somewhere within the folds of his robes and rang it three times, silencing it completely between each peal.

Gail was fascinated. It's all so precise, she thought.

Folding his hands together at chest level, Pra Chhay began to chant. One by one, all the refugees joined in until soon, the tones of their chanting swelled and filled the tent. Most of the Cambodians closed their eyes as they prayed, some swayed to the subtle variations in tone and rhythm that swirled about them like an ocean current.

Closing her eyes, Gail felt soothed by the ebb and flow of the chants. "I'm glad I don't know the words," she thought. She felt her muscles relax, her brain unwind. She felt as though tonal vibrations were passing straight through her body. Maybe they were. The chanting had a drone-like quality to it that made her think of bees buzzing in a sunlit field. The soft claps, three of them, popped her eyes open quickly enough to see several of the townsfolk jerk in their seats, glance around and smile at their neighbors.

Gail was disappointed that the chanting ended so soon, but she was also hungry. As she watched, the Cambodians hung back and let the townspeople leave the tent first, then just as they'd planned about half of the folding chairs were scooped up by the men and carried into the house to supplement Phally's meager seating.

Gail let the crowd thin out before wheeling herself around to the new ramp at the front of the house. It was getting dark now, but she had no trouble navigating her way. She paused for a minute on the porch, looking through the windows into the brightly lit living room.

A throng of people, plates and utensils in hand, crowded around the food tables in the center of the room. Everyone was smiling, pointing at particularly attractive platters of vegetables, meat and curries, heaping their plates and choosing seats. Father Ralph and Teresa stood by the kitchen door, darting in to retrieve empty dishes and replace them with full ones.

It's perfect, Gail thought. Exotic foods to sample, a new experience to chat about. This is going really well.

Quietly, Gail eased the door open. Instantly, Nary was there, holding the door so Gail could roll inside with a minimum of fuss. She must have been waiting, Gail thought.

Nary guided her to a place of honor near the fireplace, its gas flame glowing. The girl disappeared for a moment then reappeared with a full plate, warm from the kitchen, laden with all the best delicacies.

"We keep special for you," she said, with a happy grin.

"Yum. Thank you." The aroma was heavenly.

Gail tore her eyes away from the brimming plate and caught sight of Phally standing in the kitchen doorway, smiling at her. Gail flashed a thumbs-up sign and tucked into her food. It was delicious, even the mysterious bites. "I'll ask what I'm eating after I've digested it all," she said to herself. Just in case.

After finishing their meals, the townsfolk began saying their goodbyes. Soon, just Father Ralph, Gail and Teresa remained, comparing notes on the party, among the nine or ten refugees staying late to help clean up.

"Phally ordered me to sit down and rest," Teresa laughed. "I hadn't noticed how tired I was until just this minute. My feet are killing me."

Gail watched a tall youth working his way around the room gathering dirty dishes, creating a precarious stack of plates, platters, utensils and cups that he cradled in his arms. As he passed the mantle, he stumbled and lurched sideways, bumping into Khath then teetering back against the mantle. His shoulder brushed the frame of one of Phally's family photos and toppled it to the floor.

"Oh dear, I hope it didn't break," Gail said, nudging Teresa. "Phally would be devastated—it's her only photo of her husband."

Khath waved the youth into the kitchen and bent to retrieve the photo. He glanced at it as he was lifting it back to the mantle, and his arm froze. As Gail watched, he passed his hand over his face, over his eyes. Carefully, he rubbed his sleeve over the photo glass and looked at it again. He shook his head and replaced the photo on the mantle. Turning away, he took a few steps toward the kitchen, then, halted.

Gail noticed Khath's fingers clenching into fists, then he unclenched them and shook his hands lightly as if to relax them. She saw him take a deep breath and exhale. Very slowly, as though fighting against some invisible force, he turned and took one faltering step back toward the mantle, then another. His right hand reached slowly for the picture and even from where she sat, Gail could see that the hand, the whole arm, was shaking. He grasped the photo and stared hard at the face of Phally's husband. His mouth opened, but no sound came out. He raised his eyes from the glass, an expression of shock on his face.

"Look," Gail said, nodding in Khath's direction. "What's wrong with Khath?"

Khath's free hand flew to his throat and he moaned. His chest heaved as he took one great gulping breath after another. Mouth open, he stared wildly around the room for a moment, then he staggered backwards a step, shaking his head. His face contorted, his lips moved and a garbled torrent of words poured from his mouth, rapidly gaining volume until he stood shouting, the photograph clenched in his raised fist.

Pra Chhay ran to his side and reached for the photo, but Khath held it aloft for all to see and began jabbing an accusing finger at the face in the frame while tears streamed down his cheeks and he shouted the same words over and over.

"What's he saying?" Gail asked Teresa. "Does he know Phally's husband?"

"I don't know. I don't think so," Teresa said. "I have no idea what's happening."

By now everyone was converging upon Khath. Father Ralph and Pra Chhay tried to sooth him, but he turned on them with a great burst of impassioned speech.

Some of the Cambodians began muttering, shaking their heads and moving away. Others stared with impassive faces at the scene playing out in front of them.

Phally appeared now in the kitchen doorway. She looked stunned, and then spoke with great anger, a fierce scowl on her face. She pointed at the door and though Gail could not understand the words, the meaning was clear: Get out.

Pra Chhay and Father Ralph hustled the raging Khath toward the door. Sareth pulled the photograph out of Khath's hand and set it on the table.

As Sareth passed by, heading for the door, Gail grabbed his sleeve.

"Wait," she said. "What just happened?"

Sareth paused, gently pulling his sleeve free of Gail's fingers.

"Pardon my rudeness, Miss Gail, Miss Teresa. I really must be brief." He bowed slightly. "It's quite unfortunate to see such a pleasant evening end on such a peculiar note. Khath says the man in the photo, Phally's husband, is Khmer Rouge. He insists that this is the man who murdered his wife and son."

# Nineteen

Phally swallowed hard to ease the tightness in her throat. They won't even look at me, she thought, watching the few of her Cambodian neighbors who yet remained in the house, helping to clean up. The women sidled around her, working faster now, obviously impatient to be done so they could go home and discuss this evening's disturbing incident with their families.

Of course Phally had vehemently denied Khath's accusation. The man is not well, she had said. He's mistaken. It just isn't true. In the morning, things will become clear.

Her neighbors had nodded their heads and clucked sympathetically when her tears had fallen at the dishonor being heaped upon her beloved husband, Boran. But Phally wondered what they were really thinking. Who did they believe?

Khath would not make such accusations if my Boran were still alive to defend himself, she thought angrily.

Most of the Cambodians had gathered their belongings and left soon after Khath's outburst. Only her closest neighbors remained, people she had considered her friends. Now, she was not so sure. Phally felt a tense silence pressing down upon them all, a deep, uncomfortable thoughtfulness furrowing brows and pursing lips.

This question of the Khmer Rouge and their killing fields was not a subject that her countrymen liked to talk about. It was so dangerously easy to become mired in thoughts and memories of things better left forgotten. Until today, Phally and her neighbors had lived together harmoniously, in the here and now.

But with Khath accusing Boran of being a blood-crazed Khmer Rouge murderer, this would change. Sides would be taken in this conflict. Of that, Phally was certain.

Someone's elbow knocked a heavy cooking pot to the floor with a loud crash. Phally jumped. The pot's lid clattered off and rocked back and forth, back and forth, while everyone stood still and watched it. Enough.

Phally stepped over and grabbed the lid. Someone handed her the pot. Even this simple kindness made her eyes well with tears.

She forced a smile to her face. "My friends, you have worked long and hard today. Thank you. I can finish this."

The house emptied quickly. It was a relief to be alone, away from the silent scrutiny of others. Phally sat for a few minutes in the living room, settling herself before going to check on Nary.

Gail had told her that the child had stared in horror, first at Khath, then Phally, her little head swiveling back and forth during all the shouting and confusion. She had begun to back away, making herself smaller and smaller, crouching, hunching, drawing inward, until she had bumped against Gail in her wheelchair.

Nary had turned to flee at that point, but Gail had swept her up into her arms and held her tightly, cradling the girl in her lap until Phally was able to take her. In the quiet of Nary's bedroom, Phally had rocked her daughter and stroked her hair until Nary, exhausted, had slept. Poor little mouse.

Moving quietly on the balls of her feet, Phally glided down the hallway to Nary's room. Slowly, she turned the doorknob and cracked the door wide enough to see inside the room. She'd left a dim light on so Nary wouldn't be frightened if she awoke in darkness, but still it took Phally's eyes a moment to adjust to the change in lighting. What she saw caused her breath to catch. Nary was not in her bed. Phally swung the door wide, letting more light into the room.

"Nary?" she said softly.

There was no answer. With mounting dread, Phally checked under the bed, in the closet and in the bathroom. She checked her own bedroom and closet and rushed through the rest of the house. Nary was gone. Phally grabbed two coats and shoved her feet in some flip-flops. Maybe Nary was in the tent in the backyard. Panicked now, Phally ran to the back door and skidded down the steps by the light of the full moon. She stumbled over the uneven ground and felt a sharp pain in the bottom of her left foot. Ignoring it, she burst into the dark tent.

"Nary," she called. "Are you here?" Bumping into chairs and tripping on the edges of the mats, she made her way to the altar and found the matches where she'd left them earlier. She lit a candle and prayed that when she turned around, she would see Nary somewhere, anywhere, in that tent. But the big tent was empty.

"Nary, Nary, where are you, child?" Phally whimpered and brushed tears out of her lashes. She blew out the candle and let her eyes adjust to the darkness for a moment, then made her way out of the tent and around to the front yard. She searched the porch and peered underneath the decking. "Nary, my child. Don't be afraid. Are you there?" She listened intently, but all she heard was the croaking of frogs and the rush of her own blood pounding in her ears.

Desolate, Phally wandered to the edge of the wheelchair ramp and sank down to her haunches. Her left foot throbbed. Surprised, she noticed her feet were bare. Her flip-flops must have fallen off somewhere as she rushed here and there. She dropped her head onto her knees. Think. Where would Nary have gone? To Gail and Teresa's? No, they would have brought her back immediately if she had.

With a rush of bitterness, Phally thought, *Khath would know.* How was it that her child trusted this man more than her own mother? Why was she unable to break down the wall between herself and Nary? If she were a good mother, she would know where her child would wander off to in the dead of night. Jolted by an awful thought, Phally sprang to her feet. Nary wouldn't go *there,* would she? Was she even now creeping around outside Khath's house? Or, even more hideous a thought, had he *taken* her? Was she in danger?

Phally began to run down the driveway. Gail and Teresa would help her. They would call the priest and together they would find Nary. Out of breath, she slowed to a rapid trot. And it was then that she noticed, coming toward her, a small figure with drooping shoulders and hanging head, dragging her feet in a weary shuffle.

"Nary, are you all right?" Phally closed the distance between them. "I've been so worried. Where have you been?" Relief tinged with anger surged through Phally's chest. She draped an arm around the child's shoulders, and began to walk back to her house.

Back in the house, she washed Nary's face and sat beside her on the couch. "Where did you go, Nary? I want you to tell me," Phally said.

Nary's gaze wandered around the room for a moment and came to rest on the photo of Boran, now back on the mantle. "There was no place to go," she said. "So I just walked until I was tired, and then came back."

"But child, I was so worried about you. Didn't you think to tell me?"

"Why, Mama? Why would you worry? What is there to be afraid of here?" Nary frowned.

Phally drew a deep breath. "Nary, I am your mother. Of course I worry." She struggled for words. How do you teach a child to be a daughter? Nary had survived without her for years in the youth brigades of the Khmer Rouge. But unlike other children in the camps, she had never come back to visit Phally. Sometimes, the Khmer Rouge would give their permission for such visits. Sometimes, the children would sneak away. But Nary never had. She seemed indifferent to the idea of a mother. It was beyond Phally's comprehension. What could have happened to her little mouse in that camp to so completely deaden the child's soul? Phally ran her hands over her face and tried a different tack.

"Nary, do you remember when you were very young, before the war started, how we would eat together as a family, you, your father and I? Do you remember those times, little mouse?"

Slowly, almost grudgingly, Nary nodded.

"We played games, you and I. We were happy. Do you remember?"

Nary stared at the floor.

"Nary, those things that Mr. Khath said about your father, you know they are not true, don't you? We were a normal family. Your papa worked for the Cambodian government. We were not Khmer Rouge. Do you understand?" It seemed to Phally that the more she tried to reach Nary, the more distant her daughter became. She plunged on. "You may hear things for a while. People will talk. Don't listen to them. We are not Khmer Rouge. The Khmer Rouge killed your father."

Nary's head snapped up. "Yes," she said. "They killed him. I know that." Her face reddened. She looked close to tears.

"I know you miss him, Nary. I do, too. He was a good man. I trust that you understand, and that you won't pay attention to what other people say."

Phally reached out and brushed the hair back from her daughter's face. "You are such a pretty child. You're smart. You're strong and sometimes, mouse, you are very helpful and kind. I want us to be a family again, like before the war." Phally felt a lump rise in her own throat. "Maybe, now that you're growing up, we can help each other not to feel so sad when people say unkind things about Papa."

At the word "Papa," Nary's eyes turned again to the picture on the mantle. The girl's lower lip quivered. She hardened her jaw and straightened her spine stiffly, pulling away from her mother.

Phally watched this sadly. *It's as if I'm not even here beside her on this couch.* Her earlier thoughts came back to haunt her. *Sides will be taken.* What if Khath's influence proved too strong, and she and Nary somehow ended up on opposite sides?

———

Khath dared not go to sleep. He straddled a chair in his bedroom, his arms resting on the window ledge, letting the cool breeze wash in from the open window. The fresh air felt moist and soothing against his throbbing temples. He was tired, so very tired, but sleep would bring no rest.

If he slept, the dreams would come. Layered on top of what he had seen tonight, he knew that he simply could not face the nightmarish visions that would torment him. He would crack. His mind would shatter. If so, he would not be the first.

Like an echo that refuses to fade, he heard again the cruel taunts of the Thai guards at Khao I Dang refugee camp. *"Ba-ba, bo-bo,"* they jeered, pointing to their heads and twirling their fingers as they dragged some poor howling, spitting refugee off to the medical building. Crazy.

One thing was certain: Khath would end his own life before he burdened his brother, or for that matter, his daughters, with the care of a crazy man. It was not a difficult task, to end one's life. It would be the least of his problems, should it come to that. After all, he would have as many additional lifetimes as needed to erase the bad karma of his suicide. And anyway, he was fairly sure his good intention to relieve others of the burden of his care would counterbalance the suicide itself to some degree. Wouldn't it? He choked back a hoot of hysterical laughter, for the only one who could guide him in this small ethical dilemma was Pra Chhay himself. What a conversation that would be.

From the corner of his eye, he saw the light underneath the door wink out. He knew Pra Chhay was out there, though. Sitting in the darkness on his prayer mat, his sandalwood prayer beads in hand, murmuring. He would sit in the hallway all night, at the ready, should Khath cry out or rush from his room in a panic. It was no use telling him not to worry. It would be a long night for both of them, Khath thought, feeling the shame of it.

Cautiously, he let his mind approach the events of the evening so that he could examine them here in the calm of his bedroom.

He felt so bad to cause such trouble, to destroy an evening set aside to honor his brother; especially now, when life in Glenberg was beginning to develop a normal routine. For the first time in a long while, he had begun to feel like he was living his own life instead of someone else's. He was confident in Teresa's friendship and finally, with her help, he was doing something useful to find his daughters.

And now, what would happen? Had he ruined everything? Was he supposed to say nothing? He'd been so shocked, to see that face above all others, staring back at him from the picture, transporting him to a hot and dusty roadside, the smell of blood thick in his nostrils, a voice like hard steel smashing his world to bits. *Clean up this mess.* This "mess" was all that remained of his wife and son.

He knew many would not believe him, would twirl their fingers as the Thai guards had done. And what would become of Nary? Nary, who needed him to help her find her way back from the jungles of Cambodia. Nary, who had turned away from her mother and chosen him. There was a reason for that, and now that Khath knew who Phally's husband was, it made sense. Phally would never admit to being Khmer Rouge, never let her family's honor be so stained. But Khath knew what he had seen in that photograph.

"Are you sure?" "So many years have passed." "You must be mistaken." "The lighting was dim." "Can this really be true?" For more than an hour, Father Ralph, with Sareth's assistance, had questioned, soothed, doubted, and in the end, left with pity and confusion etched into his tired face. Sareth had soon followed, telling Khath to get some rest and they would discuss it further in the morning, as if getting some rest were a simple matter.

Pra Chhay had surprised him by staying in the background while Sareth and Father Ralph had questioned Khath. He was usually so quick to act as a buffer between Khath and the rest of the world. But this evening, apart from offering tea, which was declined, and murmuring his mantras, the monk had not said a word until bidding the priest and his interpreter good night. Khath had watched his brother stand at the window until Sareth had driven away. When Pra Chhay finally faced back into the room, he wore the saddest expression Khath had ever seen on the monk's face.

"And you, brother?" Khath had asked. "Just what are your thoughts on this matter?"

Pra Chhay had lowered himself into the corner of the couch, and now he angled his body to meet Khath's gaze.

"I believe you," Pra Chhay said.

Khath's breath whooshed out of his lungs and his body sagged. Only then did he realize how it had been several moments since he'd last taken a breath, and that every muscle was tensed to do battle. To convince, to persuade, to beg if necessary, for his brother's support.

Pra Chhay had continued on. "I believe that a man who has looked upon the face of his child's executioner does not forget that face. You gazed into his eyes, Khath. You looked into his soul. Your destinies are entwined."

And then Pra Chhay had leaned forward and looked hard into Khath's eyes, speaking slowly for emphasis. "Do not tie your heart in malice with this man and his family, Khath. Do not carry the blood feud forward." Pra Chhay had leaned back against the couch then and spread his hands wide in a gesture of appeal. "You don't have the whole story yet, Khath. Please, do nothing foolish. Promise me you will keep a cool heart as we look into this."

Khath had nodded his head, and watched the worry lines soften in his brother's face at his response.

Now, in his bedroom, Khath wondered. Was it a promise he could keep?

# Twenty

Sareth drove slowly through the darkness, his staid pace at odds with the excitement racing though his body. A chuckle started low in his throat and soon he was laughing out loud. He guided the car to the edge of the road to give himself a moment to savor this feeling, his shoulders shaking with mirth mixed with relief.

As far as Sareth was concerned, the party could not have ended on a more perfect note. "Phally, my girl," he said to the night. "You have just lost the contest with my wife."

He grinned. Life was about to take a turn for the better. Once Chea felt secure in her place in the community, she would stop pouting and poking at him to fix her unhappiness.

These thoughts of his wife stirred up a small concern, however. He had best hasten home before Chea managed to do something that might jeopardize her victory. He hoped she had left quickly and quietly, as he'd instructed, and had not spoken with anyone yet. It was a delicate situation, and Chea would require his guidance to handle it properly.

A few minutes later, he swung into his driveway. As he hurried up the walkway, the door opened and Chea stood framed by the light, her face shadowed. But the moon was full, and as Sareth came nearer, he could see that her lips were spread wide in a smile of welcome. As always, her beauty took his breath away, and he paused for a moment, gazing up at her before mounting the stairs.

"Chea, my dear," Sareth said. "Tonight we have much to celebrate."

Seating himself on the couch, Sareth waited for Chea to bring him tea. "Sit with me, Chea, and let's discuss how best we should handle Khath's accusations about Phally's family."

Chea nodded eagerly and sank down beside him. "I came straight home, as you said."

"Good. I knew I could trust you," Sareth said. At least I hoped I could, he thought. "Chea, for now you must not openly take sides in this dispute. It is well known that you and Phally do not agree on many things. If you were to take sides now, people will think you are taking advantage of the situation. Do you see how that is?"

Chea nodded. "I should say nothing?"

Sareth sipped his tea. "No, I did not say that, my dear. You must show that you are concerned, but say only neutral things. You can frown and say, 'How could this have happened?' or 'I just don't know what to think now.' In this way, you will get other people to talk, and then you tell me everything you hear."

"And what will you be doing, *Bong*?" Chea asked. She refilled her husband's cup with tea and took a sip of her own.

"I will be busy, stirring the pot. Don't you worry about that. Slowly, we will turn the community against Phally, make her feel uncomfortable, even a little unsafe, about staying in Glenberg."

"So she will leave and take that horrid child of hers away. I can hardly wait for that day." Chea spoke heatedly and her eyes flashed.

"But you must wait, Chea," Sareth spoke sternly, and then softened his words with a smile. "Though I promise you it will not be for long."

The next morning, Sareth awoke refreshed, dressed carefully and drove to the church. His polished leather shoes tapped on the floor as he made his way to Father Ralph's office. Perhaps someday he would buy a pair of tennis shoes and glide quietly through the halls, but he doubted it. He liked to announce his presence as he made his way in the world.

The priest was not in his office. Sareth glanced at his watch, frowning. Had Father Ralph forgotten their appointment? On impulse, Sareth stepped through the arched entrance to a private passageway leading from the priest's office to the church. He'd never used this passageway before, but Father Ralph had told him it led to a small door which opened onto a side aisle near the front of the church. "In case I want to pop in and have a word with my boss," the priest had said with a smile.

The door at the end of the passageway was open, and Sareth paused to peer into the church's dim interior. As he expected, Father Ralph knelt at the railing in front of the altar, his head bent over clasped hands, deep in prayer. He gave no indication that he had noticed Sareth's presence. As Sareth watched, the priest looked up at the crucifix hanging over the altar, and beat his chest softly, three times with his right fist, then bowed his head again and continued praying.

Sareth glanced at his watch again. It was too bad to interrupt the priest—he certainly had a lot to pray about after last night—but they were due at Gail and Teresa's house in half an hour. Sareth wanted a chance to see where Father Ralph's thoughts were taking him at this point before they met with the volunteers.

Putting a grave expression on his face, Sareth coughed lightly. Father Ralph glanced over, gave a slight nod and turned back to the crucifix. He mumbled a few more words, then made the sign of the cross and rose up, coming to meet Sareth.

The priest's face was lined with fatigue, his eyes red and squinting. He looks as though he hasn't slept at all, Sareth thought. He felt a twinge of guilt. Father Ralph had always treated him fairly and well. He didn't deserve the havoc that was about to descend upon his small community.

Sareth bowed his head slightly. "Good morning, Father Ralph," he said. "I'm so sorry to interrupt, but I know you like to be punctual, and I thought I would offer my services should you want to talk before we go visit the ladies."

"Kind of you, Mr. Sareth. Let's go back to my office and have a quick cup of coffee."

Seated on Father Ralph's couch, Sareth sipped at the strong brew Father Ralph had handed him.

Opposite him, the priest heaved a sigh. "I feel this is my fault somehow," Father Ralph said. "You warned me against accepting Khath and Pra Chhay into our community. But what are the odds of something like this happening?" He looked at Sareth. "What *are* the odds, Mr. Sareth? Do you know? Have you heard of anything similar in other communities?"

Sareth shook his head. "I have not," he said. "But at this point, we don't really know where the truth lies, do we?" Best to keep the priest off balance for the moment. "All we know is that a very serious accusation has been made. One we must not ignore."

"No, of course not," Father Ralph agreed. "But we need to proceed carefully, don't you agree? I want to make sure that Gail and Teresa don't get in over their heads on this one. As volunteers, they're my responsibility. I'm not worried about Teresa so much, but Gail is a little impulsive at times."

Sareth nodded gravely, pursing his lips to keep them from erupting into a grin. Things were unfolding just as he wanted them. "A very insightful observation, Father Ralph," he said. "Perhaps we should waste no time in delivering this message to Miss Teresa and Miss Gail."

Father Ralph drained the last of the coffee from his cup. "I'm ready. Let's go," he said.

Gail tapped a pen against the pad of paper she held in her lap, waiting for Father Ralph and Sareth to finish exchanging small talk with Teresa by the front door. Good God, hurry it up already, she thought. We've got important things to discuss. Who cares about the damn weather?

When at last they were settled, Father Ralph began. "Well, I'll get right to the point," he said. "I wanted to check in with you both after what happened last night, see if you have any concerns about your volunteer work with the refugees."

"How is Khath this morning?" Teresa said. "He was so upset last night."

"We have not seen him yet today," Mr. Sareth said. "We, Father Ralph and I, thought it best to wait until later in the day. Let him have some time to rest after his ordeal."

What about Phally's ordeal? Gail thought. Is anyone but me worried about Phally? She cleared her throat. "Can you fill us in on what happened after you all left the party?"

Father Ralph nodded. "Yes, we took him straight home, of course. I spent a good hour there questioning him, trying to see if there was some mistake, but he was adamant in his belief that Phally's husband killed his wife and son. Quite unshakable, in fact."

"Well, he must be deluding himself, poor man. All those years have passed. A lot of people have similar appearances." Gail shook her head. "It can't be true."

The priest leaned forward, resting his elbows on his knees, hands clasped. "That's what I thought, too. But there were some distinguishing physical characteristics. The person who killed Khath's family was missing half of his right ear lobe and had a scar under his left eye. So did the man in the photo."

Gail straightened in her chair. "That's it? You're going to condemn someone on the basis of a few facial wounds? Come on. There was a war going on. Lots of people stuck their faces in the wrong places and got disfigured as a result." She hesitated for a moment, and then said, "And you've got to admit, Khath's not the most reliable witness."

"Hold on," Teresa stiffened. "You can't just assume Khath's wrong about this just because he's a little on the rocky side, emotionally. He's way better than he was. And anyone would come unglued at a shock like that."

Gail stared at Teresa, who met her eyes without flinching, a firm set to her jaw.

Oh my God. She thinks Khath is right. Speechless with dismay, Gail realized her own jaw was slack, and she shut her mouth and swallowed. "Teresa," she said, her voice coming out an octave higher, just short of squeaky. "This is *Phally* we're talking about."

Mr. Sareth shifted in his seat. "If I may interject, this is Phally's *husband* we are talking about."

"Well, sure," Father Ralph said. "But I imagine people will assume at least some degree of guilt by association in this case?"

"You are probably right," Sareth sighed. "It is difficult to explain. There are so many degrees, so many levels, of guilt when it comes to my people's relationship with the Khmer Rouge. You see, the roots of this movement go back to the 1950s and '60s, when there were no colleges in Cambodia. The wealthy sent their sons to Paris to study, where some of them were exposed to the teachings of Mao Tse Tung."

Gail watched Sareth closely. Where is he going with this, she wondered. He almost sounds like he's trying to defend Phally, which is sure not what I expected given all the bad blood between her and Chea. "Interesting," she said. "Then what happened?"

"These young men brought the teachings back to the countryside, where there was already resentment among the peasants toward the upper classes. Many of the villagers were eager to join a movement that glorified their humble way of life. They were the farmers, the backbone of the country. They were designated the "Old People," and were better treated by the

Khmer Rouge than those who later were forced from the cities—the "New People," who were very harshly treated.

"So by no fault of your own, just by being a village farmer, you could be assumed to be Khmer Rouge?" Gail asked.

"The Old People often were sympathizers, if only to keep their own necks safe," Mr. Sareth said. "Spying was rampant. Turning someone in for an infraction would curry favor with the Khmer Rouge leaders. So, if you report a New Person for stealing a potato to feed his starving child, which in turn earns you an extra half-scoop of rice to feed your starving child, are you Khmer Rouge or are you a desperate parent?"

A small silence followed Mr. Sareth's words. Outside the window, a bird twittered.

Gail rubbed her hand over her jaw. "So, I'm confused. Are you trying to say that Phally is Khmer Rouge or that she isn't?"

Mr. Sareth smiled grimly. "I'm trying to say that it is a delicate situation. And that people will react to it according to what their own experiences have been, Miss Gail. We are none of us blameless, but neither can most of us be blamed entirely for our actions under the Khmer Rouge." He paused for a moment, studying his fingers. "I cannot say at this point how people will react. But make no mistake, they will react. Maybe not today or next week, but they will not let this lie."

Father Ralph heaved a deep sigh. "I brought the refugees here to get them away from all that, to give them a chance to break free of it and go on with their lives." He shook his head. "What a terrible turn of events. It could tear this community apart." He paused and his face grew thoughtful. "Or perhaps with the grace of God, it could bring great healing."

Again, silence fell. This time it felt a little awkward. *Does Father Ralph know he's sitting in a room full of heathens?* Gail wondered.

Mr. Sareth stepped into the void. "Your prayers may bring great comfort, Father Ralph," he said vaguely. "I'm sure they are of great value."

"What about the rest of us?" Gail said. "What do you suggest we do?"

Mr. Sareth appeared to think for a moment, and then he gave one decisive nod of his head and began to speak. "For the moment, do nothing."

"Nothing?" Teresa said. "What do you mean, nothing?"

Mr. Sareth smiled. "Forgive me. That was unclear. What I mean to say is to go on about your activities as usual. Keep helping Khath write his letters." He looked toward Gail. "Miss Gail, you should foster your friendship with Phally however you like."

"But?" Gail said. She could sense that there was a very strong "but" in there somewhere.

"Yes, Miss Gail is correct," Mr. Sareth said. "Carry on as usual, but keep your eyes and ears open. And let me know if you hear anything that troubles you. I, of course, will do the same."

"Of course," Gail said, dryly. She locked eyes with the man for a moment. It's like looking at a billboard, she thought. You only get the intended message, never the whole story.

Father Ralph cleared his throat. "At the same time, Mr. Sareth and I will be looking into ways to try to discover the facts of this situation. And Gail, Teresa," Father Ralph nodded at each of them in turn, "I want to be sure that you both know that you can walk away from this at a moment's notice. I don't want you doing anything you are not comfortable doing."

Teresa smiled at the priest. "I can't wait to get back to working with Khath on the letters, but thank you for making that clear." She glanced briefly at Gail.

Gail felt the sting of Teresa's glance. Her sister might as well have drawn a line in the sand. Teresa would throw her support behind Khath, no matter what.

Gail looked at the priest. "Sure, no problem," she said. But in her bones she could feel the heaviness of a gathering storm.

# Twenty-One

"Don't squirm, child. Do you want your hair to be all in a zig-zag?" Phally scolded gently, scissors in hand, poised to make the final few snips to Nary's black bangs.

"It tickles, Mama. There's hair all over my face now." Nary screwed up her nose and forehead.

Swiping lightly at Nary's face with a soft rag, Phally resisted the urge to gather the girl into her arms, afraid that Nary would stiffen and pull away. It was better to be satisfied with fleeting moments of intimacy like these than to risk being rebuffed by her daughter yet again.

"Nary, I will be going to English class soon, but today I want you to stay home." Phally did not want Nary exposed to the stares and whispers that she knew awaited her in the classroom. She would go first, and see just how bad it was, before she let Nary come back to the Sunday afternoon family class.

Nary looked at Phally briefly and then rubbed her hands over her face, brushing away the last bits of tickling hair.

"You can clean up our lunch dishes, and then do your homework for Monday, all right mouse? I don't want you to let anyone inside, and you are not to leave the house."

Nary nodded. "Okay, Mama."

"I won't be gone long, and when I get back, we'll go have a visit with Gail." Phally turned her daughter to face the mirror in the bathroom. "There, see how nice you look?"

Next, Phally gave a few strokes to her own hair with the brush, and then twisted the strands into a bun on the top of her head. Boran had always said she looked beautiful with her hair up, and today, she wanted his memory close to her while she braved the stares of her neighbors.

Boran. She remembered the day the Khmer Rouge took him away like it was only yesterday. The two young soldiers had ambled through the village like any two country boys out for a stroll, except for the deadly guns slung casually across their chests. Polite messengers of death they were, and everyone knew it. They always came in twos, with smiles for the families as they took the men away, "just for a few days, for a special project." Sometimes they came for a single man, sometimes for a village full of men. And always they lied, softening the death sentence with a piece of candy for a crying son or daughter, a ball of sweet rice for a pale and stricken wife.

On the day Boran was taken, nine others were selected as well. They were marched to the outskirts of the village, where they were trussed like fowl and loaded onto a truck. For days after the men were taken, everyone pretended: pretended that there was a special project, that the men would return if not today, then surely tomorrow. When they were too exhausted by hours of fieldwork to pretend, they simply avoided looking at one another.

After a week, a work brigade stumbled upon the men jumbled together in a shallow trench, their skulls smashed and broken, their flesh eaten away by starving dogs. And shortly after that, all the children eight years or older were taken away to work in a youth brigade.

Phally sighed. Poor Nary barely had time to accept the fact that her father was dead before she was taken away from her mother, she thought. Maybe that is the root of our problems now. It would just take time, she decided, for Nary to realize that she was safe now, here in Glenberg with her mother.

It was getting late. Phally checked her reflection in the mirror, looking for stray hairs escaping from the knot at the crown of her head.

"Is it done right, Nary? I can't see the back," Phally said. But her words were swallowed by the stillness of an empty room. Her daughter had already slipped away. Setting the brush on the counter, Phally went to find her. Just once, she thought, I wish she would come looking for me.

After saying goodbye to Nary, Phally set out for the 20 minute walk to Father Ralph's church, where the classes were held. As she approached the building, she noticed that her steps had slowed, heavy with the dread of what might lie ahead. Then, a surge of anger propelled her forward in a rush. How dare anyone judge her? She had done nothing wrong nor had Boran. A crazy man had made wild accusations. That was all.

Phally held her head high and marched up the steps and down the hallway. She heard the buzz of conversation coming from the ESL room, but when she stepped through the door, the din subsided. One by one, people nudged one another and nodded toward the doorway. Phally felt her face grow warm. She searched for one smile, one friendly nod and found none. Not even one.

Trembling, she crept to the back of the room and sank into a seat near the door. She opened her notebook and stared fixedly at it, realizing after a moment that she was scowling at a blank page. She sighed and shut the notebook. *I'm not brave, like Boran. I dishonor his memory with my fear and shame. So what if no one smiled. No one scowled either. Their faces were neutral, blank like the pages of this notebook, waiting to be filled. Maybe they don't yet know what to think, who to believe.*

She raised her head and looked around, noticing that Khath had not come to class today. Good. She would have a chance to talk to some of her closest neighbors, to express her own outrage at the terrible things Khath had said. Outrage, yes, but sadness, too, an overwhelming sadness that made her heart so heavy she wanted to sink to the floor with the weight of it.

Phally closed her eyes for a moment, then jerked them open as Mr. Sareth swept through the door, all business and bustle. He slapped a thick stack of papers onto the table at the front of the room and nodded curtly at the assembled adults. Odd, Phally thought, noticing for the first time that no one else had brought their children to class today, either.

"Good afternoon," Mr. Sareth said in English.

The class mumbled a reply. Phally wondered why Teresa was not there today either. *Is she with Khath?*

She turned her attention back to Mr. Sareth.

"Today," he was saying, "Our lesson is 'body parts.' If you hurt yourself and visit a doctor, or if you have an emergency and have to call 911, you need to know how to describe the injury. Where it hurts, and so forth."

Mr. Sareth began passing out the packets of handouts, which were covered by drawings of body parts and organs with fill-in-the-blank labels. "For some of you, this will be review. But you will notice as we go through the packet, that each page is more difficult, more detailed." He smiled at the class. "Shall we begin?"

Always an eager student, Phally soon found herself swept up in the lesson. Mr. Sareth was a good teacher, she thought, whether she liked him personally or not. He had divided the group into two teams, giving points for correct answers and making a game of spelling the name of each body part. Cheers and laughter filled the room, and Phally began to relax. At the break, she sat at her desk for a moment after the other students had left, flicking through the final pages of the packet.

"No fair looking ahead, Phally," Mr. Sareth said. "Go take your break."

She smiled at him then dropped her eyes politely. The last page of the packet lay open and exposed on her desk, and it was impossible not to see the images there. A line drawing of a man's face, disturbingly familiar. Labeling lines pointed to eyebrows, even eyelashes. And yes, there was a blemish on the cheek, under one eye. A scar? Like Boran's? Phally caught her breath and her heart began to bang inside her chest. She looked more closely at the picture. A heavy line slashed across the bottom of one earlobe, making it appear as though half the lobe was gone.

Phally's jaw dropped and heat surged into her face as she realized what Mr. Sareth had done, how he had tricked her. With a handful of subtle clues, Mr. Sareth had turned an anonymous teacher's aid into a likeness of Boran to fuel local gossip. And had she not looked ahead, she would have been blindsided by it, shamed again in front of her neighbors. The malicious intent of it shocked her.

With the packet shaking in her hands, she raised her eyes to face her accuser. Mr. Sareth leaned casually back against his table, his arms crossed, a bland expression on his face.

"Phally, my dear," he said, the concern in his voice at odds with the smirking twitch of his lips. "Are you unwell? You look..." Sareth hesitated for the barest fraction of a second, "...feverish."

Phally grabbed her things and backed out of the classroom, afraid to take her eyes off her tormentor until she reached the safety of the hall. Then, she turned and ran, away from the evil and the hatred, the loss and the pain, the memories and the unfilled blanks.

---

Bundled up against an autumn breeze that swirled the first dry leaves of the season around the yard, Gail sat in the porch rocker and studied the diagrams in her hand. Decorating the tent for the party had whetted her appetite for the work she loved, and she'd pulled some old design ideas out of her briefcase—the last project she'd worked on before the accident. Was it time to go back to work? Was she ready to face the stares and the pity of her former colleagues? Gail felt her insides contract at the thought. No, not yet. But maybe she could start small. Maybe someone in town needed some interior design work done.

Just for fun, she began to make notes on the diagrams, but her attention was distracted a moment later by the rattle of the picket fence gate.

"Phally," she said, in surprise. "I didn't expect you until later." She glanced down at her watch to make sure of the time. When she looked up, Phally was near enough that Gail could see the angry set of her friend's mouth, the wild look in her eyes.

"What happened?" she asked, laying her work aside.

Phally thrust a packet of papers at Gail. "Look," she said. "Look how he do. He very bad man. He do like that. Then people hate me. Hate Boran."

"Who? Khath?" Gail asked, confused. Phally was struggling with her English, too upset to string words together properly.

"Not Khath." Phally shook her head vigorously. "The teacher. Mr. Sareth."

Gail stared at the body parts worksheets, not sure what she was supposed to see. "I'm sorry, I…" she began.

Phally snatched the pages from her hand and flipped to the back of the packet. "There," she said, pointing at the picture. "Look same Boran." Her finger stabbed at the drawing. "There. He make scaaah." Again the finger stabbed. "There. He cut ear. Same Boran."

"Let me see that," Gail said. She held the picture close and examined it. It was subtle, just a hint, but the likeness was there. Was it just coincidence? Maybe Phally was overly sensitive. She laid the papers in her lap, thinking hard. But if Phally were oversensitive, so were her neighbors, at this point. They would see it, too. She felt the first stirrings of anger. It was so cleverly done. So like Mr. Sareth. Easily denied as a mistake, a slip of the pen, yet sure to stir up the raw and powerful emotions of a brutalized people.

"You are right, Phally," Gail said, handing the packet back to Phally. "He is a bad man. A very bad man." And so heartless, she thought.

"I no go back," Phally said. "He shame Boran, me, Nary. In my country, we very respect for teacher. Teacher good, very high. Now, no. I not study with Mr. Sareth. I no respect. I can not."

Gail nodded. "I agree. You should not go back there. At least, not right now." She sat silently, the tapping of her pencil against her fingers the only sign of the agitation in her mind. Beside her, Phally sat with bent head, looking dejected. This was not good. Without her classes, what was Phally supposed to do all day? How would she learn and get by in this country?

"Hey," Gail said, nudging Phally. "We're smart ladies, right? We are not going to let him win. I think I have a plan."

Phally looked hopeful. "You can help me?"

Gail nodded slowly. "I believe I can. Let me think this through for a bit. In the meantime, you go get Nary. Put some nice clothes on and meet me back here in an hour, okay?"

"Yes, I can do." Phally and strode from the porch, looking determined. Her packet lay discarded on the floorboards.

After Phally had left, Gail scooped up the packet and tucked it carefully into her briefcase. She would not put it past Mr. Sareth to alter the packet, if Father Ralph or Teresa asked to see it. Had Khath seen it? What a cruel stunt to pull, Gail thought, against both Khath and Phally. What else might the man do? She felt a shiver run up her spine. This would probably get ugly, she knew that. But might it also become *dangerous*?

Frowning, Gail slipped into her wheelchair and headed inside to the phone. It was time to call in some favors.

# Twenty-Two

"Go on, brother. I will be fine." Smoke swirled lazily from the glowing tip of the cigarette Khath waved toward Pra Chhay, who stood hesitating, his hand on the front doorknob. "You will be late to class," Khath said.

"I don't mind staying home with you," Pra Chhay offered.

Khath shook his head and coughed. He hadn't smoked non-stop like this since leaving the refugee camp in Thailand. Now, his tongue felt like a withered sausage wrapped in a leathery casing. He cleared his throat. "I would rather you go, see what people are saying," he replied.

Pra Chhay nodded. "Then that's what I will do," he said. "Be safe."

After Pra Chhay had left, Khath wandered restlessly around the house. He carried the overflowing ashtray from the living room to the kitchen and dumped it in the trash, then went to retrieve the one from his bedroom as well. He washed the lunch dishes and tried not to think. But what else was there to do? The house was clean. He'd spent half the night washing and polishing when he couldn't sleep. He opened all the windows, and though he shivered at the cool breeze that blew in, he preferred that to the rank odor of stale cigarette smoke that pervaded the house. Standing at the window, it occurred to him that everyone else would be in ESL class, so he could take a walk without meeting his Cambodian neighbors. Khath knew that his rage and grief were much too fresh for public display. He felt peeled, utterly raw, and the merest glance would slice to the bone.

He got a pencil and scrap of paper. *Out for a walk,* he wrote. *I am fine. Don't worry. See you this evening.*

Twenty minutes later, his footsteps crunching on a gravel shoulder, Khath drew in a deep lungful of clean, cool air and felt the tension in his chest and shoulders finally begin to unwind. Taking a walk had been a good idea. He realized he'd been striding along heedlessly, and now he paused to look around and figure out where his feet had taken him. He was standing on a country road. Up ahead on the opposite side of the street, he could see a little path leading into the forest. After a moment, he recognized it as the path that Nary had shown him on the day the farmer and his dog had chased them from the cornfield.

Khath's mind began to skitter around the thought of Nary. Too late, he tried to recite a mantra to shield himself from the images that surged toward him, overwhelming his fragile defenses. It was no use. He saw the girl wherever he looked: Nary, handing him three ears of corn. Nary, sanding the wheelchair ramp and accidentally dumping paint onto Chea's sarong. *That* thought brought a grim smile to his face. And then he remembered holding her as she shook with sobs after the piñata incident, carrying her into Phally's house and handing her over to her mother. His gut wrenched realizing he'd handed her back to the Khmer Rouge. "I didn't know," he mumbled. "The picture was not there that day." The sound of his own voice startled him. He blinked and looked around, hoping no one was watching him standing in the middle of the road, mumbling to himself like a crazy man.

Khath sighed. For all he knew he might be breaking a law standing here like this. He'd better get off the road, he decided.

And then he had an idea. He would return to the abandoned cabin he'd found in the woods all those weeks ago. It would be safe and quiet, and above all, private. At the cabin, he could be alone and figure things out without people hovering around and trying to steer his thoughts in one direction or another. Yes, it was perfect. He would clean it up and make it weather-tight, and use it whenever he felt overwhelmed.

Pleased with his decision, Khath continued along the road until he reached the edge of the cornfield and then jumped down the embankment. He didn't want to leave an obvious trail, certainly nothing that would attract the attention of the farmer. He worked his way along the edge of the cornfield and just as he was about to cut back into the forest, something caught his eye. An old shovel was tangled in the underbrush. It looked like it had been heaved over the fence. Khath pulled it out and examined it, and soon saw why it had been discarded. A long crack ran down the handle, threatening to split the wood.

Very wasteful, Khath thought. He could fix this easily with splints and some braided twine or strips of leather. No need to throw it away, and it would come in handy for cleaning up the cabin. Glancing around and seeing no one, Khath shouldered the tool and headed into the forest.

The cabin looked much as it had the first time he'd seen it. Overgrown with brambles and wearing a heavy coat of dried needles trimmed with moss, it was easy to overlook. Khath circled around the outside, parting the undergrowth gently with his shovel. With a critical eye, he decided which bushes he would thin or clear, which he would leave, and where he might selectively weave the growth into a natural barrier to keep his safe haven hidden from prying eyes. Satisfied that he had a plan, he used the shovel to scrape dirt away from the entrance so he could open the door wide and let some light in.

Pushing aside vines and brambles, Khath ducked low and entered the cabin. The dirt-floored structure was larger than Khath remembered, pacing it off now at about four meters square. Rough wooden shelves and a work bench ran nearly three meters along one wall, framing a small window. A flimsy wall extended from the end of the work bench and shelving, screening off a small space for storage, or even a sleeping alcove, he guessed. Rummaging in the corners and crannies, Khath found a rusty lantern with no wick, some rope, and a fishing pole. A dented tin pan sat on the bench, and a length of wood for barring the door completed the inventory.

Khath eyed the rope. If it wasn't too badly rotted, there was plenty for a temporary fix of the shovel handle, enough to let him beat down the brush around the door so he could pass through upright. He turned his mind to this task, grateful for any activity that would occupy his thoughts. Using his pocket knife, Khath cut a ten foot length of rope, then unraveled it so he had four thin lengths of twine. Starting four inches below the split and extending the same length beyond, Khath wrapped the shovel handle tightly with one of the lengths, laying the twine so it ran at a slight diagonal up the handle. He repeated this wrap three more times with the remaining lengths of rope, alternating the direction of each layer. When he was done, he tested the strength of the handle, flexing it over his bent leg, and nodded. It would do, for now.

Stepping outside, he raised the shovel high then brought it down with a grunt, using the edge of the blade to slice through a dense mat of vines near the cabin door. Again, he struck at the vines, and as he did so, a sickening image flashed into his brain: a man, kneeling in front of an open trench, blindfolded, hands tied behind his back, while a Khmer Rouge executioner swung a bloody shovel blade down toward his skull.

Khath gasped and stood frozen with his shovel raised for a moment, shaking his head to erase the vision, forcing a weak laugh at his trickster mind. He turned his attention back to the bushes, but they faded from his sight, replaced by an image of Boran's face sneering out at him from the shadows, a scar under the left eye, a missing earlobe, a pistol raised and Khath's wife's blood flowing into the dirt. Enraged, Khath struck at that hated face as he could not do on the day his wife and son died, for on that day he'd been forced to choose between being a man or being a father. To save his daughters, he'd let the death of his wife and son go unavenged.

Khath raised his head and screamed at the sky above, his pain and fury loosed in a guttural roar that tore at the lining of his throat. Again and again he flailed at the vines, slashing and shredding, sobbing and raging, until, spent at last, he sank to his knees and wept.

———————

"Are you ready, Phally?" Gail studied her friend, who stood on the sidewalk with hands clasped at the waist, eyes bright and eager, a half smile curving her lips. Her hair was clipped back with a barrette, and she wore a subdued green and tan sarong with a white blouse. A dark green cardigan, an addition from Gail's closet, added a polished touch to her outfit.

Phally gave a tight nod.

"You'll do great," Gail said. "Just remember to look him in the eye now and then, speak up and don't rush your words together. And don't be afraid to ask him to repeat himself, or to speak slowly."

Phally nodded again. "Yes," she said. "I can remember."

"Okay, then. Let's go." Gail turned to Nary. "Give me a push up the hill, will you?" *Why is it so much easier to ask Phally or Nary for help than it is to ask Teresa,* she wondered. *Maybe because they didn't know me before the accident. Or maybe because they have seen so many mangled people that it doesn't faze them a bit. They're not timid about it or afraid of offending me.*

Nary giggled and grabbed the back of Gail's sports chair seat and began to run, pushing Gail ahead of her up the small hill toward Dan's Fountain and Grill. Phally followed at a more sedate pace. As they approached the entrance of the eatery, the door swung wide, held open by Dan Olsen himself.

Gail grinned and waved at the older gentleman, her heart warmed by his welcome. Dan had been her father's best friend. After the accident, when Gail was still in the hospital, Dan had come to visit. "Anything you need, Gail, anything at all, you come to me, you hear?" the old man had said gruffly, standing stiff at her bedside.

Well, now she needed something. She needed a job for Phally. And Dan, she figured, could use a superb cook and a freshening up of his dated lunch menu. When she outlined her proposal over the phone, Dan had agreed to meet Phally and consider the request.

"And I can be there, too, in the beginning, teaching her things so it won't be a burden on you. She's a very fast learner," Gail had promised Dan over the phone.

"Sounds like I'll be getting two gals for the price of one," Dan had replied. "How can I turn down an offer like that?"

Now, he stood towering over the trio. He ushered them to a table for four by the window, pulling a chair from one side to make room for Gail's sport chair. Then he turned to Phally.

"Are you the little lady who cooked up them delicious egg rolls at the party?" he asked.

"She is." Gail jumped in to make introductions. "Dan, this is Phally and her daughter, Nary."

She looked at Phally. "This is Dan," she said.

After a slight hesitation, Phally extended a timid hand. "Hello, Mr...Dan. Nice to meet you."

Dan engulfed Phally's hand in both of his. "It's an honor to meet you, Miss Phally," he said. He glanced at Nary. "That little one needs fattening up. Hot chocolate to go around?" He peered at Phally, waiting for her permission to give Nary a hot chocolate.

Gail watched the smile on Phally's face grow brittle. She knows she's supposed to reply, but she has no idea what he just said, Gail thought. Of course she doesn't. How would she? We haven't taught "fattening up" in ESL class yet, nor is it likely we ever would. She was struck by the enormity of what it means to take on a new language and watched anxiously as a slight frown tightened the muscles of Dan's forehead as he waited for Phally to respond. Not good, Gail thought. He's wondering how they'll communicate.

"That would be lovely, Dan. You make such good hot chocolate," Gail said, filling the awkward silence.

Dan disappeared into the kitchen, reappearing with a tray and four mugs of cocoa a few minutes later. He handed the mugs around and placed the tray on a nearby table, then pulled up a chair and lowered his lanky frame into it. "I've got an hour before I reopen for the dinner crowd," he announced. "Plenty of time to chat."

Speaking slowly for Phally's benefit, Gail explained her idea of a part-time minimum wage job for Phally, making egg rolls and other Cambodian savories that Dan would get to sample and choose, and a few desserts. Gail would help train Phally and add a touch of Asian flair to Dan's decor here and there.

Gail paused to take a sip of cocoa. Anything would beat the limp plastic greenery currently tacked up on the walls, their dusty foliage the perfect accent to the brittle plastic table covers, she thought. With any luck, Dan would let her redo the whole interior.

She swallowed her cocoa and continued on. Dan would provide the budgets for decoration, Asian ingredients, and any special cooking implements Phally might need, and Gail and Phally would do the shopping.

Dan listened quietly, nodding his head occasionally.

Dan turned his look now upon Gail. "And you'll help her get along?" he asked.

"Absolutely," Gail said.

Dan nodded. "And you think we can figure out what each other is trying to say? I don't want any big mix-ups happening."

"I do, Dan," Gail said. "Once you've spent a little time together, gotten used to each other's accents, it's not hard. You'll develop a common vocabulary."

"Could still be a problem with customers, though." Dan stroked his chin and stared at the ceiling.

"I'll be here to help out," Gail reminded him. "I'm sure it will work, and your business will get a nice boost once people taste Phally's cooking."

"Can't argue with that," Dan said with a grin. "Those were some mighty tasty egg rolls."

When Gail finished speaking, he leaned back in his chair. After a moment, he looked at Phally. "And you want this job?" he asked, speaking slowly, clearly, and a little too loudly, as if volume would help Phally understand.

"I very want," Phally said.

Dan looked at Phally for a moment, his eyes sweeping over her tidy hairstyle and simple dress. He nodded then and turned toward Gail.

"Alrighty, then. Your word is good enough for me," he said. "We'll start Monday. Meet me here at 2:30. We'll go over the budgets and then you gals can go shopping." He glanced at his empty mug. "I need a refill. Anyone else?"

"Dan, thank you," Gail said. "This means a lot to me."

Dan blinked hard for a moment. He shrugged and cleared his throat. "Well, I reckon this town needs some quality Asian food," he said, then excused himself and ambled into the kitchen. Gail heard the honk of a good nose-blow before Dan returned with a jug of cocoa that he passed around. Then he turned to Phally. "Now, little lady, tell me about yourself. How long you been in America?"

Phally nodded and began to speak. Gail pushed her notepad to Phally along with a pen, knowing that Phally did better if she could doodle pictures as she talked, illustrating her words for back-up. Dan caught on quickly and began doing the same, using simple line drawings to help Phally understand, and soon the two of them were enjoying sharing information, while Nary looked on and occasionally added detail. When Phally learned that Dan's wife Frieda had died a year ago, an expression of great empathy swept over her features.

"I know, hurt here," she said, placing a hand over her heart. "My husband, he die in Cambodia. I so very miss."

"I'm right sorry to hear that, Miss Phally," Dan said. "I guess we got more in common than you'd think, just looking at the two of us."

Gail smiled. This just might be good for all of them, she thought. All of us.

Now that things were flowing smoothly, Gail let her eyes drift to the window. The trees were draped with autumn finery. Nearby, a vine maple shimmered in exceptionally vibrant red color, its leaves rippling in the breeze.

Coming down the street, a homeless man was shuffling along in drab clothing with bits of foliage clinging to his pant legs and scattered throughout his dark hair. Must have slept in the park, Gail thought. This was a new twist in Glenberg's growth; she'd never noticed the homeless before. The man paused and ran his hands over his face, then straightened his body with a visible effort. He raised his head, pulled his shoulders back and began to walk more briskly. Gail felt a stab of admiration. Clearly the man had known better times and retained an element of self-respect. She wondered what his story was. And then she realized it was Khath.

Oh no, she thought, a rush of guilt flooding over her. The poor man looked so devastated, so pitiful. So alone. Confused by her own emotions, Gail glanced quickly at Phally to see if she too had noticed him, but Phally's body was angled away from the window as she concentrated on talking with Dan. Not so with Nary. The girl's eyes sparkled with tears as she stared out the window at Khath as he passed by, body held rigid, staring straight ahead. Gail hoped he wouldn't look in the window and notice them. Nary raised her hand to rap on the window, and

Gail reached quickly across the table to stop her, closing her hand over the child's small one. Gail met Nary's startled gaze and gave a brief shake of her head. "Not now," she mouthed. Nary's thin shoulders rose as she drew a deep breath, swallowed and slumped back in her chair, her small body seeming to cave in upon itself.

Gail wrapped her hands around the warm cup of cocoa in front of her, her throat constricting as she witnessed Nary's misery. She looked at Phally, watching the woman smile and nod in a mighty effort to show her new boss that she was up to the challenge, the opportunity, being offered to her. Seeming to feel the pull of Gail's scrutiny, Phally glanced over, throwing a grateful look in Gail's direction. Gail nodded and forced stiff lips into a smile of encouragement as disquieting thoughts rumbled in her brain.

Was she doing the right thing, helping Phally like this? Should she have just let the Cambodians settle things within their community? What if she was making things worse, causing new jealousies and resentments?

Gail watched Dan and Phally for a moment. Well, it was done now. Clearly, those two had taken a shine to one another. She'd just have to follow it through and hope for the best.

# Twenty-Three

Crisp leaves crackled underfoot as Sareth strode up the sidewalk to Khath's front door. Two days had passed since the party. It was time to pay a call. He rapped on the front door with bare knuckles and had time to assume an expression of concern before Pra Chhay answered his knock and let him inside. At the monk's urging, Sareth settled into the couch and waited while Pra Chhay prepared tea. His gaze wandered around the room, seeking clues to the state of things in this house. It was tidy, clean, sparkling actually. And yet, a faint odor of cigarette smoke lingered in the air. Khath was nowhere to be seen.

"And how is our dear boy?" Sareth asked as Pra Chhay returned with a tray of tea and condiments. "Such a dreadful time he's had."

The monk's quiet eyes, clear and calm like a reflecting pool, gave away nothing. "As you would expect," he said. "Khath is struggling with painful memories. He is resting at present. He had a restless night."

Sareth took a deep sip of his tea. It was bitter, over-brewed, and he struggled not to grimace. He added another teaspoon of sugar and stirred, the spoon making a soft scraping noise against the cup.

"I had hoped he would be up by now," Sareth said, making sure that Pra Chhay saw him glance casually at his watch. It was 10:00 AM. "You see, Father Ralph is usually at his office this time of day. I came to offer my services to Khath should he want to make a formal request to have Father Ralph look into Phally's background."

"This is something Father Ralph can do?" Pra Chhay asked. "Some legal means to investigate?"

"I am certain there must be channels," Sareth replied.

"And making such a request will not backfire?" Pra Chhay said. "It would not cause Khath to come under suspicion or get him into trouble in some way?"

"I will impress upon Father Ralph the utmost need for discretion," Sareth said, watching the monk closely. He could see that Pra Chhay's loyalty to his brother was absolute. It was a good thing to know, Sareth thought, and possibly useful at some point.

"As I am sure you can appreciate," Sareth continued, "Father Ralph has no desire to create more problems in our community. But, as a sponsor, he bears some responsibility to act on these accusations. A formal request from Khath smooths the way for Father Ralph to take some action."

Pra Chhay nodded slowly. "Yes, I see that," he said. "Father Ralph, in all fairness, has to follow up. Yet he is not the one initiating the action. He remains neutral."

"Exactly," Sareth said. "And I am confident that he would like to get to the truth of things as well."

Sareth wondered what Father Ralph would do if it were proved that Phally was Khmer Rouge. If the choice were even up to him, would he have her deported? Or would he practice the Christian values of forgiveness and redemption? "Turning the other cheek," Sareth believed it was called. He was not sure many Cambodians had enough flesh left on their cheeks to offer them up for yet another slap. Nor would it serve his purposes if they did. The sound of Pra Chhay's voice interrupted his reverie.

"An inquiry may take weeks, even months," Pra Chhay was saying. "Perhaps this is good. It will give us all some time to breathe, to settle down."

Not if I can help it, Sareth thought. But aloud he said, "You make an excellent point. So, you agree with me?"

Pra Chhay nodded and stood up. "I will go see if Khath is awake."

A few minutes later, the monk returned to the room with his brother. Khath squinted at the light pouring in through the windows and rubbed his eyes. His hair was disheveled and his clothing rumpled.

"Have a seat, Khath," Pra Chhay said. "I will bring you some coffee. Mr. Sareth and I have been talking, and I think he has a good plan. See if you agree."

Forty-five minutes later, the three men stood in the hallway outside of Father Ralph's office. The door was partially closed, but Sareth could see that the priest was on the phone.

Father Ralph did not look especially pleased, and indeed, as he hung up he passed a hand over his brow as if the conversation had troubled him. Sareth waited for a few seconds and then tapped on the door. The priest looked up and smiled, as if relieved.

"Mr. Sareth," he said. "Just the man I was hoping to…" His smile faltered. "Oh. Pra Chhay. And Khath. Well, this is a surprise. Come in, do come in."

The priest came around from behind the desk and clasped the hands of the two brothers in turn, guiding them to the comfortable chairs clustered around a small coffee table to one side of his large office. "Coffee? Water? What can I offer you? How about some tea?"

Without waiting for an answer, Father Ralph walked to the electric tea kettle on the credenza, plopped tea bags into mugs, added hot water and shook some fig bars onto a plate.

He seems nervous about something, Sareth thought. All this busy bustling about is not like him. He walked over to help the priest. As they stood in the corner, brewing the tea, Sareth said, "Forgive me for not phoning ahead. Have we come at a bad time? We can return later."

Father Ralph took a deep breath. "No, it's fine. I am very glad to see Khath out and about. But can you stay for a few moments after we've all talked? There is something I'd like to discuss with you."

"As you wish," Sareth said. Was this about the disturbing phone call?

Once they were all settled, Father Ralph seemed more at ease, his attention focused on the two brothers. "How are you, Khath? I'm so sorry for what you've been through. I can't even begin to imagine how difficult it must be." The priest's voice was gentle, full of concern. He leaned forward and laid his hand briefly on Khath's knee.

Khath's head dropped. He gripped his hands tightly together and cleared his throat. "Thank you," he said in a low voice.

"Is there something I can do for you, Khath?" Father Ralph asked.

"Yes," Khath said. "I come, ask you..." His English failed him, and he turned to Sareth and spoke rapidly in his native tongue.

"He has a formal request to make of you, he says. But first, he wants to tell you about something that happened in Khao I Dang, the refugee camp, just before he and Pra Chhay came here," Sareth said.

"All right," Father Ralph said, sitting back in his chair. "Go ahead."

Sareth listened while Khath spoke, then translated. "He says they lived in a big hut at Khao I Dang, with six families per building. There was a nice old granny who lived across the aisle from them, taking care of her two grandsons. The Khmer Rouge had killed her son, the boys' father. One day she was very upset, weeping and shouting."

241

Sareth turned back to Khath. In spite of himself, he was interested in the story. It was so seldom that Khath initiated a conversation or provided more than a polite response to questions. This was a side of the man he'd not yet seen before.

Khath continued with the story. Although he spoke to Sareth in his native tongue, his eyes never left the priest. He told of how the old Granny had seen a known Khmer Rouge soldier from her village in Khao I Dang, and that he had worn her dead son's watch. "I was so upset to know that Khmer Rouge were in my camp, living among us like neighbors," Khath said. "And then, I met the man myself."

When Sareth translated this, Father Ralph sat upright. "But how did Khath know who the man was? Can you ask him that, Mr. Sareth?"

"There was another man, a Cambodian man who converted to Christianity," Khath told Sareth. "He invited me to visit his church group. That's where I saw Mith, passing out bibles, wearing that beautiful watch. He was pretending to be converted, volunteering at the church, so he'd have a better chance of finding a sponsor, a church, and coming to America."

Khath flushed suddenly and looked down at his hands. "I mean no disrespect. Tell the priest that. I don't mean to dishonor his work, but this is what the Khmer Rouge did. They lied, they pretended. It is who they are. Why should being in a camp change that?"

Sareth gazed at Khath with narrowed eyes. "You are sure of this?" he asked Khath. "You know that there were Khmer Rouge in Khao I Dang camp?"

Pra Chhay leaned forward. "The events are as Khath has told them. I can vouch for that," he told Sareth.

"Very well," Sareth said, then he turned to Father Ralph to translate. He kept his face grave, but his heart was singing. Khath's story provided some credibility to his claim that Phally was Khmer Rouge. If one could slip through the cracks, why not two, or fifty?

"It is possible that the man truly converted," Father Ralph said. "Did you talk to him?"

Pra Chhay spoke directly to the priest. "Khath's friend, he say some people convert in their hearts. He say could be Khmer Rouge, could be government soldier. People who do bad things in the war, they like to hear about a big God. They like God who forgive them. Make them feel okay." Pra Chhay shook his head. "Not Mith. In his heart Mith still Khmer Rouge."

Sareth turned to Khath. "*Did* you talk to him?" he asked in Cambodian. He sensed there was more to this story.

Khath was silent for a long moment then began to speak. "I was afraid Granny's eldest grandson would try to get the watch back from Mith. I decided I would take care of it. I didn't want the boy to get hurt. They'd just found sponsors, relatives in America. They were leaving the camp soon, just waiting for their travel documents." He fell silent again.

Sareth translated, surprised to feel a growing sense of anticipation mixed with dread rising in his chest. "Don't stop now," he wanted to shout. Whatever else Khath was, he was a very fine storyteller, he thought.

"Ask him what happened next," Father Ralph said quietly, his eyes never leaving Khath.

Prompted by Sareth, Khath continued his story. "I could have killed him," he said. "I surprised him in the dark and took the watch back. I had my blade against his throat. In my mind, I saw my son, my wife, my daughters. I wanted to press that blade deep, all the way through. My hand trembled, so strong was my desire to take my revenge." He sighed. "Instead, I took only the watch, and I gave him a little nick on his neck, something to think about. To this day, I am not sure if I did the right thing." As he said these last words, Khath fastened his gaze upon the priest.

Sareth began to translate, but Pra Chhay interrupted him. "Let me finish the story," he said to older man. "We knew Khath's life was in danger from that point on. We tried to stay together, but one night when I was delayed at the temple, Mith and his Khmer Rouge cronies found Khath walking alone. They beat him almost to death, three against one. Khath's friend brought him back home, and I nursed him as best I could. Two days later we left for America."

Sareth nodded. He was very pleased. There was no way that Father Ralph would deny Khath's request after hearing this story. As he translated, he watched the priest's expression change from horror to concern to pity.

"The bruises," Father Ralph said quietly, when Sareth was done speaking. "That's why you arrived here looking so bruised and exhausted. There was no 'accident.'"

Pra Chhay bowed low. "Of course you are right," he said. "I apologize for tell you that."

The priest waved off the apology.

"Father Ralph," Sareth said. "The reason Khath wanted to come here today was to formally request that you make inquiries regarding Phally's background and that of her husband, Boran. Knowing, as he has just explained, that some Khmer Rouge actively sought resettlement in foreign countries, he feels that such an inquiry is proper and just, given the circumstances."

Father Ralph leaned back in his chair. "Yes, I see," he said. He gazed out the window, a slight frown knitting his brow as he stroked his jaw in silence.

After a moment, Sareth said, "I can see that this request is troubling you. May we know the reasons why?" He kept his voice respectful, squashing down his irritation with the priest's hesitation. What was the problem here?

"I'm not even sure how to go about it," Father Ralph said. "And I really have no idea what the possible ramifications might be. But these are just logistics. On the human side, Phally has been a big part of this community for the last six months. She is making such progress settling in. I hate to disrupt that." He paused. "On the other hand, Khath is making a legitimate request, and his story is very compelling."

Sareth translated for Khath, who sat with his gaze never leaving the priest's face. He said something to Sareth in Cambodian.

"Khath wants you to know he appreciates the difficult position he is putting you in, Father Ralph. He apologizes, but says he cannot withdraw his request."

At least, he said the first part, Sareth thought, gauging the effect of his words on Father Ralph. And he would have said the second if he were more comfortable in this country and understood the culture a little better. I am merely voicing his intent, in addition to what he says. Sareth was aware that Pra Chhay had looked at him sharply when he embellished Khath's words. He would need to deal with that later.

Father Ralph straightened up in his chair. "All right. Here's what I'll do. First of all, this discussion stays in this room. Phally has enough to deal with without hearing rumors that I am investigating her. Who knows, she may come to me herself and ask me to see what I can find out about her husband." He stopped to let Sareth translate and waited until all three men had nodded before continuing.

"There's another very important reason why I don't want this getting out. If it turns out I've brought Khmer Rouge into this community, the whole town may turn against you all. They may wonder if you *all* are Khmer Rouge. The party was a huge success in building bridges between the locals and your community. All of that will be ruined if the townsfolk get wind of this. If the worst is true, I will be the one to break the news, in my own way, understood?"

Again Sareth translated and reported back to Father Ralph that everyone was in agreement.

"What I will do immediately," Father Ralph said, "is to begin to make inquiries of how to conduct this type of investigation and determine how we can stay in control of it, if that's possible. I'll let Sareth know what I find out and he can tell you both, all right?"

Sareth nodded. "A very wise course of action," he said to Father Ralph, pleased that the priest was putting him in control of what was communicated to Khath and Pra Chhay. But as he turned to the brothers to explain how things would work, he found to his irritation that Pra Chhay was speaking up before he could.

"We, my brother and me, this has much important to us," Pra Chhay said to Father Ralph, ignoring Sareth. "We say thank you to you, but we can..." he made a circling gesture encompassing everyone in the room, "...all of us have meeting, like this. Is better than one by one by one, yes? Can ask questions, think together, yes?"

Sareth felt a surge of anger. As he had feared, the monk was beginning to insert himself in matters that would previously have been privately handled by Father Ralph and himself.

He turned a polite face to the priest and cleared his throat. Putting a slightly apologetic tone in his voice, he said, "I believe Khath's brother is trying to request that we continue to meet as a group on this matter."

"I see. All right," Father Ralph said. "Perhaps we can gather at their house next time."

Sareth translated, and Khath and Pra Chhay stood up to leave. Sareth stood, too, took a step toward the door, and then turned to Father Ralph. "I nearly forgot," he said, making sure to speak loudly enough that Pra Chhay would hear. "There was something else you wished to discuss with me?" That should help put the monk back in his place. Make it clear that when there was trouble, he was the one that Father Ralph turned to for counsel, Sareth thought. And he intended to keep it that way.

After the brothers had left, Father Ralph stepped into his private bathroom and dumped his tea down the sink. He poured himself a cup of coffee. "Care for some?" he asked, raising his cup at Sareth.

"Thank you, no," Sareth said.

"Well, I'll get right to the point," Father Ralph said, sitting down at his desk. "That was Gail on the phone when you arrived earlier."

Oh no. Now what? Sareth kept his voice light. "And how is Miss Gail?" he said.

"Oh, she's fine, fine. But she had a bit of news to share." Father Ralph took a sip of coffee.

"Good news?" Sareth asked, with a smile. His heart began to thump faster in his chest.

"Good news, but bad timing I think," Father Ralph said. "She got Phally a job cooking egg rolls and such at Dan's Diner and Grill. She starts this afternoon."

"What?" Sareth was stunned. He could not possibly have heard correctly. "Phally has a job?"

A job. What a nice reward for being Khmer Rouge. Chea would be absolutely livid to be trumped in this way. Not that she wanted to work, but as the wife of the community leader, she had every right to expect that she would be the first to be offered a position. After she declined it, then Phally could have it. He sat, shaking his head in disbelief. Finally, he gathered his wits enough to say, "I fear this will not be well-received in my community."

"I didn't think so either," Father Ralph said. "I hate to think of Khath's reaction."

The priest was continuing to speak, but Sareth could not hear him over the roar of his own thoughts. He would have to move quickly. Convince Chea that this was all part of his plan to enflame Khath's emotions to the point that he would push Phally out of the community. Threaten her, perhaps. He glanced at his watch. He'd better hurry home and break the news to his wife in the proper way, before she heard it from someone else. He forced his attention back to the priest.

"So, why don't you call me once you've had a chance to think it over," Father Ralph was saying. "Then we'll work out a strategy for damage control."

Damage control. As Sareth understood it, that term meant damage prevention to the greatest extent possible. He was not interested in damage *control*. On the contrary. He intended to inflict as much damage as he could.

# Twenty-Four

Khath stood outside the Glenberg Hardware store, nervously jingling the change in his pockets. At the beginning of each month, he and Pra Chhay received their Refugee Cash Assistance checks in the mail. Now, with some funds at hand, he could buy a few things he needed to fix up the cabin in the woods.

Teresa had helped him and Pra Chhay set up bank accounts and showed them how to endorse the checks so the bank would exchange them for cash. She had encouraged them to save a portion of their money and use a checking account, insisting that it was safer to use a checkbook rather than carry large sums of cash around. You might get robbed, she had fretted.

But Khath was not worried about that. He thought of all the people wailing outside the closed banks in Phnom Penh, their money inaccessible as the Khmer Rouge clawed at the edges of the city. At least for now, Khath preferred cash in his hand and hidden under his mattress, rather than numbers written in a little booklet. Besides, a little risk could be a good thing. It kept your senses alert and your mind sharp.

Patiently, Khath waited for a customer to come along and enter the store. So far, he had only ventured into the grocery store in Glenberg, never a specialty store like this one. His plan was to watch and see how transactions were handled before he attempted to make a purchase.

In Cambodia, the shops were smaller and not all of the merchandise was displayed. You simply told the shopkeepers what you wanted and they fetched it for you. Even if you didn't see the item you needed, there was a good chance the vendor had it stashed in the back somewhere.

Khath decided to smoke a cigarette while he waited. After all, there was an ashcan, amazingly, right there, by the door of the hardware store. What a tidy country. He liked that about America. In contrast, the Cambodian countryside was dotted with piles of trash dragged about by dogs, rooted through by pigs and cows, as much a part of the landscape as the rice paddies and coconut palms. There was no garbage collection, so people burned their trash and some were more regular about it than others.

Blowing smoke out of his nostrils, Khath noticed a man getting out of a dented tan pickup truck that had parked just down the street. The man stretched, hitched up his blue jeans, then headed toward the hardware store. Khath stepped away from the entrance a pace or two. He felt his muscles tighten instinctively, still uncertain of his place in this new culture.

The man came closer and Khath felt himself raked by cool blue eyes: face, body, face. What did the man see as he looked him over, Khath wondered. A short, wiry man, tidily dressed, finishing his smoke before starting his shopping? Or did he project something much worse than that?

As he passed by, the man jerked his head in a neutral nod toward Khath, and Khath nodded back, pleased to have been acknowledged. He took three more draws on the cigarette, crushed it out in the ashcan and entered the shop. A little bell jingled overhead as he opened and shut the door, and he noticed a large round mirror hanging in the corner that gave an overview of the entire store.

A grin spread itself over Khath's face as he peered down row after row of gleaming tools, small machines and hardware. The sharp tang of metal and oil lingered faintly in the air. So much to look at, all out in the open where he could examine it all at will. It was a mechanic's dream.

Wandering down an aisle, Khath stopped and reached his hand out to touch a hammer, amazed at the variety of heads and handles: wooden, metal, rubber, a whole wall of hammers. He felt overwhelmed at such a nonchalant display of wealth.

"Help ya?"

Khath spun around guiltily. Was it permitted to touch? He had forgotten all about watching the other customer first, so delighted was he at the riches spread before him.

A tall sandy-haired man, his belly straining against the cloth of a dark green apron emblazoned with the store name, stood smiling at him.

Khath smiled back. It was impossible not to, so strong was the good humor radiating from the shopkeeper's face. "I look," he said. "Is okay?"

"Sure, no problem." The man reached out and plucked a hammer from the wall, handing it to Khath, a steady stream of words flowing from his mouth. Khath had no idea what the man was saying, but he hefted the hammer in his hand, enjoying the balanced feel of it, the solid weight in his grip. He tried a wooden handled hammer, and a metal one with a rubber grip, swinging at an imaginary nail. At some point, he realized that the man had asked him a question and stood waiting for his answer. But what had the man said?

Khath smiled apologetically. "Sorry. I don't understand," he said. "I can do. But I cannot say."

The man studied him for a moment then smiled again. Speaking slowly, he said, "A man of action, not words. I like that." He swung his arms back and forth and stomped his feet. "Action, right?"

Khath nodded. "Action, yes."

"No problem, buddy. I'll leave you to it." The man turned to go.

Then Khath thought of a question. "Excuse me?" he said. "How much?"

"Prices are right here, on the tag," the store clerk said, showing Khath where to find the price among all the other numbers and information on the display tags. "Just look for the dollar sign," the shopkeeper said, and laughed loudly. He walked away but returned a moment later with a plastic basket. "Anything you want to buy, you just put it in here, and bring it up to me, there," he pointed to a counter, "to pay for it, okay?"

Left to his own devices, Khath selected a hammer, a box of nails, screws and screwdriver, pliers, a hank of clothesline cord, a padlock and an ax. As an afterthought, he tossed a package of candles into the basket as well, along with a box of wooden matches. Khath added the prices up in his head as he moved toward the cash register. He would have more than enough to cover the cost. He placed his basket of goods on the counter and said, "I pay now."

The friendly shopkeeper wore a tag on his apron. Khath ventured a guess. "Your name, Al?" he asked.

The man beamed, his cheeks creased in a pleased smile. "That's right. I'm Al. And you must be one of those refugees from Cambodia that Father Ralph is bringing in."

Khath nodded. "I am Khath," he said.

"Khath," Al repeated. "That'll be sixty-six dollars and ten cents, Khath." He pulled a heavyweight plastic bag out from under the counter and began placing Khath's items inside.

Khath riffled through his wallet and pulled out three twenties, and a five. But he had no other small bills. So instead, he laid his last $100 bill on the counter. As he began to gather back the twenties and the five, Al stopped him.

"Nah," he said. "You keep that." He pushed the $100 bill away. "You probably need that extra dollar ten more than I do." He winked at Khath. "I'm the boss, here. It's okay."

Khath stared at the man. Really? Al's gesture of kindness was making Khath's throat tighten. "Thank you," he said, unsure what to do next.

Al handed him the bag with his left hand, and reached out with his right to grasp Khath's for a firm shake. "Welcome to America, buddy," he said. "Come back soon and bring your friends."

Buoyed by his pleasant experience at the hardware store, Khath hummed as he walked down the street, heading for Nary's shortcut to the outskirts of town. He felt that things were going well again, getting back on track. Father Ralph was going to investigate Phally, he could continue working with Teresa to find his daughters, and now, he had a project and the tools to make it happen. Fixing up the cabin was something to keep him occupied while he waited for vindication from the priest.

He turned off into the woods, following the narrow trail. After a few minutes, he heard a twig snap behind him and then another. Someone was following him. Khath shortened his stride, slowing his pace imperceptibly. He angled his head slightly and used his peripheral vision, aided by the twists and turns of the trail, to keep watch behind him as he moved deeper into the woods.

There. A movement. Fifteen meters back, a slight figure detached itself from the shadow of a tree and darted across the path. A surge of gladness swelled up in Khath's chest as he realized it was Nary. He pretended to stumble and dropped his bag, turning swiftly to pick it up and glance down the trail for Nary. Would she let herself be seen? Would she approach? Khath was disappointed to find that the child had melted behind a tree, so quickly that even he, with all his skill, was unable to determine which trunk was shielding her. He assumed that Phally had forbidden her to have any contact with him.

Knowing that nothing would be gained by forcing her to reveal herself, Khath continued on, thinking. Nary was very good at this tracking and hiding business. Whoever had taught her had done a fine job. But who had taught her? Her father? But Phally swore her husband was killed shortly after the Khmer Rouge had come to power. Even Nary said her father was dead. But maybe Phally was telling her to say that. Was it Phally then? Had Phally trained her and sent her out to scavenge food? That couldn't be because Phally claimed that Nary was separated from her, sent to a youth brigade during the Khmer Rouge years. And Nary certainly acted as though the maternal tie had been severed.

Khath walked on, puzzling. Even taking out the fact that Khath firmly believed he had seen Boran, alive, with his own eyes, there were big holes in this story. He was determined to fill them with the truth.

When Khath reached the little country lane, close to the cornfield, he slowed to give Nary plenty of time to be able to track him across the road and down the embankment near the farmer's land. He chuckled to himself. She would think he was crazy, going back to tangle with the farmer and his dog again.

Entering the forest again, he pictured her surprise when she saw the cabin. It pleased him to think of having something to offer Nary, a place to go if she needed peace and quiet, or a place to talk with someone she trusted. She certainly wasn't getting that at home. He'd never seen a child so closed off to her own mother before.

Suddenly, he stopped, struck by a new thought. What if Phally *wasn't* Nary's real mother?

His mind in turmoil, Khath moved woodenly along the path. Of course. It was the only explanation that made sense. Phally was Khmer Rouge and had used Nary to gain entry to a resettlement country. Hadn't the Red Cross officer in Portland said that people would use any means to get out of the camps?

It was so brilliantly simple. Phally must have been in charge of Nary in the youth brigade. If Nary's own family was dead, there was no one to protect her in the chaos of an occupied country. If they teamed up, Phally would get a ticket out of

Cambodia and Nary would have an adult to fend for her. It was the perfect plan.

Anger welled up in his chest, making it hard to breathe. He did not blame Nary, no, not at all. After four years of absolute dominance by the Khmer Rouge, what chance did an orphaned girl have to resist a scheme like that? Phally may have threatened Nary, forced her to go along with it.

Khath turned and looked behind him for the child but there was no trace of her. He would have to find a way to talk with Nary, a way to get her alone where Phally couldn't intervene. Obviously, that wasn't going to happen today if the child was afraid to show herself.

He glanced at his watch and quickened his pace. He would barely have enough time to drop off his tools at the cabin and get back home before Pra Chhay returned from ESL class.

Fifteen minutes later, he was carefully pulling the old cabin door open. Leaving it ajar, he walked inside and tucked his bag away behind the screened off area at the end of the counter. He stood for a moment by the thick and blurry window to watch for Nary, but the glass was too distorted to see anything clearly. It didn't matter. He was sure she was out there.

With no time to spare, he left the cabin, making a fuss of closing the door so Nary would know he was leaving. He was half-way back to the road when he realized he'd left his wallet inside the plastic bag with the tools. He'd dropped it in there to free his hand when Al wanted to shake with him, then, then forgotten all about it. Exasperated, Khath turned on his heel and jogged back through the forest.

Annoyed and breathless, he reentered the cabin and strode toward the counter, taking all of two steps before stopping in surprise, a smile breaking over his face. In the twenty minutes he'd been gone, Khath had had a visitor. The rusted tin can, filled with pond water and positioned to soak up the feeble glow from the window, held several fern fronds that framed a delicate arrangement of tiny white and pink wildflowers. Nary had left him a bouquet, a house-warming present. He moved toward the counter and, leaning close, inhaled a faint sweet scent from the flowers, subtle and ethereal, like Nary herself.

Khath groaned, his gut twisting in a storm surge of emotion. How could a child so ill-used by life still have the capacity to see the beauty around her, let alone the desire to reach out and share it with others? She was a very special little girl, and Khath vowed, then and there, he would find a way to protect her, to clear a path for her in life.

Grabbing his wallet from the bag, Khath hurried out the door and ran down the trail, hoping to catch Nary and at least acknowledge her gift. She must be close—he hadn't seen her on his jog back to the cabin so she may have been hiding in the surrounding bushes even while he was in the cabin. Or, had she heard him crashing back down the trail and simply stepped off to one side and watched him pass by?

Khath covered the distance back into town in half the time it had taken him to walk out to the cabin. When he emerged from the path onto the street, he paused, his chest heaving, looking up and down the road, searching for Nary's slender silhouette. There, about two blocks up the street, he saw her. As much as he wanted to, he dared not run. Only children could run down a street without causing suspicion. Settling into a fast walk, Khath kept his eyes fixed upon Nary's back and gained rapidly on her.

He was only half a block behind her, when abruptly she turned and entered a building. Mystified, Khath hurried to see where she had gone so boldly, without any hesitation at all. He stopped in front of the building, his curiosity increasing when he realized it was a restaurant. Why would Nary go into a restaurant by herself? There was only one way to find out. Firmly, Khath grasped the handle, stepped through the door and stood, transfixed by the scene in front of him.

Phally, wearing a white apron with her hair tucked up in a bun, stood behind a glass display case, arranging Cambodian sticky-rice desserts on a tray. Beside her, in her wheelchair, Gail was holding another tray full of sweets, and pointing to where she seemed to want Phally to put them. Nary, her back to the door, stood outside the case, admiring the tempting display, her hands flat against the glass case.

Disbelief and anger made Khath's jaw drop, then clench, at the thought that Phally, of all people, was now the public face of Cambodia in Glenberg. The insult was almost more than Khath could bear. His lip curled. That woman should be hiding herself in shame, not brazenly flaunting the culture she and her Khmer Rouge compatriots had shredded and trampled upon. Those sweets were made with the blood of his people, his family. How dare she? His gaze flickered over Gail. This had to be her doing. He felt a stab of betrayal. Did Teresa also help to bring this about?

Khath took a step forward, his hands balled into fists, his breath rasping in his throat. He saw three startled sets of eyes staring at him in dismay.

Quickly Gail shoved her tray at Phally and wheeled out around the corner of the case. "Khath," she said, reaching out to him, her hands palms up, in a calming gesture. "I'm so glad to see you. Let me explain."

Khath backed away, his throat working. "No," he said hoarsely. "No." His shoe caught on the door jamb, and he almost stumbled, but managed to catch his balance in time. He could not tear his eyes away from the three women. Talk? No. As Al had said, Khath was a man of action. He turned on his heel and walked out the door.

# Twenty-Five

Leaning back in his chair, Sareth gazed at the troubled faces of the women across the coffee table from him, while Father Ralph made some notes on a pad of paper. They were all seated in the conversation corner of the priest's office as Gail explained how Khath had reacted to seeing her and Phally working at Dan's Grill.

Sareth supposed the English word for how he was feeling was "smug." Yes, that was it. He'd told Father Ralph that this business of Phally getting a job was going to create trouble in the community, and now here were Gail and Teresa, proving his point.

"It looks like I really made a mess of things, didn't I?" Gail was saying. Well, if she wanted to be reassured that she hadn't, she'd better not be looking at him, Sareth thought. His ears were still ringing from the scolding he'd gotten from his wife, Chea, when he had broken the news to her. *I thought you had things under control,* Chea had hissed, her faith in him shaken. He had thought so, too, but he'd not taken the meddling of Miss Gail into consideration.

Poor judgment on his part. He would not make that mistake twice. For now, he was going to enjoy explaining to the worried sisters on the couch, in great and very sorrowful detail, the extent to which they truly had upset the equilibrium of the community. He leaned forward.

"Can you tell us exactly what happened when you went to visit Khath at home?"

"Well," Gail said. "Pra Chhay answered the door, and I thought he seemed startled to see us there." She glanced at Teresa. "Didn't you think so?"

Teresa nodded. "I'd even use a stronger word: 'Distressed' maybe. He definitely was not happy to see us."

"And then?" Sareth prompted.

"Pra Chhay let us in, and we sat down, but he didn't offer us tea. We were sort of waiting for him to head off to the kitchen, the way he always does," Gail said. "It took us a while to figure out he was staying put."

"It was definitely an uncomfortable few moments," Teresa added, shaking her head.

"A rather strong signal in our culture, I am afraid," Sareth said. "You see, our country is so very warm. When a guest stops by, it is of the utmost importance to bring a beverage, otherwise your guest may end up collapsed on the floor from thirst." He paused. "Or even worse, they may have to *ask* for water, which would reflect very poorly on one's reputation for hospitality. We pride ourselves on being a hospitable people, you know. Or perhaps you didn't know." Another pause.

"So what did you do then?" Sareth caught himself just in time, biting off the rest of the sentence, pressing his lips together. He had almost continued with "when you realized you were not welcome," but he doubted these obtuse Americans had realized any such thing. They had probably assumed that Pra Chhay was just distracted and had forgotten to serve tea.

"I asked if Khath was home," Teresa said. "Pra Chhay just sat there for the longest time without answering, just looking at us." Teresa's voice started to tremble. "I felt really terrible, so small. There was no judgment or anger in his face, he just looked at us."

Sareth felt anger rise in his chest. "Well, but don't you see, Miss Teresa, what a position you were putting him in? He is a monk. He has taken a vow to be truthful. He gave you both the strongest possible signal that your visit was not a good idea, but still you pressed him with your direct questions."

Sareth took a deep breath. "In my country such directness is not polite. We speak indirectly to avoid putting others in a situation where they will lose face. We do not force issues in my culture." He brought a smile to his lips to soften his words, not wanting to show anger in front of Father Ralph. "It is a major cultural difference between our two countries, no doubt frustrating to some degree for both sides."

He leaned back and glanced from Teresa to Gail. Teresa looked wretched, her eyes brimming with tears. Gail was stony-faced, with furrowed brow.

Father Ralph broke the impasse. "So, you left then?" he asked.

Gail shook her head. "No. Finally Pra Chhay said he would check and he went to Khath's room. We heard agitated voices and then Pra Chhay came back and said Khath was resting and couldn't be disturbed."

Sareth's eyes narrowed at this piece of information. "So Khath refused even to see Miss Teresa? This is very bad indeed." He paused to let the gravity of the situation sink in.

"We tried to convince Pra Chhay to go get him," Teresa said, "Which I can see now was the wrong thing to do after what you've told us, Mr. Sareth. But we wanted to explain."

Explain? Sareth marveled at the way Americans seemed to think that if they could just explain their actions, everything would be all right, as though they hadn't really done the things they'd done. Gail had gotten a job for the woman Khath had just accused of being Khmer Rouge, whose husband had killed Khath's family. What in the world did they think they were going to explain? It was as plain as a snake with a bulge in its throat and feathers on the ground.

Sareth cleared his throat. "I'm sorry to say that I doubt that your explanations would make any difference," he said. "Khath sees that you are helping his enemy. He likely feels confused and betrayed." Sareth shook his head. "The entire community will see this as taking sides, I am afraid. Forgive my frankness, but they will wonder why you support the Khmer Rouge over its victims."

Gail ran a hand over her face. "Nothing is proved," she said. "We believe in due process in this country." She stared out the window for a moment. "I was just trying to help a friend, for Christ's sake." She glared at Sareth. "A friend who was too upset by your behavior to return to your classroom, by the way. Let's not forget how this all really started."

Sareth kept a concerned expression on his face. "A most unfortunate misunderstanding," he said. "Obviously, Phally is overly sensitive at the moment. Perhaps if you'd come to me first."

"All right," Father Ralph interjected. "Mistakes were made this week. But I think we are best served by staying in problem-solving mode. So what happened next?"

After a glance at her sister, Teresa continued. "So, anyway, at that point I just pulled out the packet of letters I had for Khath to sign and left them with Pra Chhay. And then, we came straight here." She turned to Father Ralph. "Thank you for seeing us without an appointment. And you, too, Mr. Sareth."

"Of course," Father Ralph said. "I'm glad you came so promptly with your concerns." The priest glanced over at the older man. "Mr. Sareth, how do you suggest we handle this?"

"Let me think for a few minutes," Sareth said. "Why don't we take a short break."

He strolled into the hallway, his mind working furiously. The broken trust between the Americans and Khath was good. He could use that to his advantage. Khath would have nowhere else to turn, and Sareth was prepared, in private, to provide a sympathetic and supportive ear. Perhaps plant a few seeds to get

Khath thinking about avenging his family. But publicly, Khath needed to pull himself together. Become a model citizen. Earn the community's trust again. Then, when the crisis had passed and senses were lulled into complacency, Sareth, like a master puppeteer, would begin pulling strings and setting in motion his plan to oust Phally from Glenberg.

When everyone was resettled in the priest's office, Sareth was pleased to see how they all sat quietly, waiting for him to speak. He wished that Chea could witness the respect with which the priest treated him at work. Perhaps that would erase the doubt Sareth saw in her beautiful eyes when she gazed at him nowadays. In the old days, with his first wife, Sareth would have slapped that look away, but he understood that husbands were not allowed to discipline their wives in America.

Father Ralph interrupted his thoughts. "The floor is yours, Mr. Sareth. How shall we handle this?"

Sareth held his hands at chest level, fingertips together, his thumbs pressing against his sternum, resting his chin on his index fingers. "I believe, at present, it would be best for Miss Gail and Miss Teresa not to pay any more visits to Khath. Give him space, I believe you would say." He threw a gentle smile in the direction of the women on the couch. "In the meantime, I will go and talk to him, see how he is holding up and explain that Miss Gail meant no harm in helping Phally. And then, we will see."

---

The next morning was gray and drizzly. Sareth pulled his coat tightly around his body and thrust his hands into his pockets, wishing he could stay home and let Chea tend to his comfort. She could bring him hot tea and rub his shoulders and feet, and perhaps she would get lucky in the kitchen and produce something pleasing to his palate. She stood behind him now, dutifully warning him to avoid puddles and protect his head from the rain. Chea performed the role of caring wife well, but lately Sareth sensed a smoldering impatience, like a dangerous undertow hidden beneath her calm surface. He saw it in the way her fingers drummed when she thought he was not watching, in the loud clatter of pots and pans when she cooked.

It worried and angered him, this simmering turbulence layered under her placid exterior. He wished she would take some responsibility for solving the problems that bothered her, instead of expecting him to handle everything. Her feuding with Phally was a perfect example. Daily she brought some new complaint to him, her soft eyes growing hard and resentful as she described some new slight she had suffered at Phally's hands, magnified by Chea's own insecurity about her place in the community.

He sighed inwardly. It was true. Chea was not well-liked in the community. She was too high and mighty, and her beauty spurred jealousy among the women and lust in the men. His deepest fear was that his wife would tire of waiting for him to fix things for her. How easy it would be for her to find a new man, probably an American, to take her away from the difficulties and boredom of a life with him here in Glenberg. It was an intolerable thought. The loss of face for him was bad enough, but the loss of her dutiful attentions would bother him even more. She was selfish and spoiled, but she was his, and he did not want that to change.

Sareth turned and took the hat that Chea silently handed him, nodded his thanks and set out for Khath's home, walking briskly to ward off the chill. He had chosen to walk the few blocks rather than drive so that the air would clear his mind and sharpen his senses, but it was a relief to step into a warm house when he arrived at his destination.

Pra Chhay took his coat and hat, and hurried to the kitchen, returning a moment later with a thermos of hot tea and cups, which he set down on the coffee table. "It is already sweetened," he said, handing a cup to his guest.

Sareth wrapped his chilled fingers around the cup and took a deep, appreciative sip, feeling the heat slide down his throat and warm his belly.

"Delicious," he said. "I thank you sincerely."

Pra Chhay smiled. "I suspected you might pay us a visit today, so I've been keeping this warm."

"You are perceptive as well as a fine brew master," Sareth said. He set the cup down. "Pra Chhay, I am sure you can appreciate how influential Khath's behavior will be as our little community tries to navigate through the mire of this situation."

"Khath does not ask others to follow his lead. He seeks the truth, that is all," Pra Chhay said.

"As do we all," Sareth replied. He let the silence gather behind his words as he leaned back and crossed his legs, fussily arranging the material of his trousers to prevent wrinkling. "I do believe him, you know."

Sareth studied the man opposite him to gauge the impact of his words and was pleased to see Pra Chhay's eyes widen for an instant. "I cannot say this publicly, of course, because of my position here. But I will make sure that Father Ralph aggressively pursues his inquiries about Phally's background. I am confident that he sees the importance of clearing this up, though I believe his sympathies lie with Phally at the moment."

"That is understandable," Pra Chhay said. "Phally is well-established here."

Sareth helped himself to more tea. "Tell me, is your brother a patient man?"

The monk did not reply immediately, seeming to consider his response carefully. Finally, he said, "If Khath himself sees the need for patience, then, yes, he can be as unhurried as a blade of grass growing in the shade of a rubber tree."

Sareth nodded and stood up. "Excellent. I say this because he must get on with his life here. He must resume his activities and regain his footing here in Glenberg. He must show patience and fortitude while Father Ralph investigates."

Sareth stared down the puzzled look in Pra Chhay's eyes, which asked the question his lips had not yet uttered: "But what is the urgency?"

Not giving the monk a chance to speak, Sareth continued, "Because you see, Pra Chhay, he must be someone that our community can support, if it comes down to a contest between him and Phally. If Father Ralph's investigation is inconclusive, Khath must be the one we rally behind." He paused. "Do you want to live side by side in America with the Khmer Rouge? Didn't you have enough of that pleasure in our homeland?"

Taking the monk's momentary silence for agreement, Sareth squared his shoulders. "Now," he said. "Khath is in his room?"

Pra Chhay rose from his chair. "I will get him for you."

"No, no, there is no need." Sareth put his hand out to block Pra Chhay's way. It was critical that he speak to Khath privately. He smiled easily at Pra Chhay. "I understand he is quite low at the moment. He may need the shock of seeing me standing in his room to get him moving." He waved his hand toward the thermos. "I believe I have nearly emptied your pot of tea. Perhaps while I chat with Khath for a moment you can prepare a bit more of that for us all." Without giving Pra Chhay time to respond, Sareth turned on his heel and strode down the hallway to Khath's room.

Sareth stood in the doorway for a moment to give his aging eyes time to adjust to the dim interior of Khath's room before stepping inside and closing the door softly behind him.

The air was stale, and smelled sour and smoky. He could see the shape of Khath curled up under a blanket, facing the wall. Heavy breathing, not quite a snore, rumbled in the silence. Wrinkling his nose in disgust, Sareth crossed to the window and yanked open the curtains. He opened the window wide and took a welcome breath of clean air.

Khath groaned and pulled the blanket up over his head.

Angered, Sareth reached out and grabbed the blanket, jerking it off the bed completely. "Get up," he said. "Now."

Khath's eyes flew open and his mouth dropped to see Sareth. "Where is Pra Chhay?"

"Making tea. Get up. We need to talk. Quickly."

Khath rubbed his eyes and swung his legs over the side of the bed. He reached for his pants, puddled on the floor where he'd stepped out of them, and pulled them on, standing to tuck his shirt in. Still groggy with sleep, he sank back down on the edge of the bed and ran his hands over his face, pushing his hair into some sort of order.

"Now listen carefully," Sareth said. "I know about Phally and her job. I know the Americans betrayed you and helped her. You know, and I believe you, who she really is. I am on your side." He paused to stare into Khath's awakening face. "Am I not the one who came to you and helped you ask Father Ralph to investigate Phally? Is this not true?" He glared at Khath until Khath nodded his head.

"Then you must trust me, Khath. By my actions, you must trust me when I say you have to tell Phally you are sorry, that it is possible that you were mistaken."

Khath's eyes flared and he shook his head. "Never," he said flatly. "I would not dishonor my family in this way."

"Listen to me, Khath, as a soldier listens to his commanding officer. We are at war here. We are still fighting the war. We cannot let them win." Sareth stood tall, staring down at Khath. "It is a strategy, Khath. You must get Phally to trust you again, so she will let down her guard. And then, when she least expects it, you can break her. Force her to tell the truth. I will help you to arrange it. But it is between us, Khath. No one else can know the full plan. They can know only that you are patient and good and willing to let the priest get to the heart of the matter."

Khath nodded slowly.

"Work on finding your daughters and building a life for them here, Khath, a life free of the Khmer Rouge."

Sareth waited, his lips dry. Had he said enough? Too much? Would Khath go along with him? His heart was pounding, and he heard the throb of it in his ears. He did not like to take such risks, to put his trust in another man like this, but he could see no other way. It was crucial to get to Khath while he was vulnerable, to bind him in a secret pact that would lead to Phally's expulsion from Glenberg.

At last, Khath spoke. "I can do this," he said. He stood up to face Sareth. "For my daughters, I can do this."

Relief surged through Sareth, almost buckling his knees. "Good man," he said. "We are an army of two now."

He gestured toward the door. "I believe we can seal our understanding with a cup of tea, and then I must go. We will speak in more detail in a few days."

Sareth started for the door then turned back. "And Khath, remember, an army of two. No one else must know the full plan. Not even your brother."

# Twenty-Six

Gail swiped at the itchy tip of her nose with the back of her forearm, careful not to contaminate her gloved hands as she arranged twenty uncooked egg rolls on a lightly oiled cookie sheet and covered them with plastic wrap. She and Phally were almost done for the day, well-positioned to start the next morning with the sizzle of hot oil as Phally's best-selling rolls were cooked up for customers. Business was booming at Dan's Fountain and Grill, and Dan had Phally's cooking to thank for the surge in customers.

A moment later, Dan ambled up to carry the last two sheets of egg rolls off to the cooler for overnight storage.

"Quitting time, Gail," he said. "Though I have to admit, you look pretty frisky yet for someone who's worked a full day."

"I feel great, Dan," Gail said, and realized with surprise that it was true. She hadn't felt so energetic and useful since the accident had zapped her strength as well as her legs. At least the strength had come back. She wrenched her mind away from the blackness that loomed whenever she thought about her useless legs and instead smiled at the elderly proprietor. "Thanks for taking a chance on us. Seriously."

"It was a damn fine idea you had," Dan replied. He tilted his head toward Nary, perched on a stool and working on her homework in a quiet corner of the kitchen. "What's that little one's story?"

"Oh, the teachers are having a planning day or something, so we told her to come here for the afternoon. Hope that's okay." Gail said, knowing it was.

Dan shrugged. "Hardly knew she was here," he said. "Cute as a button, but she sure don't smile much."

"No, she doesn't," Gail said. "All we know is that she was taken away from her mother for several years and put to work in a Khmer Rouge youth brigade. She won't talk about it at all, not even to Phally."

But had Nary begun to confide in Khath before everything went to hell, Gail wondered? As far as Gail was concerned, the severed tie between Khath and Nary was the biggest casualty in the fallout from Khath's accusations. Anyone who cared to look could see that those two were good for each other.

And now, he wants to talk, she thought. Gail had been surprised to receive Sareth's call early this morning, asking if he and Khath could stop by later. Asking for her help in gathering Phally and Teresa to hear what Khath had to say.

"What's this all about?" Gail had asked. She was not going to agree to anything Mr. Sareth requested without knowing a bit more. But try as she might to wheedle information out of him, Mr. Sareth would only say that things were moving in a positive direction, and he was quite sure, "quite sure, indeed, Miss Gail," that she would be pleased with the outcome. He'd better be right. She'd have his head if he wasn't.

"Well, it's a damn shame," Dan was saying. "What those Khmer Rouge did to their own people. I don't know the half of it, and it's still a damn shame." He patted Gail on the shoulder. "You're doing a good thing here, Gail," he said, as he gathered up the egg rolls and turned toward the cooler.

I hope so, Gail thought. She saw Phally preparing to leave, looking around to make sure all was tidy, nothing left out or forgotten. In this new setting, Phally's inner strength, her quiet competence, was even more evident to Gail. She had learned quickly and was soon devising ways to make the cooking process easier, faster, more efficient. She was blossoming, Gail thought, a flour-dotted, grease-spattered rose.

As Gail watched, Phally grabbed Nary's shoulders and twirled her around on the stool in a playful half pivot, but the child was strangely passive in the face of Phally's attempt at fun. Dan was right. Nary had barely cracked a smile since Khath was removed from her life.

Dan saw them off at the door, replacing the *Open* sign with one that read *"Gone Fishin' Back at 4:00."* Gail and Phally worked from 8:00 AM to 2:00 PM, three days a week, preparing as many egg rolls as they could. Dan often scolded them not to work so hard. "Ladies, ladies," he would say. "The smoke's a'flyin in here. You don't need to feed the whole dang city. When them egg rolls are gone, they're gone. Tubby Joe ain't gonna die overnight if he skips a day of egg rolls."

Gail had laughed at that remark, remembering how Phally's eyes had widened at the enormous bulk of Joe Sanders, a giant of a man who had to stoop to enter the shop on egg roll days.

As usual, Dan offered to drive them home. As usual, they declined. Gail enjoyed this quiet time rolling through the streets with Phally and Nary, though when the fall rains began, she intended to take Dan up on his offer. The three trundled toward Gail's house, Phally pushing the wheelchair, and Nary alternately darting ahead and lagging behind, occasionally dropping a gift of a pretty roadside flower or unusual stone into Gail's lap.

"Phally," Gail said. "Could you and Nary have dinner with us tonight?"

Phally's rich voice radiated pleasure. "Yes, we can. We very happy to eat together."

Gail felt a stab of guilt. You won't be so happy in a minute, she thought.

"And then after dinner?" she said. "We are going to have visitors."

"Ah," said Phally. "Nary, me, we can make special dessert, give your visitors. Then we go home."

"No, no, not like that," Gail said. Ahead of them, Nary bent over to examine something in the roadside weeds. "It's Mr. Sareth. He wants to talk to you, to us all." She paused. Oh, hell. Just say it. "And Khath."

Gail heard a sharp intake of breath, almost a hiss. The smooth roll of the wheelchair stuttered. "Phally?"

"I sorry. I not see Khath. Mr. Sareth, is ok." Phally drew a deep breath. "Khath, I cannot."

Gail heard the anguish in Phally's voice. "Please, Phally. Teresa and I will be there with you. I think Khath knows he is wrong. I think he wants to say sorry to you."

Phally was silent.

"You don't have to reply to him, Phally." Gail said. "Just hear what he says. When he is finished, we will make him go. *I* will make him go. I promise you." Yes, this was what she could do for Phally. "I will tell them when they arrive that you agreed to listen, nothing more." Gail paused. "Do you understand?"

"Yes," said Phally. She sighed a deep, long sigh. "I understand. And I will do."

———

"Khath, this doesn't make sense," Pra Chhay said. He stood by the living room window, leaning on the sill.

Khath sat on the sofa, his stomach in knots. Pra Chhay was not making this easy for him.

"I told you, brother," Khath said. "Mr. Sareth says that if I apologize to Phally, she will relax her guard. She will make a mistake. And besides, the priest is still continuing his inquires. What use is it to keep our community in an uproar until the truth is revealed about Phally?"

On the surface, it was a reasonable argument, Khath thought. No one else needed to know that he and Sareth had a plan to make absolutely sure that Phally's lies would be exposed. Perhaps then, Nary would be freed from Phally's control.

"But he is asking you to lie, Khath. He is asking you to turn your back on what you know to be true. This will not help you in the end," Pra Chhay said. "It will cause Father Ralph to distrust you. He is your sponsor, not Mr. Sareth. You should discuss this with him before you act."

Khath's temper flared. "It is a strategy. Can you not understand that? But, how could you? You, who have been a monk, sheltered for most of your life behind the walls of a monastery." Khath glared at his brother. "You forget, I was a soldier for the government. Sometimes, a deception is the only way to win a battle."

Unable to stop himself, Khath watched the ugly words continue to roll out of his mouth, his tone scornful. "I will do what I have been trained to do. I advise you to do the same. Chant your chants, brother. Pray for my soul and let the wheel of karma turn."

Feeling ashamed of his outburst, Khath dropped his eyes. He was unnerved by the calm demeanor of his brother, who absorbed Khath's wrath without flinching, the angry words disappearing harmlessly among the folds of Pra Chhay's robes.

"Khath, you are already so close to winning this battle. Your theory that Phally is not Nary's true mother explains so much. We have all noticed the distance between the child and Phally. Even Father Ralph has commented on it."

Pra Chhay crossed the room and sat beside Khath. "Come with me tonight, instead of going with Mr. Sareth. We will tell Father Ralph about your new insight and tell him that Mr. Sareth wants you to lie to Phally. Let us see what the priest has to say about this."

Khath shook his head. "I am sorry, brother. You are putting too much faith in a man who does not truly understand our culture and has no way of grasping the extent of Khmer Rouge brutality. Has he witnessed the lust in their eyes as they torture and maim, the black emptiness afterward? He can never really know the depth of Khmer Rouge evil." Khath stared hard at his brother. "Phally may even harm Nary or run away with her. Have you considered that?"

Pra Chhay did not respond.

"No?" said Khath. "So, now you understand, perhaps, that we must put Phally at her ease so she will continue on with her life as normal."

"Then at least wait until tomorrow so I can go with you to Gail and Teresa's house. Why must you do this tonight? You know that it is the night of my weekly tutoring with Father Ralph. I cannot cancel so late without raising questions."

Which is why we must do it tonight, Khath thought. Mr. Sareth did not want a crowd of witnesses to gather for Khath's performance. "We'll keep it low key, intimate," Mr. Sareth had said. "This will make it easier for you, and if necessary, I can rephrase your words slightly when I translate for the Americans without your brother there to notice." Mr. Sareth had chuckled then. "The Americans have a saying," he explained to Khath. "They claim it is better to apologize afterward than to ask permission before. This is the way we will handle Father Ralph when we break the glad news tomorrow of your visit with Phally tonight."

Khath stood up, feeling restless. "Probably, Mr. Sareth is afraid I will change my mind if you have much chance to work on me." He smiled at his brother. "He didn't want me to tell you anything. But out of respect I am sharing this with you. Grant me that, brother."

Pra Chhay tipped his head in acknowledgment. "Mr. Sareth is right to worry. I have done my best to dissuade you from this plan." He sighed. "But, you have my promise that I will not say anything to Father Ralph tonight, as long as you can assure me that he will be told by tomorrow."

At Khath's nod, Pra Chhay moved to the door, pausing a moment with his hand on the knob. "Khath, no matter what happens, you know you can trust me to do my best for you, don't you?"

Khath nodded. If only we could agree on what that was, he thought.

Not long after Pra Chhay had left, Khath found himself walking through the dusk with Mr. Sareth. Though Sareth had driven to Khath's home, he insisted they walk the mile and a half to Gail and Teresa's house. "It will settle your nerves," he had said, "and give you time to rehearse."

As usual, the man was right. How gladly I would have served him in the army, Khath thought. He is a careful planner, a brilliant strategist and attentive to the needs of his men. Too bad we did not have men like him to command us during the war. Things might have gone differently. The sound of the older man's voice interrupted Khath's thoughts.

"Tell me what you plan to say tonight," Sareth said. "You must speak firmly, without hesitation."

"I...it is difficult to force the words from my throat," Khath admitted, "like trying to swallow a bitter powder without water."

"Yes, but only because you are losing focus," Sareth said. "You are thinking in a small way, of yourself, your words. You believe you are lying, betraying yourself, but you are not." They were walking past the park now, and Sareth drew Khath to a bench.

"Khath, I know you are a good man. I know that saying something against your personal belief is hard for you. But here is what you are forgetting." Sareth leaned forward, putting a hand on Khath's knee as he spoke. "Remember that we are an army of two stopping the spread of the Khmer Rouge in our own community."

Khath nodded. "An army of two," he repeated. Sareth had leaned back and was watching him now, his gaze cool.

"That's right. Because make no mistake, Khath," Sareth said. "The Khmer Rouge will only prey on us, their own people. They are too smart to do otherwise. They know they cannot win a bigger war. So it's up to us, Khath, people like you and me, to stop them from gaining a foothold in our new lives. Because the larger world does not care and will not act."

Again, Khath nodded. For four years the world had turned a blind eye to the suffering of an entire nation of Cambodians. Sareth was right. It was up to them, an army of two, to stop this evil in their own backyard.

"All right. I'm ready," Khath said, standing up, resolute, walking briskly the last quarter mile toward Gail and Teresa's home. When they arrived on the porch and their knock was answered, Khath stepped back respectfully, allowing the interpreter to enter first.

It was warm inside the house, and Khath felt himself begin to sweat, his resolve wavering as Teresa ushered them into the living room. He dared not meet her eyes.

Mr. Sareth and Khath seated themselves on a short couch across the coffee table from Gail and Phally. Vague pleasantries were exchanged, floating in the air around them, but Khath noticed that no one else was exactly making eye contact, either. No one, that is, except Mr. Sareth and Gail, who seemed to lock eyes briefly, though no smiles were exchanged between them.

Teresa brought glasses of water, and Khath could not help but reach for his eagerly, nerves making his mouth dry.

After a short pause during which no one spoke, Mr. Sareth coughed lightly and said, "Well. Here we are. Thank you for seeing us."

Gail spoke up then, a rapid stream of English that Khath, in his anxious state, could not begin to follow. He focused instead on the tone of Gail's voice, which was firm, not angry or unkind, but not open to negotiation either. What was she saying? Khath was relieved when Mr. Sareth turned to him to translate.

"Miss Gail informs us that Phally has agreed to listen to what you have to say but will not respond to us tonight," he said. "After you are done, Miss Gail or Miss Teresa might have questions, or might not. We will take our leave when they are satisfied. Miss Gail wanted us to know what to expect tonight and says she is sorry if she seems rude to speak in this way."

"No, not rude," Khath said. "I am happy you…" He waved his hands toward Gail, casting about in his mind for the right words, "…you make clear. Is good. Very kind. Thank you."

He took a deep breath, starting with the easiest sentences, the ones that were true or at least partially true. "I want to say sorry, to you, Miss Gail, Miss Teresa, and to you, Phally. I no want to make problem, here. Is enough problem in Cambodia."

Khath's heart was beginning to pound, his senses heightened. Phally sat like a statue across from him, her eyes cast down. He heard the clink of dishes being washed in the kitchen. Something pressed against his side and he realized Mr. Sareth's elbow was jabbing him in the ribs. Focus. An army of two.

Khath took another deep breath and pressed on with the hardest part. "I think maybe the room was dark. Maybe I make mistake." Khath swallowed. He had just one more sentence to utter, the most important one. "I think, is possible, maybe your husband not Khmer Rouge." There, it was done.

Phally's eyes snapped up as he uttered those words, and an instant later, a loud crash came from the kitchen.

Teresa and Phally both sprang up and hurried toward the kitchen calling, "Nary, are you all right?"

Khath never felt himself move but suddenly here he was, crowding behind the women at the doorway to the kitchen. He stared at the child, standing in the middle of the kitchen, soap suds dripping from her hands to the floor where a shattered platter cast a pattern of white against the red tiled floor.

"Oh, Nary, don't cry. It's just a plate," Teresa said, hurrying to the child's side, never even noticing that the child's eyes were not fixed on the floor or the destruction at her feet.

Did Phally notice? If so, she gave no sign, stooping to gather up the shards of pottery. It's not right, Khath thought.

Phally should be comforting the child while Teresa cleaned up the mess.

His heart breaking, Khath could only stand and watch as Nary turned her stricken face toward him, tears spilling down her cheeks.

# Twenty-Seven

Phally, wearing a light sweater, stood on her porch rubbing her hands up and down her arms to chase away the chill. Today, she and Nary were going grocery shopping, an excursion she had come to enjoy. There was so much to look at and learn from at the grocery store: new fruits and vegetables to puzzle over, cans and boxes to practice her reading skills on, fellow shoppers with whom to exchange nods and small talk. Hello. Thank you. Excuse me. She was also trying hard to master American body language so she would appear open and friendly, rather than shy and awkward as she had been.

The sun was slow to rise this morning, even slower to take the chill from the air. She drew a deep breath of cool air into her lungs, smelling the tang of drying leaves, hearing them scrape gently against the sidewalk as the breeze swept them restlessly to and fro. There's a sharpness in the air, she thought. The seasons are changing and soon it would be winter, her first in Glenberg. How cold would it get? She and Nary would soon need winter clothing.

She felt no fear of the approaching cold and darkness. Her friendship with Gail had changed all that. Before Gail, every day was filled with the small terrors of the unfamiliar. She had endured an uncertain life, treading carefully in the safety of

America. At least in Cambodia, the dangers were stark, un-disguised. The rules were crystal clear, as were the consequences of resistance. Not here. It was so easy to make a mistake, to cause embarrassment or anger. Before Gail, she had lived timidly in the shadows, searching for her footing in this strange new culture.

A tenderness softened her heart whenever she thought of Gail, so strong despite her crippled legs. The Khmer Rouge would have killed her immediately, having no use for someone who could not perform hard labor. What a loss that would have been. A shadow of sorrow passed across her mood as she thought of the ones who had died under the reign of the Khmer Rouge. By the end of the war, the air was thick with wandering souls torn from their bodies and searching for peace.

Phally sighed and mumbled a prayer for the dead. She looked around. What was taking Nary so long? She poked her head back through the door, and saw Nary standing in front of the ancestor shrine, staring fixedly at Boran's photo, a frown creasing her forehead.

"There you are, little mouse," Phally said. "Are you missing your papa today?"

Nary started, as though she were being pulled from a trance. She stared at Phally blankly.

"Shall we say a prayer for him, Nary? Make an offering?" Phally looked closely at Nary, wishing she could pry open the door to Nary's heart. "Are you all right, mouse?"

Nary blinked and took a step away from the shrine. "I'm fine, Mama," she said in a small voice. "There was something on the frame. Dirt. Maybe a bug. I don't see it now."

Phally walked into the living room and sat on the couch. "Nary," she said. "Your mind seems troubled these days. I'm sure there were things that happened in the war that you didn't understand, things that frightened you. Is there anything you want to tell me about?" If only she would talk to me, Phally thought. Why can't I reach her? Am I such a monster? What has happened to my little girl? Phally felt tears rise to her eyes, then despair as Nary shook her head and turned away.

It was a puzzle to Phally that the one problem that she had yet been unable to solve in this new country was so closely tied to the old country. It broke Phally's heart that her own daughter, her little mouse, did not love her as a child should love her mother. Nary seemed content to live with her, both in the camps and now here in Glenberg. The child was not overly rebellious. But the bond between them was devastatingly empty, a matter of convenience rather than love. Phally vowed never to give up trying to break through to her only child, but she was beginning to wonder if her efforts had any chance of ever succeeding.

Sighing, Phally followed Nary out the door and down the ramp that Khath built for Gail's wheelchair. Nary always used the ramp now, never the stairs, her choice a silent protest against Phally's ejection of Khath from their lives.

Khath had been friendly and respectful since his apology, two weeks ago. He nodded politely at her in class or when their paths crossed in town. But letting him back into Nary's life was different, something Phally was not yet sure about.

"Nary," Phally said, breaking the silence that had fallen between them as they walked toward the grocery store. "Do you miss Mr. Khath? Is that what is bothering you these days?"

Nary ducked her head, her glossy bangs shielding her eyes. She walked a few steps more and then said, "Yes. I miss him. He taught me things. I liked to learn from him."

"That's true, mouse. He was patient with you," Phally said. "But you know he said terrible things about your father. Things that were not true, yes? Khath cast a great shame on our family. It was impossible to remain friends with him after that, Nary. You're old enough to understand this, yes?"

Nary trudged along beside her without speaking. Finally, in a tiny voice, so soft that Phally had to bend to hear, Nary said, "But he said he was sorry."

A breeze rattled the leaves on the trees. Nearby, a squirrel scrambled up a trunk, its jaws bulging.

Phally laid her hand on Nary's shoulder. "Yes, child. He said he was sorry. It's a start. Now, let us wait a while and see by his actions how truly sorry he really is."

Ahead, the Country Grocery's parking lot was half full of cars. Workers were setting up a display of pumpkins in wooden crates with straw scattered about. Phally knew there was an American holiday coming, but she wasn't sure when or what the celebration was about.

"Look, Nary," Phally said, pointing to the pumpkins. "What are they doing? Have you learned about this in school?"

"It is a strange holiday," Nary said. "I don't like it. People dress up like spirits. They make themselves look dead, bloody. And then they laugh about it and eat candy."

Phally stared at Nary. "Are you sure, child? Why would they do that?"

Nary must be mistaken, she thought. What kind of people would celebrate such things? An image flashed in her mind of three heads impaled on stakes and planted at the entrance of a village as a warning to the villagers not to help the enemy. Flies buzzed loudly around the heads and the smell was terrible. That was early in the war, when such things were still shocking. Worst of all, Phally thought, she wasn't even sure which side was considered the enemy in that village. She had hurried past with averted eyes, unsure of which enemy to fear.

---

Sareth stood in line at the customer service window at the Country Grocery, waiting to pay his utility bill while Chea did the food shopping. He enjoyed this ritual of stepping up to the window to pay with a check, instead of using cash as all the other Cambodians did. With a polite greeting, he would reach into his breast pocket and remove his checkbook with its fine leather case and stand with pen poised over the check while the clerk verified the amount due on his account. Sareth had beautiful handwriting, unlike the awkward scrawl of the rest of the Cambodians in his community, who had yet to fully master the shaping of English letters. And spelling! Only the French had a worse system of spelling, in Sareth's opinion.

At any rate, he very much enjoyed showing the townsfolk of Glenberg that not all Cambodians were simple villagers, barely literate. Indeed, he considered it his duty to do so.

Bill paid, Sareth strolled the aisles, glancing about for Chea. He entered the aisle with the cooking oil and came to a sudden stop. Phally and Nary stood with their backs to him, studying the label on a large bottle of oil. Unnoticed, he stepped backwards, just around the corner and watched with idle curiosity the interactions between Phally and Nary. They stood side by side, not touching, their heads bent over the jug. Wouldn't a child and her mother be crowded together, forming a single unit of focused attention? Wouldn't they smile into each other's eyes as they puzzled and guessed over the words on the label? Frowning, Sareth turned away and continued to look for Chea.

This idea of Khath's that Phally was not Nary's real mother was intriguing. Sareth had not bothered to examine his own feelings about whether or not he believed Khath's initial accusations about Phally's husband. The truth did not matter so much and could probably never be proved. Rather, it was convenient for him to support Khath's accusations for his own purpose of ridding the community of his wife's nemesis. But now, things were different. Sareth felt his anger rise at the thought that Phally herself was Khmer Rouge, living under his nose this whole time, undetected.

Sareth hated the Khmer Rouge though not with the visceral hatred of those who had suffered under their rule for four years. No, his hatred was more reasoned. The Khmer Rouge had destroyed his country, his power base, his wealth and his way of life. He hated them for forcing him to start anew, when he should be enjoying a peaceful and privileged old age. He hated them for placing him in a position that weakened his authority over Chea and threatened his very ability to hold on to her. Who would take care of him if Chea left him for a younger, wealthier man? If he could force Phally out, Chea would see that he still had the power to take care of her and ease her way in life. It would be a start, anyway.

Sareth drew a deep breath and looked around. How long had he been standing here staring at the toilet paper? He'd been so deep in his thoughts he had no recollection of even turning into this aisle, but here he was. It worried him that these mental lapses seemed to be happening more and more. Embarrassed and irritated, Sareth strode around the corner into the produce department and came face to face with Phally and Nary.

"Pardon me," Sareth said in English, swerving to avoid a collision, the words coming automatically before he realized it was only Phally and Nary. In his country, the villagers scattered before his approach, bowing as he passed by, clearing his way. Now, he noticed, Phally merely stepped back a bit, clutching Nary by the shoulder. She bowed her head and murmured a respectful greeting, but it was hardly adequate. And that child of hers just stood staring, until Sareth saw Phally's fingers whiten on Nary's shoulder, pressuring the child into a more respectful posture.

"Good morning. *Su sidai,*" Sareth said. "It is a fine morning for shopping, yes?" After all, the pleasantries must be observed, even when staring into the eyes of your enemy.

Phally replied that the lettuces were especially fresh this morning, nodding in the direction of the vegetables. Then the natural sweep of her eyes seemed to catch, widening slightly at something she saw beyond Sareth's left shoulder. Her mouth opened slightly then snapped shut.

Sareth studied her face, keeping his own expression bland. What is it that gives her such surprise, yet seals her lips?

Ignoring the sense of foreboding that tightened his stomach, Sareth smiled at Phally. "Thank you. Freshness adds so much to the flavor." He nodded his head and turned to go, being careful to move slowly and casually.

His heart clutched at the scene before him. Chea stood, her hand resting on a watermelon, her hip cocked, smiling and exchanging words with a store clerk.

The clerk was tall, dressed in a white tee shirt with a dark blue store apron wrapped tightly around his slim hips. The man had broad shoulders and his muscles bulged as he hefted a large melon and placed it into Chea's cart.

As Sareth watched, Chea brushed a strand of hair away from her face, a useless gesture. For a moment later she smiled at the clerk and dipped into a graceful *wai*, head bowed over clasped hands, her hair cascading into a sheen of ebony around her, thanking the man for his assistance.

He's practically drooling over her, Sareth thought furiously. He forced himself to stroll, not rush, toward Chea. Clearly Chea was enjoying the man's attention. She has not even noticed my approach, Sareth thought. Coming to stand beside her, he said, speaking in his native tongue, "Almost done here?"

Chea faced Sareth with a smile. "I practice to speak," she announced with pride, in English. She turned to the store clerk, gesturing to Sareth. "My husband," she said.

Sareth watched the man's jaw drop, no doubt registering the age difference between husband and wife. He recovered himself quickly though, Sareth noted. Not a total oaf then.

"Pleased to meet you, Sir," the man said, offering a hand. "You folks have a nice day now."

Sareth breathed a sigh of relief as the clerk ambled off to arrange the mushrooms. But then he noticed Chea's eyes following the man and his anxiety returned with a rush. He was acutely aware that Phally was still in the vegetable section. He imagined she was quite enjoying the spectacle of Chea flirting with a young man, right in front of her husband.

Do not fret about Phally, he scolded himself. The most important thing right now is to handle this situation with Chea. Besides, Phally will be gone soon.

Speaking quietly but with a touch of steel in his voice, Sareth said, "Chea, are you aware that Phally and Nary are here in the store, too, watching your every move?"

"What? No. Where?" Chea's voice held a hint of dismay, and Sareth was pleased to see a blush flame suddenly upon her cheeks. So, she was aware that her behavior was inappropriate.

"Do not turn and look for them," Sareth instructed. "Let us continue shopping as normal." He glanced into the cart, nearly empty except for the melon. How long had his wife been toying with that clerk?

"Phally informs me that the lettuce is particularly fresh this morning," Sareth said. He wanted Chea to worry about how long he had been watching her, wondering what he had seen or heard.

Chea steered the cart toward the lettuce.

"I am glad that you are practicing your English, Chea. But you must remember that you are the wife of the headman of this community. People will watch you and talk about everything you do. People envy your position, Chea, and you must never give them a reason to lose their envy."

Chea nodded. "I am sorry, *Bong*."

Sareth watched her carefully. Was she sorry, chastised? Or was she simply doing what was expected of her? He decided to push her a bit, let her know that he had seen her indiscreet behavior.

"You must not lose your head over these silly American men, Chea. You are an exotic flower to them, a curiosity, nothing more. They are beneath your attention." He paused. They had reached the lettuce. Sareth picked up a bunch, holding it toward Chea as an excuse to face her and speak directly to her. She grasped the lettuce but he held on, causing her to raise her eyes in confusion.

"You are the wife of the headman, Chea. Never forget that. Do not shame me." Sareth paused. "Your behavior weakens my position, and then we will lose everything. Do you understand?"

Chea merely nodded, but Sareth was satisfied. He had seen a dawning realization reflected in her eyes. Perhaps at last she was growing from a child bride to a woman, a wife, finally realizing that even as her husband protected her, she must support him. He hoped so. Chea's support was vital to his plan to expose Phally.

Yes, the pieces were in place now. It was time to move against Phally.

# Twenty-Eight

"Come, Chea. We must not be late." Sareth stood at his bedroom door, watching Chea put the finishing touches on her hair and makeup. Was she worth it? Worth the risks he was taking, the fine line he was treading? More and more, this question troubled him.

Chea raised her eyes and glanced at his reflection in the mirror. "In a moment, *Bong*." She smiled. At him? Or perhaps she was just smiling at her own beauty, her own perfect face, with its arched brows and smooth skin.

Sareth turned away and stood near the front door, his hand on the knob, waiting, while his mind ran through the afternoon's scenario.

Khath had said he knew of a place where he could take Phally, someplace where they would not be disturbed. Sareth had not pressed him for more detail. From this point on, it was important to keep a distance between Khath's actions and his own in case things went wrong. He would be able to say honestly that he did not know where Khath and Phally were, only that Khath had wanted to speak privately with Phally.

Naturally, in the interests of resolving the conflict in Glenberg's Cambodian community, Sareth had offered his and

Chea's services to watch over Nary for several hours, perhaps feed the child an early dinner, so that Khath and Phally could talk undisturbed.

Who would fault him for that? Didn't the Americans believe that talking could solve almost any dispute? Such a naive people. What words could possibly soothe the raw wound of seeing your enemy smash your infant son's skull against the trunk of a tree?

Had he prepped Khath properly? Fanned the flames of the man's rage and anguish to just the right degree of heat? That was the real unknown. How far would Khath go to ferret out the truth about Phally? How much pressure was he willing to bring to his interrogation?

Sareth knew that the right degree was essential. If Khath was too soft, without frightening Phally sufficiently, the woman would just complain and Khath would be ostracized again. On the other hand, what if Khath lost his head, flew into a rage? If he injured or killed Phally, he surely would be deported, and if he left, Pra Chhay would follow. It would certainly be a tidy solution, as long as Sareth could keep his own hands sufficiently clean.

Hearing footsteps in the hall behind him, Sareth turned and smiled at Chea, hiding his real emotions. It was nerve-wracking to have to depend on others of lesser ability as he put his plan into action. It's not too late to pull back, a tiny voice in his brain insisted. Is it worth it? Is *she* worth it?

Courteously, he opened and held the door for her. "All ready? I do hope the child will come along without protest. She is so unpredictable." Sareth kept his tone light, his anxiety in check. "But as the leader of this community, I must help our neighbors to resolve their disputes from time to time. I'm proud of you for assisting me, Chea."

Chea gave him a dazzling smile, momentarily silencing the voice of doubt in his head. She rested her hand briefly on his arm as she passed by, her step purposeful, her head held high.

In the car, they drove in silence to Nary's school, arriving just as the bell rang and a flood of children burst through the doors.

"Do you see her, *Bong*? How will we find her among all these children? I didn't realize there would be so many." Chea's tone was anxious.

"Don't worry. She'll be one of the last out the door. She always is." Sareth had spent more than a week casually driving past the school as the final bell rang, observing Nary's habitual behavior after school. He was confident that she would come out last, and come out alone. In another minute, his patience was rewarded.

"There," he said. "In the red jacket. Do you see her?"

Chea nodded and reached for the door handle.

"Not yet," Sareth said. "Let her get closer." He watched the child come steadily toward them, her pace neither fast nor slow. Nary's face was unreadable, impassive. She showed none of the exuberance of the other children, but she did not seem unduly sad or disturbed either. She simply made her way along the sidewalk, aloof from the ebb and flow of life around her. When she was about twenty feet from the car, Sareth nodded at Chea. "All right. Now," he said.

Chea slipped out the door and hurried around the front of the car. Once on the sidewalk, she took a few paces toward the child. "Nary," she called and beckoned with her hand. "Come here. I have news for you."

Sareth watched the scene unfold. The child moved toward Chea, her steps slowing and eyes alert. Sareth rolled down his window in hopes that he could follow the conversation, but a breeze rustled the dried leaves, and all he could hear were disjointed phrases.

*Your mother. Mr. Khath. A meeting. Mustn't be disturbed. Very important. Adult things, not for children.*

"Come on, Nary," Sareth muttered. "Be a good child, for once in your life.

Chea sidled closer to Nary, still talking animatedly. She's talking too much, Sareth thought. Just order the child into the car. His hands gripped the steering wheel tightly.

*Dinner with us. Your mother will be back later.* Chea took another step toward Nary and held out her hand. *Come, child.*

Nary frowned and took a half step backward, casting a quick glance around. She's going to run, Sareth thought. Grab her, Chea, before she gets away. Sareth's hand was on the door handle, poised to jump out when he saw Chea step forward and encircle Nary's thin shoulders with her arm, getting a firm grasp on one shoulder, and propelling her toward the car. Sareth breathed a sigh of relief.

Chea opened the passenger door and half pushed Nary onto the front seat between her and Sareth. The child grunted and braced herself against the dashboard, resisting, but was no match for Chea's size and strength. As Chea slid in beside her, Nary tried to scramble over the woman's lap toward the freedom of the still open door, but Chea flung out an arm, pushing the child back against the seat.

"Gently, Chea." Sareth lifted the corners of his mouth in a smile and laid a firm hand on Nary's leg. "Come sit beside me, child. There's nothing to fear. We'll have a pleasant evening together, yes? You can do your lessons, we'll eat and then we'll take you home." The child's body was stiff and unyielding beside him, but she had ceased to struggle, at least for the moment.

Sareth put the car into gear, glancing at his watch. Right on schedule. He glanced over the top of Nary's head to meet Chea's eyes, bright with success. "Nicely done," he mouthed, and was pleased to see a genuine smile flash his way.

At home, Sareth oversaw the settling of Nary with her schoolbooks at the kitchen table, then drew his wife aside.

"All right, Chea," he said. "Keep a close eye on her. We don't want her slipping away." Again, Sareth glanced at his watch. "I should be back in 30 minutes. Once I see that Khath and Phally have met up and begun a discussion, I will come quickly to relieve you here. And then, we shall wait for Khath to return. I do hope he will have happy news for us when he arrives."

———————

Weak sunlight filtered through the canopy, brightening the woodland path that Khath hurried along. Nary's path. He'd had an absurd urge when he awakened today to tidy up the cabin before bringing Phally there. So he'd slipped away in the morning to bang nails into the walls on which to hang his few tools, to sweep the dirt floor, put down some comfortable mats to sit upon, and arrange things nicely on the wooden counter. He'd even picked a few stems of greenery and some wild flowers to put in the rusted tin can that Nary had used for her bouquet. Perhaps the homey touch would calm Phally and make her more inclined to be truthful with him.

Glancing at his watch, he broke into a jog. He wanted to be well in place before Phally passed by on her way home from Gail's house, where she'd taken to spending the afternoons since she quit the ESL classes.

But Khath also wanted to be slightly out of breath, a little sweaty, to lend credence to the story he would use to lure Phally into the forest with him. He could jog in place to keep his energy high if necessary, though as the time approached, he felt a nervous tingle along his spine, and his palms were damp. Just like any military operation. Jitters were normal and kept you alert. Even more important when so much was riding on the efforts of just two soldiers. An army of two, like Mr. Sareth had said, on a mission to clear their community of the hated Khmer Rouge.

As he neared the street, Khath could see Mr. Sareth's car parked past the entrance of the path, partially hidden by a curve of the road. Good. His back-up was in place and well-positioned, too. You'd hardly notice the vehicle unless you were looking for it.

Turning away from the parked car, Khath peered down the street, staying just out of sight of any passers-by who might wander through. He was only expecting one person though.

There. Right on schedule, Phally was approaching, striding with a loose, flowing gait. He'd never really noticed before how gracefully she moved. She looked strong, as though she could keep that gait up forever. He was glad he'd noticed her apparent strength. He'd be prepared if it came to a struggle.

He stilled himself and melted behind a trunk until Phally had passed him, waited a moment and then crashed noisily along the brushy path and ran onto the street. As expected, Phally had whirled around to face the noise, a look of shock on her face that only deepened when she saw it was him.

"Phally," Khath gasped. "I was just coming to get you. It's Nary."

"What? What has happened?" Phally took a pace toward him, eyes wide and darting, mouth agape.

"I was in the forest, collecting greenery. I noticed her behind me, at some distance. She must have followed me. I heard her call out, and then she stumbled and rolled down an embankment."

"You left her there? Where is she?" Phally brushed past Khath, staring into the forest.

"Phally, be calm. She is safe and comfortable, but she cannot walk. Just a sprain, I think. There is a cabin. I took her there to rest. I thought it best to come get you first, and we can bring her out together." Khath watched Phally's face as she absorbed all this. He saw a trace of distrust flicker over her face, fighting her natural urge to find Nary. He took a breath and played his strongest card. "She was asking for you, Phally, crying for you. So I came as quickly as I could to get you."

If Phally were Nary's real mother, Khath thought, she would run to comfort her child; if she were not, she might hesitate but the need to keep her story intact would still force her into the forest.

"I must go to her," Phally said. "Take me to this cabin."

"Of course," Khath said. "We can use this path." As Phally plunged into the forest, Khath turned briefly toward the car parked down the road. He gave a curt nod, and then hurried after Phally.

In a short while, they came to the road near the old farmer's cornfield. Khath touched Phally's shoulder and motioned to her to stay down, stay quiet.

"I will check to make sure it is clear," he said. "As you know, the corn farmer does not like refugees, and we must go quietly here." Staring at Phally, Khath forced a lightness into his tone. "Do you remember? The fool thinks all Cambodians are Khmer Rouge," he said.

Phally's eyes flicked up toward him briefly and her mouth tightened, a small frown wrinkling her brow, but she said nothing.

Almost before the words were out of his mouth, Khath realized his mistake. How stupid of him to mention the Khmer Rouge before he had Phally securely in the cabin. Focus, he thought. An army of two. To distract Phally he began to describe the way to her.

"We must cross the road and go down the embankment, staying to the right of the fence. There is a path on the right. We'll take that. In about 20 minutes, we'll be with Nary at the cabin." He climbed partially up the embankment and peered around. All was quiet. He gestured to Phally to follow him and in a few minutes they were back in the forest on the other side of the road, moving steadily toward their destination.

When the mossy roof of the cabin came into sight, Phally ran forward. "Nary," she cried, and again, "Nary." She turned a frantic face to Khath. "Is this the right place? I don't hear her answering."

I must calm her before she gets suspicious, Khath thought.

"She might be sleeping, and the walls are thick," he said. "Let's not wake her too suddenly, or she will be frightened. She might move suddenly and worsen her injury." Khath spoke soothingly, moving around Phally. "Let me get the door. It sticks."

He opened the door for Phally and waved her inside ahead of him. "She's behind the partition at the end of the counter," he said, speaking in a hushed tone. "I made her a bed of sorts out of what I could find." He pointed to a pile of rags protruding from the end of the partition, barely visible in the dim light of the cabin.

"Nary?" Phally said softly, moving toward the pile. "Is there a light? I don't want to step on her. Nary, child, are you awake?" She squatted and felt the pile of rags with her hands, patting it gently. "Where are you, child?"

Khath quietly closed the door and placed the wooden bar across the jamb. He moved to the counter and reached for the candles and matches he had arranged so carefully earlier that day. He could hear Phally's search becoming wilder as she slapped the floor and moved the rags around in confusion. Khath scraped the match head against the side of the box. As the matchstick flared, he heard Phally exclaim.

"She's not here. Khath, she's not here. Could she have left on her own?"

He touched the match to the wick of the candle. Should he light two? A candle could be a weapon, used against him. It was risky, but he decided that more light was important.

Phally turned, a puzzled look on her face that quickly turned to fear as her eyes swept the cabin and took in the bolted door. Then she straightened her shoulders and squared her jaw.

"Let me out. I have to find Nary," she said.

"Nary is fine. Do not worry about Nary. She is safe, doing her lessons, eating dinner. It was necessary to deceive you so that you would come here willingly. But I promise you no harm will come to Nary."

Khath pointed to the mats he had placed on the floor earlier. "Sit down, Phally. You see how I have tried to make this cabin pleasant for this occasion. We are going to have a talk, you and me, about your husband, and you, and the Khmer Rouge. And then, when I am satisfied that you have told me everything truthfully, then..."

Khath paused. The Khmer Rouge would torture people to force them to confess to the wildest things, to implicate others as enemies of the regime, and after all that, kill them anyway. That was the whole evil purpose of Site 21.

But this was a different time, a different place. He rubbed his hand across his forehead, where a headache was beginning to throb.

How odd it was that he and Mr. Sareth had planned so carefully up to this point, and then, nothing. He felt like an army of one now.

# Twenty-Nine

Facing Khath in the cabin, Phally felt a shock of fear ripple from her toes to her scalp, replaced almost immediately by an icy calm. How quickly her mind and body reverted to the subtle skills that kept her alive under the Khmer Rouge. The threat of death made life so simple. Survive, escape, protect her child.

Khath stood before her now, waiting in silence for her to sit. So gentle, yet so deadly. Phally tried to speak, but fear had sucked the moisture from her mouth, and her tongue stuck to the back of her teeth. She swallowed hard and tried again.

"All right, I'll sit," she said, in a voice that did not quite sound like hers. She took a step backward, moving slowly toward the mats on the floor, trying to put some space between herself and Khath. As she gathered her sarong and prepared to sit, she dropped her head slightly to hide the fact that her eyes were scouring the cabin, getting a sense of her surroundings.

What she saw only deepened her horror, for neatly arranged on the walls and counters were all the simple objects of daily life that doubled as implements of torture and death under the Khmer Rouge. An ax for smashing skulls, hung next to a shovel, which could substitute for the ax in a pinch. On the counter, a plastic bag rested under a length of rope.

Phally would never forget the first time she saw a young woman suffocated by a filmy plastic bag over the head, her hands bound behind her. She'd been clever, Phally remembered, dropping to her knees and scraping her face against the ground to try to rip the bag. Her cleverness earned her a forceful kick to the head, followed up by body kicks, but she was already dead by then.

Beside the bag, pliers, for pinching, crushing and pulling. Ears, teeth, nails, whatever body part took the fancy of the torturer: a knife, a car battery and a coil of wire, a hammer. Each tool brought to mind a story of torture, a personal experience, a memory long buried. Like a flash flood, these thoughts swept through Phally's mind in the time it took her to select a spot, smooth the fabric of her sarong, and lower herself, slowly and gracefully, onto the mat.

Would he sit as well? To Phally's great relief, Khath lowered himself into a squat, still retaining an advantage over her position, but at least not towering over her. For the moment, anyway.

"Khath, please tell me where Nary is. I cannot think of anything else until I know what has happened to her," Phally spoke in a humble tone, watching Khath's face through lowered lashes. At the mention of the child's name, she noticed a softening of his stern expression. His lips twitched upward, his brows relaxed, his gaze turned inward for a moment.

Yes, she thought. This was the path to take, treading lightly, alert for mines and booby traps, but this was the path that just might lead her to safety. Somewhere inside this stern stranger was the man who carried her daughter, sobbing against his chest, to the safety of her home after a traumatic day at school. The man who helped Nary escape from the angry farmer and his dog. The man who built a ramp for Gail and let Nary work by his side while he did so, who protected the child from Chea's wrath after the paint spill. She had to find that man. She had no doubt that her life depended on it.

Khath shook his head. "I told you she was safe, Phally. I am sorry I cannot tell you more than that at this point. Especially," Khath's gaze turned cold, "since I am not even convinced you are her real mother."

"What?" Phally was astonished. Not Nary's real mother? "Of course I am her mother. What do you mean, not her mother." She heard the volume of her own voice increasing, taking on a shrill edge. *Careful, Phally. Don't antagonize him.* With an effort, she continued in a softer tone. "Why would you think that?"

Khath stood up and moved to the counter. In an aimless manner, he picked up the piece of rope from on top of the plastic bag, and began looping it around his hand, running it through his fingers. Phally was unable to take her eyes from the sight of it slithering like a snake in the hands of a charmer. With a sudden snap that made Phally jerk, Khath pulled the rope taut, a knot appearing in the center. He gazed at the knot for a moment, and then raised his eyes to Phally.

"Nary doesn't love you," he said.

Phally opened her mouth, but the protest died on her lips. What could she say? Foolishly, she wanted to use Khath's own deception to prove him wrong. *But you said she was calling for me.* It was all lies. Tears slipped down her face. Khath's words struck at a festering wound deep in her heart. She wiped her face with the back of her hand, aware of how motionless Khath was, standing over her with that rope curled around his fingers.

"Nary is my daughter. I carried her in my womb, nourished her with the blood of my own body. You know her, Khath. She is broken by something that happened to her after she was taken from me. First, she lost her father, then…" Appalled, Phally stopped speaking. Idiot. She should never have mentioned Boran. Khath had stiffened at the word "father," and his eyes flared.

"Her father," he sneered, drawing the word out, "is a Khmer Rouge murderer. Shall I tell you what I think?" Khath took a menacing step toward her, his fists balled. Rage darkened his face.

Phally shrank away, attempting to get her feet positioned so she could move quickly if Khath lunged at her. Her heart hammered in her chest. "Please," she whispered.

Khath stared at her, clenching and unclenching his fists. He took a ragged breath. "Have you any other children, Phally? Children who died of starvation or disease because your Khmer Rouge leaders killed all the doctors who could have helped them? Is that why you chose Nary from the camps and took her for your own, as a ticket to resettlement?"

Khath shook the rope in her face, his whole body seeming to vibrate with suppressed emotion. "I met Khmer Rouge like you in the camps," he hissed, "people who would do anything to wash the blood from their hands and hide themselves in a new country."

"No, Khath. No, I swear it." Sweat trickled down her back as Phally inched herself away from the enraged man. *Calm him before he snaps.* She opened her mouth and the right words tumbled out of it, the only words that might reach Khath. "Ask Nary. Nary will tell you herself that this is not true. I am not Khmer Rouge, Khath. I hate them as you do."

Khath silenced her with a sharp gesture of his hand. "Quiet," he said. He straightened up, cocked his head.

A great hope surged in Phally. What had Khath heard? She strained to listen over the roar of blood rushing in her ears, the sound of her own panicked breathing. Was she imagining it? The crack of a broken limb, a shadow cast across the opaque window over the counter, and then, she was sure of it, a soft thud against the side of the cabin.

---

Unable to sit still, Sareth walked to the living room window and glanced out at the street. Still no Khath. He turned away, frowning. From where he stood, he could observe Nary at the kitchen table, bent over her schoolbooks. He couldn't see Chea, but the rattle of pots and pans, the thunk of knife against cutting board, the sizzle of garlic and chili peppers in hot oil attested to the efforts of his wife to produce a meal for the three of them. He hoped it would be palatable.

He raised his eyes to the wall clock. Four thirty. An hour had passed since he saw Khath and Phally enter the forest. Again, as he had so many times already, Sareth ran through every possible outcome of today's events, and what his response would be to each. If, as he hoped, Khath could break Phally and get her to confess her Khmer Rouge involvement, Sareth would insist she be deported. Maybe Nary could stay, under some type of legal guardianship arrangement, perhaps with Gail and Teresa. That would make Khath happy. Yes, that would be the best possible outcome.

The worst case, for him, would be if Phally continued to deny any connection to the Khmer Rouge. Khath would be in trouble then, especially if Phally were injured. Khath would probably try to implicate him as well. But Sareth had been so very careful, choosing his words with such care whenever he spoke with Khath, referring only to this "conversation" that he would help Khath arrange. He had no knowledge of how Khath planned to get Phally to go with him, or even where Khath planned to take her.

His own hands were clean; Sareth was sure of it. He'd merely offered to babysit the girl, so Phally and Khath could meet undisturbed. Of course, as a pure formality, he would immediately accuse himself of poor judgment and offer his resignation to Father Ralph, who would almost certainly refuse to accept it.

He became aware that Nary was standing before him, eyes downcast.

"Yes, child, what is it?" Sareth said impatiently.

"May I use the washroom?" Nary spoke softly.

Sareth gazed at her for a moment, pleased to see Nary displaying proper manners for a change. Clearly, Phally was too lenient with the child. The girl just needed a firm hand to tame her wild ways.

"Of course. You'll want to wash up before dinner," Sareth said. He pointed down the hallway. "It's just there, the door on the right. And Nary, there's no need to lock the door behind you, do you understand?" It would be just like her to lock herself in and refuse to eat with them, Sareth thought.

Nary nodded her head, her eyes still directed respectfully downward.

"Speak up, child, when you're addressed by an elder," Sareth said.

The girl raised her eyes briefly. "Yes, I understand you." She paused a moment, then added, "sir."

"Good girl. You may go." Sareth waved her away, much as one would brush away a mosquito. Children bored him.

The odor of burning food assailed his senses. Sareth strode to the front door and yanked it open to air the house, and again glanced anxiously up and down the empty street. A brisk breeze was blowing, causing him to shiver. He rubbed his hands up and down his arms. Clean hands. It was so important. Was there anything he had said or done that he could not deny, claim as a misunderstanding, or gather up under the heading of "poor judgment?"

Perhaps there was. An army of two, he had said to Khath. That phrase could be his undoing. He stood mulling it over, trying unsuccessfully to come up with an innocuous phrase that sounded similar enough to be misheard. No, if it came up, he would either have to deny having said it, or say that Khath misconstrued his intent. Easy enough to do, he thought, and no need to decide until faced with the situation. He would wait, let things play out and then choose the best tactic.

And what if Khath lost all control and killed Phally? The poor fellow would be distraught, unhinged by his own actions.

Any accusations he leveled at Sareth could be passed off as the ravings of a desperate man.

Sareth rubbed his chin thoughtfully. A loss of life was regrettable, of course, but a case could be made that the only thing that would cause Khath to kill would be some proof that Phally were Khmer Rouge.

Of course Khath would be deported, but he would leave a hero to the people of Glenberg, and that was something. Or perhaps there would be a trial, here in America. He doubted the Americans would execute any man who had defended his community against the Khmer Rouge. They were a soft-hearted people and Khath would be a sympathetic figure. There might even be a role in there for Sareth to play, as the community elder who could explain the roots of Khath's actions to the American public, an ambassador for Cambodian culture and history, so to speak.

All in all, Sareth thought, he could live with these outcomes. Indeed, he would welcome them.

Behind him, he heard Chea laying plates on the table. Sareth had insisted they adopt the Western custom of table and chairs, rather than sitting on the floor to eat. With a final glance at the street, Sareth shut the door and made his way to the kitchen. Entering, he glanced around and scowled. What a nuisance. The child was still holed up in the bathroom.

"Chea," Sareth said. "Have you seen Nary?"

Chea looked at him in surprise. "No, *Bong*. I told her to ask your permission to use the washroom. Did she not do so?"

"She did. But I wonder if she is ill. She is taking a long time." Sareth raised his brows slightly, his unspoken command clear. *You'd better go get her. No telling what she is doing in there.*

Chea wiped her hands on her apron. "Let me check on her," she said.

Sareth sat down at the table as Chea left the room. Steam rose from a platter of fish and vegetables his wife had set in front of his plate, making his mouth water. It appeared that

Chea had scraped a few burned areas off the fish, but no matter. He was hungry, and he'd had worse.

A moment later, Chea hurried back into the kitchen. "She's not in the washroom, *Bong.*"

Sareth jumped to his feet. "Are you sure?" he said, striding to check for himself. He flung aside the shower curtain. The tub was empty. His eyes moved to the small window over the toilet, up near the ceiling. The window hinged at the top and could be pushed outward and propped open with a small arm that attached to the side of the window frame. It latched at the bottom, and now Sareth noticed that the latch hung loose.

No, it wasn't possible, was it? The child was small, but small enough to squeeze through that tiny opening? He moved closer to the toilet and bent to examine the tank lid. There it was: a smudge, the barest outline of a small, dirty foot. She must have thrown her flip-flops through the window, stood on the toilet and hauled herself up and out to freedom. He stepped onto the toilet seat and examined the window sill. A reddish-brown smear at one edge caught his eye. Blood. She must have scraped herself as she wriggled through. He touched the spot lightly. It was sticky and stained his finger when he lifted it. Wiping his finger with his handkerchief, Sareth wondered how many minutes had passed since Nary fled.

A flicker of rage burned in Sareth's chest at the knowledge that he'd been duped by a willful child, his beautiful plans disrupted. Nary would sound the alarm that Phally had gone somewhere with Khath, he was certain of that. It was a complication, but nothing he couldn't adapt to.

Not for the first time, he was grateful that he had not taken Chea into his full confidence. She lacked the finesse to deal with the questions that would be raised when Phally's disappearance was discovered. Her ignorance would protect her and him both. His hands were still clean.

Sareth drew a deep breath. Don't overreact. What would a man with a clear conscience do in this situation? He'd be affronted by the child's rudeness, but he wouldn't be too concerned. After all, this was Nary, who roamed the streets routinely. She knew her way around. An innocent man would return to his dinner, eat more quickly than normal, and then set out to track the wayward child down. An innocent man would pay a courtesy call on Phally to check if she were home yet, safe with her child. If she were not, he might then drop by Gail's home. Of course, all of this bothersome activity could be averted if only Khath would show up on the doorstep. What was keeping the man?

With a heavy sigh, Sareth turned to his wife, who was standing now in the doorway. "What an ungrateful child," he said, "to run from our hospitality like that. No manners at all." He smiled at Chea. "Come, let us have a quick bite of your delicious dinner, and then I will handle this."

# Thirty

Flip flops in hand, Nary ran down the alley behind Mr. Sareth's house, ignoring the rocks that bruised her feet and mashed her toes. *Hurry.* It had taken all of her self-control to sit meekly at Sareth's house, waiting for the right moment, biding her time until she could see that both Mr. Sareth and his wife were occupied in thought or action. All the while her nerves were screaming with the urgent need to find her mother and Mr. Khath so she could explain.

For it was time to explain, Nary was sure of that. She only hoped it wasn't too late. *This is all my fault. If something bad happens… No, it can't. It won't. Hurry.* Her feet beat out a rhythm in time to the chant in her head. *My. Fault. My. Fault.* Faster and faster the words echoed in her mind as fear drove her into a panicked rush for home.

At last she arrived, racing up the sidewalk and taking the stairs to the porch in two bounds, stubbing her right big toe on the top step as her tiring muscles sputtered at this extra effort. She hopped across the porch and yanked the front door open.

"Mama?" she shouted.

The house was silent. Nary stood in the living room for a moment, panting. The throbbing in her toe caused her to glance down at her foot. Blood was seeping out around the stubbed nail, dripping down the side of her toe. She lifted her feet one by one and looked at the bottoms, crisscrossed with little cuts, embedded with bits of gravel and dirt. She noticed a blood trail down her right forearm, too, and only now felt the slow burn in her elbow.

Should she at least put some shoes on? Nary's eyes drifted to the photo of her father on the mantel. No. There was no time. She'd already wasted precious minutes, standing dumbly in her living room. She tore through the house, opening every door, even the closets. She looked under the beds, too. Just in case.

In the youth brigade, her friend Nai had taken to crawling into tiny spaces after she'd returned late one night, bruised and bloody from a disciplinary session with the camp leaders. She never talked about what they did to her, never talked much at all after that. It wasn't long until Nai stopped eating, too, sneaking her rations to Nary with the ghost of a smile on her tired, drawn face.

*Hurry.* Nary ran out the kitchen door and made a quick circuit of the backyard. Satisfied that her search was thorough enough, she continued without pause, back on the street, running, running. Her thoughts churned. Where were they? Phally would never go alone to Khath's house. There was only one other place she could think of where they might be. Khath must have somehow convinced her mother to go to the cabin deep in the forest.

Her breath rasped in her throat as she ran, trying to puzzle out what to do next. Showing up alone at the cabin might make things worse. Khath and her mother would fight and not let her explain. She had felt the depth of Khath's grief and rage—it was equal to her own—and she knew her mother was no match. Nary felt the weight of her guilt pressing in on her. *If anything happens...*

She needed the monk. Khath's brother could calm him like no one else. The monk would not hesitate to face his brother's wrath, to absorb any blows, verbal or physical. The monk would not be harmed in his mind or spirit, and body wounds would heal.

Nary stopped, her lungs on fire and heart threatening to burst. She felt dizzy and her chest heaved. Bile rose in her throat, and her limbs trembled. She hadn't eaten since the morning. How soft I've become, she thought, remembering the days of hard labor on a cup of rice gruel, a bit of dried fish, and any bugs she could find to still the gnawing pain in her stomach.

She rubbed her forehead and looked around. Her headlong rush had taken her, without forethought, to Gail's gate. Feeling faint, she pushed through the gate, dragged up the porch steps and with her remaining strength, pounded on the front door.

———

Khath kept his eyes trained on Phally, though every other sense was focused on the muffled noises coming from outside the cabin. Who, or what, was out there?

For a moment, Khath's heart had leapt for joy at the thought that Nary had come, but he dismissed the notion immediately. Nary was skilled in the ways of both the hunter and the hunted. Nary would walk as a tiger, not bumble and thrash. He moved back a pace and laid one hand gently against the cabin door, so he would feel the slightest tremor of any subtle attempt to enter.

Were there bears in these woods? The slow and ponderous footfalls could be those of a foraging bear. Given that there was a pond with fish in it nearby, it wasn't an unlikely guess. Was that a snuffling sound? Khath could not be sure, nor could he simply hope for the best. There was too much at stake.

As he listened, the noises moved away from the cabin and gradually faded. He waited for a bit, and then quietly lifted the wooden bar from the door. Without taking his gaze from Phally, holding her silent and immobile with the stern command of his eyes, Khath pushed at the base of the heavy door with his foot, until he felt it give and a breath of fresh air seeped in around the frame. He listened and heard only the rustling of a forest preparing itself for dusk. For the moment, he was safe. But he had to assume that his hideaway was discovered now.

Khath's mind raced, turning over the ramifications. Possibly, nothing else would happen. It was most likely that children had found the cabin, and they would have no reason to rush home and tell anyone. But he dared not make this assumption. He would have to hurry now. He estimated at most he was safe for 40 more minutes, the time it would take to hurry to the road and back. His thoughts churned. Maybe 50 minutes if he added in the time it would take to reach a telephone. He decided to leave the door unbarred, slightly ajar, so he could monitor the sounds of the forest more easily, and if it came to it, escape quickly.

His decision made, he turned his attention to the most immediate problem facing him now. Still holding the length of wood he used to bar the door, Khath studied the woman on the floor in front of him. He had to admit that she had him almost convinced that she really was Nary's mother. Her deep concern for the child seemed genuine. But nothing Phally could say would ever convince him that her husband was not the man who'd killed his wife and son.

So what did that make Phally? A willing and eager helpmate to her husband? A reluctant participant dragged into the Khmer Rouge madness out of fear for her own life and that of her child? So much hinged on the answers to those questions.

Khath stared at the wood in his hands. Perfect for "smashing," the word the Khmer Rouge used to describe the act of clubbing their victims to death. He had seen the notes beside the names on the prisoner lists at Site 21. This one smashed, that one died during interrogation. Again, the memories threatened to pull him from this cabin and back into the blood-stained terror of the prison. A bead of sweat traced its way down his back, making him shiver. Would he never be free of Site 21?

A muscle twitched in Khath's face, and he became aware that his teeth were aching, so tightly were they clenched. With his free hand, he rubbed his jaw and noticed Phally tense at his gesture. The woman was coiled tighter than a spring, reacting to his slightest move.

In an unpleasant flash of clarity, Khath saw himself as she must: cold and impassive, standing over her with a club in his hand. Just like the Khmer Rouge. His eyes swept the cabin and he felt sickened. Why hadn't he seen this immediately? His attempts to tidy the cabin this morning had only made it resemble an interrogation cell, neatly organized to inflict torture.

The floor seemed to rock beneath Khath's feet for a moment as a wave of vertigo swept over him. *And why not?* a voice whispered in his head. *Why not take your revenge?* Blood seemed to lap at his toes as he stood with one foot anchored on the dirt floor of the cabin, the other sliding toward the screams and broken bodies of Site 21. With a shudder, Khath pulled himself upright, shaking his head to drive the vision back into the recesses of his mind.

*Focus. Find the truth.* He forced his thoughts back to that moment in time when his world was shattered by a man with a scar and a torn ear. His hatred flared, steadying him for the task ahead. He gripped the wooden bar more tightly.

"Phally," Khath said. "You have ten minutes to tell me your story and convince me that you are innocent of the blood crimes of the Khmer Rouge." He tapped the bar against the floor of the cabin. "And I should warn you, Phally, that I will not be easily convinced."

---

Nary sat squashed into the back seat of Teresa's car, beside Gail's sport chair. She gulped the last bite of a banana and wiped her hands on her sarong. The food was reviving her quickly. Gail's chair pressed into her shoulder as Teresa steered the car sharply around a corner. A faint squealing noise was audible inside the vehicle. They were on their way to the church, where Teresa said Khath's brother would be studying English with the priest.

Nary leaned forward as if that would make the car go faster. *Hurry*. Several blocks ahead she could see the tall spire of the church.

With Teresa spinning the steering wheel, the car bounced over the church's graveled and potholed parking lot and pulled to a stop in a cloud of dust near the front doors.

Gail was unstrapping her seat belt as Teresa jumped from the car and yanked Gail's wheelchair out of the back seat and into position for Gail. "Go," Gail said, waving her sister toward the stairs.

Nary scrambled out of car and headed for the church stairs, limping as the jagged gravel raked the bottoms of her bare feet. Then a loud blaring noise filled the parking lot, overwhelming her senses. What was happening? She clapped her hands over her ears and confused, turned back to the car. Gail, a look of determination on her face, was leaning on the horn.

Nary froze, unable to choose: run to find the monk or stay with Gail?

In the next moment, the church doors banged open and Pra Chhay and Father Ralph strode out in a swirl of black and saffron robes, billowing forth into the fading afternoon sunshine. The horn fell silent.

At the sight of the monk, Nary ran forward and burst into a torrent of Cambodian, telling Pra Chhay what had happened. "We have to hurry," she said. "Please."

Pra Chhay's face became sober and then concerned. He placed calming hands on her shoulders, hands that seemed to lift the burden she had been carrying alone for so long. Tears of relief ran down her face.

"Good girl, Nary," he said. "You've done well to come to me." He turned to translate for the others, and Nary noticed that Gail had joined the group in her wheelchair now.

*Hurry.* Nary fidgeted and when the monk paused, she spoke up in English. "We go now? I can take."

"I really hate to involve the child like this." Father Ralph hesitated. "But I suppose there is no other way to find the cabin."

"No," Pra Chhay said. "Nary is right. We must go now, quickly. My brother is," he paused, searching for words. "He is not himself these days. I have been worried."

Just then, a battered pick-up truck pulled into the church lot. A dog with droopy ears and snuffly nose hung its head out the passenger side window.

Nary's heart lurched. The farmer. Had he seen her mother? Was she all right? Was she with Mr. Khath in the cabin?

The truck rattled to stop beside Teresa's car and with a screech of rusty hinges, the driver's door swung open. Farmer Taylor emerged and trudged heavily to the stairs leading to the front doors of the church. He stood at the bottom and pointed his finger at Father Ralph, then spoke loudly in an accusing tone.

Nary strained to understand, but the farmer talked in such an odd way. She heard the words "cabin" and "corn" but not much else.

If I start to run, they will chase me, she thought. Maybe that is the only way to get them to stop talking and come now. Her blood hammered and throbbed making her fingers tingle and swell. In a moment she would burst.

Then Gail's voice cut through the chatter. "Did you see them? Were they both all right?" she said, her voice shrill with anxiety.

The farmer looked over at her. He shrugged. "Course I seen 'em. I followed them to my cabin. *My* cabin." He glared at Father Ralph.

"I mean inside the cabin," Gail said. "Could you see what they were doing inside?"

Farmer Taylor shook his head. "Nah." He said more, but Nary again got lost in the man's accent. Then her ears pricked up. Had he said Khmer Rouge? Did he *know?* Was that why he was so mean?

He shook his finger at Father Ralph. He spoke loudly and clearly in a threatening tone. "I want them out of there, damn it. And I don't want them coming back."

"We'll come at once," Pra Chhay said, stepping forward. "Just show us where it is. Please. It's very important."

Father Ralph turned to Gail and Teresa. "Will you take Nary to your house? We'll come to you there as soon as we can." The priest squatted down and spoke to Nary. "You go with Miss Gail, all right Nary? Pra Chhay and I will go get your mother. It won't be long."

Nary shook her head violently. "No, no," she said. "I come with you." Her voice rose to a shout. "We go now," she said, trying to push past Father Ralph toward his car.

Pra Chhay stepped up. "Nary, stop. You have done your part. Stay with Miss Gail. We will come soon."

Nary stared wildly at the adults grouped around her, searching for support, but there was none. "Please," she said, appealing to the group at large. "I can help. I can explain." She felt the tension rising through her body, felt her hands clench. Her eyes felt dry but she dared not blink, dared not miss a second of this moment of decision. "Please," she begged.

Father Ralph shook his head. The farmer began to walk to his truck.

Nary felt her world collapsing. How could they forbid her to come? She had to be there.

Gail rolled her chair up closer to Nary and held out her hand. "Nary, come."

Nary stood, her head swiveling back and forth between the car and Gail.

"Let's go, Nary," Gail said in a gentle voice. She waggled her fingertips, but Nary took a step away from her, her hands behind her back, watching as Farmer Taylor spun his truck out of the parking lot, spewing gravel. Father Ralph and Pra Chhay followed in the church van. Anger began to burn in her chest. She should be in that van.

"Nary?" Gail said.

Nary shook her head, gliding backward another step. With tiny steps, soft and smooth, so Gail and Teresa would hardly notice the increasing distance between them, Nary inched away, just like her father had taught her. "Float backwards, like a leaf upon a stream, child, then run like a hunted tiger," he had said. "That is how you escape."

Another step, one more, just enough and then she was flying, her feet skimming the earth as the shouts of Gail and Teresa faded behind her. *I'm coming, Mama.*

# Thirty-One

Khath stood rigid as Phally spoke, slowly drawing out each word, about her life in the village with Boran and Nary before the Khmer Rouge took over, about how her husband worked for the government, how he had actually sent reports back to Phnom Penh about suspected Khmer Rouge activity in the region. "He hated them," she said. "He was not one of them. Never."

Phally's voice sounded strained, a cracked veneer barely concealing an under-layer of terror. Like a fine seamstress, she took great care to embellish her tale with the silken thread of Nary, weaving the child's presence through her narrative, binding it together.

Khath knew what she was doing. She was playing for time, trying to calm him with the drone of her voice, quavering though it was, trying to reach his humanity with memories of a world before the Khmer Rouge. She pattered on about settling down in Glenberg, creating a new life with Nary, the two of them making their way in this world.

He could see her fighting her fear, working hard not to show it, the muscles of her face at war with the emotions she tried to hide. So intense was her struggle that she hardly looked like herself. Good. It was easier for him that way.

"You are running out of time, Phally," Khath said, his voice grim. "I have been generous, given you more time than you deserve, and you have not yet told me the truth." He made a show of looking at his watch. Suppose she did not confess? What would he do then? Dusk was falling hard, compounded by the natural dimness of the deep forest. Darkness pressed against the window, the cabin now illuminated solely by candlelight. Khath could not afford to be patient for much longer.

A strained silence fell in the little cabin. Phally's eyes were wide and darting, her nostrils flared, her body taut, all betraying the swirl of thoughts that Khath knew must be racing through her brain at this moment, searching for some way out of this situation.

Soon, she would begin to bargain with him, as people always did in the interrogation cells of the Khmer Rouge. Hadn't he done so himself? Resisted, bargained, begged, to no avail. In the end, his death was postponed only because he had skills his jailers needed. He himself had seen the note scrawled in the margins of that day's prisoner list by Comrade Duch, the commander of Site 21. There, next to his name, were the eight words that settled his fate. *"We can use him. Keep for a while."*

Everyone else on the list had been transported to the killing fields for execution. He knew about the open pits at Choeung Ek, filled with the bodies of the doomed, separated by a light dusting of lime.

He'd been taken there one night to fix a generator that powered the floodlights illuminating the activity of the guards as they clubbed the prisoners one by one, then kicked the bodies into the pits. The roar of the generators muffled the screams of the dying so those waiting their turn in the small sheds nearby would not become crazed with fear. The executions were always performed at night, casting eerie shadows in a macabre dance of violence, shadow puppets enacting an epic tale.

He could have refused to do the work the Khmer Rouge assigned to him. He could have chosen death instead. But they would have found someone else to fix the machines. And despite the daily horrors of his life at Site 21, he had still wanted to live for the sake of someday finding his daughters.

Khath's gaze fell upon his hands, knuckles white from their deathlike grip upon the wooden bar from the door. Skilled hands, forced to labor for the Khmer Rouge, to keep the lights burning as they tortured and killed. How much innocent blood was splashed upon his own hands by association? Sweat broke out along Khath's hairline, a wave of nausea mixed with revulsion swept through his body, building into a rage that hammered against his temples.

The quiet in the cabin was broken by the rasp of ragged panting. Startled, Khath realized the dog-like sounds were coming from him. With a cry, he swung the bar at the neatly arranged counter, scattering the ropes, the wire, the pliers.

"These are my tools," he screamed, "my tools, for repairing the cabin." He pointed to the wall. "A shovel," he cried, "for digging, not for killing, an ax to cut wood. I am not like your husband. I am not Khmer Rouge."

Phally had thrown up her arms to protect her face from the objects flying from the counter. She sprang up now and pressed herself back against the far corner of the cabin.

Khath dropped the bar and advanced toward Phally with clenched fists. "Speak, damn you. I want the truth now. Your husband killed my family. He killed my baby just for crying. Did you know? Did you help?"

Phally opened her mouth and shut it. Swallowed. "No," she whispered. Her voice gained strength. "No, no, he could not. He killed no one. They killed him. The Khmer Rouge killed my Boran." She was shouting now, tears streaming down her face.

"You lie," Khath snarled. "I saw him kill with my own eyes. Do you hear what I say? I *saw* him. Your words, your tears, they do not change that truth. *I saw him.*"

Phally shrank away from his fury. Khath edged closer, but not too close.

*Careful, now. Be very cautious; she is strong despite her fear.* Khath studied Phally's crouched position warily. *But, see how she cringes. Surely she will break now and confess.*

But still Phally shook her head, resisted him, clinging to her own version of things. A tiny doubt entered Khath's mind.

"No, no." Phally's voice whispered on, relentless. "You must believe me. It was not him. He would not do such things." She sank to her knees, raised her arms, hands clasped, beseeching. "Please," she said. "Think of Nary. Think of your own daughters."

Khath reeled backwards a step as though struck. He had seen a woman beg for mercy just this way at Site 21. The memory overpowered him. He felt again the pain in his ribs as he did on that night when he was kicked awake from a restless sleep on the hard floor of his cell at the prison. A guard unlocked the shackles from his ankles and jerked him roughly to his feet, pushing him down the hall toward the interrogation rooms.

Strangely, the rooms were dark and silent. No one screamed or moaned. There was no smack of club against flesh, no coppery smell of freshly spilled blood.

Khath was shoved roughly into a small room filled with the metallic odor of burnt electrical wiring. The guard pushed him toward a corner of the room. Khath stumbled over a mound of bodies on the floor, shuddering as the flesh yielded beneath his feet.

"Fix the light," the guard ordered, and then Khath knew where he was and groped for the fuse box mounted on the wall.

"I can fix it faster if I may be allowed to use a candle to see, comrade." Khath stood with head bowed humbly.

A grunt and the scrape of a match were the only reply he received, but a moment later a candle was thrust into his hands. By its flickering light, he saw a woman kneeling on the floor, raising her hands to beg for her life, mistaking him for a senior cadre.

The guards laughed. "You think this one can save you?" they jeered at the woman, whose cheekbones strained the skin of her face. "Only your confession will protect you now, sister."

But Khath knew that was a lie. There was no protection at Site 21. Just ask those bodies piled in the corner.

Khath turned away in haste and searched for the blown fuse in the panel before him. Carefully he flipped the lever to reset the fuse, and in an instant the room was flooded with light. He didn't want to look—his past and present minds screamed at him, "Don't look. Don't look at the bodies," but he couldn't help himself as his eyes were drawn downward to a tangle of small limbs. Tiny limbs. Children's limbs.

His thoughts lurched wildly, approaching that lifeless pile, veering away. Needing to know, dreading the knowledge. He felt sick. His hands trembled as his mind wondered. What was happening outside this prison to cause so many children to die? Had they run out of adults to murder? Were the children resisting, turning upon their captors? A sense of shame rose in him at the thought, assaulting him with the force of a physical punch. Were the children doing what the adults lacked the courage to do? Or had life simply ceased to matter to them?

"Why do you linger, comrade? You are done here," one of the guards spoke in a softly dangerous voice.

Khath bowed. "Comrade, I was merely waiting to make sure the power would not fail again," he lied.

Even as he bowed, his eyes betrayed him, straying again to the pile of bodies in the corner. And it was then that he saw it: a leg with a tiny foot, a star-shaped mark near the ankle. It could not be, but it was. He reached his hand toward his daughter Sitha. But she was already holding someone's hand, in death as in life, clinging to her older sister, Kamala.

"Someone you know?" the guard inquired coldly.

A moan started somewhere deep in Khath's chest and worked its way up toward his throat, escaping in a howl of despair. He gazed wildly around the tiny cabin, struggling to orient himself to the present while his memory hurled painful images at him, images he had locked away in the deepest part of his being, unwilling, unable, to face the devastating loss of Sitha and Kamala.

A searing pain began in his chest and he struggled to breathe. Sweat poured from his body. "They're dead," he croaked. "My girls are dead. I remember it now. The Khmer Rouge killed them at Site 21. I saw them. All of my family is gone."

The silence in the cabin was absolute. Or perhaps it was that the roaring in his ears had deafened Khath to external sounds. His entire body throbbed in the grip of a pain unlike anything he had ever felt before, far worse than any blows the Khmer Rouge had inflicted upon him. Worse even than witnessing the deaths of his beloved wife and son, for at that time he had had things to do, his daughters to protect, a mess to clean up.

And then it occurred to him. There were things yet to be done here, in this cabin.

Khath refocused his attention on Phally. Her eyes were enormous, her mouth a round "O" of shock and dismay. Within seconds, he saw a growing unease in those eyes, a mounting horror as Phally processed this new bit of information.

For it certainly changed things, Khath thought. Kamala and Sitha were dead. And now, standing here before him like a gift of retribution was the wife of the man Khath knew to be a Khmer Rouge killer.

———

Nary flew through the forest, her feet pounding on the path leading to the road near the corn field. There was no need to be quiet now. Speed was what mattered. Up ahead across the street, she saw the farmer's truck and the church van parked along the side of the road. She slowed and moved behind a tree, watching as the farmer slid his bulk out of the truck and hitched up his overalls. He pointed in the general direction of the cabin, talking, his words indistinct at this distance. Just go, she wanted to shout. Pra Chhay seemed to feel the same, for he started down the embankment without waiting for the farmer.

It was too late now to get to the cabin ahead of the men. She would have to let them get a head start, and then follow close behind.

The noise of an approaching vehicle drew her attention. The priest and the farmer turned toward the car. Now what? With a frown, Nary saw it was Gail and Theresa, waving frantically out the windows. She had hoped they would not know where the farmer lived, but clearly they did. The car drew up alongside Father Ralph. Gail's voice carried clearly in the still air. "Nary's gone."

Father Ralph laid a hand on the roof of the car and bent his tall body toward the passenger window. Nary heard Gail say, "Okay," and then the car was nosed over to the edge of the road and parked, the rumble of its engine silenced. Teresa got out and leaned against the car, turning her head from side to side to look up and down the road. Gail hung out the other window, staring toward the forest. They were keeping watch, determined to stop her from following the men.

Nary sighed. She would have no trouble slipping past the Americans, but it would take precious time. Already the men were moving into the forest. She would have to work her way up the street, cross when Teresa's head was turned and then cut through the forest to intercept the path. She hoped the farmer would not bring his fat dog along. Now that would be a complication.

She faded back into her side of the forest and began to make her way along the road, moving with less caution the further she got from the parked cars. When Teresa was just a blurry shape in the gathering darkness, Nary crawled up the embankment, then crouched low and darted across the street. Once across and in the shelter of the trees, she paused to see if

Teresa had noticed but so far, her luck was holding. She imagined Gail blowing the horn in warning if they saw her, and dreaded to think what effect that might have on whatever might be happening in the cabin.

Nary moved deeper into the forest, then stood listening. She heard no voices, no snapping of branches, nothing to signal the passing of the three men. She remembered that the trail curved away to the left, away from the road, but how far did it run beside the road before curving? She didn't want to guess wrong, miss the trail entirely and end up lost.

Think. What would Papa advise her to do? He had spent hours teaching her how to chart a course through dense underbrush, moving from landmark to landmark in a more or less straight line. "You never know when you might need this skill." It was what he always said when he took her aside, away from her mother, to teach her survival skills. "It will be our game. Our secret," her father had said. "You must learn to keep secrets, Nary."

After a few minutes, Nary reached the trail. Again, she stood and listened. And then grinned. No need to listen at all. One sniff was all it took to tell her that the farmer's dog had pooped along the trail, quite close to where she was standing.

Looking down, she saw a dark pile near her left foot and gave it a wide berth as she took off running down the trail, relief surging as every step brought her closer to the cabin. Soon it would be all right. *I'm coming, Mama.*

But was she too late?

Fear made her careless as she rushed along the path. She was upon the men so quickly that she nearly gave herself away. Only the hacking cough and phlegm-filled spitting of the farmer saved her from that mistake. Nary froze at the sound, almost in mid-air, landing lightly on her bare feet, toes first. She peered ahead as the trail curved slightly and saw the farmer leading the group, his dog straining against a leash. Pra Chhay was next, nearly on top of the farmer. Father Ralph followed behind, looking around. Once he stopped, turned and stared back down the trail for a moment.

He's looking for me, Nary thought. But she had already stepped behind a tree when she saw the priest stop. She was sure that the man had seen nothing but forest behind him.

The dog was another matter. A breeze was pushing her hair forward, blowing her scent toward the animal. Would he notice? Would he care? Nary did not know very much about fat American dogs with floppy ears and drooling mouths, but she knew he had chased her once already, and that might be enough to trigger a reaction. There was nothing she could do about it.

The men proceeded along the trail. They must be getting near the cabin now. Nary followed as closely as she dared. She stared ahead, craning her neck to see past the men, and caught her breath. Was that a glimmer of light ahead? She squinted into the night. Was it a glow of interior light escaping through the cloudy window of the cabin, or perhaps moonlight on the pond? She tried to remember if the water was visible before the cabin or not. Her attention distracted, Nary stubbed her toe against a tree root and stumbled, pitching forward into the brush and against a tree. Immediately, the farmer's dog began to whine, quickly silenced by a yank on the leash.

The priest strode rapidly toward her, reaching a long arm into the brush to haul her out with a firm hand on her shoulder.

"Nary," he exclaimed. "Are you hur...".

An anguished howl tore through the silence of the forest.

"Jesus Christ. What was that?" the farmer said.

A scream and shouts echoed through the trees. Pra Chhay sprinted past the farmer, robes gathered over one arm to free his legs for running. Father Ralph was close behind.

Nary raced after the men. *Oh no. Oh no.* She saw Pra Chhay fling himself against the cabin door, which gave way easily. She heard him cry out, "Khath. Stop." She heard a crash, and cries of pain, sounds of a struggle. And finally, she heard weeping. *Mama.*

She reached the entrance to the cabin, blocked now by the bulk of the farmer and his dog. Squeezing past, Nary stopped, shocked at the scene before her. She first saw Khath lying on the floor, all but smothered beneath the saffron robes of his brother Pra Chhay, who pinned him firmly to the ground. She saw Khath's shoulders were shaking and realized he, too, was weeping.

"Shhh, Khath. It's over now. Shhhh," Pra Chhay whispered again and again.

In the corner, her mother crouched against the wall, tears streaming down her face, while Father Ralph sat on the floor in front of her, trying to comfort her.

"It's not true. It's not true. My husband not Khmer Rouge," Phally said through her tears. "He good man. He not Khmer Rouge."

Nary stepped softly into the room. It was time. "But he was, Mama," she said, forcing the words from her tight throat. "He was."

# Thirty-Two

Nary moved toward her mother with slow, careful steps. *A trapped, wounded animal may lunge at you, Nary, even one whose nature is normally peaceful.* Her father's words echoed in her head as she approached this stunned woman in the corner of the room. Her mother stared at her with the bewildered eyes of one who believes herself saved, then realizes that her torment has barely begun, struggling to grasp this abrupt veer in the path of her karma.

The priest moved aside to let Nary pass. A stifling stillness blanketed the room. Even Khath had stopped weeping. Nary felt the weight of many eyes upon her.

Her mother squinted a little. She seemed to be trying to focus her gaze. Her brow wrinkled. "Nary," she said, then stopped, looking her daughter up and down as if truly seeing her for the first time. "What are you doing here? Where are your shoes?" She reached her arms out. "Come here, mouse. I am so glad you are safe."

Confused, Nary hesitated. Had her mother not heard her? Was there a way to go forward now pretending those words had never been spoken? A quick glance at the others in the room ended that hope.

"Nary?" Her mother's eyes pleaded with her.

Nary shook her head. She had to go on with this before her courage failed and she was held forever in the darkness of her secrets. She felt the prick of tears stinging her eyes. "I'm sorry, Mama. Papa said I could never tell anyone. He said we would be killed if anyone found out." She wiped a tear off her cheek. "But Mr. Khath is right. Papa was…he was…" Nary's throat closed. She was unable to say those hated words, could not free them from the hidden place deep in her soul where she had carried them for so long.

"Nary, hush. You don't know what you're saying." Her mother looked angry now, her voice beginning to rise. "I am tired of hearing these accusations about Papa. And now, from you, his own daughter. Hush, child. These are adult matters."

"Let her speak," Pra Chhay said, his voice stern.

The monk turned and said something in English to Father Ralph. Nary saw the priest's jaw sag for a moment. He passed a hand over his face and then rose to his feet slowly, like a much older man.

"Stop. Just stop. We will not discuss this here," the priest said. He pointed to Nary's bloody feet and continued speaking, but Nary had stopped listening to him, her attention drawn to her mother's face.

Never had Nary seen such a look of despair and dread in her mother's eyes. Phally's mouth trembled and her face reddened. She dropped her head into her hands and her shoulders shook from silent weeping. One learned to do that in the camps, to cry without making a sound. Tears were a sign of weakness and weakness was punished.

*This is my fault. I was weak. I should have told sooner.* Nary looked at Khath. He was sitting quietly now, cross-legged, head tilted backwards against a leg of the counter, eyes closed. He seemed to feel the pull of her gaze. His head lifted, eyelids rising slowly as though battling against some great weight. His dark eyes gleamed at her, focused, and finally saw her. An expression of bleak sadness crossed his face as he gave a brief nod, then let his eyelids drop and his head tilt back. A single drop seeped from the corner of his eye, glistening in the flickering light of the candles.

Again, Nary felt the sting of her own tears. The two people left in her life that she loved the most were broken, weeping like children in their separate corners, and it was her fault. *But how could I know? He made me promise. And then he died.*

Nary flinched as a hand was placed on her shoulder. The priest stood behind her now, and from the corner of her eye she could see hair sprouting like shoots of new rice from the fingers he draped over her collar bone. Westerners were much hairier than Cambodians, she thought distractedly. She felt very tired, and a wave of nausea rose in her throat. As from a great distance, she heard the voice of Pra Chhay explaining what Father Ralph had said, something about going back to Gail's house, food, a warm fire, serious conversation.

A roaring filled Nary's ears, and as she tumbled toward the ground she felt strong arms scoop her up, breaking her fall and cradling her tenderly. Like Papa, she thought. Just like Papa used to do. Then darkness descended.

———————

Khath plodded along the forest path after Father Ralph, who carried Nary sleeping against his chest. Phally, at the front of the group, kept stopping to check on Nary, to touch the child's hand or tuck her foot out of the way of a branch. They had left the farmer behind to close up his cabin.

Behind Khath, his brother walked clacking his prayer beads, chanting the Heart Sutra, the words a soothing wash over Khath's battered soul. *Go beyond, beyond the suffering, to find peace.* Khath was emptier than he ever had been, scoured by the images his brain had vomited up to him in the cabin. And he began to understand the truth of the Heart Sutra that beyond the suffering, in the emptiness, there was stillness and grace.

Kamala and Sitha were gone, and yet Pra Chhay would say that they were here, all around him, their spirits floating through the forest at his side, free of pain and fear.

Khath took a deep breath and invited them in, pulled his daughters into the warm and protected chambers of his heart, away from the rustle of the forest, the chill of the night air. Embraced them with his love, and let them go, flowing back into the night as he exhaled. Breathe in the pain, bathe it with compassion, and release it. This was the practice of an enlightened being. Another breath, another step, one after the other. He was far from enlightened, but he could do this simple thing, moment by moment.

Ninety minutes later, they all sat in Gail's living room, a fire roaring in the hearth. It was almost too warm. Khath, in Gail's wingback chair, shifted slightly away from the embers. The glow from several lamps fell over the group, and Khath studied these people clustered around the room.

Nary sat wrapped in a blanket and snuggled between Gail and Phally on the couch, her bandaged feet swathed in a pair of Gail's brightly patterned woolen socks. Phally, from the depths of another blanket, looked upon her daughter with a strange expression on her face. Love, yes, but a certain distance there as well, as if she were wondering who this stranger was beside her. She seemed resigned to hear bad news, dreaded news.

Pra Chhay sat in the other wingback chair, his saffron robes an extension of the fire. He and Father Ralph had sparred politely over who would get the last comfortable chair, the priest winning the argument when he said, "You should be near your brother." Teresa had rolled her office chair in for Father Ralph, who squeezed it between Pra Chhay and the couch. The priest had wanted to be close to Pra Chhay, who would interpret the conversation for him. For herself, Teresa had selected a chair from the dining room, straight and hard, positioned next to Khath and closest to the door. Everyone had a cup of tea close at hand.

Father Ralph leaned forward. "Shall we begin?" he said. "Nary, why don't you tell us how you came to be in the cabin tonight."

Pra Chhay translated and nodded encouragingly at Nary.

"Mr. Sareth and his wife picked me up after school," Nary began.

"What?" Phally said, staring at her daughter.

"They said you and Mr. Khath needed time to talk alone, Mama. They said I was to come home with them for the evening."

"I know nothing about this," Phally's voice was rising.

Khath cleared his throat. "I can explain," he said. "I thought if you and I could talk undisturbed that I could convince you to confess about your husband and yourself. Mr. Sareth thought this was an excellent idea and said he would help me to arrange such a meeting."

Khath turned to Pra Chhay. "I'm sorry, brother. I ignored all your counsel, just as I did in the camp before we left, and again, it led to trouble." He paused while Pra Chhay translated for Father Ralph and the girls.

"I knew it," Gail muttered. "I knew Sareth was behind this."

Father Ralph glanced at Gail but made no comment.

Khath continued. "I meant only to talk, perhaps to frighten you a little, Phally, if you refused to tell the truth. I hoped you would be forced to leave. I could not stand the thought of living side by side with the Khmer Rouge in Glenberg. I hoped to protect Nary from you, to save her from the Khmer Rouge. I am sorry. I was right about your husband, but it appears I was wrong about you."

A short silence followed Khath's statement, then, Father Ralph spoke again.

"Tell us about your father, Nary. It's all right to talk about it now."

Khath saw Nary look up at Phally, who nodded and spoke to her daughter in her native tongue. "The priest is right, mouse.

No more secrets. You can speak without fear, child. When did you see him again, after he was first taken from us?"

Nary began to speak, hesitantly at first, then with greater confidence. As she spoke, Pra Chhay whispered a soft translation, his words a low hum, blending with hers in a duet of language.

"It was a couple weeks after I was taken to the Youth Brigade," Nary said. "I was sick one night and went to the outhouse on the edge of the woods. When I came out, someone grabbed me from behind. I thought it was a soldier at first and I was very frightened. I fought hard to get away but I was not strong enough.

Then he whispered my nickname. "Little Tiger, it is me," he said, and I knew it was Papa. I wanted to shout with joy, but he kept his hand over my mouth so I couldn't make a sound. He carried me into the woods. He told me he was an assistant to one of the leaders at the camp and had seen me brought in. He said I had to pretend not to know him if I saw him during the day, but that he would try to take care of me and bring me extra food when he could. Sometimes he got me assigned to easy work, like tending the camp garden, instead of planting rice or building roads."

"So Nary was a connection to his past as a government official?" Father Ralph asked. "I suppose to convince the Khmer Rouge he supported their cause, he would have had to cut all ties from before?"

Nary nodded as Pra Chhay translated the priest's question. "Papa said they would kill him, and probably me too, if they knew I was his daughter and caught him helping me. They didn't trust him, he said, and were always watching him, waiting for him to make a mistake."

Khath nodded. "It is true. There was no trust between the Khmer Rouge. Everyone lived in fear of being accused of a violation. And once you were accused, it was your duty to accuse others."

"But how did Papa get there in the first place, Nary? I saw him taken away to be shot," Phally said. "I heard the gunshots and we found the bodies dumped outside the village. Though they were all in a tangle and rotting in the heat, so it was difficult to tell one from another," she conceded. Then she looked around a little wildly. "The faces go first, you know. The bugs and the animals like those parts best, so you have to be quick or you'll never know, for sure. There's always a doubt." Her voice broke and she buried her head in her hands.

Gail reached across Nary and squeezed Phally's hand. "I don't know what Phally just said, but maybe we should take a little break," she suggested.

Teresa stood up and went to the kitchen, bringing back a thermos of hot water and fresh tea bags.

Khath shook his head when Teresa offered him more tea, mulling over Phally's words. *Always a doubt.* Whether you called it doubt, or hope, it was what you clung to when things looked darkest. It was what made you open your eyes in the morning. How well he knew that feeling.

After a few minutes more, Phally raised her head. She looked drained, but nodded calmly at Nary. "Go ahead, mouse. How did your Papa end up in the camp?"

"He knew some of the soldiers at the checkpoint, Mama. From home. He'd gone to their meetings sometimes."

Phally nodded. "Yes, that's true," she explained to the group. "He was spying on the Khmer Rouge organizers, sending reports back to the government on their strength, their activities. He was pretending..." Phally's voice trailed off and she flushed.

"Papa told me he convinced the soldiers he was one of them that day. They sent him to a camp to train him." Nary's voice dropped. "They made him kill and hurt people. It made him sick to do those things, he said. They always made him do the worst things to prove himself."

Again, true, Khath thought. The last assignment for many of the guards at S21 was the killing unit. Once the leaders no longer trusted you, they gave you the worst jobs, and you did your best at these horrible tasks, trying to save your own life by killing others. A lot of guards went crazy at the end. Some took their own lives. Others probably wished they had.

"So was he able to keep his promise to take care of you, Nary?" Father Ralph asked.

Nary nodded. "I was lucky. Papa left me food, balls of rice, a piece of fish. He made me promise to eat it myself and not share it with anyone." The child looked down. "I felt bad sometimes to have food when no one else did. But Papa said he risked his life to save mine. 'Don't let all my effort be wasted,' he said. 'You must eat this food, and remember all the things I taught you so you can survive. Promise me, Nary.'"

Khath felt his throat tighten. Such a heavy burden to lay on a child. He tried to reconcile this portrait of an anguished, desperate father with the cold, hooded eyes of the man who'd shot his wife, and he couldn't. He simply couldn't. His mind veered away and refused to look too closely into the dark well of human complexity. It would be too easy to lose one's balance peering into the depths. Maybe later, but not now.

"He must have known," Father Ralph was saying. "If he was sending reports back to the government, he must have known that the Khmer Rouge were getting stronger. So he tried to give Nary a fighting chance. What a tragic story. But I'm curious, Nary," the priest leaned forward in his chair. "How did your father manage to get the food to you if he was being watched so closely?"

"We had a system of signals," Nary said. "If he had left food hidden for me, he would leave me a sign. Like turning a particular rock upside down, or draping a string over a branch. I knew where to look. Depending which sign he used, I would know which hiding spot to check."

"Did you get to see him, talk to him again, mouse?" Phally smoothed a lock of her daughter's hair, tucking it behind the girl's ear.

"Sometimes, maybe once a month, when I sneaked out to collect the food, he would be there waiting," Nary said. "He never stayed long or said much. He was afraid he would be missed or someone would hear us talking. He mostly just held me in his lap or touched my face."

Khath saw tears welling in Nary's eyes as she said this. Then the little girl sighed and looked at her hands. Her voice began to tremble as she continued her story.

"The last time he came, he said he couldn't come anymore but would try to keep leaving me food. He said new leaders were coming to the camp, very strict leaders, and we must be extra careful. About a month later, I saw them take him and the other old leaders out into a field and force them to dig a hole."

Khath felt the burn of anger. He knew what was coming. He saw tears running down Nary's face now and ached for her. Children should not have to witness such things.

"They tied everyone's hands. Then they made them kneel blindfolded at the edge of the hole." Nary's voice quavered. "They hit them on the head with an ax, one by one." She looked around the room, her words anguished as she said, "I never told anyone, Mama, and still they killed him."

Phally pulled her daughter close, murmuring softly to the child.

Khath let his breath out in another long sigh. "It was not your fault, Nary. Don't ever think that any of this was your fault. By the end, they were all killing each other as well as killing us," he said.

"Things weren't going well," Pra Chhay explained to the Americans, "with the war or with the grand plan to reform society. It was all crumbling, and someone had to be blamed. And by that time, killing was all they knew how to do."

Silence fell over the group, broken only by the crackling of the fire. The sadness of Pra Chhay's last sentence settled over Khath like a shroud. If Pra Chhay is right, he thought, then there is no hope for Cambodia.

"Well, now, things can't be as bad as all that."

Khath jerked his head up, startled. As one, all the eyes in the room turned toward the speaker.

Mr. Sareth stood at the edge of the living room carpet. "Forgive me. I heard your voices and let myself in," he said, then paused, sweeping his eyes over the group. "I have been searching all over town. How very fortunate to find you all here together."

# Thirty-Three

Sareth watched the priest with a vague unease in his heart. A day had passed since the incident in the cabin. The two men were seated now in Father Ralph's office, not in the comfortable chairs but facing each other across the expanse of the priest's large mahogany desk. It was not a good sign, this distance, this formality.

Sareth had listened closely to the priest's recounting of all that had happened at the cabin and of Nary's revelations about her father, gasping, murmuring and shaking his head at the appropriate places in the tale. Through it all, he had tried to hear the unspoken story, to anticipate the questions the priest would have for him, and to formulate his responses in advance.

When Father Ralph was done, Sareth took a moment to arrange his thoughts before speaking. "I so regret the lapse of judgment on my part," he began, putting a bleak expression on his face. "I feel I have done you a grave disservice. I am afraid I have been over busy of late with concerns of my own, though that in no way excuses my lack of foresight."

Sareth paused to let the priest speak, but when Father Ralph said nothing, Sareth rushed on. "Indeed, I am quite shocked. I hardly know what to say. I just never thought that Khath was desperate enough to *kidnap* Phally and drag her to a cabin in the woods, resort to violence as he did." Sareth leaned forward in his chair. "Father Ralph, I hope you know that if I'd had any idea of the depth of the man's desperation, why, I would never have let him out of my sight. Knowing now that I played some role in helping Khath, by watching over the child," Sareth ran his hands over his face and played his trump card, "well, I feel I have no choice but to offer you my resignation."

At these words, Father Ralph held up a hand. "No," he said. "It is I who should apologize. I have put far too much responsibility on you, relying on you to be my eyes and ears instead of looking and hearing for myself." He'd smiled ruefully then. "You are so talented, Mr. Sareth, so good at what you do, that I never thought to question how you were getting along and what challenges you might be facing here in Glenberg. No, I do not blame you for what has happened. I blame only myself."

Sareth's heart gave a happy leap at hearing these words. This was more than he had hoped for. "You are very gracious," he said to the priest. "But it is not right for you to shoulder this responsibility alone."

Father Ralph inclined his head toward Sareth in silent acknowledgment of his interpreter's assessment. "I am sure there is more than enough blame to go around," he said dryly. "But there is one thing that bothers me."

"Something I can assist with, I hope," Sareth said, feeling his body tense again.

The priest leaned back in his chair, a faraway look on his face. "It is a great tragedy," he said. "I think about everyone involved: Khath, losing his daughters, his whole family; Phally, left without a husband and with a daughter who is cold and distant; Nary, living with this terrible secret, seeing her father killed, unable to love her mother openly."

Nodding his head slowly, Sareth agreed. "A great tragedy."

"And yet," Father Ralph continued, "when I look at the actions of all those involved, I see that they are motivated by love. Khath, after all, was trying to save Nary from the clutches of the Khmer Rouge, in the form of her mother. Nary was trying to honor and protect the memory of her father, who risked his life to protect and save her from the very evil he had perpetrated on others. Phally was trying to save Nary from her memories and give her a better life. All of these people, acting with such good intentions."

Sareth felt a prickle of sweat gathering along his hairline. "It is admirable," he murmured.

"Mr. Sareth, I will speak frankly here," Father Ralph said, leaning forward now, his forearms resting on the desk. "Like I said earlier, you are very skilled at this work. But for you, it is merely a job, not a calling. I understand that you have not gone through what the others have, but I am concerned by what I perceive as a lack of empathy on your part. I question if you can still be effective in your role here after what has happened."

Sareth felt his jaw drop, blood rush to his face. "I…" he began.

But the priest held up his hand again. "Let me finish," he said. "I meant it when I said I bear the responsibility for what has happened. I feel that I did not supervise your actions properly and relied too heavily on your assessments, instead of forming my own. And so, though I do accept your resignation, I have spoken with some friends about another position for you. One in Portland that I believe is better suited to your talents and interests. I'm sorry. I have enjoyed working with you, Mr. Sareth, truly I have. Your help has been of immense value to me. But after all this, it seems impossible for you to stay on, don't you agree?"

Sareth struggled to control his emotions. Anger, fear and humiliation were washing over him in such churning waves that he felt quite ill. He closed his eyes for a moment, his stomach churning as he struggled to absorb the priest's words. When he opened them, Father Ralph was standing before him, handing him a cup of tea.

"Are you all right?" the priest said. "Would you like a few moments?"

Sareth shook his head and took a sip of the tea, clasping the mug tightly with both hands to still their trembling. He cleared his throat. "Perhaps you are right," he said, with all the dignity he could muster. "It would be unpleasant for Chea and me to remain here."

Father Ralph looked relieved. "Difficult, to say the least," he said.

Gathering his thoughts, Sareth said, "And this new position? What can you tell me about that?"

Father Ralph smiled. "It is actually a great opportunity for you, Mr. Sareth. The State of Oregon needs interpreters and translators to help out in the court system. It's a State job, well-paying, with opportunities for advancement. They badly need people with your level of fluency and sophistication. I'm sure you'll find the work more challenging and interesting than anything you could find in Glenberg."

Slowly Sareth nodded. Chea would like living in Portland, once she got used to it. And a bigger paycheck would go a long way towards reestablishing his authority in the home.

An unfamiliar feeling of gratitude towards Father Ralph rose in his chest. He stood and faced the man. "I bow to your superior wisdom," he said with a brittle smile. "And I do thank you, very much, for this new opportunity." He extended a hand toward his benefactor. "I trust we may part as friends?"

---

Khath ran a gentle fingertip along the carved teak frame protecting his most treasured belonging, now displayed on an easel in his living room. Teresa had taken the battered and grimy photo of Kamala and Sitha to a photography shop in Portland to be repaired, cleaned and enlarged for today's *Prachum Bend* ceremony, and the results were beautiful. There, carried on his hip, his daughter Sitha, smiling down at Kamala who held tight to Khath's hand, an impish grin lighting her face.

When he had first gazed upon the renovated photo, seeing his daughters' features so clean and clear, free of the blurry edges of time, Khath's heart had cracked open wide and a flood of love and grief surged against the hard, frozen places deep in his soul. He had wept then, great shuddering sobs, and afterward, had felt cleansed of something heavy and dark and dangerous.

Waiting for his guests now, Khath rearranged the funeral flowers slightly, careful not to dirty his white mourning shirt. The details were important today to ensure that as much good merit as possible could be transferred to benefit his daughters' rebirths.

Would the ceremony help, even now, after so much time had passed since the date of the girls' death? This he had asked his brother. Pra Chhay had reassured him. You have held your daughters so tightly, Khath, so deeply hidden that you may have impeded their passage to the other side, Pra Chhay had said. You can use this time to release them with your blessing. Khath had seen the truth in those words.

"I was always so sure that I would know it if they were dead," he'd said to Pra Chhay. "And I *did* know it. I just couldn't bear to think of it. And so I looked outward, instead of inward, where the truth lay."

Pra Chhay had smiled a gentle smile at this. "You have directly experienced a powerful teaching in all this turbulence, Khath," the monk had said.

Now Khath could hear his brother chanting in his bedroom, performing cleansing and purification rituals in preparation for the merit transference ceremony. With a sense of shame, Khath remembered how he'd asked Pra Chhay to renounce his vows so they could find a Christian sponsor. *How glad I am that he was the stronger one, steadfast in his path. What would I do, where would I be without him now?*

A short while later Pra Chhay joined him in the living room. "Is everything set up the way you want it?" he asked glancing about the room. "The others will be arriving soon."

Khath nodded. "It will seem strange without Mr. Sareth here. I cannot say that I will miss him, but I will notice his absence."

"We may yet see him from time to time," Pra Chhay said. "If not him, his work."

"What do you mean?" Khath asked. "I assumed he was moving to Portland to be with relatives. Is he still working for Father Ralph?"

"No, Father Ralph accepted Mr. Sareth's resignation," Pra Chhay said. "But he also referred him for a job in Portland translating for the courts. Apparently they hired him immediately. Father Ralph asked me to tell you."

Khath stood silent, letting his feelings sort themselves out before he spoke.

Pra Chhay filled the silence, watching him closely. "I think in this new job Mr. Sareth can do much to help our people. I think Father Ralph made the right choice."

Pra Chhay walked to the window and looked out for a moment. "He made it clear to the new employer that Mr. Sareth needs close supervision."

The monk paused for a moment, as if unsure whether to continue or not. "Khath, Father Ralph blames himself for being too trusting of Mr. Sareth. He said he let Mr. Sareth become a barrier between himself and the very people he wanted to help. It was easier that way. I am sure he will tell you how sorry he is for not reaching out to you when it was so clear that you were struggling."

Khath glanced briefly at Pra Chhay. "I bear him no ill will," he said.

"He will be glad to hear that, Khath. But because he holds himself responsible, he also thinks Mr. Sareth should have a second chance in Portland. Is it a good decision, do you think?"

After a moment, Khath nodded. "Yes, Portland will be a good place for Mr. Sareth. There is no option, really. He would not survive long if he were sent back to Cambodia. And there are so few educated Cambodians left."

"You are not upset?" Pra Chhay asked. "Father Ralph feared that you would be. He discussed it with an immigration lawyer. The lawyer could not guarantee that Mr. Sareth would not be deported if complaints were filed, and Father Ralph did not want to risk it."

Khath shook his head. He imagined Mr. Sareth kneeling at the edge of a ditch while someone clubbed him senseless, and shuddered. "No," he said. "The Khmer Rouge would make short work of our Mr. Sareth. I would not wish that fate on him."

"I did not think you would," Pra Chhay said. "But I am glad to hear you say it. This way it keeps you safe as well, though Phally told Father Ralph she would never press charges against you, not after what her husband did to your family."

Pra Chhay went to the kitchen and returned sipping a glass of water. "There's an awful lot of food in the kitchen, Khath. Has Phally been here?"

"Yes, she brought it earlier while you were doing your purification rituals," Khath replied. "It's far more than we need, but I couldn't refuse." Khath sighed. "She looks as though she has not slept or eaten for days. She begs my forgiveness every time I see her, though I have told her there is no need for this. She is not the one who pulled the trigger."

"I hope she can adjust," Pra Chhay said. "I am sure it will take some time."

Khath sat down on the sofa where the Americans would sit, facing the photo of Kamala and Sitha. He let his gaze rest on his daughters' faces. It calmed him to see them so joyous, to know that they had at least known some happiness in their brief lives.

"Nary asked me about her father the other day," he said to Pra Chhay. "Was he good? Was he bad? He protected her, but he killed other people. He was the enemy, but he was also her father."

"It is a wonder that her secret did not break her," Pra Chhay said. "What did you tell her?"

"I said only that I was sure that her father had loved her."

Their conversation was interrupted by a knock on the door. Khath stood to answer it and welcomed Father Ralph, Gail and Teresa into his home. The women wore white shirts and light-colored pants. Good. Pra Chhay must have explained to them that in Cambodia lay people wore white rather than black to a funeral. It was not so important, really, just another ceremonial detail that Khath wanted to get right today.

With a jolt, he realized the letter writing project Teresa had designed to find his daughters was over now. *Even when I refused to see her, she left me packets of letters to sign and address. She never gave up, never stopped helping me.*

He turned to Teresa and said, "I want to say thank you to you for help me look for Kamala and Sitha. You work very hard, believe me when I say my girls still alive. You very kind with me. In my heart, I thank you."

Teresa's eyes watered but she smiled as she dabbed at them with a handkerchief. "I am always happy to help, Khath. I hope you know that now. Always."

A moment later Phally and Nary tapped on the door and entered, leaving their shoes outside. Phally wore her hair pulled back tightly from her face, the severe style making her face look gaunt, her cheeks hollow. She bowed low as she greeted Gail and Teresa and the priest, then lower still when she turned to Khath and Pra Chhay, as though apologizing for her very presence on the earth.

Khath bent over and captured her clasped hands between his own, drawing her upright. "Enough," he murmured, for her ears only. "I intended to harm you in that cabin, yet by your actions you helped me regain my memory. Our karmic debt is settled now, Phally. It is done." He showed her and Nary to a mat on the floor, noticing with pleasure that Nary seated herself close to Phally and whispered something in her ear.

It was time to light the candles. Khath went to the kitchen to get matches. Pra Chhay followed him in and they spoke quietly for a moment, watching their guests settle in for the ceremony.

"They are closer now," Khath said, nodding toward Phally and Nary. "In the past, Nary would not have sat so near or whispered to her mother like that. Look, she is resting her hand on Phally's leg. She never used to touch her mother at all."

Pra Chhay nodded. "I think they will be happier now that there is no big secret between them."

Khath nodded. "Nary said she was afraid to show her love for her mother. She feared she would not be able to keep her secret if she let her guard down." He shook his head. "What a terrible burden for a child. I am so glad it is over now, that some good has come from all this madness."

As the two men watched, Phally laid her hand over top of Nary's, curling her fingers around the child's hand in a gentle squeeze, her lips curving into a soft smile as she gazed down on her daughter.

Seeing this, Khath felt his heart lift. This is how it should be between mother and child, he thought. He glanced at his watch and smiled at Pra Chhay. "It is past the hour. Remember what Mr. Sareth said to us on our first morning here? We must learn to be punctual. Rule Number One!"

Pra Chhay laughed softly. "And then we found wristwatches in our "Welcome to America" basket, a not so subtle hint from Mr. Sareth." Pra Chhay took out his prayer beads. "All right, brother. Are you ready?"

"Yes," Khath said. "Yes, I am."

# Saving Nary

## Carol DeMent

## Readers Guide and Discussion Topics

---

1.  On page six, Khath tells Youk that he searched for his daughters for nine months in Cambodia, never giving up "because they could always be there, at the next village. Or the one after." What does this tell us about Khath's character? How, as a parent, does one decide when to stop searching for lost children under such tragic circumstances?

2.  How do Khath's experiences with Mith in Khao I Dang shape his perceptions and his behavior as the novel progresses?

3.  Mr. Sareth's life has been turned upside down by the war in Cambodia. He has lost his wealth, his status, his country, and his confidence in his marriage. Do these losses make him a sympathetic character? Why or why not?

4.  Gail is struggling to accept her inability to walk since being injured in a car accident six months earlier. What role does her new disability play in her relationships with the people around her?

5. Phally is uneasy about the closeness of Nary's relationship with Khath from the beginning, even though it is clear that the child finds solace in the man's company. Is her caution merited? What factors complicate Phally's choices?

6. Khath has physically lost his daughters; Phally has emotionally lost Nary. In a sense, each parent has what the other wants. How are Khath and Phally's situations different and the same?

7. Throughout *Saving Nary*, we see examples of cultural differences ranging from mundane matters, such as having to master the workings of a new household, to the complexities of learning to decipher subtle body language and verbal cues. How do these differences shape the chain of events in the book? What experiences have you had that give insight into the difficulties and rewards of learning to live in a culture radically different from your own?

8. Khath's accusation against Phally's husband splits the community between those who believe him, those who don't and those who don't know what to think. Where did you fall on this spectrum, and why?

9. Nary carries a burdensome secret until the end of the novel. How does her secret isolate her from those around her? Why is it so important to her to keep her promise to her father, and what made her finally break her silence? How would you answer her question to Khath: Was her father good or bad?

10. Father Ralph helps Mr. Sareth to move on to a new job in Portland. What considerations do you think went into the priest's decision? The scene ends on page 335 with Mr. Sareth saying, "I trust we will part as friends?" What do you think Father Ralph's response was? What would your response be?